KEEPERS
of the
CAVE

Gerri Hill

Bella
BOOKS
2012

Bella Books, Inc.
P.O. Box 10543
Tallahassee, FL 32302

Printed in the United States of America on acid-free paper
First published 2012

Editor: Medora McDougall
Cover Designer: Linda Callaghan

ISBN 13: 978-1-59493-301-1

PUBLISHER'S NOTE

ABOUT THE AUTHOR

Gerri Hill has twenty-one published works, including the 2011 GCLS winner Devil's Rock and 2009 GCLS winner Partners, the last book in the popular Hunter Series, as well as 2012 Lambda finalist Storms. She began writing lesbian romance as a way to pass the time while snowed in one winter in the mountains of Colorado. Her first published work came in 2000 with One Summer Night. Hill's love of nature and of being outdoors usually makes its way into her stories as her characters often find themselves in beautiful natural settings. Gerri and her longtime partner, Diane, live in the East Texas woods with two Australian Shepherds and an assortment of furry felines. For more, see her website: www.gerrihill.com

ALSO BY GERRI HILL

Artist's Dream
Behind The Pine Curtain
The Cottage
Coyote Sky
Dawn Of Change
Devil's Rock
Gulf Breeze
Hell's Highway
Hunter's Way
In The Name Of The Father
The Killing Room
Love Waits
No Strings
One Summer Night
Partners
Rainbow Cedar, The
Sierra City
Scorpion, The
Storms
Target, The

CHAPTER ONE

It was eerily quiet in the room, only the constant drip, drip, drip of the coffee machine disrupted the silence. At this early hour, even the other teams were absent. DeMarcus Freeman, known to everyone as Ice, stared at the empty desks for a moment, then glanced at the large clock on the wall. They would be in soon. He knew their routine better than his own, especially after closing out a case like the one they'd just wrapped up. Eight missing boys. Yeah, they found them. Found them all. Dead. The bastard had been using them for sex toys, the longest for two months. The newest one, just two days. All dead. And Ice knew exactly how his team would handle it.

His partner, Constance Jean Johnston, would go out alone to a popular lesbian bar and, after a multitude of tequila shots, would pick up a woman whose name she wouldn't remember this morning. CJ would follow the woman home, fuck her brains out, then leave before the woman woke up. No name, no phone number. That's how CJ handled things.

Billy Calhoun, whose own young son was the same age as most of these boys, would go to his ex-wife's house, where, for some crazy reason, she still had sex with him. Maybe she'd been around long enough to know how these cases affected him, even though on a normal day they fought like cats and dogs.

Billy's partner, Paige Riley, would always go home alone and drink a whole bottle of wine—sometimes two, according to Billy—while soaking in a bubble bath. Ice let his mind wander to the beautiful blond agent, picturing her up to her neck in bubbles, a hand lazily holding a wineglass over the side. He pushed it away, knowing Billy would have his ass for the thought. Billy had his own crush on her, although he would deny it to his dying day.

He sighed and made his way to the coffee, even though he knew the routine. On a normal day, after a normal case, Paige would be the first to arrive. Always. She was annoyingly punctual, never late. Billy would hurry in next, still chewing whatever he'd picked up for breakfast that morning. Then CJ would drag in, her hair still wet, evidence that she'd only gotten up in time for a quick shower, no coffee or breakfast. CJ was habitually late. Always. But that was on a normal day.

Today, since it wasn't a normal day, CJ would arrive first, reeking of sex and tequila, wearing the same clothes as yesterday. She would grunt a hello at him, then sink into her chair. He would hand her a cup of coffee, which she would complain about. Billy would pop in next, his eyes red and puffy from lack of sleep. His ex-wife, to hear Billy tell it, was a sex machine. Paige would be the last to arrive. She always brought Starbucks coffee and a breakfast treat for them. Sometimes ham and cheese croissants, sometimes tacos from a local Mexican bar, sometimes only McDonald's, but she always brought breakfast. And she would watch them, looking to see if they had recovered, her eyes undoubtedly landing on CJ with a slightly disapproving look. He often wondered if that was why she intentionally arrived late—so she wouldn't have to witness CJ walking in looking like shit.

He didn't understand their relationship, really. When the four of them went out for beers, they would flirt shamelessly with each other. Well, CJ would flirt, as was her nature. Paige took it, giving back just as well. But they always left separately and as far as he knew, they never did anything with each other outside of the four of them. He wasn't certain he would even call them friends.

He sat back down again, rubbing his newly shaved head, wondering if CJ would even notice.

***

CJ squinted in the bright sunlight, her dark glasses doing little to temper the glare. She ran her tongue over her teeth, her mouth dry and still tasting of tequila . . . and sex. She groaned, wincing at the pounding in her head as she ducked inside the building. The woman had been a blonde. Recently, they all had been blonde. She couldn't remember the woman's name to save her life.

She sighed tiredly as the elevator opened. She walked into the room, sunglasses still covering her eyes. Their set of desks was separated from the other FBI teams by rows of filing cabinets, and she saw Ice sitting at his, as expected. He was the last to leave and the first to arrive. She sometimes wondered if he went home at all. She ignored the glance he gave her and pulled out her chair with her foot, sinking down slowly, keeping her head still.

"Yeah, thanks," she murmured as he handed her a cup of coffee. She took a sip, grimacing at the taste. "Damn, Ice, this tastes like shit. When are you going to learn to make a decent cup of coffee?"

"Feel free to give it a try." he said

She blinked several times, focusing on his head. "What the hell happened to you?"

"Felt like a change," he said as he rubbed his shaved head.

"Huh. You don't say."

She laid her head down on the desk, sunglasses smashing uncomfortably against her ear, waiting for his question.

"What was her name?"

She gave her usual answer. "Hell if I know." She kept her eyes closed, hearing the elevator doors open, knowing it was Billy. His aftershave arrived long before he did.

"Jesus, CJ, aren't those the same clothes you had on yesterday?"

"Bite me," she murmured, eyes still closed.

"You wish."

"Shut up."

She sighed again, vowing—for at least the hundredth time—to stop these all-nighters with strangers. But it was the only way she could completely chase the horrors of the job from her mind. Well, not the only way, she mused, as she remembered the one night Paige Riley had shared her bed. She groaned quietly, not wanting to think of that right now. She never brought women to her own bed. It was a rule she never broke. Never. It was easier that way. No names, no phones, no addresses. But she had broken all the rules that night. Only she hadn't been the one slinking out of someone's bed and escaping into the early morning darkness. She was surprised at how much it stung when she woke to find Paige already gone.

"Jesus, Ice, what happened to the Afro we've grown to love?"

"Come on, man, that wasn't a 'fro."

***

Paige knew what she would find even before the elevator doors opened. Ice would be leaning back in his chair, watching CJ with annoyed—yet concerned—eyes as he tossed wadded up pieces of paper into the trash can. Billy would be reading the news online, his chin resting in his palm as he tried to stifle a yawn. He wasn't really reading the daily paper, she knew. He was reliving the night spent with his ex. And CJ would have her head down on her desk, eyes closed. If it were a really bad morning, she'd still have her sunglasses on.

She paused before getting off the elevator, her glance going quickly around the room. She silently acknowledged that her assumptions were right on. Taking a deep breath, she moved forward, smiling at Ice before handing him a coffee.

"Nice head," she said with a smirk.

Billy reached for his coffee before she could offer, then eyed the bag she held.

"Sausage and egg wraps," she said, handing him one.

"You're the best. Thanks."

She tossed one to Ice, then walked over to CJ, who had yet to raise her head. She placed the coffee and breakfast down beside her, slowly shaking her head.

"You really, *really* need a shower, CJ," she said quietly.

"I know," she mumbled.

Paige shook her head again, wondering why CJ put herself through this. Couldn't she be satisfied with a night alone? Perhaps a bottle of wine, maybe a hot soak in bubbles? Did she always have to chase the images away with sex? She allowed herself a brief glimpse into the past, a night where she had been the one CJ had turned to. Against her better judgment, Paige had given in to her desires, a mistake brought on by CJ's incessant flirting, too many tequila shots, and her own need to escape the job for a few hours. Even though she had regretted her decision the next morning, it was still a night she wasn't able to forget.

***

Billy watched his partner watch CJ. He glanced at Ice with raised eyebrows as Paige shook her head for the third time before taking a seat at her own neat desk. Billy ate his breakfast wrap in silence, as did the others. Finally, CJ stood—albeit slowly—and grabbed her coffee and wrap. She stared at Paige.

"Grabbing a shower," she said as she sauntered off.

"Good. Why don't you take two?" Paige called, scooting the chair away from her desk and heading in the opposite direction of CJ.

"Damn. What's with them anyway?" he asked.

Ice wadded up his breakfast wrap and tossed a perfect shot into the trash can. "I don't know. They've been acting strange for the last several months."

Billy leaned forward, his voice low. "You don't think...you know."

"No, man. Come on," Ice said. "Paige is Paige. She's perfect. And CJ...well, you know I love her, but she's got some issues."

Billy snorted. "Issues? Is that what you call it?"

"Cut her some slack, man. You know how she grew up."

"Yeah, I know." Billy leaned back again with a sigh. Yeah, they all knew how CJ's old man used her as a punching bag when she was a kid. CJ grew up just this side of trailer park trash in a bad part of Houston, and even though she'd put that behind her, they all knew she carried it around like a chip on her shoulder. She was gorgeous as hell and could have her pick of women. But she was not beautiful in the classy, clean way Paige was. No, CJ was rough-and-tumble, her dark hair cut short in different lengths, always looking a little on the messy side. But even he would admit it was a sexy look, with just enough hanging over those big brown eyes to make you want to just reach out and brush it away.

He shook himself. *Damn.* That was CJ. What in the hell was he thinking?

CHAPTER TWO

"Gather round, people."

CJ brushed the hair out of her eyes, wondering what Howley had for them this time. The Special Agent-in-Charge had given them two days off after wrapping up the *missing boy case*, as they'd ended up calling it. She hated when the victims were kids, hated it more when sexual abuse was involved. It brought way too many of her own demons to the surface. Obviously, she wasn't very good at handling them. But two days off were good. One night of drunken sex with a stranger, then last night, a blissful sleep in her own bed. She felt human again this morning.

She followed the others into the conference room, choosing her normal seat between Paige and Ice. Paige was speaking to her again. That was a plus. She hated the tension between them and she suspected Paige hated it as well. But it was what they did. When CJ pulled one of her all-night stunts like she had the other night, she knew it would take a couple of days for them to get back to normal. She glanced at Paige now, pleased to see that the disapproving look in her eyes was gone, the disapproving look that sometimes bordered on disappointed. That look cut deep. She smiled hesitantly, getting a slight one in return.

"Got a rather interesting assignment," Howley said. "Get comfortable. This will take a while."

The large monitor on the near wall came to life and what appeared to be an aerial view of a small community popped up. A smattering of buildings was nearly swallowed by a forest of tall trees. He slid a file folder to each of them.

"We're calling it Hoganville Complex," he said. "Population estimated at fifty, give or take. I say estimated because this isn't a town. It isn't even an unincorporated community. By the way, Hoganville is the informal name only. It's not an actual named town." He pulled up a map on the monitor next. "It's located between the Angelina National Forest and the Sabine National Forest in far East Texas. Lake Sam Rayburn is here," he said, pointing, "and the Louisiana border is here, in the middle of Toledo Bend Lake."

"Disappearances?" Billy asked as he scanned the first page of the folder.

"Lots of them," Howley said. "Let's get some background. This investigation was originally started eight months ago. Senator Trumbley from Dallas has a stake in this. His daughter has been missing for nine months now. College student. She was driving from New Orleans back to Dallas last October. Alone. The last communication he had from her was here," he said, pointing to the map, "in Leesville, Louisiana."

"Looks like it's far from a major highway," CJ said. "Is it a case of the GPS leading her astray?"

He shrugged. "Who knows? Car was found here in Deridder," he said. "Clean."

"If the last communication was from Leesville, why is Hoganville in question?" Paige asked.

"Hoganville is one of three investigations. One team is concentrating efforts in Baton Rouge and Louisiana State University, which on the surface, appears to be the logical location. Another is going over the senator's comings and goings in both Dallas and Washington, trying to determine if it's politically motivated or not. Hoganville is an afterthought, I believe, mainly because of the weirdness of it."

"Weirdness?" Ice tossed his pen down. "In other words, we pulled the short stick."

"I'm afraid so. It threw up red flags, that's all."

CJ was ready to push the file away, quickly losing interest. "So we're like the junior varsity team? The big boys get Dallas, Washington and Baton Rouge?"

"Look, we take the assignment we're given and do our jobs. Now take a look at the file. It's really fascinating reading," Howley said. "I think there could be something here. When the team was investigating Trumbley's disappearance, they stumbled across a rash of them, really. None appear to be linked or have a pattern to them, just random disappearances. They discovered that there have been documented disappearances going back to 1939. The disappearances are of the variety of vagabonds, the unemployed who were traveling and looking for work, college students, hitchhikers, traveling salesmen back in the day or people just passing through. Like young Trumbley there. In the most recent cases, the last twenty years or so, most of the disappearances involve women, mostly young, always traveling alone."

"And none have been found?" Billy asked. "Bodies?"

"None. Not a trace. In some cases, the vehicle has not been found either. Like I said, read the file. It's interesting."

"Is this for real?" Ice asked as he flipped through the pages. "A family compound that at one time was over three hundred people?"

"What about this school?" Paige asked.

"That's part of what's interesting. Hogan School for Girls," he said. "It's a private institution established thirty-one years ago with a federal grant. They took the name Hogan because that's the property it was built on."

"Home for troubled girls," CJ said, reading the brief description of the school.

"Yes. Girls who have been kicked out of public school, girls who would otherwise be heading to juvy perhaps. This is an alternative. It's pricey. But also subsidized by the feds."

"What's the school got to do with all this?" Billy asked.

"The school is the only outside entity there. And it's totally separate from Hoganville. It's located about three miles away, out in the middle of nowhere. It was built on property sold by the Hogans. Over the last thirty-one years, they've had six girls come up missing. None in the last ten and we can attribute that to better security."

"So what? Serial killer?"

"I think it's worse than a serial killer if we're talking over seventy, eighty years' worth," CJ said.

"Exactly," Howley said. "Unfortunately, *worse* could be any number of things. So, what we've done is replace the director of the school with an agent. A paper pusher, but an agent nonetheless. He's been there nearly seven months, getting a feel of the community, gathering information. He suggests we bring in two agents." He glanced at them one by one. "A couple."

"A couple?" CJ looked at both Ice and Billy and shook her head. "Oh no. No way am I going to pretend to be a couple with one of these guys."

Howley gave a quick smile. "That's not exactly the type of couple I meant," he said. "It's an all-girls school. Most of the teachers are women. In fact, all but two, actually."

"And?"

He glanced at Paige. Paige's eyebrows shot up into her bangs.

"A couple? *Us?*" she asked, pointing to CJ.

"Based on what Avery has told us—he's the agent posing as the director—that's the best course of action, if we want to fit in."

"What do you mean?" CJ asked. "What kind of couple?"

"What kind do you think, CJ? A couple. A *lesbian* couple," he said.

She arched an eyebrow. "Seriously?"

"Seriously. Avery says there are eight lesbian couples on staff. He thinks that's the best way for us to get a team in and to fit in."

"Eight couples?" CJ glanced at Paige. "That's pretty high, isn't it?"

Paige shrugged. "It's an all-girls' school. Stands to reason the teachers would be female."

"God, can you imagine the drama? Who's sleeping with whom? Who's cheating, who's fighting."

Paige laughed. "You'll fit right in."

"Ladies? Let's stay on task, please." Howley handed them both another piece of paper. "That's your backstory. Memorize it."

She and Paige both scanned it quickly. Paige was the first to speak.

"Six months? We've been together only six months?"

"What's wrong with that?"

CJ laughed. "At six months, you're still fucking like bunnies."

They all laughed, even Paige, who responded by tossing her pen at her. CJ read on, smiling. "Oh, cool. I get to be a campus cop."

"A gym teacher?" Paige groaned. "Really? I'm a gym teacher?"

"Look, I didn't write this, okay," Howley said. "I'm just passing it along. Live with it."

Paige tossed the paper on the table. "Okay. Just what does this all mean? We're a couple. What's the plan?"

"The plan is to infiltrate the teachers and hopefully the community."

"Where will we stay?"

"Housing is provided at the school. It's tight as a prison," Howley said. "The school is secured with a high fence and a locked entry. Remember, this takes the place of juvenile detention. A security guard operates the gate at all times. Dorms for the students, cottages or cabins for the staff. All the teachers live on campus. The only locals who work there are janitorial and cafeteria staff, and that's part-time. Less than two hundred students, thirty staff, give or take. Sixteen teachers. Your objective is to infiltrate the main staff—two of which are locals. Fiona Hogan, a science teacher. And Gretchen Hogan, the nurse."

"So we'll live on campus too?"

"Yes. Like I said, you're going in as a couple. This isn't going to be a quick fix, ladies. It's likely to run several months."

CJ glanced at Paige, seeing the stricken look on her face. "Months?"

"As you'll see in the file there, there have been documented cases all throughout the years, very random. The most recent records are more accurate, as far as where the victim was last seen and so on. Earlier records are speculation only. The victims are not necessarily from this area. In fact, they rarely are." He pulled up another file on the monitor. "This is Ester Hogan. Descendant of the original Hogan who founded the town. Avery tells us she's the matriarch."

"Age?"

"We have no idea. It's a very closed-off community. Everything we have is speculation. It took months to get as much as we have." He glanced from one to the other. "They are very secluded. They don't venture out very often. Not for Sunday church. And as far as we can tell, not for funerals."

"Meaning?"

"Not sure what that means," he said. "We can assume people die there. What they do with the bodies is anyone's guess."

"Okay, now it's getting weird," Billy said.

"You think it's just *now* getting weird?" Ice asked.

Howley pulled up another photo of the community on the monitor. "Everything is basically funded by Ester Hogan. They got their original fortune in timber back in the early 1900s. They acquired hundreds of thousands of acres. It's one reason they've been able to remain isolated. It's hard to tell if other families might have moved into the community, but judging by the age of the houses, I'd say it's been forty, fifty years, maybe more."

"What about utilities?" CJ asked.

"They're pretty much off the grid. They have a community water system. Basically, it's just a large well and cistern that feeds all the houses. Again, built at the expense of the original Hogan family. It's considered a private water well so there's no state inspection. There is no evidence of phone lines. I would assume, but don't know for sure, that some have cell phones. Avery says there are no TV antennas and no satellite dishes. There are generators and solar panels. Not very many cars. Like I said, pretty much isolated."

"So...are we looking at something like the *Stepford Wives* here?" Paige asked. "Or a situation like Waco?"

"We're not sure what we're looking at," he said. "Like I said, on the surface, things appear perfectly normal. Dig a little and you find all this. There are no birth records, no marriage records, no death records."

"But what evidence is there linking this community to the disappearances?" Ice asked.

"None. No evidence."

They all looked at him questioningly.

He shrugged. "It's all we got. It threw up red flags because, frankly, it's a little too similar to David Koresh's setup in Waco."

Paige leaned back in her chair, twirling a pen between her fingers. "Evidence of firearms?"

"No."

"I thought this was a family, not some religious cult," CJ said.

Howley shrugged. "We don't know. Your job is to find out. Again, there's no evidence linking Hoganville to the disappearances. This is purely a precaution."

"Well, this is going to be loads of fun," Paige said dryly.

CJ nodded. She hated cases like this. *Precaution.* In other words, killing time. She glanced at Paige, wondering what her take was on the "couple" thing. That part of it was going to be uncomfortable as hell.

"Okay, that's all I have. Read the file. Ice, you and Billy will stay here in Houston. Your job is research. I'm sure after CJ and Paige get there, they'll have lots of questions. Your job is to find the answers."

"Cool with me," Ice said. "I have no desire to go to the woods."

He looked at CJ and Paige. "The cabin you'll be staying in is furnished. Avery has given me an inventory list so if there's something you can't live without, bring your own. That list is in the file. You leave in five days."

Howley left them alone, and CJ could feel the tension in the room. The guys were glancing between her and Paige. She wondered what they were expecting. So, she did what she normally did with them. Reverted to flirting.

"So," she said, wiggling her eyebrows teasingly at Paige. "Should we go practice kissing or something?"

Paige rolled her eyes. "In your dreams, tiger."

"Oh yeah, baby," she called after her, staring at Paige's backside as she retreated. "You've definitely been there." CJ grinned at the guys. "My lucky day, huh?"

"Damn right," Billy said. "Man, I would trade places with you in a heartbeat."

CJ raised her eyebrows.

"What? I'm just saying, she's smokin' hot. She may be my partner, but she's still smokin' hot."

CJ had to agree. But Ice came to her rescue.

"Paige is the lucky one, man. She gets to be with my woman, CJ. Now this is hot," he said dramatically, motioning to her. "CJ Johnston, the woman with abs of steel."

CJ stood up and pulled her shirt out of her jeans on cue, showing off her stomach, eliciting whistles from both men.

"Wow," Billy said, reaching out to touch her, but CJ slapped his hand away. He looked up sheepishly. "Okay, so, yeah, that's hot too. I mean, if you're into that sort of thing."

"Yeah, man," she said. "Chicks love it."

"Chicks love what?"

They all turned, finding Paige standing in the doorway. CJ quickly lowered her shirt but not before she saw Paige's eyes glued to her exposed skin. She didn't know why she was the one blushing, but she was. Paige's expression shifted to one of boredom as she walked away.

CHAPTER THREE

Paige methodically packed her clothes, her thoughts not on her impending role as a gym teacher. Rather, they were bouncing around, scene by scene, from a night six months ago. She had no interest in CJ Johnston romantically, of course. None at all. CJ was attractive, sure. If CJ were playing a role, she would have made a perfect female version of James Dean. She had just the right amount of rakish charm, was just enough of a rebel with that *bad boy* attitude to pull it off. Plus, she had brooding down to a fine art. She paused in her task, sighing as she stared off into space. Yes, CJ was very attractive, but CJ was definitely not her type. Definitely.

Which brought her back to the night she went home with CJ. What in the world had possessed her to follow CJ to her apartment? Was it the flirting mixed with tequila? Was it that she, too, wanted to forget about the case they'd just wrapped up? Or was it the needy, nearly desperate look in CJ's eyes that had propelled her on? Perhaps a combination of things, but she could still see that haunted look on CJ's face. A home invasion had turned into a hostage situation. Only on TV did those end well. A husband and wife, two kids—all dead at the end of the day. They had been bound and gagged and doused with gasoline. The fire took them quickly, but it was a horrific scene. When it involved kids, CJ always took it harder. She knew CJ had been abused as a child, but she didn't know the details, just bits and pieces she'd picked up over the last three years. She and CJ weren't friends, really, and she never thought it was her place to ask questions about it.

But that night, for some reason, she'd followed CJ to a bar. She'd kept her distance, watching from afar as CJ made the rounds. She obviously knew quite a few of the women there. Paige wondered how many of them she'd slept with. Then their eyes had met across the room. Paige had been rooted to the spot as CJ sauntered over in that distinct walk of hers, with a sexy, mischievous look on her face.

"Special Agent Riley, this is sinking a little low for you, isn't it? Shouldn't you be at some high-dollar bar sipping martinis?"

Paige smiled at the memory. It was the one and only time she'd set foot in that bar. Her wine was quickly replaced with a shot of Patrón tequila and CJ had pulled a chair close to her, her eyes dancing as she shamelessly flirted with her. It was a game they played and played quite well. Ice and Billy expected it of them now.

Only that night, Ice and Billy were nowhere to be found. Nonetheless, they slipped into their roles, moving past the verbal flirting when CJ had boldly touched her, her hands moving with a purpose between her thighs. Paige had been stunned by CJ's bravado but was more surprised by her own reaction. Instead of pushing CJ away, knowing she had crossed the line, she parted her thighs invitingly, feeling a thrill as those hands moved higher. She had been shocked by how aroused she was. Shocked that she hadn't wanted those hands to stop. It was then, looking into CJ's eyes that she saw it—a desperate need for contact, for physical intimacy. She told herself to stop, to get up and leave, to run. And fast. But she couldn't look away—couldn't pull away—not even when CJ leaned closer, her lips brushing against her mouth teasingly. Instead, she turned her head, finding CJ, their first tentative kiss deepening quickly, her mouth opening, allowing CJ inside.

The rest was a complete blur. CJ's hands finishing their trek between her thighs, the wetness she couldn't hide from CJ, the soft moan she heard—hers—as CJ's fingers rubbed against the seam of her jeans, pressing intimately against her. Then they were up and walking, hands clasped, hurrying outside. She had been in a daze as she listened to CJ's directions to her apartment, surprised to find herself following CJ, too aroused to come out of her stupor.

They didn't speak. Not one word. CJ closed the door behind her, then pinned her against it, her hands making quick work of the jeans Paige wore. Shaken—dazed—Paige found herself helping CJ undress her, found herself grabbing CJ's hand and bringing it inside her panties, the desperate need now hers, not CJ's. She barely registered CJ's fingers on her, inside her. Her orgasm was hard and quick, and she bit down on CJ's shoulder to keep from screaming out. Then CJ led her to her bedroom, closing the door to the world as they fell together. How many hours they were there, she no longer knew. Sleep came intermittently, the sex between them thrilling and exhausting, electrifying and exhilarating all at the same time.

She had slipped out of CJ's arms and out of her bed, gathering her clothes quietly while CJ slept. It wouldn't do for her to still be there when CJ woke. What would they say? How could it be explained?

She drove home, once again feeling like she was in a fog, her thoughts muddled, confused. And for the next week, maybe two, she and CJ avoided each other, speaking only when necessary. If the guys noticed—which surely they did—they never mentioned it. Then another case came around, giving them something to focus on and little by little, she and CJ reverted back to what they were accustomed to. The gentle flirting over beers with the guys looking on, the teasing, the taunts. Things got back to normal. Never once in the last six months had they mentioned the night they'd spent together. Truth was, they'd never once been alone together. By choice or coincidence, she wasn't sure.

Now, they were heading off to Hoganville—alone.

As a couple.

Pretending to be lovers.

CHAPTER FOUR

"They're acting really weird," Billy whispered. "I wish you'd ask CJ what's going on."

Ice watched Paige and CJ as they headed off to Howley's office for their last briefing. "If you want to know so bad, why don't you ask her?"

"She's your partner."

Ice absently rubbed his head, still not used to the smoothness of it. "Then ask Paige," he said.

"You don't ask Paige stuff like that. She's...well, reserved."

"Reserved? Just because her family has more money than God doesn't mean she's reserved," he said. "You've been partners for four years, man."

"She's not like us. You can't just ask her stuff like that."

"Well, then, what do *you* think is going on with them?" Ice had his own suspicions, but he would never voice them to Billy. He long ago suspected that, like them, CJ had her own little crush on the lovely Paige Riley. And in CJ's mind, she was nowhere close to the same league as Paige. Paige grew up in a mansion, CJ in a mobile home. Maybe CJ was afraid it would become known—her little crush—now that they had to play the part of a lesbian couple. Of course, that didn't explain Paige's actions. The two women had been blatantly avoiding each other ever since Howley gave them the assignment four days ago.

"I think there's enough sexual tension between them that they're afraid of this case, that's what I think," Billy said.

"Yeah? That's what you think?"

"The way they flirt with each other when we go out? Yeah, that can't be just for show."

"I think it is. They're just playing around. I've never even seen them alone together. Have you?"

"That doesn't mean anything."

"You never see them here alone," he said, motioning to their desks. "They never go to the restroom together. They're never up getting coffee at the same time. They never talk about them seeing each other outside of work. No lunches, no dinner. Nothing. In fact, the only conversations they have are work related."

"Except when we go out for beers," Billy said.

"Yeah. So, since they're leaving tomorrow—"

"Then it must be a beer night," Billy finished for him with a grin. "Yeah, maybe a night out can get them back to normal."

***

It's funny how some bars just become cop bars. This one was no different. It wasn't located that close to the police department. Wasn't real close to the sheriff's department either. And it was a good ten blocks from the building where the FBI offices were. Yet Ice guessed ninety percent of the clientele were from law enforcement. A wraparound bar was the main attraction and where they normally gathered. The front part of the bar was filled with tall, round tables—where they'd chosen to sit tonight—and the side wall housed a row of booths. Five large TVs were spaced about, giving the place a sports bar feel. The only food served was burgers and fries or spicy buffalo wings, nothing else, yet the place was packed nearly every night of the week. Above the noise of the crowd, the whacking of pool balls could be heard from the three tables at the back of the bar.

"Man, you two are going to be crazy after a few months together," Billy said as he tipped his beer bottle at CJ.

"Crazier," Paige murmured.

"Speak for yourself," CJ countered.

Paige leaned her elbows on the table and rested her chin on her hands. "You don't snore, do you?"

Ice watched them, their stare intense, and he actually saw CJ clamp her mouth shut, keeping in the words that were about to spill out. Instead, she leaned closer too, her gaze lowering to Paige's lips. Ice stared in fascination at the exchange between them.

"Baby, I'll have you so tired and sated, you won't be awake long enough to know if I snore or not."

Ice saw just a ghost of a smile cross Paige's face. "What makes you think that *you* won't be the one satiated?"

Billy leaned closer to Ice. "What does 'satiated' mean?" he whispered.

"Seriously, man?"

Paige smiled affectionately at Billy, her gaze finally leaving CJ's. "Let me buy the next round."

It wasn't her turn, but no one complained. Just like no one complained when she ordered dinner for them all when they were working late. Or when she brought in breakfast or coffee. She was genuinely generous and didn't expect anything in return. Like he'd told Billy, just because she had more money than the rest of them, it didn't mean she wasn't one of them. She was. She just dressed better and drove a more expensive car.

"Are you nervous?" CJ asked.

Ice noticed the teasing was gone and was surprised by the question. He was even more surprised by Paige's answer.

"Terrified."

Billy, as usual, was oblivious to the underlying tension. "You'll be fine," he said. "Sounds like a crazy place, yeah, but they're still just people."

Paige and CJ exchanged real smiles, and Ice would have sworn it was the first time he'd ever witnessed that between them.

"Yes, I'm sure we'll be fine," Paige said. "Gonna miss you guys though. It'll be weird not seeing you every day."

"Just a phone call away," Ice said. "We're your research, remember."

An unusual silence followed until Billy—apparently feeling brave after three beers—asked the question that had been bothering him all week.

"Is everything okay with you two?"

Paige and CJ looked at each other, then away. "Yes, of course," Paige answered. "Why?"

"You've just been acting a little strange. Kinda like you're avoiding each other."

He expected them to protest, CJ at least, but neither refuted Billy's words. It seemed like they couldn't even come up with a good lie.

"Well, how would you like it if you and Ice had to go undercover as a couple?" CJ asked. "It's a little unnerving."

"Yeah, but you two are gay. What's the big deal?"

Paige stared at him, her blue eyes narrowing. "Why would you assume I'm gay?"

Billy swallowed. "Well, you never talk about guys. About dating."

"Do I talk about women and dating?"

"No. You don't really talk about your personal life."

Her gaze finally softened. "Right. And let's keep it that way. Now, back to your point, pretending to be in love with someone, someone who you work with, is a little disconcerting. CJ and I, while I would consider us work friends, don't really know each other all that well," Paige said. "So being suddenly thrown together, having to pretend we're in a relationship, is making us both a little nervous." She looked at CJ. "Right?"

"Yes. Definitely." CJ downed her beer and slid the empty to the middle of the table where the other bottles had landed. "Not only that, but we have to *live* together."

Ice could see the wheels turning in Billy's head. "Sleep together?"

"Share a bed," Paige corrected quickly. "Howley informed us that our cabin is a cute one bedroom, one bath. Very intimate," she said.

"You are so going to get on my nerves," CJ murmured.

"Me?"

"Yes. You're a neat freak," CJ said.

"Yeah. So?"

"So? Can you say OCD?"

Paige actually glared at her. "Obsessive-compulsive disorder? Really?"

CJ grinned. "Tell me everything in your desk is not either color-coded or alphabetized. You're probably one of those people who rotate your underwear and towels and stuff so you don't use them out of order." She raised her eyebrows. "Am I wrong?"

Paige blushed and Ice couldn't contain his laughter.

"Okay, so maybe I have a *touch* of it," Paige conceded. "I doubt living with you will be a bed of roses either."

"Baby, I'll try to make it as pleasant...and satisfying for you as possible."

Paige again leaned forward. "Tiger, I don't think you can handle me."

CJ's eyebrows shot up. "Oh? Is that a challenge?"

"No. Just a fact."

Ice and Billy exchanged glances again, surprised at how quickly the two of them reverted back to flirting.

"Well, I guess we'll have a few months to see if that's true or not. I think I'll break you."

"We'll see who breaks whom," Paige nearly purred.

CHAPTER FIVE

"Are you sure you're not lost?"

CJ flicked her eyes at her. "Despite the fact that we have a GPS and she's not *recalculating*, I know where I am."

Paige turned doubtful eyes her way but said nothing.

CJ kept her gaze on the road, the forest nearly swallowing up the highway on both sides. It looked inviting from the comfort of the air-conditioned car, but she knew outside it was hot and humid. It was still early June, but the temperatures had been steadily climbing closer to the century mark. The tall pines and oaks were nearly motionless, no breeze penetrating them. Out of the corner of her eye she watched Paige, who was again reading through files on the fancy laptop she had. *Notebook*, she mentally corrected. Well, at least she had something to keep her occupied. Their conversation thus far had been stilted and nearly nonexistent. It had made for a long, stressful trip. Stressful, because she knew eventually they had to talk. And eventually, *it* would come up. That night. It had to.

And she didn't want to talk about it. Not at all. Unusual for her, but she was the one who had woken up alone in her own bed. Alone, but completely sated. She hadn't slept that well in years. Of course, it wasn't something she was going to admit to Paige, should they discuss that night. She still had a hard time wrapping her brain around the fact that they had slept together. Not just slept together, but spent hours pleasuring each other. Paige was so not her type. She was too pretty, too classy, too smart, too... too *everything*. She glanced quickly at her, afraid Paige could read her mind and see the direction of her thoughts, but Paige seemed engrossed in her reading.

She gripped the steering wheel a little tighter as images flashed through her mind—Paige lying naked on her bed, legs opening to her, Paige's face etched in pleasure, her mouth slightly open, her hips bucking wildly with yet another orgasm. And Paige's hand parting her thighs, her fingers filling her, Paige's mouth at her breast. Then Paige's mouth moving lower, claiming her with a hunger that still brought chills to CJ's body.

"What?"

CJ turned, blinking several times. "What?"

Paige arched an eyebrow. "Is something wrong?"

CJ looked quickly back to the road, cursing her thoughts, praying Paige wouldn't notice the flush on her face. "Sorry. Nothing," she mumbled.

Paige closed her laptop and sighed. CJ waited, knowing what was coming.

"Do you want to talk about it?"

What kind of crazy question was that? She shook her head. "No."

Paige sighed again. "Are we going to be able to do this?"

For the first time, CJ heard—and understood—the trepidation in Paige's voice. She realized she wasn't the only one fighting with the demons of that night. How out of character was it for Paige to not only end up at the lesbian bar in the first place, but to allow CJ all that she did? She played along with her, flirting like they always did. It was different, though. Maybe because they were alone, without the guys, but the flirting became real. At least to her it did. And she'd had just enough alcohol to dampen her good sense. She remembered how bold she felt when she slipped her hands along Paige's inner thighs, remembered the look in Paige's eyes as she touched her. And God, she remembered how wet she'd been. So wet she could feel it through Paige's jeans. What came next was inevitable. But it was something Paige didn't do. One-night stands. No, that was CJ's specialty, not Paige's. Although, that morning when she'd found her bed empty, it seemed like Paige was the expert, not her.

But now here they were, heading to Hoganville with clothes and knick knacks, things to make it look like they were a real couple. A couple who'd been together only six months. A couple madly in love. Could they pull it off?

"I think it'll be fine," she said. "It's our job. We've both had undercover assignments before. This is nothing different."

"I hope you're right."

***

Paige watched as CJ effortlessly slipped into character, her arm hanging out the window as she smiled up at the security guard.

"Yep. We're the new ones," she said. "Can't wait to get settled in."

"You'll need to see the director first. The admin offices are on the first floor of Mathis Hall." He handed CJ a map. "Follow Campus Drive around the little lake here," he said, pointing to the paper he'd given her. "It's the first building. Flagpole out front."

CJ frowned. "Okay, but it's Saturday. The admin offices are open?"

"Not usually, no. But the director likes to greet the new staff."

"Is there a lot of turnover?" she asked.

He laughed and held his arms out. "What do you think? There's not a whole lot for entertainment out here."

"Got it. Okay, thanks. I guess we'll be seeing you around."

"Yeah."

She put her window back up, closing off the afternoon heat. "Well, we're in."

Paige nodded. "Yes. And I agree with Howley's term of compound. This place is like a prison."

"I think that is the intention," CJ said. "Because if these girls weren't here, a lot of them might be in juvy."

"Oh, that's pretty," she said, spotting the small lake to their left. "Do you think they let the girls out here?" She pointed. "Look. Picnic tables."

"I don't know how much freedom they get. The whole place is five hundred acres. That's a lot to fence off securely. I can't imagine the girls would have run of the place."

Paige took the map that CJ had tossed on the dash. She had already downloaded the one that was on their website, but she hadn't studied it much. She knew the cabins for the staff were located well away from the dorms. That led her to believe that the girls did have some access to the grounds. She knew from her research that some of them were allowed to have bikes but no vehicles. She actually found the hike and bike trail appealing and had to remind herself that she was working, not vacationing.

The security guard must have announced their arrival. The door to the admin building opened and another security guard was waiting.

"Right this way," he said.

CJ nodded at him, then politely let Paige go in first. She just barely resisted rolling her eyes as she reminded herself they were playing roles. An older man with graying hair stood in a doorway, a smile on his face.

***

He hadn't quite known what to expect of the two agents they were sending him. He had assumed they would be older, but these two looked to be in their early thirties. They would fit in well with the other teachers.

"Good afternoon. I'm Director Avery." He held his hand out to them, and they both shook it. "I see you found it," he said.

"It's definitely back in the woods. I'm CJ Johnston," the dark-haired one said. "This is Paige Riley."

"Nice to meet you. Come inside, please." He nodded to the security guard. "Thank you, Richard."

"Sure thing. I'll lock the door on my way out."

Once the door was closed, Avery let out a breath. "I'm glad you're finally here," he said. "I was afraid they weren't ready to move on it yet."

"No. We're ready to move. I just think no one knows who or what to move against," CJ said.

"That's true. I trust you've both read my notes?"

"Yes," Paige said. "Thoroughly."

"Well, like I reported, the community is isolated. They keep the school isolated from them as well. From what I've seen, everything goes through Ester Hogan. Everything."

"She's the...matriarch, right?"

"Yes. She also owns the café. Well, I guess she pretty much owns everything. The little grocery store and the service station." He motioned to the visitors' chairs. "Please sit." He waited until they were both sitting before resuming his position behind the desk.

"Are staff from the school welcome there at the café?" CJ asked.

"Not welcome, no. As far as I know, I don't believe anyone from school ever goes there."

"You said in your notes that it was an *old* community," Paige said. "Can you elaborate?"

"I haven't seen any kids. Ever." He sat back in his chair, watching them, wondering at their line of questioning. "Now that doesn't mean there aren't some. I would say the age of most of the residents is above fifty, maybe closer to sixty. You don't see young people, like twenties and thirties."

"So people move away and don't return. That's not unusual for a community like this," Paige said. "I wouldn't imagine there's much to hold people here."

He shook his head. "That was my assumption at first," he said. "But the longer I've been here, I don't think that's the case. I wouldn't imagine anyone would be allowed to leave without approval."

"Approved by whom?"

"I would assume Ester Hogan."

CJ laughed. "Oh, come on. No one is going to have that much control. Who would allow that? If you're just out of high school and you want to go to college, you're telling me they'd have to clear it with Ester Hogan?"

"There is no school. Everyone is informally homeschooled. From what I've learned, that's how it's always been, long before it was fashionable. Another thing is birth records. Officially, there have been six births in the last thirty-five years."

"Officially?"

"That's how many birth certificates were issued and Social Security numbers applied for. Six."

"Okay, this whole thing is really strange," Paige said. "It's going to take a little time for us to get the feel of it. You've had seven months." She paused. "There are two people who work here from town. They had to have gone away for their education," Paige said. "Let's research them more thoroughly."

"Yes. Fiona Hogan is a science teacher. She's very good and the girls love her. Gretchen Hogan is the school nurse. She's much more reserved than Fiona. She's also much older. I'm certain the only reason they were allowed to go to college was so that they could come back and infiltrate the school, if I may use that word," he said. "Of the six official births, three are Fiona, Gretchen, and the town's so-called doctor, Don Hogan. I know it sounds strange, but trust me. Once you've been here awhile, you'll understand."

"Who do the other three belong to?"

"I have their names," he said. "That's it. If they are still around,

I've not seen them or heard mention of them. Two should be eighteen now. The other was born the same year as Fiona."

CJ stood, pacing. "Okay, we get that the community lives off the grid. But babies are born but not documented?"

"*If* babies are born, yes, that's what it appears. Like I said, I haven't seen children. I've asked for them to research it as far back as they can. The community was quite large at one time. Birth certificates—and death certificates, for that matter—don't exist for most of the residents."

"Yet some are documented. Predestined?" Paige guessed. "Fiona was documented and went to college. Gretchen too. And the doctor. Of course, presuming at birth that someone is going to be brilliant enough to be a doctor is really rolling the dice."

"His medical degree is suspect," Avery said. "From a college in the Dominican," he said. "That's the only record of him. Nothing here. If he is actually practicing medicine, it would be very basic."

"What about here at the school?" Paige asked. "You have a nurse. But what if the kids need emergency care?"

"San Augustine has the closest medical facility. We also have two doctors who come by on a rotating basis." He smiled to himself. Seven months on the job and suddenly it was "we" when speaking of the school. Perhaps this assignment had grown on him more than he'd realized.

CJ ran her fingers through her hair in what he assumed was a nervous habit. "Okay, let's get back to the reason we're here in the first place. The mysterious disappearances. The town's quirky, sure, but are you suggesting there's something sinister going on here? As far as I know, there's not one shred of evidence that links this town to the disappearances. And as weird as this town seems, we're here to investigate the disappearance, not the community. Right?"

"All I can say is take a drive there. Go by the café. See if you don't feel it too. It's a dead town, that's how I describe it. You won't see smiles or hear laughter. Muted conversations that stop suddenly. You may only see one person, yet feel eight pairs of eyes on you." He shook his shoulders as if trying to ward off something. "It's creepy."

"Okay, so it's like a cult of some sort," Paige said. "Is that what you're suggesting?"

"That's your word, not mine," he said quickly. "You start throwing the *cult* word around and people get nervous. But something of the sort, yes."

CJ sat down again. "What about the staff here? Do they stay away? Are they warned when they take the job?"

"I wouldn't say they're warned by the administration, but I'm sure the other teachers fill them in. Turnover rate is very high here. On average, most teachers stay only three years. There are two, a couple, that have been here five. They have the longest stint, if that tells you anything. Gayla Grumfeld is who I've assigned to be your mentor," he said to Paige. "She can fill you in on the intricacies of the school and whatnot."

"The school has been here, what? Thirty years?"

"Thirty-one," he corrected.

Paige nodded. "If the town is so isolated and wants to be isolated, why was the school located here? I mean, they obviously have influence on what happens here. Why would the Hogans sell land and allow the school to be built?"

"Money," he said simply. "Without the school, I think the community would have died long ago. I know what the estimate is on the population, but I'd say it is less than fifty people. To the person driving down the highway, they wouldn't even notice it."

"But how does the town handle visits by parents? Assuming that parents visit, that is."

"It's very regimented. Parents are allowed one Saturday visit per quarter in which they can take their child out of the compound. Surprisingly, Hoganville puts on a good show. It's very staged. They welcome the parents in the café with signs. In fact, one of the guys has this huge smoker that they'll bring out front and barbeque brisket and ribs. It's quite a hit with the parents," he said. "Of course, a lot of the parents take day trips out of town. The girls aren't allowed to be gone overnight. Bed check is at ten p.m. on those days. Nine p.m. on normal nights."

"How many parents actually come visit? I would imagine a lot of the girls aren't exactly from model homes and families," Paige said.

"I've been here for two of the quarterly open houses. I would guess less than half of the eligible girls get visits. The school is expensive, so there's an odd mix here," he said. "I'm surprised it's worked, but it has. There are two sectors—blue and red. I classify the reds as just this close," he said, holding his thumb and index finger an inch apart, "from being sent to a traditional juvenile lockup facility. Those were sent here by a judge and are obviously funded by the state. These are girls who got into trouble and need guidance. Petty thefts, drugs, mostly. First-time offenders really. But still, just basically your run-of-the-mill juvenile delinquents. Then you have those whose families have money and can afford to send their child here." He shook his head. "Even though they are kept separated, I personally would not send my child here."

"I'm assuming it's diverse? More so than the town, anyway," CJ said.

"Of course. I would say sixty percent white, thirty black, ten Hispanic. But like any school—or prison, for that matter—you have your cliques. You have a group of leaders and a bunch of followers."

"Gangs?"

"Let's call them mini-gangs. Again, there's a lot to go over. That's why I've asked Gayla to assist you, Paige. CJ, you'll get the rundown from the chief."

"Okay, how will we communicate with you? Face to face?"

"Not often. It might raise suspicions. Especially CJ. There's really no reason for one of the campus cops to visit my office."

"What's the layout on that? Security guard at the gate. Another here? What else?"

"There are ten security guards, who don't carry weapons. They split the day and night shifts. Besides the gate, they are in and out of classrooms, the cafeteria and the dorms. There are also six police officers, including yourself. An armed officer is always in the red sector's classrooms. The gate closes and locks at ten each night, except Saturday. No one else knows the two of you are plants, by the way. We need to keep it that way."

"How did you manage two new positions?"

"The gym teacher position was actually available. It's hard to get a single teacher to come here. That's why most are in pairs.

The vacancy in campus security came about quite suddenly," he said with a smile. "I believe Officer Nelson got an offer he couldn't refuse."

"And as far as you know, none of the staff associates with anyone in town? Well, besides Fiona and Gretchen."

"They both live here during the week but stay in town over the weekends. Fiona is very friendly with the rest of the staff. Gretchen, not so much. But I don't believe Fiona mixes her two lives. Meaning, she's not introduced any of her personal friends to the staff. At least, not that I'm aware of."

"Don't people find that odd?"

"You mean any odder than the rest of it?"

Paige smiled at him. "We really have no idea what's going on, do we?"

"None whatsoever," he agreed. He leaned back, deciding not to warn them of the strange cries—screams—he sometimes heard at night. He would let them experience that on their own.

CHAPTER SIX

CJ stared at the bed, then glanced at Paige. Their eyes met for a second, then Paige turned, following Avery back out into the small living area.

"It's not much, I know. But it's the only one that's vacant and clean. The one Officer Nelson lived in is a bit larger, but it'll need a thorough cleaning."

"This is fine," Paige said, going to the window. "It's like a little suburban neighborhood out here."

"Yes. But for the most part, everyone gets along well. I'll let you integrate yourself with them naturally, but they have a weekly potluck dinner or a cookout. There's no entertainment in the compound, so they've learned to make their own. We're forty-five minutes to the nearest town of any size."

CJ shifted uncomfortably, still trying to wrap her mind around the fact that she and Paige would be sharing a bed. Avery apparently took her silence as his cue to leave.

"Well, I'll let you get settled in. You both have my number and e-mail. Most of our communication should be done that way. After you've met the staff—I have no doubt some will be over shortly—you might want to take a drive, check out Hoganville. I'd even suggest breakfast at the café tomorrow morning. That should prompt a call from Ester Hogan. She'll want to know your background. She likes to keep her hand in everything."

"Oh, what about a uniform?" she asked.

"Yes. You've been issued five. They are already in the closet."

"You've thought of everything, it seems."

"I believe in being organized." He opened the door, his expression changing. "Again, welcome to Hogan School for Girls," he said louder than necessary. "I hope you'll enjoy your stay with us."

They watched him walk down the steps and across the yard to his car, then Paige closed the door, leaving them alone. All alone.

CJ swallowed. "Well," she said, her voice trailing off. She saw movement outside the window. "Wonder why we didn't close the blinds," she said.

"Do we have company already?" Paige asked quietly, their eyes meeting.

CJ nodded.

"Great," she murmured. "Showtime. And I don't believe I'm ready." A knock sounded shortly thereafter and again their eyes met. "I'll get it...*honey*."

CJ took a deep breath, forcing a smile to her face. As Paige had said, showtime. They hadn't even had time to practice.

"I know you two want to get unpacked and all, but we just had to meet you," said an exuberant redhead with long, straight hair pulled back into a ponytail. "I'm Suzette. This is my partner, Becca."

"Hi," Paige said. "I'm the new gym teacher. Paige Riley," she said as she extended her hand. "And this is CJ Johnston."

She held her hand out, beckoning CJ to take it. She did, stiffening only slightly as Paige's fingers entwined with her own.

"We're kinda new," Paige explained shyly. "Is it proper to say partner already?"

"Oh, newlyweds," Becca exclaimed with a clap of her hands. "I love it. How long?"

"Just six months," CJ said. "I can't believe we're here together. This is exciting."

"Oh, honey, it's a good thing you're newlyweds then." She gave an exaggerated wink. "It'll give you something to do," she said with a laugh. "Because exciting is not how I would describe this job."

"Don't jade them already," Suzette said. "Come on, let's get out of their hair. Burgers at Jules's place tomorrow. You're both invited."

"Jules?"

"Three houses down. Bring your own burgers to grill. There'll be plenty of side dishes."

"We're kinda empty on the food department," Paige said. "We're told there's a grocery store here."

"Oh, there is, but, honey, I wouldn't recommend it. Drive the forty miles to San Augustine and be done with it."

"Is something wrong with the one here?" CJ asked, feeling a light squeeze from Paige's fingers.

"We don't have enough time to go into all that's wrong around here," Suzette said with a short laugh.

"I think they should stop in," Becca said. "It's an experience everyone should have at least once. If they're open. They keep odd hours."

"They don't like lesbians?"

They both laughed. "That's not it. *That*, at least, you could explain." She shook her head. "No, it's just a weird little place." She smiled broadly. "Nice to meet you both. Don't forget burgers tomorrow."

They let their hands fall apart as soon as the door was closed. CJ tried to lighten the mood.

"Look at that, baby. We've already made new friends."

"I wonder how long they've been here," Paige said, ignoring her comment. "They seem to know enough about the town."

"Wonder if they know anything about the disappearances?"

"Depends on what local TV stations they get here. I'll assume Lufkin stations."

"If they watch local. I think every cabin has a satellite dish."

"Shame we don't have a TV," Paige said, looking at the empty spot on the small entertainment center.

"Good thing we're newlyweds," CJ said with a grin.

***

"So you really think it's just some sort of cult?"

"A cult can have many meanings," Paige said. "Are you referring to a satanic cult? Or something less sinister, like pagans or even Scientology? Or perhaps occultism, with magic and witches?"

"I don't know," she said. "Just, you know, a cult."

"Well, that's a broad statement. The Nazis in Germany were considered a cult. White supremacists are a cult. Jim Jones and the People's Temple. David Koresh and the Branch Davidians. Terrorists." Paige smiled. "Catholics."

CJ laughed. "Okay, I get your point. Maybe I should wait until I've actually seen the place before passing judgment."

"Of course, a community of over fifty people, that's a large number to control, to manipulate. I mean, that's what cults do. But if it has no outside influence, I suppose that makes it much easier."

There were no signs signaling their approach to Hoganville. The two-lane road sliced through the tall pines, a link between the two national forests where the school was located—the school and the tiny, secluded community. CJ slowed when they first spotted the buildings. They were as Avery had described. Neat and well kept, unpretentious to say the least. An almost too simple sign hung above each door. *Hogan Grocery. Hogan Café*. The service station had no sign of any sort, only faded numbers advertising the cost of fuel. All three appeared to be closed.

CJ stopped in front of the small grocery store. There was

no open or closed sign that Paige could see, and there didn't appear to be posted hours on the door.

"Where the hell is everyone?" CJ asked.

"Let's check it out," Paige said, already opening the door.

The parking lot was gravel, with only cement stepping stones at the entryway of the store. The afternoon heat was hot, but not unbearably so. They stood side by side, both frowning at what they saw.

"Who has blinds on grocery store windows?" CJ asked quietly.

"There aren't any signs. No advertisements. No sales. Isn't that odd?"

CJ smiled at her. "Let's take a bet on how many times we say the words odd, strange or weird."

Paige leaned closer. "Is it just me or do you feel people watching us?"

"It's not just you, baby."

Out of the corner of her eye, Paige saw movement. She nudged CJ. "The blinds just moved, far window," she whispered.

"This place is creepy."

"Yes. Let's add that to the list of words we'll use to describe Hoganville."

CJ turned, looking around the empty parking lot. "No noise," she said. "No dogs barking, no cars. Nothing." Behind the store—beyond the woods that nearly blocked her view—she had a glimpse of the neat, white houses of the Hogan clan.

Paige took her hand and tugged her back to the car. "I vote we drive to San Augustine for groceries. This whole thing is just...eerie."

CJ smiled at her. "And another word to add to the list."

CHAPTER SEVEN

Ester Hogan ran her fingers over the deep purple robe, still amazed at its softness after all these years. It had been her mother's, handed down to her thirty-some odd years ago when she took over the flock. It was predestined, she knew, and she had been prepared, but oh, how she had loved it the day her sickly mother gave her the robe. It was with pride that she admitted she was probably the most prepared *mother* of them all, even more than her beloved grandmother. She closed her eyes, making a mental note to go visit her grandmother later.

She slipped the robe on, leaving the hood off. For now. The elders would be gathering in the chambers soon, but she would have time to dress fully. The summer heat was already upon them and she allowed herself that little indulgence. The meeting would be longer than they all anticipated, she knew. Fiona, the good sheep that she was, had alerted her to the strangers. Two new women were due at the school. That was why she had ordered the lockdown. She hadn't had time to place her inquiries. This new director was proving hard to break.

She smiled slightly, her gaze going to her fingers—her nails—and she brushed them softly against the robe. Perhaps Director Avery needed some persuasion. And that too could be fun, she thought. It would give Belden something to do. After all, he had broken the guard, the one they called Richard, in record time.

The ancient grandfather clock chimed the hour, and she dutifully lifted the hood over her head, making her way to the stairway that would take her underground to the tunnels. She used to be afraid of the tunnels when she was young, but now she could find her way blindfolded through the maze and on to the cave and the chambers beyond.

They awaited her—the elders. Then she stopped, smiling broadly. She'd come to love all this ritualistic rhetoric that her great-grandmother had started. She knew the history behind it, of course, but most of the flock did not. To them, this was all they'd ever known.

And all they would ever know.

***

Paige glanced away from the squash she was slicing, still wondering how she'd gotten saddled with fixing their dinner. CJ was on the phone, mostly listening, nodding occasionally. It was Howley, she knew that much, but most of their conversation was one-sided. When CJ put her phone down, Paige waited expectantly.

"Nothing new, really. They're doing some background checks. Or trying to. The café and grocery store, as well as the gas station, are all legally owned by the Hogan estate. Financially, those appear to be the only assets they have, other than the adjoining acreage. And they're trying to get records on the medical school guy, Don Hogan. Other than that, nothing." CJ came closer, inspecting the pile of vegetables Paige had chopped. "So are you just making this up or what?"

"Unless you want to volunteer to cook, I would suggest you keep your comments to yourself," she said. "And no, I'm not making this up. It's a dish I cook frequently."

"Vegetables. What else?"

"Brown rice. And I'll make a sauce to put on it."

"I meant, you know, protein."

"Navy beans, kidney beans. A mixture."

CJ's eyebrows shot up. "Beans? I went shopping with you. I saw us buy chicken breasts, fish, a couple of steaks. So beans?"

"We're having burgers tomorrow. I thought we'd do a vegetarian meal tonight. It will go wonderfully with that chardonnay."

CJ sighed. "I'm going to miss takeout. That's how I survived, you know."

"No doubt. Lucky you, I love to cook."

"Yeah, lucky me," CJ murmured as she plopped down on the sofa. "I get vegetables and rice. And no TV."

"So ask Howley for approval to purchase one," she suggested.

"Yeah. We should."

Paige put onions and peppers into the hot olive oil while she finished slicing the squash. Their first night together was not going well. There was a visible tension between them, and she knew it stemmed from the fact that soon, they would be retiring into the bedroom together, to share a queen bed that was getting smaller by the minute. So now seemed as good a time as any to bring up...*that night.*

"Why haven't we ever talked about it?" she asked. Thankfully, CJ didn't pretend to not know what she was talking about. CJ couldn't, however, hold her gaze.

"Because that's what we do. We don't talk about things. We do our job, we see what we see and we deal in our own way. That night, we just happened to deal with it together."

Paige was amazed by her honest answer. It was better than any she could have given. But she did feel she owed CJ an explanation.

"I know you. I've worked with you for several years now. You have this persona that you project to everyone—always a different lover. You go out searching, after we've had a particularly bad case. You go to the bar, find some stranger, someone you don't know, someone you won't have to know after it's over with. You go home with her and then you leave and forget all about her."

"Hey, wait a minute," CJ said. "I'm not the one who left. You did."

"Yes, because I knew you wouldn't want to talk about it, to deal with it. That's not your style. What would we have done if I'd stayed? I wasn't like the others where you could make your escape before I woke up and never see me again."

"No. But you made *your* escape," CJ reminded her.

"Yes. I did that so you—*we*—wouldn't have to face it. I left because that's what you wanted. I left because...well, because I knew it would be awkward. And I knew we wouldn't have any rationalization as to why we did what we did. And I didn't want us to be uncomfortable at work." She gave a quiet laugh. "Which, of course, was impossible. We spent the first few weeks acting weird with each other, so much so that Ice and Billy started to notice. It got back to normal, but..."

"But? What would we have talked about? We had sex. It was one of those things. It was a bad case and..."

"And what? I was there? I was available?"

CJ shook her head. "That's not what I meant." She paused. "Well, yeah, maybe it is what I meant. You were there. You were someone who could relate. You weren't a nameless stranger who didn't know me, didn't know the job." CJ met her eyes, finally holding her gaze. "Why did you come to the bar that night?"

Paige turned away. She knew if she brought up that night, CJ would ask this question. Despite being prepared for it, she still had no answer. She supposed that night, surely, she had a reason. And if she were to guess, she would say it was because of CJ. Because of the kids. Because she knew how personal CJ took those things. And for some reason, that night, she didn't want CJ to find solace in some stranger's arms...and a stranger's bed.

"You're right. I knew no one else could possibly understand what you'd gone through that day. No one would understand what you needed," she said quietly, surprising herself with the honest answer. She looked back at CJ. "And I think maybe I needed someone who understood me as well."

CJ was quite possibly stunned by her words because for once, she had no comeback. Their eyes held for the longest moment, then CJ nodded, finally glancing away. Paige went back to her dinner preparation, wondering if that was to be the extent of their conversation on the matter. If so, it was actually more than she'd thought they'd ever say.

CHAPTER EIGHT

CJ scrolled through Avery's notes for at least the fifth time, rereading every line, still finding the whole thing bizarre. It was like a bad TV movie. Maybe Paige was right when she said *Stepford Wives*. From all accounts, the residents in town acted more like robots than anything else.

She glanced up when she heard the water turn off. Getting used to sharing a bathroom was going to take a while. Trying not to imagine Paige naked, drying off as she finished her shower, was going to be damn near impossible. She remembered every exquisite curve of Paige Riley's body.

She shoved away from the table and stood by a window, looking out into the woods across the road. She wouldn't really call it a street. The cabins, while all relatively close together, were staggered and offset, allowing a little privacy. She tilted her head, hearing the bathroom door open, then the bedroom door, knowing Paige was dressing. She ran her hand through her hair, thinking back to last night. She'd been surprised at Paige's confession. She had often wondered how Paige had ended up at the bar that night. It was just your average lesbian bar—loud music, dim lights and lots of alcohol and laughter. Not a place Paige Riley frequented, she knew. The circumstances which brought her there...well, CJ wasn't really sure how she felt about that. Should she be grateful Paige cared enough to do that? Or was it as Paige had indicated? That they both needed each other that night.

Regardless, it seemed to ease a little of the tension between them. Dinner had been good, the conversation light, and it was nice to share a bottle of wine knowing there were no expectations at the end of the evening. They had actually made light of the fact that they were sharing a bed, and Paige drew an imaginary line down the middle which CJ promised not to cross. And she hadn't. She slept soundly, and that surprised her. She wasn't used to sleeping with someone, but she found Paige's presence reassuring, if nothing else.

All of which was great and wonderful...if only her mind wouldn't continually flash back to that night. It was a night she remembered in great detail, which was unusual for her. Normally, the lingering effects of the tequila would erase most of her dalliances from her mind. On that particular night, they'd left the bar long before she'd succumbed to the tequila. She was quite lucid in her seduction of Paige Riley. Or was it Paige's seduction of her? It didn't matter. She could remember every detail with delicious clarity.

"Hey."

She turned, finding Paige looking as beautiful as ever—pressed khaki shorts, a soft-looking, low-cut blouse that showed off far too much cleavage, with leather belt and matching sandals. CJ raised an eyebrow as she spied the red nail polish on her toes. That was something she never considered and she found it extremely sexy. She glanced at her own outfit. Her shorts were khaki as well, although worn and wrinkled. Her T-shirt hung loose, her shoes were sports sandals.

"I feel underdressed," she said.

"You look fine. It's a barbeque."

"Then why are you so dressed up?"

Paige glanced at herself. "This is hardly dressed up."

"Oh. I see. That's your casual. That would be *my* dressed up."

Paige smiled and it was actually a sweet smile, CJ noted.

"Yes, well, you are you and that's what you feel comfortable in. And this is what I feel comfortable in."

CJ let the conversation end with that. If they'd been with the guys, she would have made a crude mention of the low-cut blouse, of the enticing cleavage. But she refrained. They were getting along well and why spoil that with a crass comment.

"I've packed us some beer and water bottles. Not sure what kind of party this is," she said. "Or would you rather have wine?"

Paige shook her head. "I'll have a beer. Or the water. It's fine."

"And I didn't touch the meat patties you made up. They're still in the fridge. What was all that stuff mixed in there anyway?"

"Just some green onions and peppers and herbs. Nothing fancy."

"It looked...interesting," she conceded.

Paige laughed. "Is that your way of saying you'd rather have just a plain old burger?"

"I'll give anything a try. Once," she added.

***

Paige was startled when CJ took her hand, then she relaxed, trying to ease into her role as loving girlfriend. They heard laughter in the back, so they skipped the front door and headed around the side. Suzette waved them over.

"I'm so glad you came," she said.

"Hi, I'm Robbie," a short blond woman said, holding out her hand. "Let me take that for you."

Paige handed over the plate with their burgers. "Thanks. I'm Paige. This is CJ."

"Nice to meet you both. It's always exciting to get new members in our community."

"I see you found a grocery store," Becca said. "I trust it wasn't in Hoganville."

CJ laughed. "No, you were right about that. We stopped by. It looked deserted. Are you sure people live there?"

"Oh, it's a weird little place. I'm Julia. Everyone calls me Jules."

"Hi, Jules. Thanks for having us over," Paige said.

"We take turns and do this every weekend. Entertainment is scarce around here."

"We go dancing every other Saturday night," Suzette said. "Do you dance?"

Before Paige could say no, they definitely did *not* dance, CJ slid an arm around her waist and pulled her closer.

"We love to dance," she said. "In fact, that's how we met."

Paige smiled through gritted teeth. "Oh, honey, don't tell that story," she said, hoping CJ wasn't going to ad lib on their backstory, which had them meeting on a blind date. Their backstory never even *mentioned* dancing. Paige smiled at Suzette. "I had a little too much to drink," she explained.

"You fell for my charm anyway, though, didn't you?" CJ teased.

"I think I'm going to love this story," Suzette said with a laugh. "The nearest gay bar is nearly two hours away, but we still make the trip. Come on, grab a lawn chair and I'll introduce you to everyone."

***

CJ was having a fabulous time, and she had to remind herself that they were working. She would pay for it later, when they were alone, but right now, with her hand resting comfortably on Paige's bare thigh, life was good.

"I will *get* you for this," Paige murmured. "There is no need to overplay it."

"Now, now. We're supposed to be in love. Isn't this what you do?"

"I wouldn't know. But if you move your hand any higher, I'll chop it off."

CJ barely controlled her laughter, instead, she leaned closer and grazed Paige's cheek with her lips. "Just wait until we go dancing. Now *that* will be fun."

Paige glared at her. "We met on a blind date," she whispered. "You can't improvise, for God's sake."

"Lighten up, baby," she said. "I love to dance. Slow songs," she added with a wink.

Thankfully—before Paige could respond—Suzette joined them, holding out a platter of deviled eggs. Paige politely took only one. CJ grabbed two, popping one in her mouth immediately.

"So good," she murmured with her mouth full.

"It's Becca's specialty," Suzette said. "Don't tell her, but I'm actually sick of them."

"This is fun," Paige said. "Thank you for including us. It's been nice to meet everyone."

"Oh, sure. We do this every weekend, either Saturday or Sunday. Not everyone comes, of course, but all are welcome."

"Well, we'll have to host one soon," Paige said, surprising CJ when she covered her hand, letting their fingers entwine.

Becca joined them, pulling a lawn chair closer to their circle. "So, what did you think of Hoganville?"

"Not sure what to think," CJ said. "It looked like everything was shut down. We didn't see a single car."

"Car? We didn't even see any *people*," Paige said.

"Yeah, it's crazy. It's like they flip a switch and the place shuts down."

"Surely some of the staff at the school is from Hoganville," CJ said. "Has anyone asked them?"

"Really, there are only two locals at the school. Well, if you don't count the part-time janitorial staff and cafeteria workers. We never see them anyway. But you'll like Fiona. She's nice. Teaches science. Now Gretchen, the nurse, no. Very standoffish. She doesn't have anything to do with us."

"Just two? Wow," Paige said.

"Yeah. That's weird too, I know. Even maintenance, they hire from outside."

"What does Fiona say about the town?"

"Not much," Suzette said. "When we comment on how strange everyone is, she just laughs and says that's how it's always been in Hoganville."

"She lives right on the other side of you, by the way," Becca said. "Not on weekends. She always leaves. Stays with her mother, I think. Comes back Sunday nights."

"How old is she?"

"Thirty something," Suzette said. She leaned closer and grinned. "Now, I want to hear how you two met."

CHAPTER NINE

Fiona stared at her reflection in the mirror as she continued brushing her long, dark hair. Mother Hogan had summoned her and she had no idea why. She'd followed every instruction ever given to her. There had been no missteps. She had seen her friends culled long ago for not being true to the flock. She had no wish to suffer their fate.

With one last brush, she stood, reaching for the white robe and slipping it on. She longed for the day she could replace the virginal white for the black robe worn by most of the others. She was more than ready to couple, if only Mother would allow it. She didn't know who she would choose if it were left up to her, as there wasn't anyone her own age in the flock other than Don, and Mother had forbidden the two of them to talk.

"Fiona? It's time."

She met her mother's eyes questioningly, but the older woman said nothing. With a nod, Fiona walked past her, heading into the kitchen and to the door that would take her downstairs and into the tunnels. She closed the door behind her, her eyes adjusting to the darkness. She felt along the wall, finding the torch. As always, she did a quick inspection. The damp, musty smell was familiar to her, but she felt a slight surge of fear. The fear that the tunnels would collapse on her was something she'd carried with her since she was a child. She took a deep breath, finally pushing down the anxiety and making her feet move. She followed the maze of tunnels, turning right at the junction where she normally would turn left if going to the monthly gathering in the chambers. She had only been summoned to Mother Hogan's twice before. Once, when she was told she'd go to college to become a teacher. The second time was when she'd gotten hired at the school.

Belden was standing guard outside the door that would lead up to Mother's rooms. She nodded at him but didn't speak.

"Fiona," he greeted. "Mother is waiting," he said, ushering her inside.

She followed Belden up the stairs and into the Hogan estate. The house had been built over a hundred years ago, she knew, and it used to house five families. Today, only Mother Hogan and her brother lived there, along with the child they'd produced. The child who didn't speak.

As she had been the first two times, she was taken into the study. The large room was showing its age, the furniture old and worn, the drapes dusty and faded, drawn against the afternoon sun. Mother sat on the large leather chair, her purple robe covering her body, the hood nearly hiding her face. As before, Fiona felt a chill in the room.

She swallowed nervously, waiting for instruction.

"Fiona, thank you for coming," Mother said. "Please, sit."

"Yes, Mother," she said, sitting down opposite her.

"I'm sure you're wondering why you've been called. A couple of reasons," Mother said. "First, thank you for alerting us to the two new teachers at the school. I will need you to find out what you can about them. We can't be too careful, Fiona. We must shield ourselves from the outsiders. Always."

"Yes, Mother. I'll do my best."

"I know you will, child." She smiled then, reaching out to clasp Fiona's hand, her thin, cold fingers surprisingly strong. "There is something else. It is time for a coupling. Our flock is getting smaller. It is time to replenish."

Fiona's heart beat wildly. "Me?"

"Yes. In the large chamber. On the sacrificial altar. Tonight."

"Who have you chosen for me, if I may ask?"

"There is only one pure Hogan left," Mother said. "My brother, Antel."

Fiona couldn't keep the gasp from her voice. "But he...he coupled with my mother."

"Yes. You have Hogan blood in you. What better way to improve the line than for him to father your child as well?"

"Yes, Mother," she said, feeling relief when Mother released her hand. She rubbed her hands together nervously.

"We will have the ceremony at eight. Afterward, you will be presented with your new robe. You will stay here with Antel tonight and not return to the school," she instructed. "You will have to miss a few days, perhaps a week."

"Yes. Thank you, Mother. I'll be ready."

"I know you will, child. You have always been ready when I've needed you. Now, go. I've already sent word to your mother. She will prepare your bath."

Fiona made the trip back through the tunnels much slower than before. She paused at a junction, her gaze traveling down the corridor that would take her to the chambers...and beyond that, the deep, dark caves. Tonight, the flock would gather to watch the coupling. She had witnessed five couplings herself. She remembered the fear she felt at the first one. She'd been young and didn't understand. As she got older, the fear turned to arousal. Now, it was finally her turn.

***

Paige took her time in the shower, mainly because she still wasn't sure of her reaction to the afternoon. She had no illusions to the roles they were playing. Or at least she didn't think she had. When in public, they would pretend to be lovers. She was prepared for that. What she wasn't prepared for was the hand holding, the touching. The kiss.

She stuck her face in the water, wanting to be angry with CJ. Paige thought they were being convincing enough. Did CJ have to kiss her? Granted, it was quick and nearly closed mouth. In fact, it could have been considered almost chaste. Almost.

If not for the fact that—to her horror—she wasn't sure which of them started the kiss. Thankfully CJ had pulled away, had averted her eyes. Paige, however, was acutely aware of how her pulse had raced from the contact. She thought she'd forgotten about their night together, but apparently her body had not.

So yes, she wanted to be angry with CJ. She supposed CJ thought she would be angry too. As soon as they had left the party, CJ had dropped her hand and they'd walked home in silence. CJ had shut her out by putting in her earbuds and listening to music. Paige had retreated to the shower.

Despite it all, she couldn't help but smile as she recalled CJ's tale of how they met. God, it's a wonder she was able to play along, seeing as how they were making it up as they went. At one point, as CJ was about to launch into yet another story, Paige had clamped her mouth shut, covering it with her hand. This led to a quick brush of CJ's tongue against her palm, causing her to drop her hand. They had both laughed, and it had seemed natural, even to her, to lean in for the kiss. Before her mind caught up with her body, the kiss was over.

Well, maybe they just needed some ground rules. Holding hands? Okay. Occasional touching? Only if necessary. Kissing? Definitely not. There should be no reason for them to kiss in public. None.

Now with a purpose, she quickly finished her shower and dressed, finding CJ in the same position as she'd left her—

sitting on the sofa, bobbing her head to the music she heard. Paige walked over, yanking the earbuds from her ears.

"We should talk."

"Why?"

"*Why?* I think you know why," she said, noting that CJ wouldn't meet her gaze. "Let's go over some do's and don'ts," she said.

CJ rolled her eyes. "Seriously? It was barely a kiss," she said. "And it seemed like the right thing to do at the time."

"Yes, it did," she conceded. *Crap.* "I would just prefer to keep things as simple as possible. It would be odd if we didn't hold hands or...or touch occasionally. But I don't see the need for... kissing."

CJ looked at her then, an evil twinkle in her eyes. "Why? Afraid you might like it?"

Paige forced a laugh. "I assure you, no. You're not my type. In the least," she added. As soon as the words were out, she knew they were a mistake.

"Really? I recall a night about six months ago that begs to differ," CJ said. "I seemed to be your type that night."

"Yes, well, an aberration, for sure," she said, as if that was excuse enough. "We both saw how well that turned out."

"Well, if it makes you feel any better, you're not my type either. This is as uncomfortable for me as it is for you."

Paige had to bite her lip to keep from replying. Actually, she had to turn away to keep the words from tumbling out. CJ promptly put her earbuds back in, and Paige went into the bedroom with a slam of the door, dragging out her laptop to check e-mail.

"Right," she finally murmured. "As if CJ Johnston *has* a type. Any woman with a pulse would do."

Of course, she was being ridiculous. She had no clue who CJ's type was really. She'd never seen her out socially and made it a point not to listen when the guys quizzed CJ about her dates. She simply wasn't interested.

***

"I'm scared."

Fiona's mother smiled reassuringly. "It'll be fine. You should feel honored Mother Hogan chose you."

"Yes, I know." She took a deep breath. "Will it hurt?"

"You've witnessed couplings, Fiona. What do you think?"

Yes. And she also had a bachelor's degree in science. Nonetheless, this was still a foreign concept. When she went away to college, all the other girls would talk about sex and guys. She had nothing to contribute. It was the closest she'd come to forsaking the flock, to disobeying Mother Hogan. She was exposed to so many things, so many things that were not allowed in Hoganville. But in the end, she remained faithful. She knew she could still be culled. Her place was in Hoganville, not out *there*. She was glad she hadn't succumbed to the outside. Mother Hogan had warned her and she had heeded that warning.

"I suppose I'm ready," she said, letting her mother tie the robe at her neck, then put the hood over her head.

"I must join the others. Belden will lead you."

Fiona nodded, taking several deep breaths before following her mother down the stairs. Belden was waiting, and she could see the excitement on his face. Couplings in the chamber only happened a few times each year. Recently, those times occurred less and less as the flock grew older and older. Once you wore the black robe, however, couplings in private were allowed, as long as it did not produce a child. Mother Hogan was the only one who could sanction a new birth in the flock. Fiona felt honored that she was chosen. If she bore a daughter, then the Hogan bloodline would continue. When she was of age, her daughter would then move into the estate and live with Mother Hogan. She would be next in line. That thought made her heart swell. Her own daughter could someday lead the flock.

"You look beautiful, Fiona."

"Thank you. I'm nervous," she admitted.

"Mother Hogan favors you. Do not be nervous."

Easier said than done, but she kept that thought to herself. Antel Hogan was a big man, much older than herself. Older, even, than her own mother. As far as she knew, Antel Hogan and her mother had only joined the one time, that in the same chamber she was being led to now.

She was trembling with fear, with anticipation. They were all there, dozens of black robes with only one remaining white robe. Mother Hogan was standing near the sacrificial altar, her deep purple robe appearing almost black in the dark chamber, which was lit only by a handful of torches. Antel Hogan stood to her left, his hood covering his gray head, only his face visible.

Fiona paused, accepting the inevitable, yet clinging to a long-ago dream—when she had dared to dream. She had no reference as to what to expect from her life other than what she saw in Hoganville. There were no marriages. They were not needed. But she had a glimpse of another life and only then did she dare to dream of falling in love, of finding a young man to marry, to bond with. But it was just a dream. She stood now before Antel Hogan, about to give him her innocence at thirty-one years of age. The same man who had taken her mother's virtue as well.

Mother Hogan held out her hand, beckoning her to come closer. In her other hand was the potion she was to drink. Fiona took the final steps, her gaze landing on that of Antel Hogan's. She was afraid.

She was suddenly very afraid.

***

"Our neighbor is not home yet," CJ said as she sauntered into the bedroom at ten. At Paige's raised eyebrows, she added, "Fiona."

"Maybe she stayed in Hoganville," Paige said, closing her laptop.

"I suppose. I was looking forward to meeting her, though."

"Why? You think she might have horns or something?"

CJ laughed, turning her back to Paige and pulling her shirt over her head, leaving herself naked from the waist up.

"Must you? Really?"

"Just getting ready for bed. Don't look if it bothers you," she said, smiling as she heard Paige leave the room and slam the door. She shouldn't tease so, she knew. Not if they expected to make it through this assignment without getting a divorce.

Of course, they had to do other things as well. Like get a TV. With Paige holed up in the bedroom, CJ had stayed in the living room, her only entertainment was the music on her phone. It would be much easier if they could get along for an extended period of time. She really didn't think the kiss was overdoing it. In fact, they had been so playful with each other, it would have seemed odd *not* to kiss in that particular moment. And if she really thought about it, she could almost say Paige was the one to initiate it.

"Was barely a kiss anyway," she muttered as she climbed under the covers, tugging at the sleep shirt she was not used to wearing. *God, how many months of this?*

"Are you decent?" Paige called.

CJ grinned. "I'm always decent, baby." She could picture Paige rolling her eyes.

Paige stood at the door, hands on her hips. "I think you're enjoying this way too much."

"On the contrary. I'd much rather be back in Houston with the guys. You're a little...uptight."

Paige glared at her. "Uptight? *Me?*"

"It was barely a kiss."

"Jesus, are we back to that again?" she asked as she jerked back the covers on her side of the bed.

"Isn't that what's got your panties in a wad?"

Paige took a deep breath, then pursed her lips. "Goodnight, CJ," she said. "Please turn out the lamp and stay on your side of the bed."

"God, this is going to be a long assignment," CJ murmured.

"Tell me about it."

CJ punched at her pillow, trying to get comfortable. She smiled devilishly as she slid her foot across Paige's imaginary line. She was rewarded with a swift kick to her calf. She couldn't contain her laughter.

"You're such a child," Paige muttered.

CJ sighed and closed her eyes, willing sleep to come. She tried to ignore the warm body only a few feet from her. Just as she was dozing off, a sharp, piercing scream shattered the quiet around their little house. They both jerked up, barely breathing, as Paige gripped her arm tightly.

"What the hell was that?" CJ whispered.

"I have no idea. What do you think it was?"

"I don't know. Maybe a coyote?"

Paige cocked her head. "Do you even know what a coyote sounds like?"

"Hell, I'm a city girl. So maybe it was like a cougar or something," she said.

"Do they have cougars out here?"

CJ shrugged, then jumped as the scream was heard again, this time a little farther away. "It sounds like it's hunting."

"It?"

"Let's go with cougar," she said as she settled down again. She was thankful Paige did not remove her hand.

CHAPTER TEN

Paige felt a little nervous and just a twinge of anxiety when she dressed for her first school day. Of the two of them, CJ would have made a much better gym teacher. Of course, CJ made a much better cop too, she thought, as she spied her tucking in her uniform shirt. Well, maybe not a better cop, but she certainly looked better in a uniform than Paige did.

"I saw you looking, quit pretending you're not," CJ said with her normal arrogance.

"I was not *looking*," Paige said. "I just happened to glance over and see you." She rolled her eyes. "God, she's so full of herself," she muttered.

CJ laughed but made no further comment. "You ready for coffee, *dear*?"

"Yes, please." She was thankful she'd insisted on packing her gourmet coffee from home. The grocery store they'd shopped at was sorely lacking and had only a limited variety.

"This is pretty good," CJ said. "What is it?" she asked as she handed Paige her cup.

"Guatemala Antigua. Medium roast," she said, closing her eyes, savoring the first sip. "I always taste just a tiny hint of chocolate in that first sip," she said. "You?"

CJ shook her head. "Not really."

"No, I suppose not. You've already killed the flavor with sugar and cream."

CJ laughed good-naturedly. "You should know, since you bring me coffee all the time."

"Well, what we serve in the office, I wouldn't exactly call *coffee*," she said, not caring in the least that she sounded aristocratic. There was a distinct difference between well-blended gourmet coffee and the cheap, low-grade coffee that made its way to their office.

CJ stood back, eyeing her. "Are you going to manage this?"

"What do you mean?"

"Off-the-rack clothes," she said.

Paige looked down at herself. "These aren't exactly off-the-rack," she said. "They are made to appear that way."

CJ lifted a corner of her mouth. "Okay, so if they're made to appear that way, why don't you just buy the real thing? It'd be a hell of a lot cheaper."

"Obviously, you don't see the point."

"Obviously, you don't either."

Paige sighed. "Okay. Perhaps I should scope out the other teachers, see what they wear," she said. "And then we can plan a shopping trip."

"Oh no. Don't lump me in with *we* and *shopping*," CJ said. "At least not clothes shopping. I'd rather go to the dentist."

Paige smiled. "That's not really a surprise. I've seen how you dress."

"Good. So you won't have to try to change me when we get into our golden years."

Paige couldn't contain her laughter—it bubbled out before she could stop it. CJ's eyes were dancing with amusement and

Paige just went with the moment, enjoying CJ's playfulness this morning. Oh, maybe she did need to lighten up.

"You know, I think you're making a big deal out of this anyway," CJ continued. "I mean, you're a gym teacher. My gym teachers wore workout gear. Maybe you could get some short shorts or maybe some tights and a sports bra setup. That'd be really hot," she said with a grin.

"I so do not see that happening," she said, still smiling.

But later, as they were parked in front of the admin building, her smile vanished and she gave CJ a threatening look.

"Don't even think about it," she warned.

"Look, let's just make it quick, then I'm gone."

"I don't believe that it's necessary."

"You don't think everyone is watching the new teacher? Do you want to pull this off or not?"

Paige stared at her. "This is not necessary. You're doing this just to piss me off."

CJ grinned. "Well, that too. This is the worst assignment I've ever had." She leaned closer. "So humor me. Kiss me and get it over with."

Paige's gaze dropped to her lips, then back to her eyes. "Didn't we just have this discussion last night?"

"Yes."

"And?"

"And I never concurred with your line of thinking." CJ smiled and it was almost a sweet smile, Paige noted. "We're in love. Now kiss me goodbye and go start your day, *honey*."

Paige relented. She was making far too big a deal out of it anyway. She closed the distance between them, touching her lips to CJ's. To her horror, she felt them linger there. She pulled back quickly, unable to meet her eyes.

"That wasn't so bad, was it?"

Paige cleared her throat, then opened the door. "Don't shoot anyone today," she said dryly as she slammed the door behind her.

She took a deep breath, making her way to the administration building where she was to meet Gayla Grumfeld. She was ten minutes early but was pleasantly surprised to find Gayla waiting for her in the lobby.

"I was hoping you'd be early," the older woman greeted her. "I'm Gayla. You *are* Paige, right?"

"Yes. Nice to meet you," Paige said, extending her hand.

"I'm afraid the whole tour will have to wait for another day, but I do have time to go over the position somewhat. Fiona Hogan called in sick this morning," Gayla said as she began walking down the hall. "Very unusual for her, but I'll have to cover her classes," she explained.

"I hope it's nothing serious," Paige said.

"Don't know. There was only a message left very early this morning." She held the door open, motioning Paige to go first. "We call this the breezeway, even though it's enclosed," Gayla said. "This links the admin building to the classrooms. There is another one on the other side of campus that links to the dorms and cafeteria. The students are allowed outside—supervised sessions—twice a day. Those who get good marks for behavior get some hours out alone on the weekends. They can go as far as the lake and the hike and bike trail. Everything else is off limits," she explained.

The long corridor had windows on both sides. On one side, there was a view of the parking lot and beyond that, the small lake. On the other side was a small courtyard with tables and chairs, a few of them occupied.

"The courtyard is for staff mainly. Some of us use it for breakfast and lunch. The only times students are allowed to use it is on visitation days when they can sit with their parents."

"How many students?" Paige asked.

"We can house up to two hundred. Currently we have one fifty-eight," Gayla said. "Has Director Avery explained the color codes?"

"He mentioned it, but no, he didn't really explain it."

They were now in the building that housed the classrooms. The hallway was large and seemed endless, their shoes echoing loudly as they made their way deeper into the school.

"Red and blue," Gayla said. "The reds are a mixed group. Some are just bordering on being a juvenile prisoner who should be at a detention center. Those who have committed violent crimes are not allowed here, thank goodness. Reds are sent here

by a judge's order. This school gives them the chance to get their
life back together and to make a fresh start. The blues—in my
opinion—should not be here. Most are just troubled girls whose
parents didn't know what else to do with them. Some parents
look at this as some kind of boarding school, which is crazy.
Others think it's a boot camp that will instill the discipline that
they obviously didn't."

"Surely they're kept separate," Paige said.

"Somewhat. The blues have the most freedom, especially at
night with a couple of TV and game rooms. With good behavior,
reds are allowed to get sent down to Blue Hall each evening, if
they wish. The reds have a small TV room, but watching privileges
are limited to two hours each evening, so that's incentive right
there."

"How do you coordinate the classrooms?"

"Times are staggered. The blue rooms are just like your
normal high school, basically. Reds have an armed guard in
them." Gayla smiled. "Your partner will no doubt be assigned
that job. You make a cute couple, by the way."

Paige didn't know why, but she blushed at the comment.

"I saw you in the car earlier," Gayla explained. "Very
attractive."

"Yes, she is."

"I heard you went to the cookout yesterday. We went to
Dallas instead. I needed a city fix. Real restaurants, shopping,
movies."

"Yes, I know what you mean. CJ and I are from Houston so
this will be an adjustment, I'm sure."

Gayla stopped in front of a pair of double doors. "The gym,"
she said, pushing them opened. "It's not full size, obviously, but
it'll give you enough room to work with."

A basketball hoop was attached to one wall with four balls
tossed haphazardly around it. A net stretched across the two
shorter walls, for volleyball, she supposed. Other than that, the
room was vacant.

"Curriculum is standard?"

"We're sanctioned by the state but also have some federal
guidelines to follow. There are six other schools like this across

the nation, this being the only one in Texas. Unlike a juvenile detention center, once the girls are here, they're here until they graduate."

"So a fourteen-year-old could be sentenced to two years, but if they come here, it's four?"

"Exactly. Our youngest is thirteen, oldest nineteen. For the most part, the system works. And it's rewarding when they graduate and you know they now have a life ahead of them." Gayla shook her head. "Not all, of course. Some leave here and go right back to where they were, but we do our best."

"You've been here how long?" Paige asked.

"This will be our fifth year. I do love it. And, as you know, you can't beat the pay. But there's a reason for the high salary," she said. "We live mostly isolated. And the main gate locks at ten so it's not like you can make a late night of it. Except Saturdays." She smiled again. "Shopping is a real challenge. I hesitate to even call Hogan Grocery a real store."

Paige nodded. "I know what you mean. CJ and I drove to it on Saturday, hoping to find something for the cookout. The store was closed. In fact, the whole community looked shut down. We didn't see a soul."

"Well, not trying to sway you or anything, but that whole place gives me the creeps," Gayla said with an embarrassed laugh. "In fact, I haven't been there in two years, at least. If we need gas, we make a point to drive to San Augustine and do our grocery shopping at the same time."

"You keep saying 'we,'" Paige said. "Married? Partner?"

"Sorry. Husband. Dave. One of only two male teachers. He's a history buff and loves teaching."

"One of two?" Paige said, hoping she showed enough surprise in her voice. "He must really feel isolated."

"Oh, we've adjusted. And we're all great friends here. You have to be. The weekend cookouts are what keep us sane." She leaned closer, her voice low. "Well, that and a good bottle of wine."

Paige laughed with her. "I hope we fit in," she said. "We were actually looking forward to living in a small town, but now that I've seen it, Hoganville isn't really a town."

"Oh, no. They keep very much to themselves. The first month we were here, we went into the café for a Saturday brunch. We sat there for ten minutes and no one came to wait on us. My husband went to the counter and asked if there was a problem. The lady just stared at him, her face expressionless. The next thing we know, someone comes out with two plates and puts them in front of us. Of course, we hadn't ordered and I was afraid to eat it. We just got up and left and never went back."

"That is weird," she said. "CJ will want to try it just for spite," she said, knowing it was the truth.

"I've been tempted to gather a group of us to all go together and see what they do," Gayla said, laughing. "I'm not sure how they stay in business. Although it seems it's only people from here at the school that they shun, which is odd. That whole community is a little on the spooky side."

"Unusual spooky or scary spooky?"

"I'll go with scary," she said. "Did you meet Valerie?"

Paige nodded. "Yes, she was at the cookout yesterday."

"Good. Ask her about the time she went into the grocery store."

"What happened?"

"No, no. Get the story from her. It's amusing now. Not so much at the time," Gayla said with a glance at her watch. "I must get going. Let me show you your office," she said.

It was small, housing only a desk and chair and one file cabinet. Paige looked at her questioningly.

"You'll be assigned a laptop. There's a closet over here," she said, pointing out a door adjacent to the office. "There's some equipment and stuff in there. Only the blues get gym, so you shouldn't have a problem. And I'm not certain about your schedule yet. Director Avery was supposed to put all that together."

"How long have you been without a gym teacher?"

"Months. We've done the bare minimum to meet state requirements, that's it." She lowered her voice. "And let's say we didn't exactly meet them."

Paige pointed to her outfit. "I wasn't sure what to wear," she said.

"Oh, nothing like that," Gayla said. "What did you wear at your previous school?"

Paige frowned. *Crap. Was that covered in their backstory?* She went with CJ's advice instead.

"Just workout clothes," she said evasively.

"Yes. That's what Carol wore. She gloated over the fact that she had on shorts each summer when it was hot like it is today." Gayla patted her shoulder and smiled. "You'll do fine. Check with the director about your schedule."

"Okay. Thank you for meeting me. I'm sure I'll see you around."

"Oh, sure. And once you two are settled, Dave and I must have you over for dinner. Have fun today," she said as she turned to leave.

"Gayla?"

Gayla stopped, her eyebrows raised.

"Well, we heard this...this *scream* last night. Some animal. It was really loud. Have you heard it?"

Gayla nodded. "Yes. It scared the crap out of us the first few times we heard it. It's still unsettling."

"What is it?"

She shrugged. "We don't know. It's been passed down that there's a black panther that lives in the woods around here. Just a tale, though. Black panthers have never inhabited this area."

She gave a reassuring smile before hurrying away, leaving Paige staring after her.

CHAPTER ELEVEN

Fiona groaned, her eyes opening slowly. She knew she wasn't alone and she tried to focus, seeing a shadowy figure standing near the bed. It was Mother Hogan. She turned, sharp eyes settling over Fiona.

"You're awake finally. How do you feel?"

Fiona tried to swallow, but her throat was dry. "Groggy," she said, her voice hoarse. The air was cool and damp. "Where am I?"

"Down in the chambers. This is your room for now." She held a cup to her mouth. "Drink this."

It was bitter and Fiona had to force herself not to spit it out.

"Antel will visit you each night until you are with child."

Fiona looked away, trying to remember what had happened

last night. When she realized it must be daylight by now, she tried to sit up. "School. I need to—"

"Not this week," Mother Hogan said. "You could not explain."

"Explain?"

Mother Hogan came closer, gently touching Fiona's wrist, causing her to flinch in pain. She looked down, seeing bruises on both arms. She closed her eyes. Yes, the shackles. Wrists and ankles. She remembered Antel coming to her but...nothing else. Her body was sore, her muscles weak. Her head still foggy.

"As soon as you are able, you'll have a bath," Mother Hogan said. "I have everything ready."

Fiona nodded. "I'm so tired," she said.

"Of course you are, dear. You rest as long as you need. Belden is standing guard at the entrance. Let him know when you are ready."

Fiona's eyes slipped closed but not before she saw another shadow in the room, this one much larger, coming to her. She whimpered when she felt cold hands on her but didn't have the strength to protest, didn't have the strength to even open her eyes. Mother's magic potion had worked quickly on her.

CHAPTER TWELVE

CJ loved the sound of the leather holster. It reminded her of her early days before she became a detective, before she joined the FBI. Simpler days, for sure. The chief, Horace Aims, had been with the school for twenty years. While his officers and guards came and went, he was a fixture. Divorced and childless, he devoted his life to the school. Unfortunately, none of his officers did the same. Most stayed only a few years before moving on. The pay was good, but even that wasn't enough to make them stay.

Her first day had been nothing more than an orientation. Tomorrow, she would begin sitting in on classes. He'd given her a file to study; the girls who needed extra attention were identified, along with those who were considered the leaders of the various cliques. She pretended to be interested, but being a guard at a juvenile prison wasn't exactly a career path she would have chosen. A few weeks of this was going to be a chore. She also wondered how beneficial it was going to be. Having them infiltrate the school wasn't the same as integrating with Hoganville itself. Investigating Hoganville from a distance seemed to be the only way inside. Investigating the disappearances themselves was futile. She'd read the files. There was no pattern to them. Skin color was different, gender was different, age was different. It seemed to be an abduction by opportunity rather than intent.

She parked in front of the admin building where she and Paige had agreed to meet. After today, she would be assigned a souped-up golf cart to use around campus. That would probably be the highlight of this whole assignment. She'd at least have a toy to play with.

She grinned when she saw Paige coming toward her. She'd actually found that she'd missed her today, which surprised her. She was also surprised to see a matching smile on Paige's face.

As soon as Paige got in, CJ leaned closer.

Paige shook her head. "Seriously?" she asked, but she didn't pull away.

CJ felt a tiny twinge of arousal when their lips met. She had to stop herself from deepening the kiss, but she did allow her lips to savor it a few seconds longer.

"And how was your first day?" she asked when she pulled back, daring to meet Paige's eyes. She tried to read them, but Paige looked away.

"You were right about my outfit," Paige said. "Shorts."

"Cool."

"I also realize I know nothing about teaching a gym class."

"How hard can it be?" CJ asked as she drove down the narrow road that would take them to their home.

"I'm not really into sports. That's how hard it's going to be. You should have this role. Not me," Paige said. Then she tilted her head. "How was your day?"

"Boring. Visited with Chief Aims most of the day."

Paige smiled quickly. "You look cute."

CJ laughed. "Oh, yeah. A gal in a uniform." She wiggled her eyebrows teasingly. "Is that what gets you off?"

Paige blushed, but her smile didn't fade. "I like guns."

"Well, baby, I've got a big one. I'll show it to you later, if you want."

Paige laughed. "No doubt you've used that line before."

Their easy banter continued into the evening as Paige cooked dinner and CJ tried to give her some pointers on teaching a gym class.

"You could play handball," she suggested. "Or Ping Pong."

"I don't think Ping Pong ranks as a fitness class, and I know nothing about handball."

"What about dodgeball?"

"CJ, these are high school kids, not elementary."

"So do three-on-three basketball. Hell, have them run sprints."

Paige shook her head. "I'm going to blow our cover, I just know it." She walked over, holding her hand under a spoon. "Here, taste this," she said, shoving the spoon into CJ's mouth.

"Mmm," she murmured. "Good," she said as she swallowed. "What is it?"

"Just an Italian sauce. I'll pour it over pasta and bake it."

"Spaghetti?"

"No. Penne pasta and some vegetables. We'll have garlic bread too."

"I think I'm going to love having you cook for me," she said.

"The idea of doing a large dish is for leftovers. I don't plan to cook every night you know."

"I don't mind leftovers," CJ said. "I'm surprised you like them, though."

"What does that mean?"

"I imagine growing up, you never ever had to settle for leftovers," she said. The tone of the conversation had shifted with that one statement, and Paige had an uneasy look on her face, her smile long gone.

"What are you saying?"

CJ knew she should stop, but she didn't. And she didn't really know why. Paige's social status had never been an issue. But no sense in backtracking now. "I'm saying you're used to prime rib. I'm used to Hamburger Helper."

"I can't help who my family is or how I grew up," Paige said. "But I never, *ever*, bring that to work."

"You're right. You haven't. But we all know where you live. We all know what kind of car you drive."

Paige's expression changed from offended to wounded. CJ wished she had never brought the subject up.

"I bought the car for safety and reliability, nothing more. It isn't some sort of a status symbol," she said.

Anything CJ said would only further their argument, so she said nothing.

Paige raised her eyebrows. "What? It's just a Mercedes. Lots of people drive Mercedes," she said.

CJ shook her head. "Not cops."

***

The week crawled by as Paige struggled daily to come up with activities to appease the girls. After their argument, she had grudgingly taken CJ's advice and had ordered several popular exercise DVDs. Overnight shipping was a godsend, in this case. Zumba was the favorite, and Paige even found herself dancing along. She found that only a handful of the girls liked basketball anyway so there wasn't really much complaining.

But still, she was nearly bored out of her mind. She only had three classes each day, with each being smaller than twenty students. That gave her a lot of free time.

Time to think. Unfortunately, it wasn't the dead-end case that her thoughts went to.

She rested her chin in her palm, her gaze going out the small, lone window in her tiny office. The area they were in was really pretty, she noted. Tall pines towering over lush oaks and other hardwoods, it looked inviting. And if not for the humidity and hot temperatures, she might be tempted to ditch the office and take a walk along the path that led to the lake. CJ's morning runs took her to the lake, and she said it was very peaceful in the woods. Paige sighed. Shame she wasn't into running.

She took a deep breath and slowly released it, trying to reconcile her growing irritation with CJ. She had to admit, it was mostly an irritation with herself; she just took it out on CJ. The hello and goodbye kisses had ceased. Thanks to CJ's new mode of transportation, they were no longer riding together each day. Of course she was happy about that. Kissing CJ Johnston was not high on her list of things she wanted to do.

Oh, God, who was she kidding?

She was a woman with a pulse. That much was painfully obvious each time they did kiss. And tomorrow—Saturday—was the weekly get-together. It was at Suzette and Becca's place. Mexican food. And they would be in public, they would hold hands and, knowing CJ, she'd find any excuse to cross the line that Paige had tried to establish. She would take liberties that she shouldn't, and Paige would have to pretend that it didn't bother her when they both knew it did. They were playing a dangerous game, and she didn't know why she didn't just put an end to it. CJ would push her as far as Paige would allow. She just wasn't sure what CJ was getting out of all of this.

Her phone rang, startling her. She smiled when she saw Billy's name displayed. She hadn't spoken with him in the last week.

"Hi, Billy Boy. What's up?"

"Wow. It's nice to hear your voice," he said.

Paige smiled. "Thank you. Yours too."

"Howley wanted me to give you a heads-up. Got a missing person. Another college student."

Paige sat up straighter, her brow furrowed. "When?"

"Reported this morning. A female, driving from Baton Rouge to Lufkin. Didn't show last night. Her parents called it in this morning."

"LSU student again?"

"Yes. Nineteen. Leah Turner."

"Okay. Last visual on her?"

"Lafayette. She stopped for gas and a burger. Three p.m. Called her parents while she was there."

"And is now gone without a trace?" She shook her head. "What do we hope to find here?" she asked. "We've got nothing. We haven't even been into Hoganville since the first day."

"And nothing strange is going on?"

"Well, one of the teachers from town, Fiona Hogan, hasn't been in all week. She's called in sick every day. From what I understand, it's the first time she's ever missed. I guess that would constitute strange."

"Howley said he would send you a file with whatever information we can put together on Leah. BOLO out on her car, of course, but no hits. The lead teams are linking this to the other disappearance last year."

"Okay. I'll pass this on to CJ. We feel really out of the loop here, like we're just killing time." She paused. "I miss you guys," she said.

"Yeah. Us too. Sure quiet here without you two." Billy laughed. "Has CJ driven you crazy yet?"

"She's working on it."

After they disconnected, she pondered whether to call CJ or just wait until this evening to tell her. She decided to call. She didn't have CJ's schedule memorized yet so she would assume she wouldn't answer if she was in class. Oh, but she did answer, in typical CJ style.

"Hi, baby," CJ said, her voice low. "To what do I owe this pleasure? Do you miss me today?"

"Hardly," Paige said. "Got a missing person. Billy just called me."

"Oh, yeah? Details?"

"Another college student. Same as Trumbley. LSU. This one was heading nearby. Lufkin."

"LSU? That'll just trigger the team there to assume it's LSU related."

"Exactly."

"Calculated? Or a coincidence?" CJ asked.

"For something that's been going on this many years, it has to be calculated," she said.

"I agree."

"So now what?" Paige asked.

"I think we need to pay Hoganville a visit in the morning. Maybe drop in the café for breakfast. What do you think?"

Paige remembered Gayla's story about their attempted café visit. She wondered if she and CJ would suffer the same fate. But she nodded.

"Sounds like a plan."

CHAPTER THIRTEEN

"Look, there's a car," CJ said as they slowed near the café. "That's a first."

"It's parked by the grocery store. Maybe they're open today."

"Well, the café is open at least. That's a good sign," she said. She parked in front, scanning the area behind the café, looking for movement and seeing none. The homes appeared deserted. "Craziest thing I've ever seen," she said quietly.

"I feel silly saying this, but I'm actually afraid," Paige said. "It's like the hairs on the back of my neck are standing at attention."

"I know what you mean," she said. She felt it too, that sixth sense kicking in, making her more attentive, no detail escaping notice. Like the blinds being pulled down on the grocery store window or the slamming of a door down the street, the only sound to disturb the silence.

There were eight people in the café and all sets of eyes turned away from them as they entered. Even the woman holding the pot of coffee seemed frozen in place as she turned her head away. It was so quiet, she could actually hear the ticking of a clock. Her gaze landed on the round face on the wall, where the second hand was moving in jerky motions. It was nine a.m.

Paige was the first to gather her composure, perhaps her upbringing dictating proper manners. She smiled at the woman as she pulled out a chair.

"That coffee looks great," Paige said. "We'll start with that, please."

CJ followed suit, pulling out the chair opposite her. The coffee lady finally moved, but not to bring them a cup. She hurried back behind closed doors. The kitchen? The others, four women and three men, remained frozen and unmoving, their conversation still halted. CJ looked at Paige and shrugged.

Paige, for her part, was trying to appear as normal as possible. She smiled, looking around for a menu.

"I'm starving. I'm thinking two eggs, hash browns. Maybe I'll splurge on bacon. What about you?"

"Pancakes," CJ said. "I haven't had pancakes in ages." But seeing as how the coffee lady hadn't returned, she thought the prospect for pancakes was slight. She met Paige's eyes questioningly.

Paige leaned closer, her voice barely a whisper. "I feel like I'm in an episode of the *Twilight Zone*."

Before CJ could answer, the door to the kitchen opened, but it wasn't the coffee lady returning. It was a much older woman, her skin pasty white, matching the gray on her head. She appeared nearly ghost-like, and she moved with light, nimble steps toward them.

"I am Ester Hogan," she said, the smile on her face forced. "I'm sorry, but we are not open for business this morning. We have a private party today. We should have locked the doors."

CJ looked pointedly at the other occupied tables, then sniffed the air with exaggeration. "But the breakfast smells really good," she said, smiling broadly. "Are you sure you can't make an exception?"

"I'm sorry, but no." Ester Hogan swept her glance between the two of them. "You are from the school?"

"Yep. Just started," she said. "CJ Johnston. This is Paige Riley."

Paige nodded politely. "Nice to meet you. We were looking for a nice, country breakfast. Someone suggested we come here," she said.

At this, Ester Hogan cracked a smile. "Someone playing a joke, perhaps. But again, I apologize. We are not open to the public today." She motioned to the outside door. "I must insist you leave."

"Wow. I thought this was a real café. It looks like a real café— standard white dishes, sugar and ketchup on the tables. Even little napkin holders," she said, fingering the chipped metal container. "Do you close like this often?"

Ester Hogan's facial expression did not change. She leaned forward, her dark eyes boring into CJ's. "You will leave now." The air around her grew cold, and CJ felt as if there was a hand around her throat choking her. She had a hard time drawing breath.

Ester straightened up, her glance going to the coffee lady, who nodded and left. CJ felt the pressure ease up, and she immediately touched her neck with her hand. The door opened again; this time a large, broad-shouldered man filled the space. He said nothing. He didn't have to. His biceps were as big as her thighs. He looked like—if he chose—he could snap her in half like a twig.

"Okay. I guess this is our cue," she said to Paige. "Pancakes are out."

Paige surprised her by walking around the table to stand in front of Ester Hogan. "Is the grocery store open this morning? If I'm to cook breakfast, I'll need some eggs," she said, a slight smile playing on her lips. "Maybe bacon too."

"I'm sorry, but no. The grocery store is not open on Saturdays. Besides, we don't carry much. Everyone is self-sufficient. Gardens, chickens."

"Oh. There was a car out front. I was hoping it was open."

"No. But I do have some to spare." Ester glanced at the coffee lady. "Selma, eggs and bacon for our new friends."

"Yes, Mother Hogan," she said before hurrying away.

"You will wait outside. Belden will keep you company."

CJ pushed her chair back in against the table. "That's not necessary. Thank you for your kindness," she said.

Paige paused at the door. "By the way, how is Fiona? We have yet to meet her."

If the question caught her by surprise, Ester didn't show it. "Yes, Fiona has been ill this week. I believe she's feeling a bit better."

"Good. We look forward to meeting her." Paige nodded slightly. "Thank you again for the breakfast items."

CJ had just opened the door to go wait outside when the coffee lady—Selma—returned with a wicker basket covered with a cloth. Instead of handing it to Paige, she handed it to Ester Hogan. Ester lifted the cloth, revealing not only the eggs and several thick slabs of bacon, but a loaf of homemade bread as well.

"Very nice, Selma. Thank you." She offered the basket to Paige. "Enjoy."

"Thank you. We will." She held up the basket. "I'll be sure to return this."

"No need. Perhaps you could drop it off with Fiona one day."

"Very well."

***

"Lock the door," Ester instructed as soon as the women drove off. "Thank you, Selma. You may resume your duties."

"Yes, Mother Hogan."

"Belden, I think we need to pay Director Avery a visit. Apparently he did not heed our warning to keep his staff away from the community. We can't have them here, especially this week."

"Yes, Mother. Should I visit him tonight?"

"Call the guard that you broke...Richard. You can take Fiona back tomorrow. Visit the director then. Return through the woods. Nothing too severe now, Belden. This is Celebration Week. We don't want anything to disrupt our plans." She smiled, thinking of the young girl they would offer up as a sacrifice. She could already smell it, taste it. She closed her eyes for a minute, imagining the warmth of blood on her hands. "No, we don't want any distractions this week." She opened her eyes again, finding Belden waiting. "Make sure everyone uses the tunnels to travel. There may be eyes on us."

"Yes, Mother."

She watched him leave, her gaze going back out the window where the strangers' car was long gone. Something wasn't right, she knew, but she didn't have time to dwell on it. It was Celebration Week. She must get Fiona ready.

"We should close the blinds," she said, turning to leave, hearing Nevelene hustle over to do her bidding. She smiled. *Like a good sheep.*

***

"You think it's safe to eat that stuff?" CJ asked.

Paige smiled. "I think so. It's probably from the stash they were using for breakfast there. The bread is still warm. Probably baked fresh this morning."

"Why do you think she gave that to us?"

"Wanted us out of her hair, most likely. God, can you believe that place?"

CJ shook her head. "No. And the coffee lady called her *Mother* Hogan. How weird is that?"

"Did you notice her fingernails?"

"Whose?"

"Ester's. When she handed me the basket, I saw them. They were like claws, filed to a point. Creepy."

"What was creepy were the other people in there. I mean, it

was like they froze. And they wouldn't look at us. They turned their backs to us," CJ said.

"Yes, they appeared to be terrified of us. And maybe they were. They don't see outsiders often, I suppose."

CJ glanced at her. "You think they're brainwashed?"

Paige smiled. "They appear to be *conditioned* to behave certain ways, I don't know if I would call it brainwashed. They are obviously subservient to Ester Hogan. I guess Avery was right in that she's the matriarch, she runs things."

"She also controls them by having the resources to run the café, the grocery store." She glanced at Paige. "I felt something," she said.

"What do you mean?"

"When she was staring at me. I felt this...this pressure on my chest, around my throat. Like I was lying down and someone was sitting on me or something. Like maybe there were hands around my throat."

"Okay," Paige said slowly. "And? You think Ester Hogan did something?"

"I don't know. But it was definitely real. I had a hard time breathing."

CJ turned into the entrance to the school, pausing at the locked gate to show her ID. Richard Barr, the security guard who had let them into the admin building that first day, waved them through without a word.

"He doesn't talk much," she said to Paige. "This may be an all-girls school and most of the teachers are women, but on my side of things—being the only female—I'm the outsider. Chief Aims doesn't really talk to me either."

"I'm assuming you're being your usual charming self?"

CJ laughed. "What are you implying?"

Paige smiled but didn't elaborate. "Nothing."

CJ parked in their tiny driveway, her gaze sliding to the basket Paige held. "So, are you really gonna make me breakfast?"

"I'm going to make *us* breakfast." Paige met her gaze across the top of the car. "And if you really have a fondness for pancakes, we'll need to add that to our grocery list."

"Thanks. I used to be a nut for pancakes when I was a kid. My mom—" she stopped, the happy memory she was about to recall replaced with one of her father throwing the hot griddle across the room, embedding it in the cheap paneling of the kitchen wall. Her mom had gotten a phone call and had forgotten about the pancakes. Soon, the ripe smell of their burnt breakfast had filled the old trailer. CJ had been maybe nine or ten, she couldn't really remember. When the yelling started, she and her sister Cathy had hidden under the table. That was the last time her mother made pancakes. She closed her eyes for a second, picturing her mother's battered face before pushing the memory away.

"What is it?" Paige asked.

CJ shook her head, not able to meet Paige's eyes. "Nothing. It's nothing."

CHAPTER FOURTEEN

Ester made her way through the maze of tunnels, not bothering with a torch. She preferred the darkness, really. The damp earth smell was comforting to her, familiar. Most of the tunnels had been built many, many years ago, linking the main Hogan house and the underground cave—the chambers—with the main buildings, like the grocery store and the café. Since she'd had the reign, she'd orchestrated the construction of the newest ones, linking the homes. They could move about freely now without having to step outside. There was no chance of prying eyes then. They were free to do as they chose. She smiled in anticipation of the upcoming week, knowing the sacrifice they'd chosen was more for the celebration week her great-grandmother had started than for him. Regardless, he seemed to enjoy it as much as the flock now did.

She followed the tunnels directly to her home, missing Belden being there to greet her. Belden had been her protector since he was twenty, long before her mother handed over the flock to her. Belden's family had always been the shepherds, his father looking after her beloved grandmother for years. They were the shepherds, yes. They were also the hunters, having learned their skills from birth, the bloodline long and thick.

She didn't concern herself that Belden was the last of his family. Only his younger sister remained and she was of no use to Ester. It was her mother's fault. She didn't have the steel hand that her beloved grandmother did. Her mother didn't control the coupling. There was no selection. Those born to the flock weren't of good linage, her mother knew that, but she couldn't cull them, not like her grandmother had. Fortunately, her mother grew ill. Ester allowed a small smile at that thought, shaking it away quickly. Her mother had been forced to hand the purple robe to her. Ester was prepared. She culled the flock quickly, ruling with an iron fist, taking instruction from *him*. Unfortunately, there was now a gap. And for the first time in over a hundred years, there was no true Hogan to carry on.

Fiona was as close as she had, and Fiona had proven to be faithful. If she bore a female child, then he would be happy. He would be able to mate again. The true Hogan line would end, but her reign would continue. The thought thrilled her, almost as much as the upcoming ceremony.

She paused at the door to her rooms, looking back down the dark tunnels. She had heard a noise, a scraping sound. She tilted her head, listening, but all was silent.

A rat perhaps.

***

"Why a cop?"

Paige halted in mid-pour, the wine bottle the only thing separating her eyes from CJ's. She hated this question. She wished she'd made up a lie years ago.

"I mean, considering your family and all," CJ continued, "that hardly seems what they had in mind for you."

"No. Hardly," she said. Actually, she was surprised by CJ's attempt at conversation. She'd been distant, withdrawn most of the day. Brooding. Paige had finally given up trying to talk to her. So now, at dinner—which she'd assumed would be another quiet affair—CJ asks *that* question.

"So?"

Paige shrugged. "I wanted to help people," she said. "I went to law school—"

"To *help* people?"

"I know. After the first year, I realized it wasn't for me. It was all about money and politics." Paige met her eyes. "I applied for the FBI without my parents' knowledge. I really didn't think it would get as far as it did," she said.

"So they freaked?"

"That's an understatement," she said. "I was raised—trained— to be some rich man's wife. They tolerated law school because that was considered a noble profession. And if I insisted, they would allow me to join the firm that served as my father's counsel." She sipped from her wine, remembering the conversation well. "Until I was married, of course. Then I would resort to being a proper wife."

"And the FBI?"

She smiled. "What can I say? They demanded I quit, but really, they had no hold over me. Certainly not monetarily, even though they tried to play that card." She looked away. "I had trust funds. They couldn't touch that. But they tried to threaten my stake in *their* wealth." Paige set her wineglass down, uncomfortable with the conversation. "When they realized I didn't care about that, they backed off. I think they assumed I would give it up eventually."

"Well, if they were thrown for a loop about the FBI, I bet they really freaked about the gay thing," CJ said, pushing her plate away to cup her wineglass with both hands.

Paige felt a blush coming to her face but was unable to stop it. She picked up her glass, hoping CJ wouldn't notice but knowing that she would.

"Paige?"

Paige cleared her throat. "They don't...well, I've never mentioned it."

CJ stared at her. "You're in the *closet*?"

"I guess you could say that."

CJ met her eyes, her own widening. She stood quickly, pushing her chair back, her head cocked to the side thoughtfully.

"Okay, wait a minute." She turned away from Paige for a second, then looked back around quickly. "What are you saying exactly?"

"What do—"

"You weren't—"

"What?"

"I mean, with me, God, it wasn't your first time?" CJ's eyes widened. "Jesus, was it?"

Paige raised her eyebrows. "Oh, come on. Really?"

"Granted, you knew what you were doing," CJ murmured, almost to herself. "No. Couldn't be. You were too—" She glared at Paige. "Right?"

"Please sit down. You're overreacting," she said. "And as if I'd have been the first *virgin* you'd ever slept with," she added.

CJ again had a panicked look on her face. "Paige, seriously. I wasn't the first woman you'd been with, right?"

Paige frowned. "Where is this coming from? Was I that bad that you thought it was my first time?"

"No. God, no. You were fantas—" She paused. "That's not—" CJ sat down again. "I'm sorry. Of course it wasn't your first time." She tried to grin. "What was I thinking?"

Paige stared at her. "What is wrong with you?"

CJ shook her head. "Nothing. I'm sorry. I just don't like to be anybody's *first*. It's scary." She took a big gulp from her wine. "So you're in the closet? Wow. I mean, with *everyone*?"

"Obviously not with you."

It was CJ's turn to frown. "Paige, the guys—Ice and Billy—I mean, we flirt all the time."

"Yes. And that's expected now. I play along with it, as do you."

"But you know they think you're gay. Right? I mean, they know, they don't think. Well, they think they know. Christ—"

Paige laughed. "While I haven't brought my personal life to the job—ever—I don't doubt that they assume, simply from the lack of me mentioning a boyfriend."

"And you don't think your parents assume the same?"

Paige smiled, hoping it reached her eyes. "I'm very busy. I don't have time to date," she stated.

"Oh my God," CJ murmured. "There's not some guy, is there? I mean, that your family is holding out hope for?"

Paige looked away. *Crap.* She sighed. "Seth Buchanan."

CJ stared at her. "Come on. Seriously?"

She stood, picking up both of their plates. "Seriously." She had hoped that would be the end of it, but CJ followed her into the kitchen, bringing their wineglasses with her.

"So how often do you see this Seth person?"

Paige took the glass CJ held out to her. "Family get-togethers, that sort of thing," she said evasively.

"And how often is that?"

"Not too often. My family is in Dallas, remember." She set her glass down. "Why so curious?"

"Are you kidding me? You drop the *I'm in the closet* bombshell and you think I'm not curious?" CJ arched an eyebrow. "Are you sleeping with him?"

"Of course I'm not sleeping with him," she snapped.

"Does he know you're gay?"

Paige sighed, wishing this conversation would come to an end. "He does not. At least he has not said anything to me."

"Yet you date?"

"We don't date, CJ. He's much like you. He likes to play the field," she said, wondering if that was really how she would describe CJ. "He has no more interest in me than I do in him."

"I don't understand."

"Look, when we're around the family, we're . . . friendly with each other. That's it. Enough to make my parents think we see each other and enough to make his parents stop worrying about his playboy ways." She didn't add that it would be much easier to pretend if Seth wasn't such an ostentatious ass.

"So where did you meet this guy?"

"I've known him most of my life. We went to law school

together. He works for the firm that represents my father's company."

CJ studied her, and Paige had to steel herself from shifting nervously beside her. She knew, of course, what the next question would be.

"So have you *ever* slept with him?"

Knowing the question didn't make it any easier to answer. But she wouldn't lie about it. "We slept together in law school. I was still...confused," she said.

CJ laughed. "Confused? You obviously hadn't slept with a woman yet. You know what they say, once you go chick, you never go—"

Paige covered CJ's mouth with her hand, smiling too. "Please don't say it."

"So when *did* you sleep with your first woman?"

"That's a little personal, don't you think?"

"It was obviously after Seth." CJ reached for the wine bottle, adding a bit to both of their glasses.

Paige thought back to those awkward days, days when she was terrified of her attraction to women, terrified of what her family would say if they knew. She actually slept with Seth in the hopes that it would chase away those attractions. In reality, it only reinforced them.

"It was before Seth, actually," she said. "Seth was my last attempt at normalcy." She smiled. "It didn't work."

"So why not just tell your parents then?"

"Because it doesn't work that way," she said. She moved away, ending the conversation. "Did you talk to Ice today?" she asked, changing the subject.

"Yes. There's nothing new. I asked him to act like a historian and get some background on Hoganville. Maybe something will turn up."

Paige eyed the dirty dishes. "Your turn," she said, heading off to the bedroom and her laptop.

CHAPTER FIFTEEN

CJ stood at the window, staring absently into the woods. She heard Paige in the kitchen and soon smelled bacon, but she wasn't really interested this morning. She felt restless. She blew out a breath. Okay, she was bored. This sleepy little assignment was boring her to tears.

"What's wrong?"

She turned, accepting the cup of coffee Paige offered her.

"Wrong? Everything," she said. "What the hell are we doing here? I mean, I feel like we're wasting our time. We're not really investigating anything, you know."

"Yes, I know."

"I'm sitting in a classroom full of goddamn juvenile delinquents—literally—and doing what? Babysitting them?

You're teaching a gym class, for God's sake. We haven't even met Fiona, who is at least a person of interest. I just feel like we should be doing something," she said. "This has got to be the most boring, waste-of-time assignment I've ever had."

Paige went back to the kitchen, flipping the bacon. CJ could see the wheels turning in her head. Finally she looked up, only to shrug.

"I agree, CJ."

"That's it? I agree?"

"What do you want me to say?"

"I don't know. Something," she said as she turned back to the window. "We don't even know if Hoganville is just a creepy little place or what. I'd like to feel like there's a reason we're here and not just that we drew the short end of the stick."

"Hoganville threw up red flags, that's why we're here. You know that. But you're right. We don't know if Hoganville is the center of the disappearance or not. A long shot at best, considering there is no evidence pointing to it. But I have a feeling *something* is happening here. Just being at the café, seeing them all like that. There's something weird going on."

"Weird, yes. Whether it's criminal in nature is yet to be determined." CJ let out a deep breath, finally turning from the window. "You need some help?" she offered, pointing to the stove.

"You can set the table, please," she said.

CJ went to the cabinets, finding amusement in the mismatched plates. "Are you going to be able to eat off of these for six months?"

Paige glanced at her and smiled. "I'm not a snob, you know. But really, how hard would it have been to buy a matching set?" She set the spatula down. "Okay, I'll admit, it's driving me crazy. And on our next trip to San Augustine, I'm buying new ones."

CJ laughed. "Yeah. Can you buy a TV too? Howley said no on my request."

"You're kidding? He really expects us to stay here for possibly months without one?"

"He said the budget was too tight for frivolous purchases."

Paige put her hands on her hips, staring at her. "Frivolous?

Does he know where we are? The closest entertainment is forty-five minutes away and most people wouldn't even call that entertainment. I'd like to see him stuck out here for a few months." She turned back to the stove, then paused again. "And if this were Ice and Billy, they'd have whined enough by now that he'd have had one delivered. I swear," she mumbled. "Men."

"You don't really seem the TV type," CJ said.

"I'm not. But if we don't get one soon, you're going to drive me insane."

***

Fiona sat up, her head pounding. It was cold in the chamber, and the lone torch above the bed was blinding. She turned away from it. Her thoughts were muddled, drifting back and forth, leaving her not knowing what was real and what was a dream. She finally opened her eyes, daring to lift the covers. She gasped, quickly letting them fall. She leaned her head back, stretching out her legs, expecting there to be shooting pain. Surprisingly, she felt nothing. All that blood and she felt nothing. What had happened to her?

She jumped when she heard footsteps. Mother Hogan seemed surprised as she came closer.

"You're awake, Fiona." It was a statement, almost accusatory.

"Yes."

"How do you feel?"

"My head hurts."

"Yes. It will stop soon." She handed her a cup. "Here. Some broth. You haven't had much to eat this week."

This week? "What day is it?"

"It's Sunday, dear." Mother Hogan smiled. "Tonight you may return to the school. Will you be up for it?"

Fiona frowned. She'd lost a whole week. "I don't know. I don't think I can drive."

"The broth will help your head. As soon as it is dark, we'll prepare your bath. I've summoned your mother to assist."

"There's...there's blood," she said quietly.

Mother Hogan smiled. "Yes. Unfortunate. Antel was...beastly with you, I'm afraid. The bath will help." She stood. "Lay back now. Belden will come get you when it's time."

Fiona did as instructed, too tired to protest. She saw the hulk of a shadow behind Mother Hogan, then it was gone. Instinctively, she reached down and covered her belly, her pulse racing. Was she with child? Had Antel succeeded? She tried to remember what had happened during the week. She had no memory of Antel except on the first night in the chambers. The rest was blurry. All she could recall were cold hands, a shadowy figure...and darkness.

She rolled her head to the side, away from the entry to the chambers. She was anxious to return to the school. There, at least, she felt like she had some control.

CHAPTER SIXTEEN

"That smells good," CJ said, but Paige slapped her hand away as she tried to swipe a taste.

"Don't you dare."

"I'm surprised you can cook," she said. "I mean, growing up like you did. You had servants, cooks. Right?"

Paige looked away, and CJ noticed the nearly embarrassed expression on her face. "We did. That doesn't mean I didn't learn from them," Paige said. "I enjoy cooking. Something my mother has not done a day in her life."

There were so many things CJ could say to that but she kept quiet. Paige didn't share much about her upbringing, but that little statement spoke volumes. She couldn't help but be impressed with Paige. Here was a woman born with a silver spoon in her mouth, yet she nearly shunned it, slumming at a job with the FBI instead. CJ believed Paige when she said she wanted to help people. After all, that was the reason CJ became a cop. To help people...kids.

They walked next door to Suzette and Becca's place as soon as they saw another couple arrive. CJ had no qualms about being first, but Paige had given her a look to indicate that it was just *wrong* to be the first at a party. Today's theme was Mexican food and CJ brought Coronas and lime for them to drink. Paige had made a casserole that was bubbling with cheese. Another one of her vegetarian dishes, nonetheless, it looked delicious.

Valerie and her partner, Ella, were there ahead of them, and they both greeted them warmly. CJ was hoping to get Valerie alone. Paige had shared Gayla's hint about Valerie's trip to the local grocery store. CJ wanted to question her about it. At least she'd feel like she was working then.

"Oh, that looks scrumptious, Paige."

"Thanks."

"What makes you think I didn't make it?" CJ asked with a grin.

"Sorry, dear. I just assumed Paige was the cook in your family," Suzette said, taking the dish from Paige and setting it on the table that would later serve as a buffet.

"That's okay." CJ flicked her eyes to Paige. "My sweetheart won't let me in her kitchen except to do the dishes."

"Can't say I blame her," Becca said. "Suzette has two left feet when it comes to cooking. I'd just as soon she stay out as well."

Suzette laughed. "Which is fine by me. I hate to cook."

CJ kept a smile on her face, mentally rolling her eyes. She was already bored, and they had the whole afternoon ahead of them. She spied the lawn chairs that had been set up in the shade, noting with amusement the two oscillating fans that were brought out to help chase away the summer heat. She grabbed Paige's hand, pulling her along. She chose a lounge chair, sitting down and drawing Paige after her, making room for her between her legs.

"We should share," CJ said.

Paige sat stiffly, her hand digging into CJ's arm in warning.

"I think there's plenty," she said. When she saw no one was watching, she turned, glaring at CJ. "What the hell do you think you're doing?"

"Now behave, sweetheart," CJ said, a smile playing on her lips. "I just can't get enough of you," she murmured.

"You will pay for this," Paige hissed, then forced a quick smile as Valerie came over.

"You two are so cute," Valerie said as she pulled up a chair. "When Ella and I first got together, we didn't leave the house for the first six weeks," she said with a laugh.

"You mean this feeling will stop?" CJ asked as she let her fingers rub gently against Paige's stomach.

"Well, if you're in love, I guess it doesn't stop, it just tempers a bit."

Paige linked her fingers with CJ's, effectively stopping her caresses. With her other hand, hidden from Valerie, she pinched CJ hard on her leg. CJ had to bite her lip to stop from grimacing, then nearly choked as laughter threatened.

"I think CJ sometimes forgets that we're not alone." Paige smiled sweetly at her. "Don't you, *sweetheart*?"

"Maybe I just can't keep my hands off of you."

"Maybe you should try," Paige murmured.

CJ cleared her throat, not releasing Paige's hand. "So, Valerie, I hear you had an experience at the grocery store in Hoganville. Paige and I tried to go there last weekend, but it was closed."

Valerie shook her head. "No, don't do it. That's one creepy place."

"That's what we thought about the café," Paige said. "We went there yesterday."

"Wow. You actually got inside?" Valerie asked. "What was it like?"

Paige turned slightly and CJ met her eyes, both with identical questions. They hadn't discussed how much to share with the others. CJ took the lead.

"It was pretty weird," she said. "We sat down, but the coffee lady wouldn't serve us. The others in there turned away and wouldn't look at us. Then some older woman showed up, Ester Hogan, and she said they were closed, that they were having a private party."

Valerie nodded. "Yeah. That's kinda what happened at the grocery store. I went in. All I needed was flour. I was having a craving for banana bread and I didn't have any flour," she said with a smile. "There were maybe five or six people in there. They literally scattered when I went inside. I mean, like ran. But it was like they just disappeared," she said, snapping her fingers. "Not a sign of them anywhere. I mean, the store is not that big. So I'm standing there, wondering if I should look for the flour and just leave money or what, when this woman—Ester Hogan—just appeared out of nowhere. Scared me half to death." She laughed.

"I knocked over a whole shelf of canned goods, ending up on my ass with this very scary woman standing over me." Her smile faded. "Then it got cold. Really, really cold. And there was this... I'm not sure how to describe it. It was like a shadow, a presence, something. Then I couldn't breathe, like someone was choking me." She shivered, and CJ felt Paige's fingers tighten against her hand. "The woman picked me up like I was a doll. She said her store was not for outsiders. I think I blacked out or something because that's the last I remember. Next thing, I'm sitting in my car." She paused. "That's weird and all, but what was really weird, there was a bag of flour on the seat." She tried to smile, but CJ could tell it was forced. "How did she know I went into the store for flour?"

"Wow," Paige said. "We went in for breakfast. They wouldn't serve us, but Ester Hogan sent us home with a basket of eggs, bacon and a loaf of homemade bread." Paige laughed. "So did you make the banana bread or what?"

Valerie laughed too, her tension easing somewhat. "Yes. After all of that, I deserved a treat."

CJ smiled. "Yeah. I will say that breakfast was the best I'd had in years. Fresh eggs, probably home-cured bacon. Wonder why they're so afraid of outsiders?" she asked.

"Don't know. Fiona is just as nice and *normal* as can be. I find it hard to believe she's from that town."

"We haven't met her yet," Paige said. "She's our neighbor, we're told."

"She's been out sick all week. Really unusual. I don't think she's ever missed a day," Valerie said. "I hope it's nothing serious."

"What about this animal scream we heard the other night? What the hell was that?" CJ asked.

Valerie shrugged. "We don't have a clue. I'd like to say you get used to it, but you really don't. Sometimes it sounds so close."

"How often do you hear it?"

"Oh, it's not like it's every night or anything. Once a week, maybe. It's probably just a mountain lion or something."

"Well, it scared the crap out of us," Paige said.

They were interrupted by the arrival of others. Paige and Ella both got up to help, as Robbie was loaded with three dishes. CJ took that opportunity to snatch one of the beers she'd brought. As she popped the top off of the bottle, her interest was piqued when she spied a portable margarita machine on a table. The man setting it up was unfamiliar to her so she extended her hand in greeting.

"I'm CJ Johnston," she said.

"Hi there. Dave Grumfeld. Nice to meet you."

CJ nodded. "You're Gayla's husband," she said.

"Yes. You're one of the new ones, right? Paige Riley?"

CJ grinned. "That's us."

"How do you like it so far?" he asked.

"Well, coming from Houston, I'm in culture shock," she admitted truthfully. "The pace is a little slow."

He laughed. "I know what you mean. Before here, we were in Atlanta. I didn't think we would make the first month. I would say you get used to it, but maybe you just learn to tolerate it," he said. "We make a monthly trip to Dallas to get our city fix. You might try that. It's only slightly closer than Houston but not nearly the traffic nightmare. At least for us. You're probably used to it."

"I will say that's one thing I don't miss," she said. "So what you got here?"

"We bring it out every time there's a Mexican themed get-together."

"In that case, we should have a Mexican theme every weekend," she said, tipping her Corona at him.

He nodded with a short laugh. "I see we have a shared

interest then. Give me about fifteen minutes and I'll have the first batch ready to go."

"Thanks, Dave. I'll be back."

She spotted Paige talking to Suzette, and she walked up behind her, snaking an arm around her waist, laughing as Paige jumped.

"Didn't mean to sneak up on you," she said.

Paige smiled. "Of course you did." She glanced at the beer, then back at CJ. "I would love one. Thanks."

CJ took that as an invitation and leaned closer, kissing Paige on the mouth. "Be right back. Suzette, can I get you anything?"

"Becca beat you to it, but thanks."

CJ winked at Paige, glad there was a hint of a smile in her eyes instead of the daggers she'd been expecting. Maybe Paige was bored as well and didn't mind a little playing. After all, they did it with Ice and Billy all the time. Of course, the flirting they did while around the guys was never physical. Today, here, they could expand on that. The roles they were playing gave them permission, she reasoned. Maybe she would test her luck and see just how far Paige would take it.

Could be fun.

Or she could kill you.

***

"She's so affectionate," Suzette said. "You're very lucky."

Paige had to bite her lip to keep from laughing. "Yes. *Very* lucky."

"Becca was never like that. I don't know that she's ever touched me outside of our own home," she said almost pensively. "I think being a lifelong teacher does that. It's fun to watch you two. So in love, always touching. I miss that."

Paige didn't know what to say to that comment. *So in love?* Was their acting that good? She glanced up as CJ approached, their eyes meeting. There was a suggestion of a challenge in CJ's eyes, and she felt a moment of panic at what CJ intended.

"Here you are, babe," CJ said with a charming smile.

"Thank you."

CJ's hand glided over her hip, dipping lower for a split second, then back to her waist. Suzette was watching intently and Paige leaned closer to CJ, affectionately brushing her shoulder with her own, feeling Suzette's eyes on them.

"I met Dave," CJ said. "He's got a margarita machine. I think he's going to be my new best friend."

Paige and Suzette both laughed. "Having tequila withdrawals, are you?" Paige teased.

"Yes." Then CJ wiggled her eyebrows. "You know what tequila does to me."

Paige smiled. "Indeed I do."

"Well, I'll leave you two lovebirds alone," Suzette said. "I should help Becca set up."

As soon as she was out of earshot, Paige turned to CJ, intending to chastise her but found herself being pulled closer. Before she could protest, CJ's mouth was on hers, her tongue brushing teasingly against her lower lip. To her horror, she found herself responding, barely able to keep her mouth from opening and inviting CJ inside.

CJ pulled back slowly, her eyes shadowed. "I love the way you kiss," she murmured.

"What the hell is wrong with you?" Paige whispered, unable to keep her hands from sliding up CJ's chest.

CJ drew her closer, mouth at her ear. "Just trying to fight off boredom," she said. "Kissing is an acceptable cure." Again, her mouth moved to Paige's. Paige had time to turn her head, if she had chosen to. Unfortunately, her body didn't catch up with her brain in time, and she accepted the kiss, her eyes slipping closed at the contact.

To the casual observer, it would appear that they were nothing more than lovers having a quick, intimate moment. Which, of course, is what they were trying to portray. But *damn*, did CJ have to make it seem so real?

"I thought we decided that kissing was *not* acceptable," Paige said quietly, her eyes drawn to CJ's lips.

"I never agreed to your rules."

They were just a breath apart and had they been real lovers, Paige would have leaned closer, again taking the lips that were tempting her. Instead, she stepped back, out of CJ's arms. Whatever game CJ was playing, she wanted no part of it.

"Take it easy on the tequila, tiger. You wouldn't want to sleep on the sofa tonight, would you?"

Paige went to help the others, hearing CJ's light chuckle as she headed in the direction of the margarita machine. She would speak to her tonight, she decided. No, this assignment wasn't at the top of the excitement scale for her either, but that didn't mean CJ could improvise in their role playing. And it certainly didn't mean she could touch her and kiss her at will. The fact that she responded to the kiss made her angrier at herself than CJ. She was no longer in the mood for a party, but she plastered a smile on her face, vowing to avoid CJ for the rest of the evening. Which might not be hard to do. She spotted her chatting with Dave, a margarita in her hand. Paige went in the opposite direction.

***

"How long are you going to keep this up?" CJ asked as Paige silently stepped around her in the bathroom. Again, Paige didn't answer as she brushed her teeth. CJ wasn't one to keep things inside. If you're angry about something, say it. She couldn't take silence. So, she childishly blocked the door so Paige couldn't flee to the safety of the bedroom. She raised her eyebrows. "What's your problem?"

Paige crossed her arms defensively, giving CJ a blank stare. "Do you have to ask?"

"Obviously I do. You avoided me at the party. You're not speaking to me. So you're pissed about something."

Paige smirked. "You're a genius. Now please let me pass."

"No. I want to talk about it. Is it because I kissed you?"

"Wow. Great deduction." Paige moved to walk past but CJ stopped her.

"You're mad because I kissed you? Come on, Paige.

Really?"

Paige lifted her chin defiantly. "I'm not comfortable with this, okay? I don't want you touching me. I certainly don't want you kissing me."

"No. That's not it. You're pissed at *me* because *you* responded to my kiss. That's it, isn't it?"

Paige glared at her. "I did no such thing. I told you, I don't want you to kiss me. Ever."

"Oh, come on, Paige. What was it? Was it too real? Did it remind you of that night?"

"I assure you, I never think about that night."

"And I know you're lying."

"I'm not. I have no need to recall that night. It meant nothing."

CJ's laugh was bitter. "Oh, right. Because I'm *so* not your type. What? Am I not refined enough for you? Am I not proper enough? Is my hair not perfect? My clothes? Am I too butch for you?" She was surprised that some of the anger left Paige's eyes.

"That's not it and you know it. We're pretending to be lovers, but no, you are not someone I would date. And it has nothing to do with your social status or your clothes or whatever. It's because of who you are," Paige said. "You pick up women and then discard them like they're nothing. I don't think you know how to treat women."

CJ would be lying if she said that didn't sting. It did. And perhaps it was true. After all, she had her father as a role model. Her anger at her father bubbled out and she took it out on Paige.

"Right. And your perfect partner wouldn't have any of the terrible past history like I do. I'm not quite good enough for Paige Riley, am I? Your lover would be someone with a better paying job than mine. Your lover would always be nice to you, do everything for you, make love to you slow and easy. She would treat you like a lady. Is that it?"

Paige held her gaze but didn't say anything. CJ leaned closer. "Except for that one night," CJ said quietly. "You didn't want it slow and easy. You didn't want it like a lady. You just wanted someone to fuck you that night." Paige's eyes flashed at her and she tried to walk past but CJ stopped her. "No. I was good enough for you that night, right? You wanted me to fuck you until you couldn't think, until you couldn't feel, couldn't see. Couldn't walk. You wanted someone to chase it all away. I was good enough that night."

Paige jerked her arm away. "Yes. Yes to all of that. I was just like you that night."

"Yeah. Yeah you were. I guess we both got what we wanted."

"Problem is, you're like that every night."

CJ let her brush past. The bedroom door didn't slam shut like she expected. Instead, Paige closed it quietly behind her. CJ turned, staring at herself in the mirror, her anger turning to sadness. Paige was right. She didn't know how to treat women. Oh, she could play the seduction game. She was good at it. And once she got a woman into bed, she knew exactly what to do with them. She was good at that too. But Paige was right. That's as far as it went. She didn't bother with their names, she had no interest in seeing them again. She had no interest in a *relationship*. She had seen firsthand how those things turned out. The yelling, the screaming...the hitting. And when that failed, turning to the kids to take it out on.

She turned away from her memories. It would do no good to travel down that road again. God knows she'd done it enough in the last fifteen, twenty years. She sighed, then went about her own nighttime routine. Maybe she would take the sofa tonight. She doubted Paige wanted her in the same room with her, much less the same bed.

They had no extra pillows and the other set of sheets was in the bedroom so she rested her head against the rounded side of the sofa, trying not to think about who—and what—had been on it before her. She wasn't fastidious by any means, but sleeping on a used sofa was disgusting. She twisted and turned, trying to get comfortable, but sleep eluded her.

She was no closer to falling asleep when, an hour later, headlights flashed across the window. She got up, peering quietly outside. The car stopped next door. Fiona? She squinted into the darkness, seeing a man—the hulk from the café—open the passenger door and help a woman out. He waited at the front door, never going inside the house. When she closed it behind her, he took off on foot, disappearing into the woods.

"What the hell?" she whispered. She made a mental note to check with the chief tomorrow to find out who was working the gate. She eyed the sofa again, then glanced at the bedroom door. The bedroom seemed the lesser of two evils.

Paige was asleep, taking up more than her share of the bed. CJ stared at her, her face so calm, peaceful. Beautiful. And so not her type. CJ tended to gravitate toward women who were a little on the raunchy side. Ill-mannered and foul-mouthed, the sex always rough and raw. Paige was just the opposite. Clean, refined. Stylish. Truth was, what started out as rough and raw with her had ended up being slow and languid. Down and dirty sex gave way to leisurely gentle lovemaking. Something she didn't think she was capable of.

She stared a few seconds longer, then quietly slipped in beside Paige. To her surprise, Paige mumbled something in her sleep, her hands reaching out for CJ. CJ's heart beat just a little bit faster as a warm hand curled around her arm. She should move, she knew. Paige would be embarrassed. But it felt good. She felt...needed. So she stayed where she was, her eyes slipping closed as Paige's hand tightened reflexively.

CHAPTER SEVENTEEN

Paige waited impatiently while the secretary, Ms. Miner, called the director. No, she didn't have an appointment but really, was it that big a deal?

"He's not answering."

Paige looked at the closed door. "Are you sure he's in?"

"Yes. I brought him coffee earlier. Now, Ms. Riley—"

"Paige, please."

"Paige, then. I think I need to remind you that we're having a state audit this fall. Your *lesson plans* are sorely lacking. I mean, Zumba? The girls need activity, games. Sports. Not dance class."

"Excuse me, Ms. Miner, but you're a secretary, right? Not an educator?" She flashed a smile. "Perhaps I should discuss my *lesson plans* with the director and not you." She looked pointedly at the phone. "Please try him again."

She made no move to pick up the phone. "You're new here. I'm not. I've seen people come and go. I'll be here long after you're gone too. So I think I'm qualified to pass along advice."

Paige was five seconds away from smacking the snotty little woman when her cell rang. She took a deep breath, excusing herself. She was surprised at the number that popped up.

"This is Paige," she said quietly.

"I need to see you."

Paige looked at the closed door, then back to Ms. Miner. "I'm right outside your office," she nearly whispered.

"Okay. I've been avoiding her. Ask her to call me again."

Paige put her phone back in her pocket as she approached Ms. Miner's desk again. "Do you mind giving him another call? I really need to speak with him this morning."

"He's obviously occupied with something."

Paige gritted her teeth. "Please. Once more."

"Very well." Ms. Miner looked surprised when he answered. "Sorry to bother you, Director Avery, but Paige Riley is here to see you." She looked at Paige. "Yes, sir." Disappointment showing clearly on her face, she motioned to the door. "He will see you now."

"Thank you."

Paige opened and closed the door quickly, leaning against it. Avery's back was to her, the coffee cup that Ms. Miner delivered earlier appeared to be untouched.

"Avery?"

He turned slowly and she gasped, moving quickly from the door.

"What the hell happened?"

"I had a visitor last night."

She lifted his head gently, seeing the split lip and swollen, discolored eye. "The bodybuilder guy from town? The one they call Belden?"

He nodded. "How did you know?"

Paige pulled her phone out, scrolling through her contacts for CJ's number. "CJ saw him."

"Who are you calling?"

"CJ."

"No. It would look odd for me to summon her here without going through the chief."

"You're not summoning her. I am." Paige stood, waiting for CJ to answer, wondering if she was in a classroom or not. When she did answer, it wasn't her normal "Hi, baby" but rather a very businesslike greeting.

"What's up?"

"Can you come to the director's office?"

"Did you tell him?"

"Didn't have to. He had a personal visit."

CJ paused, her voice low. "I'm watching some damn training movie on how to be a good little prison guard. I'll be there as soon as I can think of an excuse to leave."

Paige smiled as she disconnected, but it faded as soon as she looked at Avery.

"Did he threaten you?"

"I suppose that's what it was, yes. A reminder to keep my staff out of Hoganville." He touched his lip and grimaced. "Couldn't even drink my coffee."

"Why didn't you call us last night?"

"It was very late. I didn't want to cause a scene. You leaving your house at that hour to come to mine would have caused a fuss." He touched his lip again. "I'm not a field agent," he said. "I don't have the training to—"

"You did what you were supposed to do," she said. "You played the part of a director of this school, nothing more."

"I was scared, I don't mind saying."

Paige actually felt sorry for him, and she touched his shoulder reassuringly. "He brought Fiona home last night. CJ was—" What? She couldn't very well tell him they'd had a fight and she was sleeping on the sofa. "She was still up," she said lamely. "He walked her to the door, then left on foot. That's why I came here this morning. CJ wanted to see how closely the gates are monitored."

"There's a record of all traffic. It's logged. Quite sophisticated, actually. The ID tag has a bar code, much like toll roads do. But on Sunday night, the gate should have been locked at ten."

"Can we pull that information?"

"The chief would have it. I can request his secretary to pull it. Say it's for an audit or something."

His phone rang a second before the door opened and CJ waltzed in, a furious Ms. Miner holding her phone uselessly behind her. CJ slammed the door in her face.

"Nosey little biddy, isn't she," CJ said.

"Yes, Ms. Miner, it's okay," Avery said to the fuming secretary on the phone. "I understand. I'll tell her." He tried to smile as he hung up. "Office protocol," he said.

"Whatever," CJ murmured as she bent down, surveying his battered face. "Gonna have a nice shiner there. What did he want?"

"A warning."

CJ raised her eyebrows.

"For us to stay away," Paige supplied.

"What makes them think you won't call the sheriff and press charges?" CJ asked. "That's kinda ballsy of them, isn't it?"

It was a question that didn't require an answer. Paige watched as CJ paced, her hand running through her hair time and again. *She's so damn attractive.* Paige blinked several times, trying to get that thought from her mind. Of course, on the heels of that came the reminder of the predicament she'd found herself in that morning. In bed. With CJ. Her arms—not CJ's—had wandered inappropriately during the night. She woke to find herself snuggled close to CJ, her hand wrapped possessively around CJ's arm. Thank God she woke first. She could only imagine the merciless teasing if CJ had been the first to wake and found Paige nestled against her.

"How about this?" CJ said. "I go into the café in uniform. I confront him. Find out what the hell is going on."

"I don't think that's a good idea," Avery said. "We would like to think the school is secure, but apparently it is not. Having the gates unlocked after hours requires special permission from me. Obviously that was not the case."

"If they did this as a warning, I can only imagine the retaliation should you confront them," Paige said.

"So we just let it go?"

"I think that's what they're used to," Avery said. "They control Hoganville, they control the school."

CJ looked between the two of them. "Yeah, but who is *they*?"

***

Fiona sipped her coffee, listening to the concerns of her friends. *Friends.* That thought struck her as funny, and she looked up, smiling as Robbie rubbed her arm affectionately.

"You just look so pale, Fiona. Have you been to a doctor?"

"Yes," she lied. "Just a bug. I couldn't keep anything down."

"Well, do you need anything? I can ask Charlotte to make some soup," she offered.

"Thank you, but..." Fiona was about to decline, but she was genuinely touched. "That would be nice," she said instead.

"Great." Robbie paused. "I don't suppose you've met your new neighbors yet, have you?"

Fiona shook her head. "It was late when I got home. Are they nice?"

"Yes, they seem nice. They've joined us at our get-togethers. I wish you would stay one weekend, Fiona. We have so much fun."

"I know. But my mother expects me home."

"You're over thirty, Fiona," Jules said. "Surely you can do your own thing."

Fiona shook her head. "It doesn't work that way," she said, recognizing the sadness in her voice. She immediately felt guilty, knowing she owed Mother Hogan everything she had. "I mean, family comes first." Maybe more so now, she thought.

"Okay. Well, if you need anything, you let us know," Jules said.

"And I'll bring some soup over this evening," Robbie added.

Jules rubbed her shoulder as she passed by. "I hope you feel better."

Left alone again, Fiona set her coffee aside. Yes, they were her friends. Not in the traditional sense, of course. She essentially led two lives, which she'd resigned herself to years ago. She was one of very few who had to leave the security of Hoganville to venture out in the world, all to keep Hoganville—and the caves— safe. There was a certain safety in numbers, and she'd known for some time that their flock was shrinking. She never made mention of it, not even to her own mother. It seemed a little late now for Mother Hogan to be concerned with it. She instinctively ran her hand across her belly, rubbing lightly. It was growing in there, she knew. She could feel it. But a chill ran over her as she remembered the blood between her legs and the cold, reptilian hands on her body. Even though Mother Hogan insisted it was Antel who visited her each night, she knew better. Antel took her innocence in the chamber during coupling. She suspected Antel had never touched her again.

She felt a tear slide down her face and she wiped it away quickly. No tears. She was not allowed tears. It was far too late for that.

She got to her feet, her legs sore. The bruising had not entirely faded, but no one had made mention of her slacks and the long-sleeved shirt she wore during the heat of summer. She glanced to the clock on the wall, then eyed the coffeepot again. Her first class wasn't for another forty-five minutes. She could spare time for another cup. Then she would make her way to her classroom to get ready. Even though she felt zapped of energy, she was looking forward to getting back to it. In there, at least, she felt normal.

She surprised herself by the quick smile she felt tugging at her lips. *Normal?* This was Celebration Week. Any one of her co-workers would be driven mad by the ceremony...and the chase that would occur within the caves.

Her smile quickly left her face, the taste of coffee no longer appealing. She shuffled out the door without it, her mind blank as she walked the familiar corridor to her classroom.

CHAPTER EIGHTEEN

Despite their earlier interaction with Avery, the tension between them was still thick and conversation was inconsequential, to say the least. Paige knew she needed to apologize. She had started the argument. Whatever *game* they were playing while in public, she needed to just go with it and not take it personally. Kissing? Okay, she could handle it. She couldn't get mad every time CJ did something that she deemed inappropriate. That would make for a very long assignment.

After seasoning the chicken breasts and getting them in the oven, she found CJ where she'd left her earlier—stretched out on the sofa, eyes closed. She wasn't asleep, she knew. She glanced at the empty space against the wall where the previous tenants no doubt had kept a TV. Perhaps as a peace offering, she'd suggest a trip into San Augustine to purchase one for them. She wasn't a big TV watcher, but maybe CJ was. If nothing else, it would provide mindless entertainment.

She cleared her throat, about to engage CJ in conversation when CJ's phone rang. Without opening her eyes, she reached out and picked it up. CJ nodded, then sat up, switching her phone to speaker mode and placing it on the table.

"Okay. You're on," CJ said.

"Hi, Paige."

Paige smiled. "Hello, Ice. How are you?"

"Bald and beautiful as ever," he said. "How are you two?"

Paige and CJ looked at each other, both with eyebrows raised. CJ finally grinned.

"She hasn't killed me yet," CJ said. "She's thought about it, though."

Paige smiled too. "Yes. I've considered it three times."

"And it hasn't even been three weeks yet." He laughed. "But I don't blame you."

"Sure. Take sides," CJ said. "What's up? You got something new?"

"Let me just say I'm sick to death of researching all things Hoganville. Because it's very hard to find. Apparently they've always kept a low profile."

"Did anything come up on birth certificates?" Paige asked.

"Hit and miss. They're still going through data, but Avery appears to be correct on that. Listen to what we found today," he said. "We first found mention of this in a book published in the '60s about the history of Angelina National Forest. We found the story in the Lufkin newspaper dated 1959." He paused. "Can you believe they've got that shit archived going back that far? Anyway, a sheepherder went missing after telling quite a tale," he said.

CJ got up and went to the fridge. "Hang on. I think I'll need a beer for this," she said. She glanced at Paige, who shook her head.

"Apparently something was stealing this man's sheep. He suspected coyotes, not rustling, as only one or two at a time would come up missing. One morning, he's out with the herd and he finds one mutilated and gutted, but not eaten. Again, he assumed a coyote. So his plan was to stake out the herd that night—with his gun—and kill the blood thirsty coyote," he said.

CJ laughed. "Seriously? That's what the paper said? Blood-thirsty?"

"No. They said rascal. I'm ad libbing."

"Rascal?" CJ shook her head. "Okay. Go on," she said, taking a large swallow from her beer.

"Right. So he's out with the herd, keeping watch. He says at midnight, on the nose, he sees movement in the woods. But it's not coyotes. He counted fifteen people, all dressed in black robes. They had ropes and were trying to lasso one of his sheep. So he fired his gun up in the air to scare them. Instead of running away, they ran after *him*," Ice said. "Obviously, he made it home safely. He told his tale the next night at the local dive. No one believed him."

"And he ends up missing?"

"Yep. Two days later. Never found a trace of him."

"Any evidence his story was investigated?"

"Not in this article. Billy looked for the next two months, I think, but the only mention of this again was just reporting that there were no leads in his disappearance. So no."

"Where did this guy live? How close to Hoganville?"

"He lived near a little place called Straw," he said. "Twenty miles or so from Hoganville. And yes, we looked that up. Nothing there. The beer joint where he told his story is long gone. There are a few homes, nothing else."

CJ shrugged. "Interesting story," she said. "Robes? Mutilated sheep?" She looked at Paige. "Satanic?"

"Something of the sort, I suppose. I'm certainly no expert," she said.

"We keep coming back to cults, don't we?"

"So you've been into town, right?" Ice asked. "I heard about your café visit."

"Yes, the café was quite fun. But you know it's not really a town, right? But even the houses, they all look deserted," CJ said.

"Like the community is dying," Paige added. "Avery calls it old. There aren't children or young people."

"So is it as creepy as it sounds?"

"And then some," CJ said. "Something's going on there. But obviously most of it is speculation. One of the teachers relayed her story of a visit to the grocery store. Now that was downright scary."

"Let me just say that I'm glad it's you guys there and not me and Billy." He paused. "So, what's the nighttime entertainment like?"

CJ looked at Paige. "What do you mean?"

"Well, you know. You met some lady friends already?"

"We're supposed to be a happily married couple, remember," CJ said.

"Yeah, of course. But if Paige is threatening to shoot you, I imagine you've been scoping out ladies with wandering eyes."

CJ looked pointedly at Paige, one eyebrow arched. "Want to tell him why you're mad at me?"

"No," she said. "Ice, if there's nothing else?"

"Oh, I see. My cue to hang up. Okay, girls. Try not to fight. We'll be in touch."

The apology she'd originally planned to utter was forgotten as the smirk on CJ's face grew. Paige turned on her heels and retreated to the kitchen instead, eyeing the bottle of wine that she intended to have with their dinner. She sighed, reaching for the corkscrew.

CHAPTER NINETEEN

Fiona felt her excitement grow as she joined the others in the chamber. With her new black robe, she no longer felt like an outcast, relegated to the back wall where the innocent, white-robed flock members were placed. She looked back there now, seeing only one white robe. It was Elizabeth, Belden's sister. She had to be in her fifties by now, Fiona guessed. She wondered what she had done to displease Mother Hogan. She looked away, feeling sorry for Elizabeth. At the last celebration in October, Fiona had been standing beside Elizabeth, the last two innocents left. Of course, that wasn't always the case. She remembered a time when there were eight or nine of them. Little by little, they were culled, mostly for disobedience. Randal had run away, something Fiona had secretly dreamed of. Belden and the hunters had found him and brought him back. Randal had not simply been culled. He had been offered up as a sacrifice. He had been taken beyond the chamber into the caves where his screams were heard in the deathly silence. Hearing that had chased away any thoughts of fleeing. She knew her place and was resigned to her fate. Mother Hogan had plans for her and she absorbed everything she could from the books, knowing she was going to be sent out so that she could learn to teach. Her mission was to integrate with the school, something she'd accomplished. Unfortunately, the four years she'd spent on the outside only fed the dream of leaving here...and leaving the nightmares that haunted her.

Ultimately, fear won out and she remained faithful to Mother Hogan and the flock. Now she feared she was more involved than ever before as she gently rubbed her belly, knowing something was growing inside her. Was it Antel's child? Or was it something else? She closed her eyes, chasing the elusive dream that remained just out of her reach. No face, no body. Just cold, cold hands.

The scream shook her out of her musings. Belden and the others were bringing out the girl who had been chosen for the sacrifice. Fiona watched in fascination as the girl struggled, her screams loud and shrill. Mother Hogan liked that, she knew. She watched the older woman's face, her smile broadening with each scream. Tonight would only be an appetizer. Tomorrow, the girl would be forced to drink one of Mother Hogan's potions. Tomorrow, she would not scream. Tomorrow she would be offered up to *it*. Tomorrow they would feast. They would all feast as the girl ran for her life in the caves.

Mother Hogan stepped forward, eyeing the girl. Fiona could feel the excitement in the chamber. It was a ritual that had been going on for more years than anyone knew. Mother Hogan nodded at Belden and the girl was lifted easily up on the altar. Her struggles didn't last long as the leather straps were secured with practiced ease. Fiona could see the girl trembling, her eyes wide with fright. Mother Hogan reached into the stone altar where she kept the knife. She heard the soft scraping as it was removed from its protective sheath. Mother Hogan held it high, its long, smooth surface reflecting the light of the torches and it glistened pleasantly overhead.

"No! Please, no," the girl screamed then, her eyes riveted on the knife.

Mother Hogan laughed delightfully as she teased the knife back and forth in front of the girl, her screams turning into sobs.

"Please don't hurt me," the girl cried. "Please."

"Yes. We have heard that plea hundreds of times before," Mother Hogan said. She turned to the elders, all of them watching her every move.

The knife struck quickly, slicing into the girl's arm as if it were nothing more than butter. Fiona, like the others, cheered as the first blood was spilled. It was expected of them. The girl mewed like the wounded animal that she was. Mother Hogan ran her fingers through the blood running down the girl's arm, then held them up for the flock to see. They all watched with bated breath as Mother Hogan licked her fingers dry, then went back for more.

The girl's head rolled to the side, her eyes glazing over in despair at the hopelessness of her situation. For a second, Fiona felt sympathy for her, knowing what was coming tomorrow night. She pushed it away. It would serve no purpose for her to empathize with this girl. Her fate was sealed.

Instead, she watched as the six elders mimicked Mother Hogan's actions, partaking of their appetizer for tomorrow's feast.

CHAPTER TWENTY

"I met Fiona today," Paige said as she scooped out potatoes for her.

CJ raised an eyebrow. "And? Does she have horns?"

Paige smiled, the first true smile CJ had received from her in days. "No, she does not have horns. She was very friendly, but there was definitely something odd about her," Paige said. "She was *overly* friendly, yet distant, if that makes sense."

"Pretending to be open but not?"

"I suppose, but she was nice. I think I would call her sweet. The visit didn't last long though. She was bringing her class down for their *exercise* period." Paige laughed. "I swear, this is the worst assignment I've ever had. We ran sprints and the girls hated it. And as punishment, they didn't speak to me."

"That's punishment?" CJ asked, taking her plate from Paige. "Thanks."

"You're welcome. And no, it was a bonus, they just didn't know it," she said with a grin. "I've decided I hate kids. Teenagers, anyway."

CJ cut into the baked fish with her fork, eyeing it suspiciously. She only ate fish one way and that was fried. But considering how frosty things had been between them, she didn't want to piss Paige off more by commenting. So she steeled herself on the first bite, preparing to have to force it down. It was surprisingly good. She looked up, seeing Paige's amused expression. "What?" she said around a mouthful.

"All prepared to hate it, were you?"

"I'm used to southern fried fish," she said. "But this is good."

"Thanks. I don't normally put a cornmeal batter on when I bake fish," Paige said, "but I figured you would like it better this way."

CJ was touched that Paige would even concern herself with what CJ might or might not like. Especially since their argument the other night, of which they had yet to speak or apologize for.

"Thank you," CJ said. "But since I don't cook, I can't exactly be picky. You don't have to alter things for me."

"I know I don't have to."

The silence lengthened, their earlier levity giving way to suppressed tension again. CJ, for one, had had enough of it. She reached for her wineglass, taking a large sip. She had never been one to talk about things—feelings. She knew it stemmed from her childhood, where talking never happened. As an adult, she'd never been in any kind of relationship where it was required. But she was stuck here with Paige for what could be several long months. If these first few weeks were any indication, they would end up killing each other before they reached the end of their assignment.

"Let's talk about it," she said. "Let's get it over with, clear the air."

Paige put her fork down. "What do you mean?"

"Let's talk about that night. Let's talk about us having sex. Let's talk about our argument last week. Let's just do it and get it over with. I feel like I'm walking on eggshells around you," she admitted. "I hate it."

Paige stared at her for a long moment, and CJ thought she was going to refuse to talk. But apparently she had only been gathering her thoughts. She nodded. "Okay."

"You go first," CJ suggested.

"I don't—" Paige cleared her throat. "I don't normally do things like that. Like that night," Paige said. "That's your game, not mine."

CJ shook her head. "No, Paige, you're just like me. You just don't want to admit it."

"That's not true. You don't date. You probably don't even bother learning their names."

CJ tilted her head. "And *you* date? I mean, other than Seth?"

"I don't date Seth, but yes, I date. Occasionally. If I wanted to, I would. If I met the right person," she said, taking a sip of her wine. "This job makes that somewhat difficult."

"Right. And that's part of the problem. I don't have the time or the energy to devote to dating," CJ said. "And on occasion, I like to have female company."

Paige snorted. "On occasion?"

"Yes, on occasion. When we have a bad case, I like to just forget it all and escape. I'm no different than you in that regard."

"Yes, you are. I normally go home and take an hour-long bubble bath and drink a bottle of expensive wine. I don't lose myself in anonymous sex."

CJ laughed. "What makes you think I don't do the same?"

"Oh, come on. Really?"

"What? You think every morning when you see me looking like crap that means I've been out with a woman the night before?"

Paige smirked. "Doesn't it?"

"Not necessarily."

"Come on, CJ. Ice and Billy gossip worse than a bunch of girls. I know everything that goes on, just like you do."

CJ sighed. "Okay, so sometimes I don't want to come home to an empty house. Sometimes I don't want to be alone. The bar is the alternative, to find a willing partner and go to her place."

"Why always her place?"

"To keep it anonymous. I never bring anyone to my place."

Paige stared at her, eyebrows raised.

"Okay, well, you, but you were the first," CJ conceded.

"You really expect me to believe that?"

CJ thought maybe she should lie and tell Paige that many women had shared her bed. For some reason, the fact that Paige was the only woman she'd ever brought to her apartment stunned her. She thought back to that night at the bar, when their touches had become more urgent, their kisses blistering. With other women, she would have walked away before inviting them into her personal space—her apartment. But with Paige, that thought never crossed her mind. The only thought crossing her mind had been getting naked with Paige as quickly as possible. She looked up, locking gazes with her now, wondering if she, too, was remembering their time together. Did Paige realize the hold she'd had on her that night? Did she realize CJ would have begged her to come home with her? Which, of course, hadn't been necessary. Paige had willingly followed her to the apartment. Obviously, now, Paige had nothing but regrets about that night.

She finally nodded, answering Paige's original question.

"Yes, it's true. There hasn't been anyone but you in my bed."

Paige looked astonished, an eyebrow arching. "Why?"

"Why what?"

"Why me and no one else?" she asked quietly.

CJ looked away uncomfortably. She didn't know the answer. Was it because she knew Paige and knew it was safe? If so, it was completely subconscious. The fact was, at the time, she was too aroused to care. She'd always been attracted to Paige, even though she knew Paige was out of her league. She decided that was not the answer to give.

"I don't want anyone to know where I live," she said instead. "I don't want the complications." She shrugged. "I don't know. Maybe because I knew you," she said, meeting Paige's questioning gaze. "I felt...safe with you," she finally admitted.

Paige nodded. "Do you regret that night?"

CJ smiled. "Probably not nearly as much as you regret it."

Paige smiled too, then added more wine to both of their

glasses. "I don't know if regret is the right word," she said. "I was actually terribly embarrassed to face you the next day."

"Why? We were both willing participants."

"Yes. But like I said, it's not something I do."

"It's not like I was a stranger, Paige."

"True." She looked like she wanted to say more, and CJ could nearly see her warring with herself. She apparently lost the battle. "I was embarrassed that I was no different than any of the other women you snag at the bar and have sex with. Another notch for you, as it were."

Those words hurt more than they should have, CJ knew, but the pain was acute. The other women, they knew the game. A quick hookup, then right back out there. It was different with Paige. As she'd said, it wasn't a game she played. CJ felt like she'd dragged her down in the gutter with her. In truth, it wasn't like that at all. It was probably the most satisfying night she'd ever had. A wonderful give and take between them, they'd made love as if they knew each other's touch well. In fact, she'd be lying if she said she hadn't looked for Paige again at the bar, hoping for a repeat.

"You weren't a notch, Paige. It wasn't like that with you."

Paige only gave her a sad smile. Apparently she didn't believe her. "So? Any word on the gate log?"

CJ acknowledged the change in subject, knowing their discussion was over with. "I sent the file to Ice this morning. I looked at it. It looked like a text file but it's just numbers all running together. Avery gave me a list of everyone's ID numbers on the vehicle bar code," she said. "If Ice tries to decipher this himself, it might take a while. I hope he requests help with it."

"Let's hope it's not Billy's help he solicits. We all know how he is with numbers."

"Yeah, he flips them. And I found out Richard Barr was working the gate that night when Belden paid a visit to Avery."

"Did you tell Chief Aims what happened?"

"No. Avery thinks we shouldn't call attention to it."

"So what about Barr? Any idea why he'd let Belden in? Especially since it was after hours?"

"I'm guessing it's because Fiona was in the car." She shrugged. "Security is obviously not as tight as it's made out to be."

CHAPTER TWENTY-ONE

Ester opened the door slowly, as if not to disturb anyone inside. That thought always struck her as funny, but she kept her levity to herself. This room was hallowed, viewed only by a select few. The beds were all handcrafted, made by Devin, Gretchen's father. His hands were riddled with arthritis now and useless to her, but her final resting place was already prepared. She hoped she wouldn't need it for many years yet, but it still unsettled her to see the bed made for her. Perhaps she was premature in having Devin construct it. There was no one coveting the purple robe. Not like she'd been when her mother wore it. Of course, her mother's reign was short-lived, thanks to her sudden illness.

Ester looked at the bed where her mother lay, a small smile playing on her lips. Her mother had been a fool and far too trusting. Ester had learned to make the magic potion quite by accident. Her mother simply loved the taste of it.

There were eight beds in all, seven occupied. She moved slowly past them, stopping in front of her beloved grandmother. Everything she knew, she learned from her. If only she had lived longer, the flock might still be thriving. As it was, even she had to admit the flock was dying a slow death. Of course, *he* lived through the flock. If the flock died, what would become of him? Would he be satisfied just hunting? The way the world was today, it was too dangerous. No, he needed them to protect the caves.

They first discovered him when her ancestors were settling the area after the Texans had defeated the Mexican army. They stumbled upon the entry to the underground caverns and, because of the stream that flowed through it, settled here. She often wondered how it would have been if it hadn't been a *Hogan* who had discovered him. Even then, it was always the females who he bestowed the gift to—the power to *see* things, the power to *do* things. All but her own mother. For some reason, she had been skipped over. All the better, as Ester had been strong enough to end her reign and take over. She glanced slyly over at her mother. Near the end, her mother had discovered the poison, but it was too late by then. At least Ester had given her a place of honor here in the burial room. She looked down the line of beds, not really knowing the history of them all. Some had been quite young when they died, their reign short. She knew that both Velma and Opal had only lived into their thirties. Of course, her grandmother had only been in her fifties when she took ill, forcing her unprepared mother to lead the flock.

But now there was no true Hogan to pass the gift on to. She had coupled several times, always unsuccessfully. The men were deemed flawed and were culled. She'd coupled with her brother, Antel, hoping for a pure bloodline but that failed as well. A male child was born. He should have been culled when she realized he would not—could not—speak, but he had proven to be her only weakness. In punishment, she had very nearly had Antel offered up as a sacrifice, but *he* hadn't been interested. Rodel, her child, was gone now, put out of his silent suffering by one of her magic potions. No one knew of his passing. Not even Antel.

She had always kept him secluded from the flock, not wanting to see the doubt, the questions in their eyes as to why she—Mother Hogan—had produced a flawed child. But now there was hope for their future.

Fiona.

Desperate times, they were. While Antel had coupled with Fiona, it was not Antel's child she was carrying. She smiled at the thought, thinking this, finally, would save the flock.

She touched the lace covering her grandmother's leg, her eyes traveling up the skeletal remains to the face, no longer able to make out her features.

"Goodbye, Mother Estelle. I'll come visit again soon."

She closed the door quietly, pausing to lift the hood of her robe over her head. It was time. The flock would be gathering in the chamber. They would offer up their sacrifice tonight.

Then they would feast on the lamb the men had been preparing all day.

And *he* would feast on the young girl after he toyed with her, giving chase in the caves.

CHAPTER TWENTY-TWO

Paige drove slowly down the winding country road, feeling nearly claustrophobic as the giant pines that lined each side forbade any glimpse of the horizon. Nonetheless, she found the pace enjoyable, so different than the constant rush she was used to in Houston. The backseat was filled with groceries from her shopping trip to San Augustine, along with a TV she'd purchased for CJ. The deal they'd made was for her to get the TV and CJ to secure satellite service. Whether they were going to be there for another month—or six—they would at least have some sort of entertainment.

She didn't really mind the solo shopping trip. It gave her time to think, time to reflect on the week. She'd left the school at two, after the group of girls had come to what they were now calling dance class. She really didn't care what the other teachers thought, the girls were enjoying the Zumba DVDs and even she could see a difference in them. Some were quite good at it and at least they were exercising. But she supposed, at some point, she would have to actually learn something about basketball and volleyball so they could do real team sports. CJ had offered to teach her, but so far she'd declined. She and CJ had enough interaction as it was.

The past week had been unbearably hard. Not because she and CJ argued or didn't get along. Quite the opposite. CJ had been on her best behavior, flirting teasingly with her at times, even surprising her in the gym one day with a cup of *real* coffee. Paige had been so touched by the gesture that she'd very nearly kissed her, a seemingly natural reaction. She'd backed off at the last minute, then blushed freely as CJ chuckled good-naturedly.

Of course, the nights were the worst. On two occasions this week she'd woken during the night to find their arms and legs tangled. The first time, she'd tried to move away only to have CJ mumble something incoherently as her grip tightened around her waist. Paige had stilled, praying CJ wouldn't wake. And last night, again, she'd found herself curled around CJ, her head resting on her shoulder. And it was *her* hand, not CJ's, which was in a compromising position. She'd managed to reclaim her hand, but she couldn't make herself move out of CJ's arms and she had fallen back into a peaceful sleep. When the alarm had gone off that morning, CJ was already up and Paige found herself—thankfully—on her own side of the bed.

All of which was making her extremely nervous about the dancing trip they were taking with the others tomorrow night. Knowing CJ, she would take full advantage of the situation.

"There's going to be kissing," she murmured, surprised by the sudden jolt of arousal that thought brought to her. She wouldn't lie to herself. She was attracted to CJ. She didn't *want* to be, but she was. Why else had she followed her to the lesbian bar in the first place? She could tell herself CJ wasn't her type—and she most definitely wasn't—but that didn't change anything. There had always been an attraction there. She wished she could just throw caution to the wind and go out with the group, play her role with CJ without any worries that their actions while in public would carry over to their private time alone.

She let out a deep breath, quickly shaking her head, trying to dispel the image of them in CJ's bed, doing much more than kissing. She hated when memories of that night surfaced. Being around CJ every day like she was, those memories were becoming more vibrant, becoming much more than just fuzzy snapshots.

***

CJ turned the TV on, thrilled to finally have some form of entertainment. The satellite had been hooked up that morning and she settled back now, clutching the remote possessively as she flipped through the channels.

"Are you happy?"

She glanced at Paige with a smile. "Very. You're the best girlfriend ever," she teased.

"Thank you."

"So, you need some help in there?" she offered.

Paige shook her head. "Stay out of my kitchen."

It was just enough of a challenge for CJ to bite. She forgot all about trying to find a good movie to watch. Instead, she sauntered into the kitchen, moving up close to Paige, brushing her body against her.

"Where's the meat?"

"There is none," Paige said, taking a step away from her.

CJ stared at the hands that held the knife, the sharp blade fading to the background as she remembered waking during the night to find Paige's hand under her T-shirt, dangerously close to her breast. She should have done the proper thing and rolled away but she didn't, secretly hoping Paige's fingers would finish their journey.

"Are you trying to turn me into a vegetarian or what?"

"Well, since the only exercise I've seen you do is jog, I thought you might need a low-fat meal." Paige waved the knife at her stomach. "You know, to keep up those rock-hard abs that chicks love so much," she said, obviously remembering CJ's description of them.

CJ grinned and lifted up her shirt. "You want to check them out? See if I've lost anything?" She leaned closer. "You remember what they feel like, don't you?"

Paige turned on her, her eyes glaring. "I have a knife in my hand. Don't tempt me to use it."

CJ laughed. "Oh, baby, you're so damn beautiful when you're angry."

"And don't call me *baby*. I hate it. I'm not your baby." Paige slammed the knife down. "And even if I was your baby, I don't want to be *called* baby. Got it?"

CJ arched an eyebrow, wondering how their teasing exchange had turned ugly so quickly.

"Are you PMSing?"

Paige literally growled at her, then spun on her heels, slamming the bedroom door with enough force to rattle the walls.

"I'll take that as a yes," she murmured. She eyed the pile of vegetables and the two pans that were on the stove, trying to figure out what Paige had been making. A stir-fry of some sort? She was about to grab the vegetables and toss them in one of the pans when the bedroom door opened.

"Don't touch it."

She held her hands up defensively. "Okay."

"Get out of my kitchen."

"Absolutely," she said, backing up.

Paige picked up the knife again, going back to her chopping. CJ slunk back to the sofa, keeping a wary eye on Paige...and the knife.

CHAPTER TWENTY-THREE

Paige rolled over with a weary sigh and punched her pillow. She'd not been able to fall into a comfortable sleep until CJ had left the bed before dawn, presumably to head out on her morning run. After a very silent dinner, she had retreated into the bedroom and CJ had claimed the TV. She kept the volume low and Paige had not been disturbed. She'd half expected—hoped—that CJ would sleep on the sofa, but she had come to bed not long after Paige had turned out the light.

She slept fitfully, guarding against her desires to snuggle with CJ. She groaned at the thought. *Snuggle? With CJ?* Oh, she was really in a pitiful state.

She smelled coffee and even though she felt like she could sleep for another hour, the enticing aroma lured her from bed.

Apparently CJ was back from her run. After a quick trip to the bathroom, she poured a cup, pausing to close her eyes and savor the smell before taking her first sip. She noted that CJ had chosen her favorite blend this morning. She glanced in her direction, finding cautious eyes on her. She put her cup down, just then realizing how childish she'd acted last night. They'd been getting along great all week, and even last night, she knew CJ had just been teasing with her. But the fact that she was actually beginning to *like* the domestic situation she found herself in with CJ—that she was beginning to *like* CJ—threw her completely off-kilter. And when CJ had lifted her shirt, revealing those killer abs, Paige had snapped. Literally.

"Paige, listen, I'm sorry about last night. I don't—"

"Stop," Paige said. "You don't have anything to apologize for. I do." She took her cup and joined CJ on the sofa. "I'm sorry. I bit your head off for no reason. I was way out of line."

"I was just playing around," CJ said.

"I know you were. I reacted poorly. I'm sorry." She reached over and touched CJ's arm, squeezing lightly. "By the way, I *did* start my period, so..."

CJ smiled. "I see. I'll be sure to mark that on my calendar."

Paige smiled too but said nothing. She'd never lived with anyone before. PMS was something she paid little attention to. If there was anyone to snap at, it was Billy and he was used to it by now, she was sure.

"Know what I miss?" CJ asked unexpectedly.

"No. Tell me."

"There's this little Mexican food place a few blocks from the hike and bike trail where I run. On Saturday mornings, I always go there for breakfast. Read the paper, spend an hour or so drinking free coffee. I miss that routine."

Paige nodded. "I miss my Starbucks."

CJ laughed. "I should have known it would involve coffee."

"I also miss Whole Foods. It was a once-a-week stop for me."

CJ leaned closer, still smiling. "I miss eating real burgers."

Paige leaned closer too. "Then maybe you should learn to cook."

CJ didn't pull away and her close proximity caused Paige's

heart to flutter. *Damn*. She sighed and leaned back, avoiding CJ's eyes.

"Is that a challenge? Would you like me to try my hand at breakfast?"

Paige looked at her suspiciously. "What did you have in mind?"

"Fried egg sandwich?"

Paige wrinkled up her nose. "Omelet?" she suggested instead.

CJ rolled her eyes. "Scrambled?"

Paige shook her head. "Fried potatoes and an omelet."

"I take it you really want an omelet." CJ smiled. "Does that mean you're going to cook?"

"Was there ever any doubt?"

***

CJ couldn't believe that they were heading out for their Saturday night dancing date at the early hour of seven. She tried to keep in mind that Suzette and Becca were older than they were, but still, it just didn't seem right with the sun still out and all. She tapped her foot impatiently as Becca tried to find a radio station.

Paige leaned closer, putting a hand on her thigh to keep it from bouncing. "You're fidgeting."

She closed her eyes for a second, the words whispered in her ear having caused a chill to run down her body. While she was looking forward to the evening for completely personal reasons, she did fear that—should she overplay their roles tonight—it would dampen the efforts that she and Paige had both made to keep their relationship on an even keel. But damn, it was going to be hard keeping her hands to herself. Regardless, she would try. She stared at the hand on her thigh, then covered it with her own, letting her fingers entwine with Paige's.

"Do you know what I'm looking forward to?"

Paige smirked. "Dancing."

"Well, besides dancing," she teased, wiggling her eyebrows.

"Then my second guess is going to be the greasy hamburger you're about to consume."

CJ laughed. "It's because you're starving me to death."

Suzette turned around in the front seat, glancing at them. "Are you tired of cooking?" she asked Paige.

"It's become a chore, yes. I don't mind it, really, but it would be nice to have other options."

"That's one reason we take advantage of our night out. It's more than an hour's drive to begin with, so stopping to eat is always a treat. We all have our favorite places so we alternate," she said. "Jules chose the burger place. You'll love it."

Finally, Becca smiled in triumph as country music filled the air. She heard Paige groan beside her.

"What? Don't like country?"

"Not particularly," she said quietly. "I'm surprised you do."

"Only when I'm dancing. I like all types of music. When I'm running, I like upbeat, driving music. When I want to get down and dirty, I like—"

"Okay," Paige said, squeezing her hand hard. "I get it."

CJ grinned. "Oh, but country music," she said. "You get to hold your baby tight." She leaned closer, her words just a whisper. "I can't wait to get you out on that dance floor."

Paige kept a smile on her face, but her words contradicted it. "I swear, CJ, don't make me hurt you. Because I will."

CJ felt laughter bubbling up. "Is that a threat? Or a challenge?"

Paige leaned over, her mouth actually touching CJ's ear, causing her pulse to race. "Remember, I do carry a gun," she said, her whisper tickling her ear.

Any retort CJ may have had died in her throat. God, that mouth, that tongue. She turned her head, looking out the window, seeing nothing but the blur of pine trees. She remembered exactly what that mouth and tongue could do to her.

***

Paige clung to CJ's hand, the crowded, noisy bar making her feel uneasy. She had never been one for bars. In fact, the night she'd followed CJ was only the second time she'd gone to a bar of any sort. The first being a dance club Seth had dragged her to when they were in college. Thankfully, CJ seemed to feel her discomfort and pulled her closer, almost shielding her.

"There's a table," Becca said loudly, pointing toward the back.

One of the advantages of coming early, Suzette had told them, was being able to secure one of the larger tables. There were eight in their group this evening, which had made for an interesting dinner. To its credit, the small-town burger joint hadn't seemed fazed in the least when eight lesbians descended on it. Finding tables and following conversation had proven to be the most challenging. Paige managed, after all she had been bred to host large dinner parties, but CJ—who normally exuded such confidence—had seemed out of her element and been fairly quiet throughout. Now, though, it was Paige who was in a foreign environment. CJ looked right at home.

"This is a large bar for being out in the boonies," CJ said to Becca. "Are they always this crowded?"

"Pretty much. It's not like there's a lot to choose from."

CJ leaned closer to her. "You want a beer? Or something else?"

She nodded. "Beer is fine."

She watched CJ saunter off, noticing women perusing her as she passed. She'd seen firsthand how CJ worked a bar and was surprised she wasn't checking any of these women out. But then, they were in their roles this evening. She wondered if it was hard for CJ to remain the faithful girlfriend with so many opportunities about.

Suzette grinned at her from across the table. "She's so damn attractive," she said. "And you're like Cover Girl gorgeous. You make a striking couple."

Paige felt herself blushing and was thankful for the muted lighting. She certainly didn't mind the comment about CJ. She *was* damn attractive. But she always felt self-conscious when others remarked on her own looks. She'd found it to be almost a hindrance as far as her career was concerned. Men, especially, failed to take her seriously. She always had to prove herself first. CJ, on the other hand, had the boyish good looks that most men envied, not desired. When she spoke, they listened. When Paige spoke, they stared at her breasts, oblivious to everything else. But her good manners didn't fail her, and she smiled politely at Suzette.

"Thank you."

"The honeymoon period never lasts," she said, "but then I see you two together and I think you might still be like this ten years from now." She leaned across the table, her voice low. "The sex must be fabulous."

Paige blushed yet again, thankful that CJ had returned, preventing her from answering.

"Here you go, *baby*," CJ said, flashing an evil grin as she handed her a beer.

Paige nearly laughed, acknowledging CJ's dig at her with a slight nod. "Thanks."

"Drink up," she said. "I'm about to haul you out on the dance floor. It's been too long since we last danced."

Mindful of Suzette watching, Paige gave CJ what she hoped was a sexy smile. "I can't wait, tiger."

Apparently, neither could CJ as she barely let Paige finish half of her beer. Before she could protest, they were out on the dance floor, CJ pulling her into her arms. Of course the song would be a slow one and CJ took full advantage of that, the hand on Paige's back slipping lower, bringing their bodies into contact. Paige stumbled, causing CJ to tighten her grip. At the cookouts, they sat together, they touched, but it was never like this, not the full body touching of an intimate dance. Paige tried to remind herself that they were only role-playing, but her body betrayed her, coming alive as CJ's lips brushed her neck.

"Fair warning, but I'm going to kiss you," CJ whispered into her ear. "Your buddy Suzette hasn't taken her eyes off of us."

It should have been a simple pretend kiss—it *was* a pretend kiss—but when CJ's mouth met hers, Paige forgot all about the roles they were playing as her body responded. Whether CJ forgot as well or if she was just testing her boundaries, Paige would never know. But when CJ's tongue brushed against her lower lip, Paige's mouth opened voluntarily, inviting CJ inside. It was a mistake, a *huge* mistake. She contained the moan that tried to escape, but she couldn't stop her body from pressing even closer to CJ, their breasts smashing together as the hand she had behind CJ's neck found its way into her hair. She closed her eyes as her pulse raced uncontrollably, memories flooding her mind, visions of CJ's tongue in the most intimate of places.

Thankfully, the kiss came to an end, and she was surprised there was no gloating sign of victory in CJ's eyes. She almost wished there was. Gloating she could deal with. But the desire she saw, desire that CJ apparently felt no need to hide, was causing her heart to race even faster. She ducked her head, afraid CJ might see the same in her eyes. Amazingly, they were still dancing, her feet moving by rote. They said nothing, and when the song faded away, CJ took her hand and led her silently back to the table.

Knowing eyes watched them, Paige felt embarrassed. It was a kiss between lovers, as they were pretending to be, but it was a kiss that promised that there was so much more to come. For them, that would not be the case. Not for the first time—or even the tenth—she wished they had separate bedrooms. She feared she would get no sleep tonight.

The rest of the evening passed quickly, both of them dancing with the others in their group. And even though they danced together again several times, CJ chose faster songs and made no other attempt to kiss her. For that, Paige was thankful.

The drive home was filled with chatter, CJ participating much more than she did. Apparently they had agreed to return to the bar next weekend as a live band was performing, one which Suzette claimed was *awesome*. When Becca stopped the car in front of their house, Paige thanked them politely for driving, already dreading being alone with CJ.

Her worries were for naught, though, as CJ promptly claimed the bathroom for a shower, and Paige busied herself with preparing the coffee for morning. By the time she finished her own shower, CJ was in bed, the lights out.

Paige's heart was literally pounding as she crawled in beside her. CJ had her back to her and appeared to be well within the imaginary line Paige had created for them. She wasn't certain if she should feel thankful...or disappointed. She sighed and rolled over, mimicking CJ's position. There were only a few moments of silence before CJ spoke.

"I'm sorry."

Those weren't the words she was expecting, and she didn't know how to respond to them. For that matter, she wasn't sure what it was CJ was apologizing for. For kissing her? For not speaking? For the desire Paige saw in her eyes? Paige knew she was guilty of all three herself.

Without knowing what to say, she said nothing. She was surprised to find sleep claiming her and she relaxed into it. Perhaps tomorrow they would talk about it.

CHAPTER TWENTY-FOUR

CJ's morning run was longer than normal, and she knew that was because she was avoiding going back home, avoiding seeing Paige. She'd crossed the line, to say the least. She'd meant for the kiss to be like the others, her teasing Paige just enough to annoy her. When she found herself deepening the kiss, she expected Paige to pull away. She never expected her mouth to open to her, never expected to feel Paige's tongue sliding against her own. She never expected Paige to respond to her like she did. She nearly stumbled from the jolt of arousal that hit her even now. She slowed to a fast walk, her body still remembering the kiss, the feeling of their bodies as they touched, the gentle touch of Paige's hand in her hair, holding their mouths together for seconds longer. Memories of their one night together came back in vivid detail.

The ride home had been filled with mindless babble, anything to distract her from the warm body sitting next to her. She hadn't known what to say to Paige so she said nothing. She took Paige's silence to indicate her anger. That's why she apologized. She didn't know what she expected Paige to say, but the continued silence wasn't it. So she'd escaped the house before Paige got up, delaying the inevitable talk they would have. Just how angry Paige was, she could only guess.

She wasn't going to be able to take much more of this, she knew. It had taken all of her willpower to not repeat the kiss each and every time they danced together. Of course she knew she was attracted to Paige. She'd always been attracted to her. But Paige was so above her, she never thought anything would happen between them. Only in her dreams did she imagine Paige would come to her, would find her at the bar, would go home with her to her bed. Only in her dreams did she think they'd ever be together. Yet they were. And it had been hell afterward and took weeks for them to get back to normal. Now here they were again, playing with fire. She knew Paige was attracted to her too. She wasn't blind to that. She also knew Paige didn't want to be attracted to her. The dance, the kiss—all CJ's doing. But it was Paige who turned the kiss into something more.

She stopped, catching her breath. Yes, Paige was the one who turned the kiss into more, not her. She shook her head. No, Paige wasn't angry. Paige was embarrassed. The silence wasn't because she was angry, it was because she didn't want to talk about it.

This caused a smile to form, and CJ took off running again, wondering if they were going to be adult about it all and talk or if they were going to continue in silence until one of them broke. Judging by their track record, she would assume the latter.

When she got back, breakfast was underway, and she tried to keep things as normal as possible.

"Smells great," she said. Paige just nodded, going back to her cooking. "Gonna grab a quick shower, if there's time."

Paige glanced at her then, and CJ wasn't sure if it was her imagination or if Paige was really doing a slow perusal of her body, but she felt her skin burning as Paige's eyes traveled slowly over her. Her habit of jogging in short shorts and a sports bra did have its advantages. Or disadvantages, in this case, as she felt very underdressed...and exposed.

"Shower, yes," Paige said, her voice sounding an octave lower than normal.

CJ turned the water to cold, trying to chase away the image of Paige's lingering inspection. She was going to end up doing something stupid, she just knew it. Something that she and Paige wouldn't be able to get past. Something that might compromise the mission, although that could be a blessing. So far they'd done very little FBI work.

Breakfast was the silent affair she suspected it would be, with Paige avoiding eye contact as well. CJ finally put her fork down. She never thought she would be the one to take the adult track.

"You want to talk about it?"

"No."

"So we're just not going to speak then? If you're angry with me, say so."

Paige looked at her then. "I'm not angry with you, CJ. I just don't want to talk about it. When we're out in public, I understand we have a certain image to portray. And...and kissing is...a part of it, I suppose."

CJ picked up her coffee cup, studying her. Paige's face was slightly flushed, and she knew her guess that Paige was more embarrassed than angry was right on. "Okay. Then why aren't you speaking to me? I said I was sorry."

"You don't have to apologize." Paige met her eyes this time. "If that's the case, I should apologize as well."

CJ grinned. "And what exactly are we apologizing for?"

Paige's blush deepened, but a smile played on her lips. CJ found herself staring at those lips and had to drag her eyes away. Paige didn't answer. Instead, she stood, pointing at the table.

"You get to do the dishes. I think I'll take a turn with the TV."

***

Fiona was nervous as she walked up to the door. While she got along well with everyone, she didn't normally go out of her way to interact with them. But Mother Hogan had insisted because she thought it odd that the two new ones would so boldly enter the café the way they did. Mother Hogan felt they were a threat and had asked Fiona to monitor them. Fiona knew how paranoid she could be. She once accused Ryan Hogan of disobedience, suspecting him of spying and taking his tales to the authorities. Despite pleading his innocence—which Fiona believed to be the truth—he had nonetheless been culled in a most brutal fashion. There was no magic potion from Mother Hogan to dull his senses. He'd been taken past the chamber, deeper into the cave. His screaming was...oh, it was so loud, so piercing. It stopped abruptly, with finality. She shuddered as she remembered the sounds of bones snapping. Like the others, she could only imagine what lived in the caves. As far as she knew, no one was privy to that other than Mother Hogan. No one dared set foot beyond the chamber and into the dark earth. Only Mother Hogan ever ventured deeper into the caves. Well, that wasn't exactly true. Others were forced to go, those being culled. And the girls, of course. The ones being sacrificed and offered to *him*.

She shook those thoughts away, going back to the task at hand. She knocked lightly, hearing the sound of a TV, then silence. Soon, the door opened, and the woman she hadn't met yet, the one they called CJ stood at the door. Fiona smiled in greeting.

"Hi. I'm Fiona Hogan, your neighbor."

"CJ Johnston, pleased to meet you."

Fiona looked past her, hoping Paige was around. She'd met her the other day at school and had found her to be both charming and friendly.

"I actually came over to invite you two over for lunch," she said. "Assuming Paige is home, of course."

CJ stood back. "Sure. Come on in," she invited.

Fiona found the inside to be much the same as her own house, although there was very little in the way of decoration. No pictures or prints adorned the walls. In fact, very few personal items were on display.

"Hi, Fiona," Paige greeted her. "Would you like some iced tea?" she asked, holding up a glass.

"Oh, no. Thanks. I just wanted to invite you over for lunch. That is, if you don't already have plans." She smiled. "I've learned that on Sundays following the dancing trip, no one gets together for cookouts."

"True," she said. "Sure, we'd love to join you for lunch." Paige looked at CJ, as if for confirmation. CJ nodded.

"Great. It's nothing fancy, but I thought it would give us a chance to get to know one another." She made a show of looking at her watch. "About an hour?"

"Sounds good. What can we bring?"

She was about to say *nothing*, but she knew in her haste to plan this she'd forgotten about beverages. "Whatever you'd like to drink. I'm afraid I don't have anything."

"Okay. We'll be over in about an hour then," Paige said. "Thanks."

Fiona left feeling a little uneasy. Mother Hogan expected her to grill them for information, but she found she was looking forward to their company. She smiled to herself, wondering if pregnancy was affecting her good senses. She knew if Mother Hogan deemed them to be a threat, Belden and the others would capture them and take them to the chambers.

True to their word, an hour later the women were knocking on her door. Lunch was simple but she couldn't take credit for it. Mother Hogan had had Selma prepare the chicken salad that morning. It was a special recipe that was quite delicious. She had sent a loaf of freshly baked bread as well. The only thing Fiona could claim was the lettuce and tomatoes she'd picked from the community garden earlier.

Paige was holding two bottles of wine. "I wasn't sure what you were having," she explained.

Fiona knew nothing of wine so could offer no suggestion. Mother Hogan did not allow alcohol in any of the homes. "Nothing fancy. Just chicken salad sandwiches." Paige's grin was infectious, and Fiona felt herself smiling too.

"The Riesling will go beautifully then. And if we're daring, we can have the Beaujolais for dessert."

"Careful honey, or you'll give her the impression that you're a mad drinker," CJ said.

"Oh. I thought you were going to say I was a wine snob."

CJ laughed. "Well, that too."

Fiona was jealous of their playful interaction, never having been a couple with anyone herself. They were both looking at her expectantly, and her lack of social skills became glaringly obvious. While she often joined the other teachers for lunch in the small lounge they shared at the school, this was the first time she'd invited anyone over to her house. She was out of her element, and her anxiety must have shown because Paige squeezed her arm reassuringly.

"Can I help you with anything, Fiona? I see you have the table all set. Shall we have a glass of wine before we eat?"

Fiona let out a nervous breath, thankful Paige had offered a suggestion to move the lunch along. Otherwise, she would have simply taken the food out and started eating. But as she saw the wine bottles Paige had set on the table, she panicked.

"I'm afraid I'm not prepared," she blurted out.

CJ raised her eyebrows questioningly, but Paige apparently knew what she meant.

"You don't have a corkscrew, you mean? No problem." Paige turned to CJ. "Do you mind running over and getting ours?"

"Of course not."

"I don't have glasses either," Fiona said. "I've got regular drinking glasses. Will that do?"

Paige laughed. "Okay, so maybe I am a bit of a wine snob. We *must* have wineglasses."

"I'll get those too. Be right back."

Fiona apologized as soon as CJ left. "I'm sorry. I'm not used to having company," she admitted.

"It's okay, sweetie," Paige said. "It was nice of you to invite us over."

She relaxed, feeling a little more comfortable as Paige didn't seem fazed in the least. For a moment there, she almost felt as inadequate as she had when she left for college. Arriving in Nacogdoches from Hoganville, she'd been as lost and confused as if she'd been dropped off in a foreign country. Which, in a sense, it was. But then, she hadn't minded the scrutiny she received. She knew she would be leaving there and never see those people again. It was different here, as this was her job. Mother Hogan expected her to fit in, to be involved at the school. And, of course, to keep her informed.

The school was something she was familiar with so she decided that was a safe topic of conversation.

"Do you like it here so far?" she asked.

"Well, it's definitely different," Paige said. "CJ and I are both from Houston so the pace is a little slow. But everyone has been super nice. Suzette and Becca, especially."

"Yes, they are. For the most part, everyone gets along very well." Never having been curious about the other teachers' personal lives, she was surprised by her next question. "How long have you and CJ been a couple?"

"Not long," Paige said, smiling. "Six months." She raised her eyebrows. "What about you? You have a nice, handsome guy waiting on you in Hoganville?" Then she grinned. "Or a woman?"

Fiona felt herself turning red. "No." Thankfully CJ returned, saving her from elaborating on her answer.

"Okay, so since I was digging around in the cabinets in *your* kitchen, I just now realized how many wineglasses we have," CJ said with a laugh. "I counted twelve of them."

The look Paige gave her caused Fiona to laugh.

"You can never have too many wineglasses," Paige said. She turned to Fiona and grinned. "She's not normally allowed in the kitchen."

"Except to do the dishes, don't forget," CJ corrected as she twisted the corkscrew.

"Yes. And you are an expert at that."

A muted pop and CJ held the cork up triumphantly. She was rewarded with a quick kiss from Paige. Fiona felt herself blushing once again, this time at their display of affection. It apparently surprised CJ as well because she too looked a bit flushed.

She accepted the glass Paige handed her, hoping she didn't gag on the wine. She'd only had it once before, when Gayla and Dave had hosted a birthday dinner. She had wanted to fit in with everyone and she took a glass. The wine had tasted dry and bitter to her, and she had nearly spit it out. But since Paige and CJ had gone to the trouble, she would at least try it.

"I don't know your preference in wine, Fiona, but this Riesling is on the sweet side, as is the Beaujolais," Paige said. "I hope it's to your liking."

The wine was cool in her mouth, and she was pleasantly surprised by the fruity flavor. "I taste apple," she said without thinking.

Paige laughed. "Very good. You must have a natural palate for wine." She turned to CJ. "And what do you taste?"

"It tastes citrusy to me." When Paige shook her head, CJ added, "What? Too vague?"

"A little."

"Well, maybe my...tongue is not as talented as yours...in the taste department."

Fiona was fascinated by the look they exchanged, and she could swear the temperature in the room rose ten degrees in a matter of seconds. Paige cleared her throat, turning to Fiona. Her gaze held none of the intensity that she'd just shared with CJ. Again, since she'd never had the closeness that these two obviously shared, she couldn't relate to what had clearly passed between them with only a glance.

"How long have you been at the school, Fiona?" Paige asked.

"This is my ninth year," she said.

"I guess you plan on staying then?"

"Yes. It would be hard for me to leave Hoganville." She shared a silent laugh with herself. Not hard to leave. *Impossible.*

Whether it was the wine that relaxed her or the company, Fiona didn't know, but their lunch passed quickly. She was pleased that CJ enjoyed the chicken salad enough to request a second sandwich. By the time they were ready to take their leave, Fiona realized she had not asked even one of the questions Mother Hogan had demanded of her. Well, she would have a week before returning home. Perhaps she would run into Paige at school.

"Thank you again, Fiona. We had fun," Paige said. "Maybe one day this week we could grab lunch together," she suggested.

"Yes," she answered quickly. "I would like that."

"Great. I'll see you at school then."

She watched with envy as they headed to their own house, their hands clasped together, lightly swinging between them. They made a cute couple. She closed her door and leaned against it with a sigh, her eyes landing on the empty bottles of wine and the wineglasses which CJ had placed on the counter. Paige had told her to keep them for the next time they were over.

Would there be a next time?

She hoped so. She'd had fun. She couldn't remember the last time she'd laughed and enjoyed someone's company as much.

CHAPTER TWENTY-FIVE

CJ took her shower first, so while Paige was taking her turn, CJ took advantage of the empty bed. It was a queen, but when you live alone and are used to a king, it was a little small and a challenge to stay on her side of Paige's imaginary line. She spread out now, arms and legs both, loving the feel of the cool, smooth sheets. Paige had excellent—and expensive—taste. She'd never given much thought to her sheets before or their thread count, but after this, one thousand thread count Egyptian cotton was her new favorite.

She rolled over, staring at the pillow Paige used. She sighed, wondering what was up with her. The lunch had actually been enjoyable. Paige was loose and carefree, and there appeared to be no tension between them at all. That was evidenced by the spontaneous kiss Paige had given her, the first one Paige had initiated between them. Yet when they left Fiona's, Paige had reverted back to silence, staying in the bedroom, on her laptop while CJ had watched TV. Dinner had been leftovers, which was fine with her. She didn't expect Paige to have to cook every night. She just wished things weren't so strained between them. The only time it wasn't strained was when they were around other people.

When the bathroom door opened, she dutifully scooted back to her side, mindful of Paige's line. When the light went out she squinted in the darkness, watching Paige move to the bed. Just the sight of her coming to their bed caused her libido to kick into gear and she turned away.

"I had fun today," CJ said, trying to break the ice.

"Yes, it was."

CJ rolled toward her. "You know, I was thinking, maybe we could lose this imaginary line here," she said.

"I don't think so."

"I like to roll around a little bit. I'm used to a king."

"So am I."

"Good. Because I hate the line. Every time I roll over I have to be careful not to get into your space."

"As it should be."

"Come on, Paige. Please?"

"No. Stay on your side."

"No. We've played by your rules long enough. My turn. I'm giving you official notice that I will not abide by the imaginary line." *So there.*

"No."

"Yes."

CJ let her hand drift onto Paige's side, only to have it slapped. She very nearly giggled.

"Don't make me hurt you," Paige threatened.

"As if."

Without thinking, CJ moved her foot, rubbing it lightly against Paige's leg. This earned her a growl as Paige slammed her fists onto the bed.

"God, must you?"

"I must."

"I feel sorry for your mother. You were probably a horrible child."

The words were said in jest, she knew, but they hit home all the same. She felt the tightness in her chest, and she drew a shaky breath.

"Yeah, sorry. I was apparently a terrible kid," she murmured, squeezing her eyes shut to try to keep the memories away. Terrible kid. She learned quickly all the different ways punishment could be doled out.

Paige grabbed her arm, squeezing tightly. "I'm so sorry, CJ. I wasn't thinking. I didn't mean anything by it."

"It's okay. You shouldn't have to worry about every single thing you say." She rolled her head to look at her. "I have a few issues from my childhood still. I'm working through them. I shouldn't be so sensitive about it. I...well, it's been twenty years."

Paige loosened her grip but didn't remove her hand. "Do you want to talk about it?"

"No. But thanks."

"I...I don't really know what happened," Paige said. "Just hearsay and gossip at the office. I don't want to assume."

"Whatever you've assumed, it's way worse."

She rolled over then, her back to Paige. She kept her eyes closed, almost wishing she could cry. Now, she wished that. As a kid, she refused to cry, refused to give in. He would win then. But now, she just wished she could cry and get it out. She was startled to feel Paige's hand on her back, rubbing, soothing her. How nice would it be to roll over and let Paige hold her? *Would Paige hold her?* Her touch was comforting, yet it felt strange. She never felt a comforting touch before. Not even in those darkest times when her father visited her did her mother ever come to her aid, ever come to comfort her. That job was left to her sister, who needed her own comforting. She relaxed now, her eyes closing, her mind easing as Paige continued to rub lightly back and forth across her back.

As she was about to drift off to sleep, she felt Paige move, sliding up behind her protectively. Paige slipped an arm around CJ's waist, then let out what CJ thought sounded like a contented sigh, her breath on her skin.

"I think you're over the line," CJ whispered.

"Yes. I am."

CJ smiled, then took Paige's arm and pulled it tighter against her. She didn't try to analyze the meaning of Paige's actions. She simply closed her eyes, loving the feel of Paige resting close behind her.

***

Paige knew she should move. CJ was already asleep. She allowed herself a few more seconds before slowly unwrapping herself from around CJ. God, what game were they playing? What game was *she* playing? Yes, they had sex. More than six months ago now. Just a one-night stand, basically. A one-time lapse in judgment.

And she couldn't seem to get past it. She wasn't comfortable with casual sex. CJ, on the other hand, had perfected it to a fine art. She rolled over onto her back, her fists balled together. *We had sex.* And all of this, this *acting* they were doing, was blurring the line. It was becoming too real. When they were around others, Paige could pretend that it was all just for show, she could let go of her inhibitions, but here, alone, she tried so hard to keep things professional between them.

She nearly laughed out loud. *Professional?* No. There was nothing professional about the situation they were in. Like now. The need to comfort CJ had been overwhelming. She had sounded so wounded, so defenseless, her voice conveying a *need* that Paige didn't understand. And all Paige wanted to do was protect her. But in reality, all it did was blur the line even more. She rolled her head slightly, looking at CJ's sleeping form, wanting nothing more than to go to her again, to slip her arm around her, to feel CJ pull her closer.

God, don't do this.

Maybe they should just do it. Just sleep together again and get it over with. Maybe it would ease some of the tension. She groaned. *Did I just think that? I do not want to have sex with CJ.*

Yes. I do.

She rolled over in frustration, her back to CJ now. No, she did not want to have sex with CJ. Been there, done that. So no. No, no, no.

She heard a scraping noise and she opened her eyes, the eerie feeling of someone watching her making the hairs on back of her neck stand up. She glanced at the window, the blinds lowered haphazardly, an inch of space remaining on one corner. The loud scream was out of her mouth before she could stop it, and CJ shot out of bed, her eyes wide.

"What the fuck?"

Paige scooted up against the wall, clutching the sheet up to her chin. She pointed to the window with a trembling hand. "Someone...something...was at our window." She was nearly panting and she tried to catch her breath. "There was something outside there," she whispered. "It was looking at us."

"Something? What do you mean *something*?"

"It could have been a person, but I don't think so."

CJ rubbed her eyes. "Well, you scared the shit out of me." She opened the tiny nightstand beside the bed and took out her service weapon. "I'll take a look. You stay here."

Paige threw the sheet off. "Are you out of your mind? Do you know what happens to people in movies when they stay behind?" She found her own gun, holding it tightly in her hand. "I'm ready."

CJ stared at her. "In the movies?" She shook her head. "Come on then."

They went into the kitchen, CJ stopping her when she lifted her hand to turn on the lights. She motioned silently to the back door located at the edge of the kitchen. Paige could feel her heart pounding in her chest as CJ reached for the doorknob.

"No. Don't," she whispered.

CJ frowned. "What is it?"

"Don't open the door," she said. "I have a bad feeling."

CJ stared at her. "We *are* both FBI agents. You do remember that, right?"

Paige smiled, then motioned between them. "Yeah, and we're both in underwear and bare feet."

"But we have big guns." She motioned to the door again. "Besides, whatever was out there is long gone by now."

Paige sighed, still hesitant. She realized she was being ridiculous. "You're probably right. Can we at least take a flashlight?"

CJ nodded, going quickly to her bag and pulling out a small one. She clicked it on, then opened the door slowly, flashing the beam toward their bedroom window, then to the woods behind it. There was no sign of movement.

"Come on."

Paige followed closely, looking from side to side, imagining... *something*...leaping out at her from the woods.

The air was warm, humid. The nearly full moon shrouded by thin clouds, making the shadows long and dark. A light breeze rustled the leaves of an oak tree over their heads, making them both jump.

"Jesus, we're acting like a couple of kids," CJ whispered.

She stopped next to the window, bending over, looking inside. Paige did the same, shocked at how well she could see inside the bedroom. CJ flashed the light around on the ground and Paige pointed to what looked like crumbled leaves. The area was disturbed, as if someone had been standing there.

"Could be tracks," CJ murmured, following them until they disappeared into the woods. A bare, sandy spot had a perfect imprint of...what? CJ knelt down, holding her palm out, the print larger than her extended hand. She glanced up at Paige.

"Bear?" they asked simultaneously.

Paige looked back down at the print. "Claws," she said, seeing the indention in the dirt.

"Yeah."

"What would a bear be doing looking in our bedroom window?" she asked.

"Well, hell, I don't know what it is. Do they even have bears around here? I know we're out in the middle of the woods, but I don't think bear run rampant out here."

Paige jerked her head around, hearing twigs breaking, then the sound of something running. Something...*large*. Just as she grabbed CJ's hand, they heard the loud, piercing scream that they'd heard last week. It sent chills down her spine and she gripped CJ's hand harder. "Let's go back inside."

"Good idea."

They both hurried back to the house, and Paige quickly locked the door behind them. She then turned on the lights and went to the front door, making sure it was locked as well.

"You think that'll stop a bear?"

Paige met her gaze. "No." She shook her head. "I also don't think it was a bear."

CHAPTER TWENTY-SIX

Ice rolled the piece of paper between his fingers expertly, a grin on his face. It was good to hear CJ's voice.

"Bored out of my mind," she said in response to his question. "There is nothing, and I mean *nothing* out here. Forty minutes to the nearest restaurant and it's a little dive that I'm wondering how it passed inspection."

"So they have a cafeteria there for you or what?"

CJ laughed. "Yeah. It's called Paige Riley."

Ice and Billy exchanged grins.

"She hasn't killed you yet then?" Billy asked.

"Let's say she's come close," CJ said. "My lone entertainment is pushing her buttons and waiting for the explosion."

"Really, are you two getting along okay?" Ice asked. "It wasn't like you hung out or anything around here."

There was only a slight pause before CJ answered. "It's hit-and-miss. Some days we get along great. Others, not so much."

Billy leaned closer to the phone and Ice knew exactly what his next question was going to be. It was one he'd asked Ice on numerous occasions.

"So, like, are you sharing a bed and everything?"

"Yeah, Billy. And we're having wild sex every night too," she snapped.

"You don't have to bite my head off. I was just curious."

"I'd like to see you and Ice share this one-bedroom, one-bath little place and see if you wouldn't go bat-shit crazy too."

Ice laughed. "Man, I've missed you. Been so quiet here without you."

"Yeah. I miss you too. A few months of this and I'll be out of my freakin' mind. We drove an hour and a half to the nearest gay bar, for God's sake. Then—"

"You and Paige went to a gay bar together?" Billy asked.

"Yes. And we danced too. We *are* supposed to be a couple, remember?"

"So you made some friends?"

"Yes. They're a close-knit group here. They included us right away. That part was easy. We also had lunch with Fiona Hogan. She's been really sheltered, you can tell, but she was nice. She and Paige seemed to hit it off. Paige is going to have lunch with her this week."

"Well, we got the results from the gate logs," Ice said, sitting up in his chair and pulling up the chart on his screen. "Now we know why that file was so huge. It was nearly twelve years' worth of data. I guess it's everything from when they had that system installed."

"So what did you find?"

"We got some patterns. Enough to say that I think this assignment isn't the short end of the stick after all."

"Oh? You mean us stuck out here in the boonies wasting our time might not be such a waste after all?"

"Maybe," he said. "Over the course of a year, Fiona and

Gretchen Hogan both have random exits from the school during the week. Not often for either of them. But going back the last six years, there's a pattern. Twice each year, they both exit the same Monday, Tuesday and Wednesday nights. Fiona is always about an hour earlier than Gretchen."

"When do they return?"

"Late. Or early," he said. "Usually after two a.m." He could picture her pacing, calculating.

"And this coincides with the disappearances?"

"Yes. The week each girl disappeared, the following Monday, Tuesday and Wednesday Fiona and Gretchen left the school."

"What did Howley say about it?"

"They're going to put together a database with the unsolved disappearances in the area and go back twelve years, the length of our file. See if their pattern matches. But he's passed the info on to the boys in Baton Rouge. They're still investigating there as if that's ground zero. But they don't have shit to go on."

"Well, it's not like we have anything here."

"No, and we don't have anything else either. There's just not a lot out there on Hoganville. Billy found a mention of it in an old newspaper article written about forty years ago. Brief. Just mentioning how a family settlement had grown to over two hundred. It compared them to the Amish, with how secluded they keep themselves."

"Yeah, and you can tell it was larger. There are a lot of houses that are boarded up now." He heard her let out a heavy breath. "I need to go," she said. "I've got to guard a goddamn classroom. Christ, I hate this job."

He and Billy both laughed. "Prison guard is not your thing?"

"A bunch of smart-mouthed girls who think they're hot shit here. Now *this* is a waste of time. Most of them will be right back out there when they're released. The next time they go through the system, they'll be adults and they can see what a real prison is like."

"Good to hear your voice, CJ," Ice said. "You could call once in a while, you know."

"Works both ways, baldy," she said before ending the call.

Ice was still grinning when he rolled the paper wad between

his fingers, tossing a perfect strike against Billy's ear. Billy swatted at him, scowling.

"You know I hate that."

"Yeah. That's why I do it."

Billy sighed. "I miss them. I really miss Paige, but I kinda miss CJ too."

"What do you think is going on with them?"

"What do you mean?"

"Well, CJ wasn't complaining nearly as much as I thought she'd be."

Billy grinned. "You think they're doing the dirty?"

"Paige and CJ?" He shook his head. "I just don't see it. Paige is too...well, she's Paige."

"Yeah. And CJ is CJ. She's doing good to know what fork to use at dinner. But they sure do flirt a lot."

"They just do that to entertain us, man. And I miss that." He grinned, getting an evil idea. "Let's send them a present."

"What kind of present?"

"You know. Something that CJ would definitely know what to do with and something that would make Paige blush like a choir girl." At Billy's blank look, Ice rolled his eyes. "A dildo, man."

Billy's eyes widened as he smiled. "That's evil. I love it."

"Yeah. Evil." He laughed. "They're going to kill us."

CHAPTER TWENTY-SEVEN

It had been three nights since things had changed between them. Four nights, really, if she counted the dance...and the kiss. But after Sunday night, after Paige had crossed the line and comforted CJ, after the incident with the *bear*, things had changed. She knew it. CJ knew it. Yet not a word was spoken about it.

The tension between them was almost unbearable, and yes, she would admit that it was sexual tension. Especially at night, in bed. The imaginary line had disappeared completely and the last two mornings, Paige had found herself next to CJ, having moved to her during the night. Yesterday, she'd managed to move away before CJ woke. This morning, however, when she opened her eyes, CJ was awake, watching her, her hand moving in lazy circles across her back. Paige had tried to sit up, away from her, but CJ had stopped her.

"You don't have to move."

There was enough light for Paige to see CJ's expression, read her eyes. There was no teasing there, no sign of gloating because CJ had caught Paige—again—on the wrong side of her established boundary. There was just a contentment in her eyes that made Paige want to lie back down. Which she did. Her eyes drifted closed again as CJ's hand continued its ministrations.

When the alarm had gone off, CJ was already on her run. Paige was out of the shower and dressed by the time CJ got back, her skin glistening with sweat. Paige had averted her eyes, but it was too late. CJ had seen where her gaze was fixed. She had turned beet red as CJ sauntered past her, murmuring a quiet "busted" on her way.

Now she was avoiding going home, avoiding CJ. She hadn't spoken with her all day, which was unusual. Normally they would speak on the phone at least once, however brief it may be. The school was quiet, everyone already having left for the day. She stood in the breezeway, looking out across campus. She could see groups of girls sitting around in the fenced-in area they called the Rec Yard. The blues had more freedom, but the reds were allowed an hour each evening before dinner to gather outside. Suzette told her that this time of year, few took advantage of it, preferring to stay inside to escape the heat. She turned to go and ran smack into a hard body. She let out a startled gasp, CJ's hands coming out to steady her.

"Sorry."

"Jesus, CJ. This place is spooky enough without you scaring me to death." She turned away, heading down the hall, feeling CJ following her. "What are you doing here?"

"Checking on you."

"I was just on my way home," she said.

"Had some paperwork to finish? Lesson plans?"

Paige stopped, facing her. "What are you insinuating?"

"That you're avoiding me."

Paige tried to keep her expression even. "Why would I be avoiding you?"

CJ arched an eyebrow. "You really want me to answer that? Because I will."

Their eyes met and Paige felt a now familiar flutter in her stomach. "We can't do this," she said quietly. "We shouldn't even *think* about doing this."

CJ's eyebrow twitched slightly. "What is it we're thinking about doing?" she asked, her voice equally as low.

Paige sighed. "Let's don't play games, CJ. Please? Not about this."

CJ let out a breath. "Okay. Tell me what you want me to do? Start sleeping on the sofa?"

"No." Paige shook her head. "I just...we can't—"

"Do you ever think about that night?"

Paige looked away, hesitating. Would CJ believe her if she said it never crossed her mind? But she didn't want to lie. She met her eyes again, knowing CJ could see the truth there. She didn't need to answer.

CJ nodded. "Me too." She smiled, although Paige could tell it was a bit forced. CJ finally took a step away from her, putting some distance between them. "But you're right. We can't...do this."

Paige relaxed, feeling some of the tension ease. "Dinner?"

"Yeah? You want me to surprise you and whip something up?"

Paige continued down the hallway, CJ at her side. "I'll take care of it. Remember my kitchen rule?"

CJ laughed. "You have a lot of rules, baby."

"Yes, and you've managed to break nearly all of them."

"But you, my dear, broke the big one first, not me."

And just like that, the tension was back. Yes, Paige had crossed the line, not CJ. Paige was the one who had moved into her arms during the night. Paige was the one who had obliterated the imaginary line.

Once home, she tried to keep things normal between them, tried to keep the conversation light and impersonal. CJ was trying too. But despite all that, accidental touches still sent her heart fluttering. It was ridiculous how easily she could fall into CJ's eyes and how hard it was to drag herself out of them.

Thankful that dinner was over, she declined CJ's offer to share the TV with her, instead retreating safely into the bedroom. Safely, because she was alone. Later, however, she couldn't be sure just how safe it would be.

She needn't have worried. CJ was apparently engrossed in a movie and she simply murmured "goodnight," never taking her eyes from the screen. Paige allowed herself to stretch out a little, enjoying the coolness of the sheets against her skin. She would never tell CJ this, but she was accustomed to sleeping naked and she found the T-shirt she normally wore to be entirely too confining. After rolling to her side to face the wall, she did another check of the window, making sure the blinds were pulled down well past the window frame. Satisfied that nothing could see in, she closed her eyes, surprised to find herself relaxing, the sound of the TV in the other room not loud enough to be distracting but enough to lull her to sleep.

She never felt CJ join her and was surprised hours later to find the bed still empty. She rolled over, feeling the sheets. There was no evidence CJ had ever been there. So she sat up, contemplating whether she should go check on her or just leave her be. Her concern won out and she got up, walking quietly to the door. The TV was off and she could make out CJ's form curled in the corner of the sofa, her arms used as a pillow. Paige stared at her for a long moment, wondering what thoughts had gone through CJ's mind last night when she'd decided to sleep out here instead of the bed. Had she given CJ the impression that she didn't want her in their bed or had CJ simply inferred that?

She finally moved, squatting down next to her. She gently touched her shoulder. "Hey," she whispered.

CJ's eyes opened and she blinked several times. "What time is it?"

"Late. Come to bed," Paige said, standing.

"I didn't want you to...well—"

"No. Come to bed," she said again. Now was not the time for a talk.

CJ sat up, twisting her neck back and forth, then stretching her shoulders back. She followed Paige, waiting until she was under the covers before getting in herself. CJ stayed on her side and Paige was thankful. She was tired and just wanted to go back to sleep.

"Thank you," CJ murmured.

Paige smiled. "Goodnight, tiger."

CHAPTER TWENTY-EIGHT

"Oh, I know," Paige said with a laugh. "She's told me in no uncertain terms that Zumba is *not* part of the curriculum."

Fiona laughed along with Paige, wondering when the last time was that she'd laughed so heartily and sincerely. She'd run into Paige in the breezeway yesterday and Paige had suggested they share lunch today. She agreed, thinking she might get a chance to ask some of the questions Mother Hogan had passed by her. But now, sitting out in the courtyard with clouds and a slight breeze keeping the temperature comfortable, she was enjoying herself too much to be concerned with Mother Hogan's intended interrogation.

"She likes to pretend she runs the school," Fiona said. "When Director Sanchez left we were all hoping she'd retire but she stuck it out. Director Avery seems to like her."

"Maybe he just tolerates her," Paige suggested.

Fiona nodded, her gaze traveling over Paige's features—her blond hair tucked behind each ear, smooth skin, makeup applied to look like there was no makeup. Fiona didn't wear makeup, never had. Only when she went to college did she see women with makeup. One night when she'd been feeling particularly rebellious, she'd almost purchased some. But in the end, she'd remember Mother Hogan's warning not to get sucked into the outside world. She wished she had now. Paige looked so fresh, so wholesome. So beautiful. Her blue eyes had a hint of green in them today, perhaps from being outside. There was also a sparkle in those eyes that she envied, and she wondered if hers *ever* had that. She realized she was staring when Paige stopped talking.

"Are you okay?" Paige asked gently. She reached across the table, resting her hand on Fiona's forearm. Her fingers were warm and Fiona enjoyed the touch.

"Yes. I'm sorry, I was—" Staring? Yes, Fiona, she could see that, she chastised herself. She looked at her again, her eyes expressive. "You and CJ are really in love, aren't you?"

Paige seemed startled by the question, and Fiona was surprised to see a faint blush cross her cheek as she sat back.

"Yes. We are," Paige said with a smile. "Does that bother you?"

"Oh, no. I don't have a problem with that. I'm used to it now. It's just...well, it must be nice," she said and even she heard the wistfulness in her voice.

Paige tilted her head. "You've never been in love?"

Fiona shook her head. "No. I can't even imagine what it's like."

Paige raised an eyebrow slowly. "Not even with the father of your baby?"

Fiona's eyes widened in surprise. "You know?"

Paige leaned forward, her voice low. "You weren't showing last Sunday, I swear, but today..." she said, her gaze landing on Fiona's slightly protruding stomach.

Fiona covered it quickly, not knowing what to say. She knew enough about anatomy and childbirth to know she shouldn't be showing for months yet, but yes, every day she felt herself getting bigger. She didn't know what look was on her face, but Paige's fingers circled her arm again.

"Sweetie, I'm sorry. Did you not want anyone to know yet?"

Fiona didn't know how to respond to that, and she very nearly panicked but Paige squeezed her arm affectionately.

"I'm sorry. It's absolutely none of my business."

"It's just—"

"No, it's okay. I shouldn't have said anything." Paige smiled at her before removing her hand. "I take it you're not in love with this guy then?"

Fiona felt a laugh threaten and she let it out. It wasn't a joyful laugh but it was a laugh all the same. "Not in love, no. Definitely not."

Paige looked like she wanted to say something else, but she picked up her sandwich instead. Then, as if fighting with herself, she put the sandwich down. "It's none of my business, but this guy, he didn't...force you, did he?"

Fiona felt a surge of...something. She didn't even have words for it, it was so alien to her. Paige was looking at her with such genuine concern, sympathy almost, that a warmth spread through her. She wasn't used to someone being affectionate and Paige was certainly that, but for her to care, as if Fiona *mattered* to her, was something so foreign, she had a hard time comprehending it. She finally acknowledged the question, knowing Paige would be alarmed if she didn't answer it.

"No. It wasn't like that," she said vaguely.

"But he's from Hoganville?"

"Yes."

Again, Paige's eyes were filled with questions, but she smiled, then laughed. "No offense, Fiona, but Hoganville is a little weird," she said.

Fiona nearly choked on the water she'd just swallowed and was afraid she would spit it out. She wiped the smile from her face before looking at her.

"Weird?"

"Okay, maybe weird is not the right word," Paige said. "But I'm just fascinated with it."

"Whatever for?"

"We went to the café one morning, hoping to get breakfast," Paige said.

Fiona laughed. "Yes, I heard."

Paige grinned. "Ester Hogan was quite intimidating."

"Yes, she is," Fiona agreed.

"We didn't get breakfast, but she was kind enough to send us away with eggs and bacon." Paige gathered up her lunch trash and shoved it in a bag. "Why is there a café in town if they don't like people from the school to go there?"

"The café has odd hours," Fiona said. "Selma does the cooking. It's open to the public whenever they want it opened to the public." She hesitated, not knowing really how to explain it. Or if she even should explain it. "Strangers stop there and that's fine. But when people from the school come by, they don't like it," she said.

"Because we're not strangers?"

"Sort of, yes. You're here. All the time. Strangers passing by for a meal leave and don't come back."

"But there aren't any jobs around here, are there?" Paige said and it was more of a statement than a question.

"No. They're not needed," she said, knowing that would probably elicit more questions.

Surprisingly, Paige just nodded, although Fiona could tell she was curious. As happy as she was to have made a new friend, she knew there was only so much she could share with her. She was glad Paige let the subject drop.

As they walked back inside, Paige motioned to her protruding stomach. "How long are you going to try to hide it?"

"I don't know," she said honestly. Mother Hogan had given her no instructions regarding it. She made a mental note to ask her about it this weekend when she returned home.

CHAPTER TWENTY-NINE

CJ followed Paige's movements, her eyes drifting down to bare legs, then back up. She was nearly salivating. She quickly averted her gaze when Paige turned around.

"I really like her," Paige said. "She's so innocent. I mean, she's not much younger than we are, yet she's almost child-like."

"I can't believe she's pregnant," CJ said. "I just didn't see that last Sunday when we had lunch with her."

"Oh, I know," Paige said. "I told her as much." Paige brought a plate to the table for CJ. Breakfast today was fried potatoes, scrambled eggs and a soy sausage patty, which CJ looked at skeptically. "For someone who doesn't cook, you're awfully finicky," Paige told her.

"For someone who is not a vegetarian, you sure cook like it," CJ countered.

"It's healthier and you won't be able to tell the difference."

"Don't be ridiculous. Of course I will."

Paige gave her a sly smile. "Oh? I thought you enjoyed the spaghetti and meatballs I made the other night."

"I did. They were great," she said as she tasted a forkful of eggs. CJ looked at her suspiciously. "Why?"

"Vegetarian. *Meatless* balls," she said with a smile. "And you couldn't tell the difference. And I'd wager to say that if you hadn't seen the package, you wouldn't know the difference with the sausage. I can't believe how lucky we are to have found a health food store out here in the middle of nowhere."

"Oh, yeah. We're *so* lucky," she said sarcastically. CJ pointed her fork at her. "Look, I'm healthy enough. I don't need you springing these soy surprises on me," she said. She pushed the sausage patty around with her fork, reluctantly admitting that it did look like a real sausage patty. She cut into it with her fork, taking a tentative bite. Damn it all, but it *did* taste like the real thing.

Paige gave her an *I told you so* look before joining her at the table with her own plate. "Anyway, Fiona was very vague about the whole pregnancy thing," she said, going back to what they were discussing. "Like she was shocked I knew. You should have seen the look on her face when I asked about the father. I asked if he forced her and she said no, but I really hope he didn't."

CJ felt the hairs at her neck bristle. She looked pointedly at Paige. "Do you think she was raped?"

"I don't know. I don't think so. It's just...something wasn't right, but I'm only speculating," Paige said. "She didn't appear to be thrilled that she was pregnant. It was like she was embarrassed that I noticed."

"Maybe because she's single. Maybe that'll be frowned upon in Hoganville," CJ said. "Okay, so this is pretty good," she said as she finished off the last of the sausage. "I'm sorry."

"Thank you. Apology accepted." She paused. "I like Fiona. The patterns Ice found in the gate logs bother me. I can't imagine her being involved in anything like that."

"Maybe she's just a small part of a much bigger picture," CJ suggested. "That Belden guy looked scary, and we know what he did to Avery. Ester Hogan is in charge. Who knows what she can command them to do."

"And there's no way to find out. I mean, if the log file matches the other disappearances, what does that prove? Is that enough to go raid the place?"

"Let's just let it play out," she said. She leaned back, taking her coffee cup with her, watching as Paige finished her breakfast. "Laundry day?" she asked, moving the conversation away from Fiona.

Paige nodded. "And change the sheets." She smiled sweetly at CJ. "Your turn to clean the bathroom."

"God," she groaned, hating Paige's rules. "I'll trade you the bathroom for vacuuming."

Paige laughed. "No can do, tiger. It's your turn to vacuum too."

"How can that be?"

"Bathroom and sheets, once a week. Vacuum every third day."

"Is that really necessary? It's just us. We have no pets running in and out." She looked around. "It looks clean."

Paige simply gave her a look that said it wasn't up for discussion and left it at that. "I'll do dishes for you though."

"I'll trade you dishes for the bathroom," CJ offered.

"Nope."

***

Fiona made her way through the tunnels, the musty dampness nearly stifling. She paused at the fork where three tunnels converged, one leading to the chambers and beyond, one back to the cafe, and the other to Mother Hogan's house. She took that one, knowing she stood to be reprimanded for not waiting until she was summoned, but her apprehension was growing as fast as the child inside of her. She knew something was wrong when her own mother had been shocked by her appearance. She'd gone so far as to accuse her of coupling *months* ago and not waiting for Mother Hogan's blessing. How else would it explain that she looked four months pregnant in a matter of weeks?

As expected, Belden stood guard at the stairs and would not let her pass.

"Please? I need to see her," Fiona pleaded.

Belden sighed. "Okay. You wait here. I'll see if she wishes to speak with you."

She didn't have to wait long for his return. He motioned for her to follow and led her up the stairs into the house, and into the study.

Mother Hogan stood at the window, looking outside. Fiona was surprised that she didn't have her robe on. She couldn't remember a time seeing her without it. She was far less intimidating this way, dressed in an old, worn dress. When she turned away from the window, Fiona saw the surprise in her eyes, but she hid it quickly.

"My child, look at you," she said with a smile. "How are you feeling?"

Fiona cupped her belly protectively. "I feel okay...just...I've gotten so big, Mother Hogan. Something must surely be wrong," she said.

"No, no. Nothing is wrong, dear," she said, coming closer. "Everything is just as it should be."

"But, I can't possibly be this big already," she protested.

"You are special, Fiona. Your baby is...special."

"Special?"

"Yes." Mother Hogan moved to the closet, pulling out the familiar purple robe. As she slipped it on, Fiona felt a chill in the room. When she turned to her, Mother Hogan's eyes were no longer warm and friendly. They had a coldness to them that scared her. She took a step back, but Mother Hogan reached out, stopping her. "You have been chosen, Fiona. You should feel honored."

"Chosen for...what?" she asked quietly.

"The town is dying. The flock soon will not be enough for him."

Fiona's eyes widened. "Him who?"

Mother Hogan only smiled and Fiona realized just how evil it looked. "You are not carrying Antel's baby," she said.

Fiona took a step back. "Who...whose is it?"

Mother Hogan turned away. "Your pregnancy will be quick, as you can see. Two months, I would think."

"Two months?" Fiona shook her head. "I...that can't be. What will I tell everyone at school?"

"They hardly matter now, do they? Your responsibility is to the flock, to me," she said. "To *him*."

Fiona had no idea what she was talking about, and apparently Mother Hogan didn't feel the need to enlighten her. "I see them every day. I have to tell them something," she said. "They'll ask questions."

"Then perhaps we should quarantine you here," Mother Hogan suggested.

Fiona tried not to let panic set in. She could envision being tied, bound to the bed again while Mother Hogan kept her drugged. While this *thing* continued to grow inside of her. She had a quick vision of cold, reptilian hands and she pushed it away.

"I think if I don't return to school, it would cause questions," she said, trying to mollify her. "We wouldn't want them here, snooping around," she said, hoping to use Mother Hogan's paranoia against her.

"Yes. This is true," she said, turning back to the window, a finger tapping her chin thoughtfully. "Okay, you can return, but you will tell them that you are six months pregnant and are just now showing. That should be enough of an explanation for them not to question you. Another three or four weeks only, though. After that, you will remain here, under my watch. You are to give birth in the chamber, at the sacrificial altar," Mother Hogan said. "It will be quite the event."

"In front of everyone?"

Mother Hogan tilted her head. "I haven't decided yet. Probably not. Some things they don't need to know." Mother Hogan's gaze traveled down her body, resting on her belly. She took a step toward her and Fiona took a step back, to no avail. Mother Hogan's hands were on her, cupping her, squeezing tightly against her stomach. Fiona watched in fascination as her eyes literally rolled back in her head. Fear had her rooted to the spot and she had a hard time drawing breath. "Yes, yes," Mother Hogan chanted. "Yes."

Her hands were like hot irons, burning her flesh. Fiona thought she could smell singed skin and she tried to pull away, but Mother Hogan would not allow it. "It is, it is, it is," she chanted. She lifted her hands and Fiona fell backward, into the wall, her eyes darting around the room, wondering if she should flee. Then Mother Hogan laughed, a low guttural sound that didn't seem human, yet Fiona was still unable to move.

Mother Hogan's eyes flew to hers. "It's a girl. It's really a girl. Now he will have someone to mate with."

He who never escaped her lips. In a moment of clarity, Fiona saw past the reptilian hands that had touched her. She saw the hard, slimy skin, the lizard-like features, the long, cold tongue that had wrapped around her neck, holding her down as sharp claws tore at her skin, *mating* with her, impregnating her with...

Her world went black and she didn't feel the hands that caught her before she crashed to the floor.

CHAPTER THIRTY

Paige busied herself with laundry, her gaze constantly going to her watch. Their second dancing trip in as many weeks was drawing near and her anxiety was growing with each tick of the clock. After the week they'd had, she was actually afraid of going dancing with CJ, scared of what would happen between them. It would be dark, the music slow, and CJ's arms would pull her closer, their bodies touching in places they shouldn't. Paige wouldn't fight it, she knew. Would CJ kiss her? Would it be like the last time? Or would it be more?

Paige found herself staring into space, the shorts forgotten in her hand. Yes, CJ would kiss her. That thought brought a flutter to her stomach, and it was with dismay that she realized she *wanted* CJ to kiss her. Her attempts to come up with an excuse for them not to go were feeble and halfhearted, at best. That should have told her something right there. She sighed.

Yes. She wanted to go dancing with CJ. She wanted to be held by her. And yes, she wanted to be kissed. Oh, hell, she wanted it all. Kissing, touching...sex.

"Great," she murmured. "You've gone to the dark side."

"Who are you talking to?"

Paige jumped, embarrassed. "Just...thinking out loud."

"You need some help?"

She shook her head. "My turn for laundry. Bathroom?"

"All done."

She paused. "Maybe we shouldn't go tonight," she suggested.

CJ leaned against the wall. "Why?"

Paige didn't look at her. "You know why, CJ."

CJ let out a deep breath. "You want to make up some rules before we go?"

"So you can break them?" she asked with a smile.

CJ shook her head. "Tell me what you want, Paige. No dancing?"

"That would be hard to do, seeing as how we're going to a dance," she said.

"Okay. Then what? You want me to promise I won't kiss you?"

Paige turned slowly, their eyes meeting. Yes, that's what she wanted. She wanted CJ to promise she wouldn't kiss her, wouldn't tempt her, wouldn't hold her close, and wouldn't touch her. That was what she wanted. *Right?* But she remained silent, no words leaving her mouth. She couldn't even bring herself to nod. Was the dance going to be an excuse? Was it giving them permission? Permission to touch, to kiss? Did CJ want to cross that line too? Or was this all still a game, still role-playing? Were they still just pretending?

When she didn't answer, CJ shoved off the wall with a nod. "Good. I'm glad we're on the same page."

"What does that mean?"

CJ grinned. "You know. I like you, you like me," she said, motioning between them.

Paige panicked immediately. "We can't do this." She shook her head. "We can't," she said again.

"Of course we can. We've done it before." CJ's voice lowered. "I think we were quite good at it, in fact."

CJ turned and left, leaving her alone with her thoughts. Paige heard the TV turn on and she went back to the laundry, methodically folding each item, her glance going to her watch, the minutes still ticking away.

***

There was electricity in the air. At least, it felt that way to Paige. The DJ was blasting music as the band set up. Even though they were an hour earlier than last week, the place was packed. She reached for CJ's hand as bodies pressed in around them, everyone talking loudly, trying to be heard above the music. CJ followed Suzette and Becca, weaving through the crowd, pulling Paige along with her. Paige looked behind her, motioning for Valerie and Ella to follow as they had become separated. Suzette found them a table, although there were only six chairs, Jules and Sherry claiming the last two.

"Val and Ella will have to stand," Jules said, the noise level only slightly lower than near the bar.

"Or steal someone's," Becca said with a laugh.

"Dare we brave the bar?" CJ asked.

"I'll go with you," Sherry volunteered.

"Beer for everyone?" CJ asked. She glanced at Paige. "Or something else?"

"Beer is fine," she said with a nod.

CJ took the money that was offered her, then she and Sherry fought through the crowd again. Paige turned her attention back to the table, straining to hear what Suzette was saying.

"I'm still in shock over Fiona," she said. "She's never once mentioned a boyfriend."

"I didn't get the impression there was a boyfriend involved," Paige said. "She didn't really want to talk about it."

"Maybe that's why she was sick that week," Becca suggested.

"Maybe so."

"You know, as nice as she is, I don't recall her ever having a one-on-one lunch with someone. She must really like you."

For all of the closeness the teachers displayed in public, she'd found that it wasn't always the case. They did the weekend cookouts, they did the group trip to the bar for dancing, and they sometimes shared shopping trips. But other than that, everyone pretty much stayed to herself during the week. Which wasn't all that odd, she supposed. Given that it was such a small group, there was such a thing as too much togetherness.

They lapsed into silence and turned their attention to the throng of weaving bodies. As opposed to last week, this was a mostly older crowd tonight. She assumed it was because of the band.

"Here you go," CJ said, sitting down beside her and sliding a beer along the table. "Nice and cold."

"Thank you."

Their thighs brushed and Paige felt a jolt of excitement at the touch. Whether it was an accident or not, she didn't know, but she didn't move, allowing the contact to continue. *Playing with fire.* Yes, she knew she was, but the tension between them had reached a breaking point. First at home, then in the car, then at dinner—innocent touches, prolonged glances, both she and CJ guilty. She knew exactly what she wanted from this night and that nearly terrified her. She was apprehensive of the first dance, yet the anticipation was killing her. When Valerie and Ella got up to dance, it seemed to stir CJ. She turned to her, leaning closer.

"Would I be breaking a rule if I asked you to dance with me?"

CJ's breath tickled her ear and Paige turned, meeting her eyes, their mouths only inches apart. "How about...we don't have any rules tonight."

She couldn't tell if CJ was startled by her suggestion or relieved. But as had been CJ's course of action the last week, she hesitated.

"Are you sure? It could be...dangerous."

Paige managed a short laugh. "Of course I'm not sure. We shouldn't be doing this. We shouldn't even be *thinking* about doing this."

CJ nodded. "Then let's just dance. We won't think about it."

Paige took CJ's hand, letting herself be led to the dance floor. She didn't have a clue as to what the song was, but she seemed to remember it from last week. It didn't matter. It meant nothing to her. Right now, her sole focus was on CJ. Their eyes met for a brief second, then strong arms pulled her in close. She didn't hesitate...or protest. One hand cradled in CJ's, the other slipped over her shoulder. She buried her face against CJ's neck, breathing in her unique scent, allowing herself a few moments to just absorb what was happening before she lifted her head again. Her feet moved automatically, following CJ's lead, shuffling in a rhythm that came naturally to them. They didn't speak, only sharing shy smiles occasionally.

They pulled apart as the song ended. Paige avoided her eyes as she turned to head back to the table. But CJ stopped her, grinning as another song started. Once again, Paige found herself in CJ's arms.

"Love this song," CJ murmured.

"Mmm," was all she could manage as she lost herself in CJ's arms. The line she was trying not to cross was vague at best, if it was even there at all. She allowed CJ to hold her close, allowed their bodies to meet, their breasts to touch. Her hand found its way into CJ's hair and she swore she heard a soft moan in her ear. It was her undoing. She lifted her head slightly, resting her cheek against CJ's, feeling her warmth, feeling her breath. But she was tired of pretending. She turned then, blindly seeking CJ's mouth...finding it. She moaned into the kiss, dancing nearly forgotten as their feet slowed, barely moving at all. Her fingers tangled in CJ's hair, her mouth opening as she shyly brushed the tip of her tongue against CJ's.

The spark ignited—as she knew it would—and Paige could feel CJ's hands moving boldly across her body, pulling her closer still. Their kiss deepened, Paige letting go completely of the tiny bit of resolve that still existed. She started the kiss, not CJ, and she was the one to finally bring it to an end. Embarrassed, she couldn't meet CJ's gaze. Instead, she closed her eyes, shielding herself against CJ's neck. She could feel—hear—CJ's thundering heartbeat, its beat matching her own.

CJ didn't speak, didn't question her actions. If she had, Paige would have had no answer. She wasn't sure if she was relieved or disappointed when the song mercifully came to an end. She was flushed and breathless, yet she clung to CJ's hand. Much like that long-ago night they'd met at the bar, she felt like she was in a daze, unable to focus on anything but CJ. CJ led her back to their corner table, politely holding her chair out for her. The table was far from the dance floor and the band, which would be starting soon, and it afforded them some privacy.

Where CJ's hand rested on her thigh, she felt her skin burning. She covered that hand, letting her fingers entwine with CJ's. She had a wicked thought of pulling that hand between her legs and begging for relief, and she barely resisted the urge to do just that.

Her breath caught as CJ leaned closer. Her voice was just loud enough to be heard, her mouth brushing against her ear. "If you kiss me like that again, all bets are off."

Paige just stared at her, her gaze going from her lips to CJ's eyes, then back to her lips again. She wondered where her resistance had fled to, the resistance she'd clung to all these weeks. She didn't realize just how hard she'd been fighting her attraction to CJ. It was one thing to tell herself that she wasn't attracted to her, that CJ wasn't her type. It was quite another to realize she'd been lying to herself all along.

She finally gave a slight nod, acknowledging what CJ had said. But like a magnet, she felt herself being pulled to her. She could tell herself that they were still role-playing, that the kiss was for show only, but again, she'd be lying. She quit fighting it, meeting CJ's mouth, keeping the kiss light, pulling away when she felt herself losing control. Her hand was shaking as she reached for her beer, now terribly warm, but she needed something to distract her. When she was able to look at CJ, she was pleased to note that CJ seemed to be as affected by their kisses as she was.

As before, they all took turns dancing with the others in their group. Despite Paige's assertion that she didn't even like to dance, she admitted it was quite enjoyable. She found Sherry to be a good dancer, but the one time she tried to lead when dancing with Suzette, they'd ended up laughing as their feet kept tangling together.

She and CJ had not danced again, but they weren't avoiding each other like they had been the last time. Quite the opposite. They sat close together, their legs brushing, touching, eyes meeting quickly before pulling away. The tension was thick between them, dangerous. Perhaps that's why they hadn't danced again. They both seemed to realize how risky it could be.

She didn't know much about country music and only recognized a handful of songs, but the band appeared to be very good. Judging by the others there, who would sing along with nearly every song, she'd have to say they were a hit. So she sat back, trying to relax as she listened to the music. She'd finally accepted the fact that she and CJ would not dance again; she wasn't sure if she was thankful or not. Her earlier aroused state had tempered but not disappeared. CJ was sitting too close for that.

A new song started, eliciting claps from the crowd as the lights dimmed, and soon the dance floor was crowded with women. A popular love song, apparently. CJ glanced at her, eyebrows raised. Yes, she wanted to dance with her, but did she dare? Her desire won out and she nodded, taking CJ's hand. Her heart pounding loudly, she moved into her arms as if it was something they'd done hundreds of times before. The dance, apparently, was just an excuse to be close, to touch, to breathe the same air. Paige gave up any pretense of dancing. So did CJ. The floor was too crowded for that anyway. The other couples just shuffled about slowly, lovers embracing, kissing.

With both arms around CJ's neck, she couldn't stop herself from threading her fingers into her hair. CJ's hands seemed to be everywhere, soft caresses stirring her arousal even more. She was so close to losing complete control, to forgetting they were on an assignment, that she made a last effort to stop things from escalating further.

"CJ, we can't do this," she said, making a feeble protest. "Please don't do this to me."

CJ pulled back slightly, meeting her eyes. "Do what?"

"Don't make me want you like this."

CJ leaned closer, brushing her lips lightly. "Do you want me? It seems only fair," she said. "This week has been torture for me. Sleeping next to you, wanting to touch you so badly it hurt."

"God," Paige murmured, her eyes slamming closed. CJ's mouth was on hers again and there was nothing chaste about it. Paige opened to her willingly, moaning as CJ's tongue slid against her own. Their bodies were so close, she doubted light could penetrate between them. So close, yet not nearly close enough. She was shocked to realize how shameless she felt, how much she wanted this, wanted CJ.

CJ was the one to pull away, her breath coming as fast as Paige's was. Paige was actually embarrassed for the wanton way she'd kissed CJ. They were still in public, after all. But the couples around them were all lost in their own worlds, oblivious to them. That knowledge alone made her ache to continue, but she still tried to cling to the last of her sanity.

"We shouldn't do this," she murmured again, trying to resist.

"No?" CJ moved her mouth to Paige's ear. "What *this* are you talking about? This?" she asked as her hand slid low, pulling Paige's hips against hers in an unmistakable innuendo. "Or *this?*" she said, moving back to Paige's lips, kissing her slowly, deeply, Paige inevitably responding as she forgot about her half-hearted protest.

She also forgot where they were as her feet stopped moving entirely, her only conscious thoughts involved CJ...and the shocking truth that they had definitely crossed a line. There was no pretense any longer, the charade having come to an abrupt end.

"Paige...*Jesus,*" CJ murmured against her lips, taking a step away from her.

She took Paige's hand, leading her off the dance floor. Paige assumed they were returning to their table, but CJ kept going, fighting through the crowd of women. Paige didn't know an outdoor patio existed, but when the door closed—the music now muffled—she found herself being led into a dark corner, lush shrubs providing privacy. She could hear other couples in the shadows, whispered words floating around them, then away. They were alone in their corner, and Paige couldn't keep her hands to herself as she reached for CJ. Their kiss was hard, wild, and Paige was moaning, her body lost to her as CJ's fingers trailed under the swell of her breast, teasing her, finally brushing her taut nipple as it hardened even more.

She pulled her mouth away, gasping for breath, leaning into CJ's touch. If she took the time to think—rationally—about what they were doing, she might have been able to stop it. But she had no coherent thoughts, nothing to cling to other than this raging desire she had, a desire to do so much more than kiss.

Her legs parted willingly as CJ slipped a thigh between them, hands cupping her hips and pulling her closer. They were in a semi-public place and she didn't care. Her body was no longer hers to control.

"Are you wet?" CJ whispered into her ear.

Paige pressed down harder on her thigh. "Silly question," she murmured between breaths, her hips rocking slowly against CJ.

CJ nearly growled in her ear, then pushed her away quickly, shocking her. "Jesus," she said, running both hands through her hair. "No, Paige. Not here. Not like this," she said, shaking her head. "This isn't you. Not like this. I'm sorry."

Paige gripped her arms, moving closer to her again. "This isn't me? Am I too good for this?" She tried to smile, but her desire was too much. "Apparently, right now, this is me," she said. "I'm out here with you, aren't I?"

Their gazes held, neither looking away.

"I want you," CJ said quietly. "I want to take you home, to bed, and make love to you. Not...not out here. Not like this."

Paige swallowed, trying to find her voice. She moved back into CJ's arms. "You're evil," she whispered into her ear. "I could come so easily right now."

CJ groaned, pulling Paige closer again, slipping that same thigh between her legs. "God, I want to be inside you," she said, making Paige whimper. "Deep inside you."

Paige's hips jerked, the seam of her jeans pressing down hard against her clit. She held tightly to CJ, eyes closed as CJ's breath tickled her ear.

"Not just my fingers. I want my tongue inside you," she whispered, her tongue snaking in and out of Paige's ear. "Just like that. My tongue so deep inside you. I want to taste you when you come."

Paige's brain was a muddled mess and she felt nearly delirious as she clung to CJ, her orgasm hitting as quickly as she knew it would. She bit her lower lip to keep from crying out, her clit throbbing as she pressed hard against CJ's thigh.

CJ held her tightly, hands moving soothingly now against her back, whispered words that Paige couldn't decipher in her lustful daze. She rested her head against CJ's shoulder, finally able to open her eyes. Good God, had she just done that? Had she been in such a feverish state that she let CJ do that to her? *Yes.*

"I'm sorry," she whispered. "That got out of hand."

CJ held her in a tight hug. "I want to make love to you," she murmured. "Please don't pull away from me. Don't...*think* about this so much." CJ lifted her head, meeting Paige's eyes. "Let's have tonight. Please?"

"This is so wrong on so many levels," Paige said, her voice quiet. Could she deny CJ? Could she deny what she wanted herself? She leaned forward, her kiss light, moving ever so slowly against CJ's lips. No, she couldn't refuse this. She wanted it too.

The kiss apparently gave CJ the answer she needed. She smiled with relief as she led Paige back inside. She paused before opening the door.

"I don't think we should dance anymore tonight."

Paige laughed, breaking some of the tension between them. "Afraid we'll get arrested?"

CJ laughed too. "Ice and Billy would love that, wouldn't they?"

They stopped at the bar, CJ getting a plain Coke and Paige water, before joining the others back at their table. Knowing eyes watched them and Paige felt herself blushing. She dared to meet Suzette's gaze and she was surprised at the envy she saw there. And why not? She and CJ could hardly keep their hands off each other. Suzette, as well as the others, knew exactly what she and CJ were going to do when they got home tonight. And that thought, too, made her blush.

CHAPTER THIRTY-ONE

CJ felt like a fumbling, bumbling teenager on the ride home. The night had been endless and she didn't think they'd ever leave. True to their word, she and Paige didn't dance again. Although, as it turned out, that might have been the safer route. Instead, they'd sat together in their corner of the table like two horny teenagers, touches growing bolder by the second, their kisses hot enough to burn. She knew it was time to stop when she'd pulled Paige's hand between her legs. Paige could feel the wetness through her jeans; she knew that by the soft moan Paige had let out. She'd allowed Paige to touch her, but only for a second. She didn't want to totally embarrass them. Paige had taken her hand away, but the hot breath in her ear and Paige's words nearly caused her to climax right there.

"Do you remember what it felt like when I made love to you with my mouth? With my tongue on your clit, sucking it? I want to do that again. Tonight."

God. Yeah, Paige was a darling. She was innocent—she was polished and refined. But damn, she had a raunchy side that CJ couldn't wait to explore.

Suzette and Becca tried to keep the conversation going, but neither she nor Paige were contributing much. She wondered if they could feel the tension in the car. With the silence lengthening, CJ could hear Paige's breath, knowing Paige was as aroused as she was. Against her better judgment, she took Paige's hand and pulled it between her legs. Paige didn't hesitate as she spread her fingers, pressing against her.

Paige leaned closer, her words barely a whisper. "Don't tempt me," she warned. "Because I'll do it."

Paige stroked her so slowly, CJ nearly moaned out loud from the pleasure of it. She'd lost all sense of propriety and decorum, forgetting that they were in a car with another couple. Thankfully, Paige hadn't. She pulled her hand away, pausing to squeeze her thigh before removing her touch completely. "Soon" was whispered into her ear.

After what seemed like hours, Suzette finally stopped the car in front of their house. CJ didn't want to take the time for pleasantries, but Paige held her hand tightly, preventing her from sprinting into the house.

"Thanks for driving," Paige said. "We need to return the favor next time," she offered.

"Oh, we don't mind," Becca said. "You two lovebirds have a good night."

CJ matched their knowing smiles, too aroused to care if they were mocking them or not. She waved them away, then suddenly turned shy as she realized, finally, they were alone. What if Paige changed her mind? What if she had second thoughts? The darkness prevented her from reading Paige's eyes and she stood still, waiting.

Paige moved first, taking her hand and letting their fingers entwine. CJ let out a nervous breath. She thought she might just die right there if Paige decided that this was a mistake. But it was

Paige who led them inside, Paige who kicked the door shut and locked it, not bothering with the lights. And it was Paige who reached for her shirt, pulling it roughly over CJ's head before pinning her to the door.

This snapped CJ into action, her hands fumbling with Paige's jeans as Paige fumbled with hers. CJ lost the battle when Paige's hand stole inside, past the waistband of her underwear. She felt her knees weaken as, without preamble, Paige's fingers slid through her wetness, not pausing until she was inside her. They both let out strangled moans before their mouths found each other. CJ's hips rocking against Paige's hand, only to have Paige withdraw her fingers.

"Bed," she murmured against her lips.

CJ groaned. "God, woman, are you trying to kill me?"

Paige smiled slightly when she reached around CJ and unsnapped her bra, letting it fall to the floor. CJ's breath stalled as Paige's fingers traced slowly around both nipples. "This isn't like before," Paige said, her voice quiet, soft. "We don't have to rush."

CJ tried to smile but couldn't. "I'm about to explode here."

"And I'm going to take care of that for you." Paige kissed her, lips and tongue teasing. "But not with my hands," she whispered.

If CJ hadn't had the wall for support she may very well have collapsed. Paige took her hand and CJ followed her into the bedroom on wobbly legs. She was normally the one in control, the one who took the lead. But she felt powerless as she stood still, staring, watching as Paige removed her own shirt and bra. Paige was clearly the one in control. The sound of rushing blood filled her ears, and she was nearly trembling when Paige finally came to her, deft fingers unzipping her jeans all the way and pushing them down her legs. CJ kicked off her shoes and stepped out of her jeans, leaving her standing naked, watching in anticipation as Paige slowly lowered her own jeans, tossing them away haphazardly.

A part of her couldn't believe this was really happening. Another part of her—a very small part—wondered at the wisdom of this, knowing they were trampling over all sorts of rules and protocols. But when Paige's mouth and lips moved across her skin, when her hands cupped her breasts, she lost all thoughts of protocol. Her head fell back as Paige's mouth closed over a nipple, her tongue swirling around it, causing CJ to moan softly.

"Bed," Paige said again, her mouth leaving CJ's breast, urging her back to the bed.

CJ complied, pulling Paige down with her, letting Paige cover her body with her own. There was no time for thoughts as Paige's mouth, hands, skin, seemed to be everywhere at once. CJ let her have complete control even though her body was screaming for release. She spread her thighs, her hips arching against Paige's stomach, feeling her wetness coat Paige's skin, knowing Paige was just as wet. But Paige refused to be hurried. Her mouth left CJ's, making a slow and deliberate path to her breast.

"God, *Paige*," she gasped, her breath hissing between her teeth as Paige sucked a nipple into her mouth. "Please, I need you." Her voice sounded hoarse—and aroused—to her own ears as she gasped for air. "Paige...*please.*"

Paige released her nipple, her teeth raking across it in a deliciously painful kiss. CJ moaned into it, her hips thrusting against Paige, seeking contact.

"Open for me," Paige whispered against her skin.

"God, yes."

Then there was no more waiting. Paige spread her thighs even more, holding her open as an insistent tongue swept against her clit, pausing there long enough for CJ to clench her fists together, then moving on, slicing through her wetness, delving inside of her. CJ whimpered at the contact, her hips thrusting hard against Paige's face, burying her tongue deeper inside her. Paige allowed her only a few strokes before pulling out and settling over her clit. She sucked it hard into her mouth and CJ's hips left the bed, grinding against Paige. Her mouth was open, gasping for breath, her soft moans tangling with the guttural sounds coming from Paige as she licked and tugged on her.

CJ wanted to prolong it—the sweet and painful torture—but Paige's mouth, and now her fingers, wouldn't allow it. She gave in to her body's release with one last hard thrust, her throat raw as she screamed out Paige's name.

CHAPTER THIRTY-TWO

Paige stretched slowly, her body wonderfully sore. She sighed contentedly, her fingers lightly brushing against the arm that was still draped possessively across her stomach. Being with CJ was as exhilarating as she remembered. Now, like then, she wondered if it had been a mistake. If so, she'd made it willingly. Nonetheless, they were still working a case, and it probably wasn't the wisest thing she'd ever done.

"We probably shouldn't have done that," she said quietly. She felt CJ smile against her neck.

"Which time? The first or the sixth?"

Paige rolled over onto her back, turning to CJ. Her eyes were still closed, but she looked so peaceful, so..."God, you're so beautiful," she whispered, giving voice to her thoughts.

Eyes fluttered open, finding hers, then closed again. "Do you know what I regret about that first time?"

"What?"

"This, the morning," CJ said. "I regret not waking up with you." She rolled onto her back too, eyes open now as she stared at the ceiling. "I never wake up with anyone. I always escape first. That morning, when I woke, I reached for you, but you were already gone."

Paige turned to her side, her hand moving lazily across CJ's skin, her eyes raking over her small breasts, her dark nipples. She didn't know what to say. Yes, she'd been the one to take off that morning, fleeing before dawn, back to the safety of her own house. Now, here, there was no place for either of them to escape to. But unlike that first time, Paige didn't feel the need to run. She hoped CJ didn't either.

"Like I said last night, this isn't like the first time," she said. "We can't ignore this, we can't run from it. We can't pretend it didn't happen."

"Is that what happened the first time?" CJ asked. "Did we pretend it didn't happen?"

"After those first few awkward weeks, yes, I think we did. Don't you?" CJ turned and faced her, her eyes searching. Paige wondered what questions she had.

"It feels different this time. Is it?"

Paige wasn't sure what answer CJ was hoping to get. What was the question behind the question? She chose her words carefully. CJ rarely let her vulnerability show, and she never left herself as unguarded as she was now. "I think it's different this time because we don't have an excuse," she said. "Last time, we could blame it on the case, on our need of a diversion from it. It's different now because—" she paused, not knowing how much to tell CJ without having her running scared. Even then, she didn't see the point of glossing over the truth. "Last night was different because it was about us," she said. "It was about the attraction we have between us. Last night had nothing to do with this assignment and the roles we're playing. Last night was about...us."

CJ smiled slightly. "I've always been attracted to you, Paige."

Paige nodded. "I know. I've always been attracted to you too. That's why it was so hard playing this game. So hard trying to resist."

CJ leaned up on one elbow, resting her head in her palm. "You never wanted to be attracted to me though, did you?"

It was more of a statement than a question, but Paige decided she deserved an honest answer. "No. It scared me, really. You're not like anyone I've ever been with, not like anyone I'd ever date," she said. It was the wrong thing to say, apparently, as CJ's expression changed and the openness she was showing Paige disappeared.

"Yeah, you've made that clear several times. I'm not quite on your level. I'm certainly no...*Seth*," she said.

Paige wasn't going to let her retreat. She pushed CJ back and straddled her hips, holding her down by both wrists.

"We're not going to play games, CJ. Not this time. We slept together. Willingly. With no excuses." She bent her head, kissing CJ's breast softly. "I don't want there to have to be excuses. We're attracted to each other, like it or not. This was inevitable. Last night was...extraordinary," she said. "I don't want us to have to conjure up a reason as to why." She met CJ's gaze, still seeing a wariness there. "Please stop belittling yourself. I've never once said you weren't good enough. There are so many things about you that I admire." She looked away for a second, then back. "There are also things about you that I don't like. You already know what those are."

CJ nodded, then flipped them over easily, resting her weight on top of Paige now. Paige tried to read her eyes, but CJ wouldn't allow it.

"Okay. No games," she said. "And no more pretending. And no more skirting the issue."

"Meaning?"

"Meaning I'm not going to pretend that I haven't wanted to get you naked every night and make love to you." CJ lowered her head, her tongue swirling around a nipple. "And I'm going to stop pretending that I don't want to take a shower with you. That's a wonderful fantasy I've had." Paige moaned as CJ's lips closed over her nipple. "And I won't pretend that I haven't dreamed of doing this to you," she said as a hand slid between their bodies, moving unquestionably into the wetness that she'd caused.

Paige drew her closer, bringing CJ's mouth up to meet her own. "Okay. And I'll stop pretending that I don't want this. Because I do."

She raised her hips as CJ entered her, all other thoughts fading as CJ slowly, and surely, made love to her.

***

Paige closed the oven door and set the timer on her phone. The casserole was sinfully delicious, mixed with cheese and sour cream. Adding broccoli to it satisfied her healthy meter even though it was loaded with calories. Quite simply, CJ loved it and Paige wanted to make it for her. It also would afford them leftovers for a few days.

She eyed the bottle of wine, then glanced at the clock. It was early to be starting dinner, but they were both ravenous, to say the least. Breakfast had been quick and light, both more interested in the shower they were going to share than in eating. Lunch had been missed entirely. The only thing that had pulled them from bed was a call from Ice. They'd located Leah Turner's car. It had been submerged in Toledo Bend Lake. They were still going over it for evidence, but the fact that the lake was only about forty miles from Hoganville gave a bit more credence to their assignment.

It also threw up more questions than answers.

She again contemplated the wine bottle. CJ would be back soon. She'd taken a drive around campus, an excuse to allow her to stop by Avery's house. They needed to meet with him, but she wanted to make it as inconspicuous as possible. Mainly, without Chief Aims getting suspicious. They finally settled on a dinner invitation. They would leave it up to Avery to decide which night.

She was fingering the corkscrew, about to open the wine when she saw Fiona drive up next door.

"Oh my God," she whispered when Fiona got out of the car.

She had seen her on Friday and while she was starting to show, it was nothing like this. She looked seven months pregnant. Well, as she'd said before, it wasn't any of her business and she was going to leave it at that but she saw Fiona double over, in obvious pain. Wine forgotten, Paige ran out the door and across the road, reaching her just as Fiona tried to stand back up.

"Sweetie, are you okay?" Paige asked, helping her to straighten. She gasped audibly when she saw her. Pale and ashen, her face drawn, Fiona wouldn't meet her eyes. "Fiona?"

"I've felt better," she finally said.

"Let me help you inside," Paige said, still holding tightly to her arm. "Should you be driving?"

"Considering I had to stop and throw up six times, probably not."

Paige pushed Fiona's door open, no longer thinking it odd that no one locked their doors. She led her to the lone recliner and helped her to sit.

"Have you seen a doctor?" she asked.

Fiona shook her head.

"Don't you think you should? I mean, maybe there's something wrong," she said, touching her forehead, surprised at how warm she was. "You have a fever."

"Mother Hogan gave me something for the nausea," Fiona said, and Paige wondered if she even realized how casually she said *Mother* Hogan. That was twice now that she'd heard Ester Hogan referenced that way. Further evidence that she was in control of the *family*.

Paige sat down on the sofa next to her, genuinely concerned with her wellbeing. "Is there anything I can do? Can you keep anything down? Broth?"

Fiona shook her head. "The thought of eating something... well, makes me sick," she said with a quick smile. "Can you just stay and visit for a while?"

"Of course."

"Where is CJ?"

"Oh, she's just making her rounds," she said evasively. "I think it was an excuse to get out of the house."

"It's so hot today, I can't imagine why she'd want to be out."

Fiona leaned back. "How was the dance?"

"It was fun. There was a live band," she said, watching the pain cross Fiona's face. "Sweetie, I think you really need a doctor."

Fiona shook her head. "In my bag," she said, pointing to the large purse she'd dropped by the door. "Mother Hogan gave me something for the pain."

Paige hesitated, her concern for Fiona overriding her need to stay focused on the job. "Is she a doctor?"

At this, Fiona smiled. "No, not in the traditional sense."

"But there is a doctor?"

"Yes. But Mother Hogan doesn't allow me to see him."

Paige thought that statement was odd, but she made no mention of it. She brought the purse over to her, then watched as Fiona pulled out a small container and shook it. "Glass of water and a spoon?"

"Of course," Paige said, quickly going into the kitchen and filling a glass.

Fiona poured some of the powder into the glass and stirred. The water turned a chalky color. Judging by Fiona's face as she drank it, the taste was abysmal.

"Why can't you see the doctor?" Paige asked, wondering if she was treading where she should not.

Fiona didn't seem to mind the questions, but her answer gave nothing away. "It's complicated."

Paige knelt down beside her and took her hand. "You call her 'mother.' She seems too old to be your mother," she said.

Fiona shook her head. "She's not my biological mother, no. Her brother, Antel, is my father. But my mother and my father have never lived together."

"So Ester is really your aunt then?"

"Technically, yes," she said, her voice low, her eyes slipping closed.

"Fiona?"

Her eyes fluttered open for a second. "I'm very tired."

Paige wondered what kind of drug concoction Ester Hogan had given her. "Come on. Let's get you to bed."

Fiona didn't protest as Paige helped her up. Her bedroom was very simple and neat, the bed made with care. Paige pulled the covers back, then wondered if she should suggest Fiona get undressed. Fiona kicked her shoes off, then laid down on her side, her hands cupping her protruding belly. Within seconds she was sound asleep.

Paige stared at her, shaking her head. Something was very wrong, she knew. She watched in fascination as Fiona's hands moved, her baby's kick fierce enough to make them jump. With a sigh, she gently pulled the covers over Fiona. She would check on her later. If Ester Hogan wouldn't allow Fiona to see a doctor, perhaps Gretchen, the school nurse, could offer some advice. That is, if even that was allowed.

CHAPTER THIRTY-THREE

"You should have seen her. She looked...ghost-like," Paige said, putting the hot casserole dish on the stovetop and closing the oven door with her foot. "I was ready to take her to San Augustine myself."

"She can't possibly be that big already."

"I know. But she is. And all the 'Mother Hogan' stuff is weird. I mean, I like Fiona, I really do. She's sweet. I can't help but think—if this *is* some sort of cult—that she's being forced into this pregnancy."

"Are you saying she doesn't have free will?" CJ asked, trying to swipe a taste of the casserole, only to have her hand slapped.

"Well, she's got a car, she comes to the school. She has a job. I assume she keeps her salary. Hell, maybe *Mother* Hogan gets it."

CJ took her hand, stilling her movements. "This has you worried?"

"Yes. And after we eat, we need to go check on her. You'll see what I mean."

"Great. Then let's eat. I'm starving." This time Paige let her take a corner sample and she grabbed a pinch of cheese, licking her fingers of every bite. She felt Paige watching her and she paused, seeing Paige's blue eyes darken.

Dinner was suddenly forgotten as Paige moved into her arms, not shy as she pressed her body tight against her.

"Had to lick your fingers, huh?" Paige murmured against her lips.

She pulled back from the kiss. "Let's go to bed."

"I thought you were starving," Paige reminded her.

"I am." She pulled Paige after her, hearing Paige laughing delightfully behind her. She grinned too, already planning how they would spend the next hour. And it did not involve a casserole.

***

"Fiona?"

Paige knocked again when she got no answer. She turned to CJ. "I have a bad feeling."

"Let's just go in and check on her. She's probably still sleeping."

Paige hoped that was the case. She saw firsthand how quickly the drug had knocked her out to begin with. But she couldn't shake the feeling that something was terribly wrong.

Fiona was in the same position as when she left her, her breathing slow and even. Paige touched her face, then jerked her hand away.

"She's burning up." She pulled the covers away, revealing soaked sheets.

"I'm going to call Avery," CJ said, holding up her phone. "Have him get in touch with Gretchen."

Paige nodded, then went into the bathroom to get a damp cloth. She wiped Fiona's face, shaking her lightly.

"Fiona? Can you hear me? You need to wake up, sweetie." Fiona moaned, but her eyes never opened. Paige patted her cheek lightly. "Come on. Wake up."

"Avery is going to call Gretchen and ask her to come over," CJ said. She shook her head, eyes wide. "Wow, you weren't kidding. She's huge."

"I know. And two weeks ago she wasn't even showing." She shook her harder. "Fiona? Please wake up."

"Maybe we should just let her be until Gretchen gets here," CJ suggested. "We don't know what kind of drugs she took."

Paige stepped back, knowing CJ was probably right. But Fiona looked so helpless, and judging by the grimace on her face, still in pain. "I haven't actually met Gretchen. Have you?"

"No."

She looked away from Fiona, taking CJ's hand and leading her out of the bedroom. "I keep telling myself this is none of my business," she said. "Fiona just looks so innocent. So, I don't know, so helpless."

"She's obviously been very sheltered."

"Ester Hogan is her aunt. And she's very obedient, as far as I can tell. She obviously needs a doctor—a *real* doctor—yet Ester forbids it. So Fiona, as sick as she is, obeys." Paige shook her head. "I just don't get it."

"She is subservient, for whatever reason. As we saw in the café, they all are."

"So what kind of hold does Ester Hogan have on them? Fiona is educated. She has a degree. She teaches science. Why, then, does this happen?" she asked, pointing to the bedroom. CJ had no answer for her other than a shrug.

Paige paced back and forth, impatiently waiting for Gretchen Hogan to arrive. When headlights flashed across the window, she let out a relieved sigh. She hadn't really conjured up a mental picture of Gretchen so to say she was shocked was an understatement. Gretchen Hogan was nearly six feet tall and built like an ox. Her dark eyes were like daggers, and Paige automatically took a step back.

"You may leave now," Gretchen said curtly as she headed directly to Fiona's bedroom.

Paige and CJ exchanged glances. She wasn't about to be dismissed so easily, so she followed Gretchen, only to have the door slammed in her face.

"Who the hell does she think she is?" She was about to open the door when CJ grabbed her hand.

"Let's just let it be," CJ said.

"But—"

"We can't blow our cover," she whispered.

Damn. Paige took a deep breath, nodding. "Okay. You're right."

Back at the house, while CJ made a call to Avery, Paige stood at the window, her eyes glued to Fiona's front door. Fifteen minutes later, Gretchen helped a very slow-moving Fiona into her car, then sped away.

CHAPTER THIRTY-FOUR

"Can you walk?"

Fiona could barely open her eyes, and she wondered just what drugs were in the mixture Mother Hogan had made for her. She shook her head feebly, knowing she couldn't even stand, much less walk.

"Stay in the car," Gretchen instructed curtly, slamming the door behind her.

Stay in the car? Even in her hazy state of mind, she found that funny. Her head rolled to the side, her eyelids heavy. It was black dark, but she could make out the shapes of the houses. She was back in Hoganville. But it wasn't her mother's house nor was it Gretchen's. She felt her eyes slipping closed again and she blinked several times, trying to focus. The door jerked open and Mother Hogan bent down, staring at her. Behind her stood Don Hogan, the closest thing they had to a doctor.

"Help us get her inside."

Mother Hogan stepped back, allowing Don closer. Fiona and Don rarely saw each other and when they did, they were never alone. She used to think it odd. If there was anyone in Hoganville she had something in common with, it would have been Don. They had both been sent away for their education, they had both been *outside*. Of course, she came to realize that was the very reason they were kept separated. They had both been to the outside.

"Can you try to stand?"

She nodded as she grabbed his arm, trying to pull herself up. Her legs felt wobbly still, as if she had no control over them. Their eyes met for a moment and she saw genuine concern in his. And why not? She must look a sight.

"Inside quickly," Mother Hogan instructed.

It was then Fiona realized they were at Don's home, the one he used to share with his mother. She had never been there before, certainly had never been inside. He led her into a back room and eased her down into a large chair. She looked around, the white walls adorned with a few old medical posters. This must be his examination room.

Mother Hogan hovered, her eyes darting between Don and Gretchen. Fiona was surprised to see fear in them.

"She has a fever," Mother Hogan said. "Do you have something for her?"

"Yes. Let me examine her."

"Do not give her anything until I've cleared it. Understand?"

"Of course, Mother Hogan."

"Gretchen, come with me. I want to know why the two strangers were in Fiona's house."

Fiona watched them leave, their voices muted now as they stepped outside and closed the door. She raised her eyes to Don questioningly.

"What did she give you?" he asked.

"I don't know," she said quietly. "Something for pain."

He lowered his gaze to her belly, then back up. "Why do you have pain?"

She swallowed, wishing she could confide in him. "You saw the coupling. Should I be this big?"

"Of course not." But he, too, appeared to be afraid to ask questions. He glanced out into the living room, seeing the outside door still closed. He touched her face, his brow furrowed. "I think you need to go to a hospital. Your fever is very high."

She shook her head. "You know Mother Hogan will not allow it."

"No. But I'm not a doctor." He motioned to the cabinet. "Whatever pharmaceuticals Belden has been able to confiscate over the years are mostly expired. And the *potions* that she mixes up, who knows what's in them," he said. "You may have had a reaction to it."

Fiona frowned, not used to hearing someone criticize Mother Hogan, even if it was the truth. She grabbed his hand, deciding to trust him. "She kept me drugged the entire week after the coupling. I was shackled," she said. "And I was bleeding."

"In the cave?"

She nodded. "She said it was so that Antel could be with me. But I don't think he was."

He took a step away from her, glancing quickly into the living room again.

"Do you know what lives in the caves?" she asked.

He shook his head. "I try not to think about it."

"I know. Me too. But whatever it is, I think this," she said, pointing to her belly, "is his. Not Antel's."

"You're saying your coupling was your...your first time?"

"Yes," she whispered. "That's why I know this can't be Antel's baby."

Their eyes held for a long moment, then he nodded. "We need to get you out of here."

"I can't," she said. "How could I explain whatever it is that's growing inside of me?"

They both looked up at the sound of raised voices. Belden had apparently joined Mother Hogan and Gretchen. Belden and Gretchen appeared to be arguing.

Don bent closer to her. "Let's get out of here together. I'll go with you," he said quietly. "We can escape this."

"I can't," she said. "It's too late for me." She squeezed his hand. "Why do you stay? Why haven't you left?"

"I've been afraid. Afraid to even think about it. Mother Hogan always seems to *know*. So many have been culled." He stepped away from her again. "I didn't want to meet their fate."

She closed her eyes, feeling very tired again. "Come to the school tomorrow night. Come up the trail and through the break in the fence. We should talk."

He shook his head. "I don't know if I can chance it."

They heard the outside door open, and Don went to his cabinets, making a show of looking through his medications.

"Beware of the guard named Richard," she whispered. "He is a spy for Belden."

She closed her eyes again as she heard footsteps approach. There was a sudden chill in the room and she knew Mother Hogan was near.

"What do you think?"

Fiona's eyes fluttered open as Don handed a plastic wrapper to Mother Hogan.

"That should help get her fever down," Don said. "I think she may have had a bad reaction to something she took. An allergic reaction, perhaps," he said vaguely.

"Yes, maybe Fiona overdid it with my potion, hmmm?" Fiona felt cold fingers digging into her shoulder, and she glanced up at Mother Hogan. "Did you take it as I instructed you?"

Fiona nodded. "Half of it mixed with water, yes."

Mother Hogan shook her head. "No, child. I told you to mix up half of it, but to sip it sparingly. Are you saying you took it all at once?"

She nodded, remembering no such instruction from her. Mother Hogan bent lower, her words meant for Fiona and no one else.

"You must be very careful. Your child is special. We can't have anything happen to you."

"Yes, Mother Hogan," she dutifully answered.

"Good." She straightened back up. "Now, Gretchen is waiting

to take you back. Do you feel up to it? Perhaps you should stay with me tonight," she suggested.

"I should go back," Fiona said quickly. "We don't want my absence to cause questions," she said, hoping this would appease her.

Mother Hogan stared at her, her eyes boring into her own. Fiona prayed she could not read her thoughts. She finally nodded.

"Very well. The two new ones from the school are nosing where they shouldn't. We don't need to add to their curiosity." She handed over the pills that Don had given her. "For your fever," she said. "You will check in with Gretchen in the morning. She will report back to me."

"Yes, Mother Hogan."

CHAPTER THIRTY-FIVE

Avery paced, waiting impatiently for the agents to arrive. He didn't like the idea of them showing up at his house like this, but CJ thought it was important for them to talk. If anyone questioned it, he would have to make up some excuse. He hadn't seen Fiona himself, but he'd heard from some of the other teachers that she was very pregnant. That certainly surprised him.

A light knock on his door had him moving quickly to open it. CJ and Paige walked in and he closed it behind them, locking it out of habit.

"Do you know anything?" Paige asked. "Gretchen left with her. We assume she took her to Hoganville."

"That's all I know," he said. "Gretchen has not called me

back. I wouldn't expect her to. This is a family matter. It has nothing to do with the school."

"What the hell is going on here?" Paige asked. "You should have seen her. I thought she was going to die."

Avery glanced at CJ, wondering at Paige's obvious concern. They were agents on an assignment, yet Paige's distress seemed very personal. CJ seemed to understand his unspoken question.

"Paige and Fiona have become friends. Since she's a person of interest, we thought it best to befriend her," she explained. "Paige saw her drive up this afternoon."

"She was doubled over in pain," Paige said. "I went to help her inside. She had this small jar, some kind of powder that she said Mother Hogan had given her."

"*Mother?*"

"Yes. She calls Ester *Mother* Hogan. Apparently they all do," CJ said.

"She mixed it with water," Paige continued. "And just like that," she said, snapping her fingers together, "she was out. I got her into bed, then left," she said, glancing at CJ. "We went and checked on her later and found her like that. Her fever was very high, the sheets soaked. I couldn't wake her up."

"You did the right thing by calling me," he said. "Despite everything, we must keep a low profile and not call attention to ourselves," he said, repeating the words Howley had told him. He wasn't a field agent, but he knew the manual backward and forward. These two might have street smarts, but he knew the written word. "Let's don't lose sight of what our assignment is." He noted the quick glance the two of them exchanged.

"We know what our assignment is, Avery," CJ said as she went to the window, absently separating the blinds and looking out. "And so far, it's been pretty benign. Our way into Hoganville—if we ever hope to get inside—is through Fiona Hogan." She turned back around. "I assume Howley is keeping you in the loop, but really, we've got nothing. The team in Baton Rouge has nothing. The gate log proved helpful and—"

"Yes, I heard about the pattern. Quite shocking, actually, to think Fiona could be involved."

"We all know they take their direction from Ester Hogan," Paige said. "Whatever happens to those abducted—and we can all guess what that is—I think it's premature to lay blame with Fiona. Or Gretchen, for that matter."

"They appear to be involved in some capacity," he reminded them.

"I seriously doubt they have free will," Paige said. "But yes, they must have some knowledge of what goes on."

"The pattern seems odd, doesn't it?" CJ asked. "Monday, Tuesday and Wednesday nights. What do you think happens? I mean, originally, we thought it was some kind of cult, right?"

"That was mere speculation," Avery said. "Is there some sort of ritual? Torture?" He shrugged. "It's anyone's guess at this point."

Paige shook her head. "Look, I've spent enough time with Fiona to know she couldn't be involved with that. Torture? Come on, she's as sweet as can be." Paige looked at CJ. "Right?"

"I don't think she's directly involved," CJ said. "But the little evidence we have suggests her participation in *something*," she said.

"Perhaps she is playing you," Avery said. "I've been around her a handful of times, and you're right, she appears to be very nice, very amiable. It could be a front."

"No. I'm not some rookie off the street, Avery," Paige said. "I know how to read people. She's not feigning, she's not play-acting."

Avery held up his hands. "I understand you want to defend her. But as CJ pointed out, she's the only link to Hoganville. Gretchen is out of the question. You cannot get close to her." He went to the same window CJ had vacated from earlier. Mimicking her actions, he too opened the blinds a bit to look outside. "We're *sure* she's pregnant?"

Paige laughed. "Oh, yes, we're sure. I don't know how far along she is, but she wasn't showing at all the first time we met her. She looks, I don't know, six or seven months pregnant."

"At least," CJ added.

"Do you think her illness is related to that?"

"I think her illness is related to whatever the hell it was Ester Hogan had her drink," Paige said.

He sighed. It was obvious he was going to get nowhere with Paige. He glanced at CJ.

"I think we should call Howley," she said. "If this is as close as we're going to get to Hoganville, this little interaction we have with Fiona, then we're wasting our time here. We either need to raid the place and find out what the hell is going on or forget about it."

Avery shook his head. "I assure you, they don't want another Waco on their hands. There will be no raid."

"Then what the hell is the purpose of our being here? To gather evidence that seems nonexistent? To simply observe?"

"Well, obviously we have more questions than answers, I know," he said, wanting to end their meeting. They were accomplishing nothing and the longer they stayed, the greater chance they had of being seen. Howley's words echoed in his brain: *Do not call attention to yourselves.*

"Is it possible for you to confront Gretchen?" Paige asked. "Find out what happened to Fiona?"

"No. I will, of course, inquire as to her health, but confront? No." He moved to the door, intending to bid them goodnight when the now familiar shrill scream pierced the night. He jumped, his heart beating frightfully loud. He always jumped.

"Jesus," Paige gasped, holding a hand to her own chest. "That sounded close."

"Yes." He cleared his throat, now afraid to open the door. "I assume you've heard it before?"

"Twice now," CJ said. She tilted her head. "Are there any bears around here?"

"Bears?"

"Something was outside our house the other night," Paige explained. "We went out. We found some tracks. Thought maybe they were bear."

"I haven't heard anyone mention bears," he said. "I don't think that awful scream is from a bear, though. Do you?"

"No," Paige said and he noticed she'd moved closer to CJ. "Do you have any idea what it is?"

"Some say a black panther, but I think that's just a myth that's been passed down. But it disturbs me," he confessed. "So much so that I've researched it to death and can find no matching sounds. A mountain lion after he's made a kill sounds similar, yet it is not the same. Regardless, I try not to ever be outside after dark." He offered a small smile. "That must sound strange coming from an FBI agent." They all jumped again, eyes darting around as the primal scream was heard once more.

"No. Not strange at all," CJ murmured.

***

Ester Hogan stood at the opened window in her study, looking out into the dark, humid night, listening for him. Was he out hunting? Was he growing weary of tracking deer? She tilted her head, hearing his call, far off in the woods. Up near the school. She waited, wondering if he'd made a kill. The scream echoed again through the woods, sending chills across her body. She imagined him ripping the flesh as he devoured his kill.

She turned from the window, the stress of the day coming back to her. Yes, Fiona was ill. She only hoped she could hang on another few weeks. The last time she'd tried this experiment, with Dovie Hogan, it had gone terribly wrong. But she had learned a lot in the last twenty years. She had perfected her potions, she was sure. She mistakenly tried to let Dovie deliver naturally. Oh, what a terrible scene that was. The *baby* had ripped her open, its sharp claws tearing at her. There was nothing she could do. The bleeding was too much. She still remembered the excruciating scream that came from Dovie when she saw her baby. Ester smiled now, thinking it probably drove Dovie mad in her final moments. It was just as well. Unfortunately, her baby did not survive. It wouldn't have mattered. It was a male. But now Fiona was carrying a female. *Oh, yes, he will be so pleased.*

Her dilemma, however, was Fiona. She didn't know how she was going to explain her absence at the school. Her mother would be curious too as to Fiona's fate but that was of no consequence. Her concern was keeping the school out of their business. Fiona's untimely death could not be explained easily. Especially when there would be no body to produce. He would take Fiona and the baby into the caves with him. When Fiona had served her usefulness, he would...dispose of her. She sighed. She would miss Fiona. She had always been so faithful. But her lot in this life was cast a long time ago.

A light tap on her door brought her out of her thoughts. She opened the door quietly, nodding for Belden to enter.

"Gretchen delivered Fiona back at the school. There was no one around."

"The neighbors? The ones who found her?"

"No. There were no lights on. They didn't appear to be there."

"Strange, isn't it? Did you check with Richard?"

"Yes. They did not leave the compound."

She went back to her window, absently fingering the worn drapes that were still pushed open. "Well, perhaps they were visiting someone." She stared at him. "The director?"

"I didn't want to take the chance of getting spotted, Mother Hogan. I left as soon as Fiona was settled," he said.

"Yes, that was the right thing to do." She motioned to a chair. "Sit, Belden. Let's talk." She took her place behind the desk, the old chair creaking as she scooted forward. "What do you make of them?"

"The neighbors?"

"Yes, the ones who came into the café that day. They seemed awfully brave. Almost as if it was a test."

"The guard, the one they call CJ, is experienced. Gretchen says the other one, Paige, the gym teacher, appears to be inexperienced."

"Meaning?"

"It must be her first job. Gretchen says it's unorthodox."

"They seem very chummy with Fiona, don't they? I know I told her to befriend them, to find out about them, but she has reported little back to me." She folded her hands together. "It's an odd time of year to bring in new ones, contracts being what they are," she said. "Something tells me they are not what they seem."

"Do you want me to pay them a visit?"

She smiled. "Not yet. But soon."

CHAPTER THIRTY-SIX

Fiona still felt weak, but she'd been able to make it through her classes without incident. Thankfully, none of the other teachers had commented, so she assumed they weren't privy to what had happened. All but Paige. Paige had sought her out first thing, making sure she was up to teaching. Fiona smiled as she recalled Paige's concern, but she'd tried to reassure her that she was fine. Paige wasn't buying it, but what could she say?

She shuffled into the kitchen. She was hungry but knew there wasn't much to choose from. She opened the refrigerator, surprised at the large container on the shelf. She lifted the lid and her stomach growled in anticipation. One of Selma's thick, meaty soups. She wondered if Gretchen had brought it, or perhaps Belden had snuck it in during the day. She didn't care. She was nearly ravenous. She poured a large helping into a pot to warm, the smell enticing. Her appetite had increased in the last month but never to this state. She was salivating as she stabbed a piece of meat from the pot. She bit into it, surprised—and delighted— that it was still nearly raw. She took the pot off of the stove, not caring that it was not entirely heated. She grabbed a spoon, eating directly from the pot as if she was famished.

She caught sight of her reflection in the shiny metal of the pot, her face that of a crazy woman as she shoveled in spoonful after spoonful, the broth dripping down her chin and onto the table. *What's happening to me?* She tossed the spoon down, disgusted with herself. She stared at the bloody piece of meat she'd been gnawing, ripping through it as if she were an animal. The meat was so raw, there was blood running down her fingers. She stared into the soup pot, seeing nothing but blood.

Her eyes widened and she barely made it to the trash can before she threw up, emptying her stomach of the soup she'd just consumed. She doubled over in pain, afraid she was going to pass out. She finally gripped the countertop, steadying herself until the wave of nausea passed. She shuffled to the sink, still holding the countertop. She turned the faucet on, watching the steady stream for a few seconds before rinsing her mouth out. She closed her eyes, then splashed water on her face several times, trying to wipe away the bloody scene from her mind.

"What's happening to me?"

CHAPTER THIRTY-SEVEN

CJ tucked the box under her arm as she entered, nudging the door closed with her elbow.

"What's that?" Paige asked from the kitchen.

"Not sure. Something from Ice," she said, placing the box on the table. "Did you talk to Fiona?"

"Just briefly," Paige said. "She looked much better, but you could tell she was still weak. I wonder why she didn't call in sick." Paige grinned. "And yes, I'm having to stop myself from going over and checking on her."

CJ walked up behind her, sliding her arms around Paige's slim waist. She felt Paige relax against her with a small sigh. Since they had become lovers, the tension between them had disappeared completely. And so had the stress of pretending they hated this undercover assignment. "Leave her alone. You know what Avery said." She kissed the side of Paige's neck, then released her, curious as to what Ice had sent.

"I know. I'll wait and talk to her tomorrow." Paige went back to slicing the tomato. "Do you mind leftovers? I made us a salad, but I wasn't in the mood to cook."

"No problem," she said as she cut into the box. She opened the lid, then moved the tissue paper aside. She stared in disbelief, blinking several times as she realized what she was looking at. "I'm going to kill him," she murmured.

"What is it?"

She slammed the lid closed quickly. "Nothing."

Paige came closer, eyebrows raised. "Nothing?"

She hesitated, then slid the box along the table toward her. Paige flipped the lid open, her eyes widening.

"Is that what I think it is?"

"Yeah. And I'm going to kill him," she said, reaching for the box. Paige took her hand, stopping her.

"Maybe we should...try it," Paige suggested, meeting her eyes with an unabashed grin. "Hmmm?"

CJ's knees went weak as she envisioned doing just that. *Jesus*.

Paige moved, brushing her body against CJ's. "Is that a yes?" she asked, kissing CJ lightly.

"God, yes," CJ murmured immediately. "Yes. That is...if you're sure," she added as her hands slid up Paige's body.

Another kiss, then Paige stepped away, handing CJ the box. "I'll meet you in the bedroom," she said with a wink.

CJ ran her hands through her hair, feeling them tremble. *God*. She opened the box again, staring inside. It wasn't like she'd never used a dildo before. But with Paige? Damn, the woman never failed to surprise her.

When she stepped out of the bathroom and into the bedroom, Paige was waiting. The sheet had slipped down to her waist, her nipples were hard in anticipation. CJ licked her lips, then tugged at the shorts she'd slipped on to hide the phallus that was strapped to her. She felt exposed, standing there in the light.

Paige lifted the sheets, revealing her naked body to CJ's greedy eyes. "Come here."

CJ nodded, going slowly to the bed, the dildo standing at attention inside her shorts. She felt nervous, and she wasn't quite sure how to proceed. Paige let the sheet fall as she got on her knees, holding out a hand. CJ took it, surprised at the confidence Paige was displaying. She felt her arousal as their eyes met, Paige beckoning her to come closer.

"Let's take this off," Paige suggested, pulling CJ's T-shirt up and off. Her bra followed, leaving her naked from the waist up.

Her worry over how Paige would receive this turned to excitement, and she pulled Paige to her, kissing her hard. She heard Paige gasp as their hips met and the bulge in her shorts pressed against Paige's center. Paige lay back down, urging CJ to follow. CJ did, seeking her lips again. "Paige," she whispered, "are you sure?"

Paige smiled as her hands slipped inside the shorts, shoving them down. CJ kicked them away, then closed her eyes as she felt Paige's hands on the skin of her thighs, moving higher.

"I've never done this before."

CJ opened her eyes, meeting Paige's gaze. "Then maybe we should—" But her words were cut off when Paige's tongue slipped inside her mouth. "God, Paige," she whispered when their kiss came to an end.

Paige lay beneath her, open and inviting. CJ lowered herself, hearing Paige moan as she rubbed the phallus against her. She couldn't believe how much she wanted her like this...desperately so. "You'll tell me if I hurt you?"

Paige smiled again. "I don't imagine you'll hurt me." She slipped her hand between their bodies, and CJ felt her take the toy, guiding it to her opening.

CJ moaned when she recognized what Paige was doing. She let herself go, relaxing as she pressed forward, feeling Paige's hand fall away as she filled her. She shuddered as she realized she was inside of her, completely. Using her arms to support herself, she lowered her hips, her gaze on Paige's face, where her pleasure was evident. Their eyes held and she stopped for a moment, not sure what Paige wanted. In answer, Paige's hands went to her hips, cupping them, encouraging her. CJ nodded as she pulled out, then pushed back inside, deeper this time, her moans mingling with Paige's as Paige arched against her.

She lost herself in this timeless dance, filling Paige with each stroke, feeling her own wetness—her own arousal—as an afterthought. Her only concern right now was Paige and the frantic hands on her hips, urging her on. She bent lower, taking Paige's mouth in another heated kiss, her breath coming fast with her exertion.

"God, yes," Paige hissed as CJ's hips moved faster, the phallus slick with Paige's wetness.

CJ vaguely heard the creaking of the bed with each thrust of her hips, its rhythm matching the force of her drive. Paige was panting now, her head rolled to the side. CJ took Paige's thigh, pulling it upward, giving herself more room. Her arms were trembling from her weight, but she continued. She slammed into her harder and harder, the base of the phallus hitting her clit with each stroke, making her painfully aware of her own aroused state.

Paige's fingers dug into her arms, her hips arching once more, meeting CJ's last stroke fully, crying out as her orgasm took her. Her body went slack, her eyes fluttering open, then closed. CJ pulled out of her and rolled over as her arms gave out. She shoved the dildo away, her fingers going to her own wetness, seeking relief.

"Let me," Paige murmured as she turned, her fingers gliding over CJ's clit. CJ arched and opened her legs, letting Paige stroke her. Far too soon her climax took her, her shuddered breath trapped against Paige's neck as she held her.

They both lay still, catching their breath. Her skin was damp with perspiration, as was Paige's. She brushed the hair away from Paige's face, meeting her eyes.

"Fantastic," Paige answered her unspoken question. She leaned up on an elbow, her fingers moving lazily across CJ's breast. "Do you want me to return the favor?"

CJ swallowed and shook her head. "No. No, I'm good." Paige looked at her questioningly, and CJ couldn't hold her gaze. *Damn.* "You must know by now that penetration is not really my thing. At least...not with that."

Paige nodded and CJ could see the questions forming.

"Do you want to talk about it?"

CJ turned away. "No."

She closed her eyes, but Paige's touch never wavered, her fingers gliding softly across her skin.

"Sweetheart, how old were you?"

CJ bit her lip, embarrassed that Paige had guessed. She shouldn't be surprised. She had hinted at it herself. She never told anyone about that time in her life. But she wanted to tell Paige. She felt a connection—a closeness—with Paige that she hadn't with anyone else. Her biggest fear was whether Paige would judge her harshly or not.

"I was ten when it started." Paige gasped and her fingers stilled. CJ turned to look at her. "My sister was two years older than me," she said. "She tried to stop him."

Paige stared into her eyes. "*Ten*? My God. What about...what about your mother? Was she there? Did she know?"

CJ nodded. "She knew. I think she was thankful he was leaving her alone." She leaned toward Paige, wiping at a tear that formed. "Don't cry for me, Paige. It's too late for that."

Paige cleared her throat and took a deep breath. "You know what I'm in the mood for? A bottle of wine."

"Yeah?"

"Yeah. In here. In bed. With you." Paige touched her face lightly, rubbing a finger across her lips. "I want to know your story. I want to know what makes you who you are. Will you tell me?"

"It's not a pretty story," CJ warned.

"No. I wouldn't think that it would be." She paused. "If you don't want to tell me, I'll understand."

CJ very nearly said just that. That was a part of her life that she rarely thought about anymore. But Paige was right. It was what made her who she was. Did she want to share that with Paige?

"Okay. I'll tell you my story."

Paige smiled reassuringly at her, then crawled from the bed, grabbing her discarded shorts and shirt and walking naked into the bathroom. CJ's gaze followed her movements, taking in the soft curves and smooth skin with a contented sigh. Her whole adult life had been spent in solitude, bouncing from bed to bed, woman to woman. Meaningless. It was all she thought she could offer anyone. The desire to share more just wasn't there.

Why then was she finding herself loving this domestic bliss

with Paige? She almost wished this assignment would drag on for a while longer. Once it was over, they would return to Houston... and their lives. Surprisingly, that wasn't something she was ready to think about.

When Paige left the bathroom, CJ took her turn. She found Paige back in the bed, leaning against the pillows. A T-shirt covered her this time, although—without a bra—CJ's eyes were drawn to her breasts and the nipples were outlined perfectly. Paige smiled.

"Easy, tiger." She patted the bed beside her. "Come."

CJ arched an eyebrow. "Again?"

Paige laughed, a laugh that had her eyes dancing in merriment. "How about we talk first?" she said, holding out a glass of wine for CJ.

CJ nodded, the levity leaving as their eyes met. There was nothing cheerful about the story she was about to tell. She leaned back next to Paige, taking the glass and holding it lightly between her fingers. She'd never been a wine drinker. She never really gave wine much thought before. Paige, however, was well versed and knew which wine was appropriate for which occasion. Like now, sitting in bed, CJ about to tell her the horrors of her childhood. A dark red wine for the occasion. CJ wouldn't even pretend to know what kind. She took a sip, then another. Paige waited quietly beside her.

"My sister and I shared a bedroom," she said. "Cathy was two years older than me." She shrugged. "I never knew that he used to visit her during the night." She gave a half-smile. "That's the word we used. *Visit*. Anyway, his temper was legendary. My mother, well, she took her share of beatings. He'd come home late, smelling of bourbon, and complain that dinner wasn't on the table." CJ glanced at her. "Of course, we'd all eaten earlier, at the normal time. She always had a plate for him. Sometimes that was good enough. Most times. Other times, he'd throw the plate against the wall and smack her around a few times for not being a good wife. He'd make her cook something for him again."

"Where would you be?"

"Oh, hell, we were hiding, hoping he wouldn't see us. I think he sometimes forgot we were there. If he was in one of his moods and beating the crap out of her, if he'd see us, we'd get it too."

"Oh, sweetie," Paige whispered.

"It was just what I lived with. Until that first time he came into my bed. I had no idea what was going on. We had twin beds in there, and Cathy jumped out of her bed and started hitting on him, telling him to leave me alone. I was scared to death, and he threw her across the room like she was a ragdoll." CJ paused, the memory of that night fuzzy. She could see Cathy coming to her defense, could remember the sound of her small body hitting the wall, could see Cathy falling. She remembered her father pulling her panties off. Other than that, she only remembered the pain... and the shame. She shook her head, clearing it. "Anyway, after that, whenever he would come into our room, it was like, you prayed it wasn't you who he picked for that night, yet you almost wished it was." She swallowed and took a deep breath. "Listening to him as he raped Cathy was worse than if he was doing it to me."

Paige's hand rubbed up and down her thigh, her head resting lightly against CJ's shoulder. She could only imagine the thoughts going through Paige's mind. She turned, seeing the glistening of tears in Paige's eyes. "Do you want me to stop?"

Paige shook her head and squeezed her thigh. "I want to know," she whispered.

CJ nodded, intending to tell her everything.

"That went on for the next three years, until Cathy got pregnant. She was fifteen then."

"Jesus," Paige murmured.

"My mother didn't even know. Cathy made me promise I wouldn't tell anyone. But then she was starting to show and we had to do something. She told me she would take care of it. So one morning, we're getting ready for school and she starts an argument with him. I don't even remember what it was. He slapped her, which was his warning to shut up. But she didn't. She kept provoking him. I was hiding in our room, watching through the crack in the door. Our mother was in the kitchen, cooking breakfast like nothing was going on. Anyway, he hit her pretty good, busted her lip. And like usual after a beating, our mother would get out the makeup to hide the bruises. This morning was different. When we walked to school, we ducked into a convenience store and Cathy washed her face, washed all the makeup off." CJ glanced at Paige. "There was a perfect imprint of his hand on her cheek."

"Cathy was hoping someone would find out?"

"Yeah. She was in high school. I was still in middle school. When we got to my school, she told me that the truth would come out that day. She said, 'When they come and get you and ask you questions, you tell the truth.'" CJ took a deep breath. "I was scared. I was scared of what he would do to us, you know."

"And did they come?"

CJ nodded. "Cathy told her school counselor everything." CJ glanced at her. "Everything. So when I got called out, there was a female police officer there. At first, I thought, crap, now we're really in trouble," she said, smiling. She had been so naïve back then. Not innocent, no. But she remembered her fear back then, fear that the police would just take her home to her father.

"But you told them?"

"Yes. I remember how shocked everyone was, how appalled." She turned to Paige. "That was our life. That was what we dealt with daily. It was no longer a shock to us. It was just the way our life was."

Paige took the forgotten wineglass from her, drinking what CJ had not. CJ saw that Paige's hands were trembling. She wondered what she thought about it all. Was she disgusted? Sure. Would she pull away from her like their friends had back then? Like they were lepers? Like they were diseased?

Paige linked their hands together, bringing them up to kiss CJ's knuckles. She let out a heavy breath. "What happened then?"

CJ stared at their linked hands, glad for contact. She squeezed Paige's fingers a little tighter before continuing.

"They took me up to the high school and they called our mother. She...she denied everything, said we were just making it all up, just wanting attention." CJ paused, remembering the defiance in Cathy's face as she stood, lifting up her shirt and pointing to her belly. *Am I making this up?* She smiled at the memory. Her mother had been shocked speechless.

"Why would she deny it? Wouldn't this have been her chance

to get away from him?"

"She was scared. She was scared of the beating she would have to take when he found out." She leaned back against the pillows, not releasing Paige's hand. "Long story short, they took us to a shelter, me and Cathy. Our mother was as guilty as our father."

"Prison?"

"Eventually, yeah. The bastard got twenty years. She served eight."

"Have you seen her?"

"Once. She found me when she got out. I was just starting the academy. Houston Police Department, not FBI," she said to Paige's silent question. "I told her not to ever contact me again. I didn't want anything to do with her." She shrugged. "And she hasn't."

"What about your sister?"

CJ closed her eyes for a moment, picturing Cathy's face. "We went to live with my aunt. She was the complete opposite of our mother. Nice home, good job. She was divorced and had no kids. She took us in and gave us someplace stable to live. But Cathy... Cathy couldn't do it." She looked at Paige then. "The pregnancy, I mean. She committed suicide."

"Oh, God, sweetie. I'm so sorry," Paige whispered, her fingers tightening around CJ's hand.

"She left a note for me. It was short, to the point. Very candid," she said. She didn't mention that she still had the note, that she still read it sometimes. She swallowed, the words coming with difficulty as she recited them. 'I love you, CJ. Don't ever forget that. You make something good out of your life. Help kids. Kids like us. But I can't do this. I can't bring a child into the world, not one that was fathered by that monster. I won't do it.'" She met Paige's eyes, just a hint of tears in them. "That's it. That was the note. She climbed a tree and hung herself," she said simply.

"Oh, baby, did you find her?"

CJ shook her head. "No. My aunt did. I had already read the note. I knew."

Paige reached out, brushing her fingers gently across CJ's

forehead, brushing the hair away from her face. "All that, that's why when it's kids, it affects you so?"

CJ nodded. "At first, her note threw me. I mean, *we* were fathered by that monster. But I didn't blame her. I tried to do what she said. I thought maybe I'd be a school counselor, like the one that helped us. Or maybe a social worker or something." She smiled. "I found out college wasn't my thing. I got an associate's degree, but the prospect of finishing was too daunting. I got accepted into the academy so I dropped out of school." She was nearly embarrassed by that fact, knowing Paige had not only finished but had gone on to law school as well.

"College is not for everyone," Paige said. "You grew into a wonderful person, CJ. Your sister would be proud, don't you think?"

"I think...yeah, maybe," she said.

Paige leaned closer, kissing her lightly. "Do you see your aunt still?"

CJ nodded. "Not as much as I should, but yeah, we talk. She's married now. I usually swing by there at Thanksgiving and have dinner with them." She rested against Paige, letting Paige hold her as they settled back against the pillows again. She closed her eyes, Paige's soft fingers running back and forth against her skin lulling her into a relaxed state, her mind freeing itself of those long-ago images. The vulnerability she normally felt when recalling that time in her life was gone now. Whether it was the fact that she was older—and wiser—or simply that she now accepted it, she didn't know. Whatever it was, she felt at peace with it all.

She opened her eyes, finding Paige watching her. There was no sign of judgment, no disgust or revulsion. Just a hint of sadness, nothing more. She stopped the hand that was still moving lazily along her arm, bringing it to her mouth and kissing it gently.

"Thank you."

CHAPTER THIRTY-EIGHT

Fiona sat in her recliner, reading. It was her lone form of entertainment as Mother Hogan had forbidden TV. Most of the others, they'd never even seen a television. Of the remaining flock, only she, Don and Gretchen had been outside. She didn't know about Don and Gretchen, but she'd been fascinated with the TV when she was in college. Whatever reason Mother Hogan used for the ban on TVs, Fiona knew the real purpose. Having TVs would expose the flock to the outside world, would influence them. It would subject them to *ideas* that most of those who lived in Hoganville wouldn't have a clue about, considering how sheltered—and controlled—Mother Hogan had kept them. As it was, there were no prospects for any of the others to go outside. Fiona was the youngest that remained. All those younger than her had been culled for various reasons.

Disobedience.

Yes, something she had never been accused of. She looked at her book fondly, knowing Mother Hogan had no idea how many of them she had devoured over the years. She was a frequent visitor to the school's library. Her only fear was that Gretchen would discover her passion for reading and would report it to Mother Hogan. So far, she'd been able to chase her faraway dreams, living through the characters in her books, letting herself slip away from the hellish existence that she'd had thus far. Yet it was a reality that she'd come to accept. Especially now, she thought, as she dared to touch her abnormally large belly. Oh, but she wished she hadn't accepted it. The events of the past month made her realize how much she really wanted out. The choices she'd made, the few choices that she actually did have, she wished she could redo. If she were stronger, she would have run away years ago. If she had only dared, she could have escaped when she was away at college. She sighed. Yes, if she had only dared. But the fear Mother Hogan had instilled in her was still strong then. And now, of course, it was far too late for that anyway.

A quick, quiet knock on the kitchen door brought her out of her musings. She tilted her head, listening, and the knock sounded again. She frowned, wondering who would be at her back door. Not Paige. She would use the front. Maybe Belden, but he wouldn't bother knocking. She opened the door, surprised to find Don there. When he hadn't shown up the night before, she'd assumed he'd changed his mind. She wouldn't have blamed him.

"Are you alone?" he whispered.

She nodded. "Yes, I'm alone. Is everything okay?" she asked, looking past him into the dark night.

"Yes. I couldn't come last night. Belden was out and about. I didn't want to take a chance."

She nodded and stood back. "Come inside." He did and she locked the door behind him.

He looked around, then laughed uneasily. "I don't mind saying, I was a little nervous leaving." He cleared his throat.

"Okay, a lot nervous. I even put pillows together in my bed to make it look like I was sleeping." He shrugged. "If Belden finds out I'm gone though..."

"Yes, I know. You came along the trail?"

"Yes. It took about a half hour at a fast walk."

Their eyes met. "Out in the woods at night, Belden would be the least of my worries," she said.

"I know. I was terrified."

She moved slowly back into the living room and her recliner, motioning to the worn sofa for him. Instead of sitting, he helped her down into her chair.

"Thank you. Every day gets harder to move around."

"I can't believe you're so calm about this," Don said, his hands twisting together nervously.

"Calm? You should have seen me yesterday. After I'd taken the potion, the one Mother Hogan told me to take twice a day, I was so hungry. But I knew I didn't have anything. Except there was a soup left for me. One of Selma's, you know. I started eating it like a crazy woman." She paused, just thinking about it making her nauseous. "The soup was bloody," she said. "I couldn't even see it at first. It was full of raw meat and...blood." She glanced away, clearing her throat. "I got sick. Threw it all up. And I haven't taken her potion at all today." She looked at him pointedly. "What do you think is in them? What do you think she mixes up?"

He shook his head slowly. "I wouldn't even begin to guess. But I wouldn't take anything she gave me." He leaned forward. "You know the rumor is that she poisoned her mother."

Fiona nodded. Yes, they'd all heard that rumor. She often wondered if Mother Hogan hadn't started it herself, just another means to keep the flock under her control. Although she had no doubt that it could have been true.

"Do you think...well, do you think there's a chance I could escape?"

"Yes. But you'll need help. There is someone I trust here. She'll help."

"A teacher?"

"Yes. The new ones. The ones who found me the other night."

"They're new? And you trust them?"

She nodded. "Yes. They'll help. I know they will."

"Will you come with me?"

She squeezed her eyes closed, feeling the pain starting again. Oh, how she wished she could run away with him. "No. You know I can't. I've been thinking about how you can do it, though. I feel certain that once I go into Hoganville this weekend, she won't let me leave again. So it must be this week." She tried to shift in the chair but couldn't. She took short, shallow breaths, finding this helped the pain somewhat. "You come here on Friday," she said. "Early. Be here when we get out of school. We'll go together." She met his gaze head on. "We need to tell them."

"Tell them?"

"Yes. Everything."

He stood up quickly. "Fiona, we can't." He paced in front of her chair nervously. "You know what will happen. Belden will take us into the caves. No one ever returns from the caves."

Her breathing was becoming labored, and she wondered if maybe she should have taken Mother Hogan's potion after all. She looked up at him, seeing the fear in his eyes. Strangely, she felt none of it.

"You are getting out of here, remember." She pointed to her belly. "And I won't be sent to the caves. Not as long as I'm carrying this."

"But if we tell them, do you think they'd even believe us? I sometimes don't believe it myself." He pulled out a small pill bottle from his pocket. "Here," he said, handing it to her. "I almost forgot. It's Vicodin. For pain. I guessed you wouldn't be taking her potions, not after the other night."

"Thank you." She stared at the bottle. "What will this do?"

"It'll make you drowsy. You may want to take only half a pill now," he suggested.

The pain was getting worse, but she thought she could hold off a little longer. "I'll take a whole pill before bed." She looked up at him. "I will wake up, right?"

He smiled and nodded. "Yes. And an added bonus, it's

not even expired." He sat down again, his thoughts obviously going back to what they'd been discussing. "If we tell them, what will happen to the others?"

"The flock?" She shook her head. "They can't function on the outside, you know that. Will they be jailed? Mother Hogan will. Belden and his crew, yes. But the others?"

"None of us were participants in this, Fiona."

"You and I," she said. "We've been outside. We know better. We should have done something to stop it years ago."

"Done what? We both know the consequences. We've seen what happens to those who go against Mother Hogan," he reminded her.

"Yes." And this too had been weighing on her. What would happen to the flock? To her own mother? She knew the answer, but she was almost afraid to say it. Had Don been brainwashed like the rest of them? Or had he been able to block it, like she had? Was it because she had an education, had been outside, that she knew to even try to block it?

"What are you thinking?"

"The sessions," she said. "I haven't let her inside." She tapped her head. "I've blocked her."

"Yellow rock," he said clearly, arching an eyebrow.

She smiled. "You've blocked her as well."

"Yes. Mother's code word for her poison potion." He stood again. "When the sessions first started, I was horrified at what she'd planned for us. I saw the others, all in their trance, all taking in her words. 'Yellow rock in the clock.'" He laughed. "You'd think she could have come up with a trigger phrase better than that."

She hated to say it, but it was the only option. "Maybe the flock should end with that phrase," she said. "Put an end to it once and for all."

"Have them die at their own hands?"

"Do you know anyone who could survive outside the confines of Hoganville?"

He slowly shook his head.

She took a deep breath, feeling more exhausted than she should. "You come back on Friday," she said. "Now you should go. You don't want to be caught in the woods."

He glanced out into the night. "Yes, I need to hurry. I don't want to be mistaken for dinner."

He said it with a laugh, but she had no doubt that he meant it literally.

CHAPTER THIRTY-NINE

"Well, you're looking better," Paige said as she helped Fiona into the chair.

"Yes. I feel almost normal," Fiona said. She pointed to her protruding belly. "As normal as can be with this, anyway." She started to unwrap her sandwich, then stopped. "Everyone is talking about me, aren't they?"

The polite thing to do would have been to lie, but Paige didn't think Fiona wanted that. So she nodded.

"Yes. Mostly they're concerned," she said. "And of course, some are surprised by your pregnancy."

"Yes. I am too," she said with a small smile. "But it'll be over soon."

"You're due already?"

"Yes. Soon," Fiona said evasively.

Paige didn't press her. She, too, was concerned about Fiona's health. Although, as she'd said, she did look better today. But she decided to keep things light during their lunch and not grill her.

"I got another lecture from Ms. Miner," she said. "She walked in the gym while we were doing Zumba."

Fiona laughed. "I bet she almost had a stroke."

"Worse. She's set up an appointment with Director Avery to go over my lack of curriculum." Paige leaned forward conspiratorially. "She thinks I'm out to sabotage the audit that's coming up this fall." She smiled. "Yes, I'm going to singlehandedly take the school down."

Fiona clasped her hand. "Oh, it feels so good to laugh. Thank you."

Paige nodded but was startled when Fiona linked their fingers together.

"I really like you, Paige. I think...I think we could have been really good friends."

Paige frowned. "What do you mean *could have been*?"

"I mean, I wish it wasn't here. I wish it was out in the real world." She squeezed her fingers. "Different place, different time."

Paige wasn't sure what she meant, and she supposed the look on her face registered it as shock because Fiona laughed again.

"No, no. I don't mean sexually," Fiona said. "Not like you and CJ."

"Oh. Okay then," Paige said, giving her a relieved smile, but she tightened her hold as Fiona tried to withdraw her hand.

"I just feel, with you, if we'd been somewhere else," she explained, "we could have been best friends." Fiona sighed. "I've never had a best friend."

Paige cleared her throat. "Well, now you do."

They went back to eating their lunch, and Paige wondered what was going on with Fiona. She seemed different. The same, yet different. Fiona's next words only confirmed that.

"Do you believe in monsters?" Fiona asked quietly.

Paige nodded. "Yes, people can be monsters." She winked. "These students can be monsters."

Fiona did not return her smile. "Not people. Real *monsters*."

Paige leaned her elbows on the table, studying her. "I don't know. We read about them in books, they're in movies, but whether they exist or not, I'm not sure." She watched as Fiona's hands went to rub her belly. "Are you okay?" she asked.

Fiona looked up quickly, the smile on her face forced. "Yes. Sorry. Must be my hormones." She cleared her throat. "Listen, will you and CJ be home Friday after school?"

Paige nodded. "Yes, but I have to make a run into San Augustine for groceries. Unless the Hogan Grocery will be open," she teased.

Again, Fiona didn't smile. "No." She met her eyes. "Don't go in there."

Paige was confused by how serious Fiona was being. Surely she knew Paige had only been teasing. "Okay." She touched her arm lightly. "What's up?"

"I have someone I want you to meet, that's all."

At this, Paige's interest was piqued. "Someone special?"

Fiona took a deep breath, nodding. "Yes."

Paige waited for Fiona to explain, but she said nothing more. She shoved the uneaten part of her sandwich in the bag and stood, using the table to support herself.

"I should get back."

"Okay." Paige gathered her trash quickly, taking Fiona's from her and tossing it all into a trash bin.

"I'm just tired," Fiona said.

"What?"

"You're worried."

Paige laughed. "Does it show?"

Fiona surprised her by taking her arm. "Thank you for being my friend."

"If you need help, you'll let me know, right?"

"Of course."

"Because—" She stopped, seeing Jules approaching. She smiled. "Hi. You getting a late lunch?"

"Oh, no. I just haven't seen you all week." She turned to Fiona. "How are you feeling?"

"Fat," she said, and they all laughed.

Jules turned to Paige. "I wanted to make sure you knew about the cookout on Sunday. It's at Val and Ella's."

"Okay. What's the theme this week?"

"Oh, no theme. We're doing steaks and a side dish. Dave has a gas grill he's wheeling over."

Paige nodded. "Great. We'll be there."

"See you two later," Jules said, waving her goodbye at them.

"Wonderful," Paige said dryly. "Steaks. CJ will love that."

"Oh? And you won't?"

Paige shook her head. "I'm just this close," she said, holding her thumb and index finger together, "to being vegetarian."

CHAPTER FORTY

CJ lay wide awake as the lightning flashed across the closed blinds and a light roll of thunder followed. The wind had picked up, and she assumed rain was not far behind. She instinctively tightened her hold on Paige, her eyes slipping closed for a second as she gently kissed her naked shoulder. Paige burrowed deeper into the pillow, her hand keeping CJ's arm wrapped around her waist from behind.

CJ thought she could stay like this forever and that surprised her. No doubt, when the case was over, when they returned to Houston, then this little *affair* that they were having would come to an end. Frankly, that sucked. Lying in bed like this with someone else, some stranger she'd just met, wasn't appealing in the least. But who was she kidding? She never stayed around long enough to hold anyone. Hell, she never wanted to hold anyone. Sometimes, she couldn't get out of their bed fast enough. God, so much had changed. She kissed Paige's shoulder again. No, she wasn't looking forward to going back to her old life.

She also was no closer to falling asleep. She eased away from Paige slowly, keeping the covers around her. Paige stirred but didn't wake. CJ grabbed the T-shirt she'd discarded earlier and slipped it on, then walked barefoot into the living room. She opened the blinds, the storm in full strength now as thunder rumbled overhead. She stood near the window, watching the show, the large pines across the road swaying mightily in the wind. She wasn't one for weather forecasts, but she'd heard Chief Aims mention to one of the other guards that these storms could produce tornadoes. She craned her neck, looking at the giant pine that stood just outside the window, figuring if it fell it would squash their little house into matchsticks.

She stepped away from the window quickly as a lightning flash sizzled over the woods immediately followed by a clap of thunder. Her gaze went to Fiona's house across the road. She assumed Fiona was in bed; it was just after midnight. She was curious as to who Fiona wanted them to meet. Paige thought maybe it was the father of her baby.

Another blaze of lightning streaked across the trees, illuminating the forest. She leaned forward, not believing what she'd just seen. She squinted, waiting for another flash of light. And there it was, a big hulk of a creature standing at the edge of the woods near Fiona's house.

"What the hell?" she murmured.

Again, darkness, and she waited. The lightning flash was nearly simultaneous with the roar of thunder and she jumped back. The... the *thing* seemed to be looking right at her, then it bolted off into the woods on all fours.

What the fuck was that?

"CJ?"

She jumped and let out a scream, her eyes wide. She caught her breath, embarrassed now.

"What's wrong?" Paige asked.

CJ turned back to the window, pointing. "I saw something. Something I'm not sure I can even describe."

Paige tilted her head. "And it scared you? Because you screamed like a girl."

CJ laughed. "Yeah, well, a little."

Paige came closer, linking their arms together and they both stared out into the dark night. Another flash of lightning illuminated the woods but there was no sign of...*it*.

"I couldn't sleep," CJ said. "The storm. So I came out here to watch it. This...this thing was over by the edge of Fiona's house. It was an animal of some sort, I guess. Four legs. But it was *standing* on its hind legs." She turned to Paige. "It was like it knew I was watching. I swear, it turned and looked right at me. Then it took off running on all four legs, back into the woods."

"What do you think it was?" Paige asked quietly.

"I have no idea. But whatever it was, I'd guess it's the thing that we hear screaming at night."

"And it wasn't a black panther?"

"No. It was too big. When it was standing on its hind legs, I'd say it was eight or nine feet tall."

Paige looked at her skeptically. "You're sure?"

CJ stared at the spot where it was, trying to picture it again. Granted, she had only seen it for a few seconds, but the image was ingrained in her mind. "Yes," she said. "I'm sure."

And off in the distance, the eerie scream was heard, loud enough so that even the rumble of thunder couldn't cover it up. Paige leaned in closer to her, her fingers digging into CJ's arm.

***

Fiona jerked awake, her eyes wide. She was surprised to find herself in her bed. She lay back down, blinking her eyes several times.

Only a dream.

But a vivid one, for sure. She'd been running. Fast. In the tunnels. And...something was chasing her. She rolled her head to the side, seeing the remnants of the storm flashing behind her closed blinds. A gentle roll of thunder, then there it was, the haunting scream from deep in the woods. No one talked about it. Not even her own mother. But they all knew what it was and where it lived. Mother Hogan assured them that they were safe, but still, Fiona made it a point not to be outside late at night. More than a couple of the flock had turned up missing over the years. She wondered if that wasn't one of the reasons the tunnels were built, so that they could move about without fear—fear of the outsiders and fear of *it*. Funny, since the tunnels linked to the chamber anyway.

A sharp pain in her gut made her gasp, and she pressed her hand firmly against her side, willing the ache to go away. When it subsided, she reached for the bottle of pills Don had left. She'd only taken a half of one at bedtime. She took the other half now, swallowing it down with the water she'd left on the table.

She rolled away from the window, eyes blinking slowly, waiting for the drug to take hold. She felt herself growing drowsy, her eyelids heavy. She was surprised to feel a tear running down her cheek. She wiped it away impatiently. It would do no good to allow her heartache and sorrow to escalate. It was too late for that.

There was only one way out of this nightmare. Fiona only hoped she was strong enough.

CHAPTER FORTY-ONE

Paige eyed the legs that were swinging back and forth beside her. CJ was perched nonchalantly on the counter, an unopened bottle of wine between her thighs. She turned the sauce down to a simmer, finally stilling CJ's legs.

"You must know you're breaking all sorts of rules by sitting on the counter."

CJ laughed. "Driving you crazy, Miss OCD?" She hopped down, the bottle of wine forgotten as CJ reached for her, tickling her sides with both hands as Paige slapped at them.

"God, will you stop," she said, laughing, trying to get away.

"You should have never told me you were ticklish."

Paige grabbed the wine bottle and shoved it into CJ's hands. "Do something useful, please."

"Okay, *dear*. I don't want to come between you and your wine." She resumed her spot on the counter, the wine bottle again secured between her legs as she twisted the corkscrew.

Paige felt an unexpected wave of affection come over her at the sight. She enjoyed CJ's company immensely, yet they were nearly complete opposites.

"I don't know why I like you so much," she said, giving voice to her thoughts. "You are so not my type."

CJ looked up, a smile playing on her lips. "Baby, I'm exactly your type. You've been such a good girl all your life, I think you like a little *bad*." CJ met her eyes, her playfulness vanishing. "That's why I like you. I need some good in my life."

"I don't know why you're so convinced I'm good," she said. She took the wine from CJ and set it aside, standing between her legs. "What's wrong?"

CJ shook her head. "Nothing really. It's just, you're right. I'm not your type."

Paige frowned, puzzled by the change in her tone. She linked their fingers together tightly. "Talk to me. What's bothering you?"

CJ shrugged. "It's just...if we didn't work together, if we'd just met somewhere, you wouldn't give me the time of day. Because I'm not—"

Paige put a finger to CJ's lips stopping her. *I'm not good enough.* She hated that CJ felt that way, but obviously her childhood, her upbringing, had a profound effect on her. But she wanted to be truthful with her.

"You're probably right, CJ. If we'd met on the street, at a party, I probably wouldn't have thought twice about you, about getting to know you," she said. "But that's not how we met. I do know you. I know the passion you have for the job, for the people, the victims. I know how much you love this, how personal it is for you. I know you just want to take care of everybody, yet you don't take care of yourself. It's like you don't think you're as worthy as everyone else." She squeezed her hand tighter. "I know all that, CJ. You have more integrity and honor than anyone I know. So don't say you're not good enough. You're better than good enough."

Their eyes held and Paige could tell that CJ was looking for the truth in hers. She opened herself, letting CJ see all that she needed. CJ finally nodded, a small smile forming.

"So, even with my good looks and charm, you wouldn't have thought twice about me, huh?"

Paige laughed. "Gee, you're so modest."

CJ laughed too, her grin chasing away the last of the somberness that had sprung up. "You know, I'm really glad we stopped all that pretending. The tension was really unbearable." She poured wine into one of the glasses. "Isn't this so much better?"

Paige nodded. "I'll have to agree with you. This is *much* better." She leaned closer, kissing CJ lightly before taking the wineglass.

CJ's legs resumed their swinging as Paige lifted the lid on her spaghetti sauce. She poured most of her glass of wine into it, then stirred it. Without her having to ask, CJ dutifully refilled her glass.

"I never used to drink wine much," CJ said. "I think you've got me hooked on it."

"Well, I try."

CJ took a sip, looking at her thoughtfully. "You know, that night..."

Paige smiled. "*That* night?"

CJ laughed. "Yeah, *that* night. At the bar. Afterward—even though it was weird for us at work—I kept hoping you'd come back."

"Oh yeah?"

"Yeah. I kept looking for you, hoping I'd see you there again." She shrugged. "I know, it's crazy. I mean, seeing as how we didn't even talk about it. Didn't even talk at all."

Paige shook her head. "It's not crazy. I actually thought about it a time or two. But I didn't want to make things any more awkward than they already were."

They were quiet as Paige stirred the sauce, but she felt CJ's eyes on her. She finally looked at her questioningly.

"You were right, you know," CJ said. "When you said I didn't know how to treat women."

"Oh, no, CJ. I'm sorry." She put the spoon down, moving to stand between CJ's legs again. "I didn't mean that. I was angry. We were having an argument—"

"No. No, you did mean it. And it's true. I don't know how." She shrugged. "I could blame it on the role models I had growing up, but that would just be an excuse," she said. "Truthfully, I never wanted anyone to know me. I didn't want there to be anyone I had to tell my story to, you know." CJ took her hand, her thumb rubbing lightly across it, back and forth. "It was easier to be alone, easier to have those one-night affairs."

"I'm glad you trusted me enough to tell me, CJ. I think if you had let anyone get close to you and you'd told them your story, I think they would have understood. You were a child. There's no blame to be placed on you."

She tugged CJ off of the counter, wrapping her arms around her tightly. She kissed her cheek, moving slowly to her mouth. They pulled apart, their foreheads resting together, eyes closed. She felt her attachment to CJ growing with each kiss, each touch. The fact that CJ trusted her enough to let her vulnerabilities show only served to strengthen the bond that was growing between them. Yes, they were very different. They grew up at opposite ends of the spectrum, their upbringing could not have been more dissimilar. Yet here they were, in each other's arms, comforting and consoling. Friends and lovers. She tucked her head, burying it at CJ's neck. Lovers? Yes. But friends? That's something that she never considered before, not with CJ. Because they were so different. But those differences meant nothing now. She would venture to guess that CJ had no friends. And if she took an honest look at her life, she would have to admit that she had no close friends either. Superficial relationships that meant nothing, really. The people she was closest to, the people she spent time with, the people who actually mattered in her life were Billy, Ice and, yes, CJ. Why had it taken this assignment for her to see that?

She lifted her head, finding CJ's mouth again. Their kiss was light, soft, neither of them deepening it. She pulled back, seeing CJ's gaze on her. She smiled quickly, then kissed her again.

"Thank you," CJ said. "I didn't mean for our conversation to be so serious."

"No. I think it's good that we can talk like this. We should be able to be honest with each other about what we're thinking." She took her wineglass and moved away from CJ, going back to her sauce. "I want you to feel like you can talk to me about anything."

CJ smiled and Paige saw the tension fade from her face. "Okay. Then let's talk about this meatless sauce you're making. I'm starving."

CHAPTER FORTY-TWO

CJ opened the blinds enough to peer out, then closed them again when she saw nothing. She glanced at Paige.

"Did she say what time they'd be over?"

Paige stood at the fridge, staring inside. "She just said after school."

CJ watched as Paige squatted down, opening the vegetable crisper and shaking her head.

"What's up?"

Paige stood again and closed the door with a sigh. "I don't really have anything to offer them. You know, hors d'oeuvre or appetizer."

CJ laughed. "And this is just...*wrong*?"

Paige put her hands on her hips. "You're making fun of me?"

"Oh, no," she said quickly. "I love that you know about hors d'oeuvres and such."

Paige tilted her head, staring at her. "I'm making too big a deal out of it, aren't I?"

"I think maybe she just wants us to meet her boyfriend or something, don't you? I mean, they'll probably pop over, say hello, then go back to her place." She shrugged. "Of course, it's Friday so maybe he's coming to get her. You know, since she stays in Hoganville over the weekends."

"I guess you're right. I am curious though, aren't you?"

"For completely different reasons, yes."

"Meaning?"

"Meaning you're looking at Fiona as a friend and you want to meet this person she claims is *special*. I want to see if he's got horns and a tail and see if he could be a person of interest in this so-called investigation we're supposed to be doing."

"Horns and a tail?"

"You know what I mean." She opened the blinds again, finally seeing Fiona coming out of her house. "Jesus, she's huge," she murmured.

"Is she on her way?"

"Yeah. And there's a normal looking guy with her. No horns. Appears to be about her age, maybe a little older," CJ said.

"Is he cute?"

CJ laughed. "I'll let you be the judge of that."

Paige opened the door at Fiona's knock, smiling broadly at them. Fiona returned her smile, and CJ could tell the genuine affection both Paige and Fiona shared.

"Come in," Paige said. "How are you feeling?"

"Honestly? Like my skin is stretched so thin I'm about to burst at any moment."

"Then I'll say again, maybe you should see a doctor. A *real* doctor," she added with a wink. Paige turned to the man standing nervously beside Fiona and held out her hand. "I'm Paige Riley," she said. "This is CJ Johnston."

"Don...Don Hogan," he said.

Although CJ and Paige both knew that everyone took Hogan as their last name—and that Don was the *doctor* in Hoganville—Paige played right along.

"Oh? Are you related?"

Fiona laughed. "We could be."

CJ walked over, shaking his hand as well. "Nice to meet you."

"I'm disappointed if you are related," Paige continued, a smile forming. "I was hoping you'd come to introduce us to your boyfriend."

Both Fiona and Don sported matching blushes as Paige led them inside and closed the door behind them. Don helped Fiona to sit, and CJ wondered if maybe Paige wasn't right-on in her assumption.

"Not boyfriend, no," Fiona said. "But I wanted you both to meet him." She glanced at Don nervously. "We have...we have something to discuss with you."

Fiona's tone was serious and Paige noticed it as well. The role she was playing as hostess disappeared, replaced by the curiosity inherent to their job.

"Is everything okay?" Then, as if remembering her manners, Paige motioned into the kitchen. "I'm sorry. Can I get you anything to drink?" She glanced at CJ who shook her head.

"No, we're fine," Don said.

Paige sat on the arm of the sofa next to Fiona, her hand rubbing Fiona's shoulder lightly. "What's wrong, sweetie?"

Fiona gave a quick laugh. "What's *not* wrong would be an easier answer." She took a labored breath, one hand rubbing her side. "Sorry. I've been cramping."

"Did you take a pill?" Don asked.

"Half," Fiona said.

Paige glanced at CJ with raised eyebrows before turning back to Fiona. "What pill, Fiona?"

"Vicodin," Don said.

"Vicodin? But...I mean, I'm no doctor but being pregnant, should you take Vicodin?"

"It may harm the baby?"

"I believe so, yes," Paige said. "It's a prescription drug. Did you finally go see a doctor?"

Don was about to speak, but Fiona stopped him with a shake of her head. She turned to Paige and took her hand. CJ could see how hard she was squeezing it as Fiona's knuckles turned nearly white.

"We need to talk to you. We need you to listen to us." She paused. "We need your help."

"Of course," Paige said immediately. She glanced over at CJ. "What's going on?"

Fiona released Paige's hand, her eyes now staring straight ahead as if she were gathering her thoughts. Don was watching her intently, his hands twisting together nervously.

"You know how you say you're fascinated with Hoganville?" Paige nodded.

"You understand how different things are here, right?"

"Yes."

Fiona turned her head slowly, looking at Paige. "We have some things to tell you—some things you might not even believe—because we need you to help Don get away from Hoganville," she said. "Once I go back tonight, I don't think Mother Hogan will let me come back."

"You mean until after your baby is born?" Paige asked.

Fiona shook her head. "No. Ever."

Paige frowned. "What are you talking about?"

This time, Fiona glanced at CJ. "Things aren't as they seem. Most of the people who live there, they've never set foot outside of those walls. Some have never even seen an outsider. They have certain jobs. Some tend to the gardens, some to the chickens, some to the pigs and cows. Some are woodworkers, some sew." She paused. "And things happen there that...well, just *things*. I'm telling you this because I need you to get Don out of here. And CJ being with the police, I thought maybe you could get the authorities to come."

CJ couldn't believe Fiona was telling them this. *Things?* Surely she was talking about the disappearances. But they needed to hear it all from Fiona. They couldn't assume that was what she was talking about. And they certainly couldn't blow their cover so she pretended ignorance.

"The authorities? For what?" she asked. "On what grounds?"

Fiona shook her head. "I don't think you'd believe me if I told you."

Paige knelt down in front of her. "What's going on, Fiona?"

Fiona took a deep breath. "I'm thirty-one," she said. "A virgin. Until recently. I was chosen for the coupling. When I missed school for that week, I was held captive and kept drugged." She looked away from Paige. "So Antel could...impregnate me."

Paige stood up quickly. "What are you talking about? *Coupling?*"

Don cleared his throat. "Mother Hogan decides who should mate so that the bloodline remains strong. The coupling is done in the chamber."

"Chamber?" CJ asked.

"The caves."

CJ and Paige exchanged glances. "What caves?"

"Underground caverns," Don said. "She has an altar in the chamber. For...well, for many uses."

Paige looked at Fiona. "But—"

"Please don't judge or try to find reason for it now," Fiona said. "There's no time. We're just trying to tell you what goes on."

"Okay, wait a minute," Paige said, holding up a hand. "At lunch one day, when you were telling me about your family, you said that Antel was your father."

Fiona nodded. "Yes."

Paige's eyes widened. "And he—"

"Yes."

"Oh dear God," Paige murmured, her glance going to Fiona's belly. "But Fiona—"

"No. I'm certain it's not his baby. It was an act put on for the flock. Mother Hogan said she wanted a pure bloodline. Antel is the only true Hogan left. I'm the next closest one."

CJ's mind was whirling. *Antel, her father, held captive, impregnate.* She glanced at Paige, still trying to sort out her thoughts. Was she trying to tell them that her own father...? Surely to God...no. Paige gave her a gentle look, one to let her know she understood the direction of her thoughts. But one also telling her to focus, to be professional. To do her job. CJ nodded. Now was not the time to dwell on that atrocity.

"Okay," Paige said, turning back to Fiona. "Go on. You're pregnant. But not by your...by Antel."

"No. It's not possible." Fiona pointed to her belly. "This happened barely two months ago."

"What are you saying?"

Fiona looked at Don, as if for help. He glanced at CJ but directed his words to Paige. "Something lives in the caves. Something we've never seen. Our community was built near the main entrance to guard the caves."

CJ went closer, trying to figure out what he was saying. She tilted her head. "*Something* lives there? What?"

"We don't know," Fiona said. "But I'm fairly certain that whatever is growing inside of me is from him."

"Fiona, what are you talking about?" Paige sat down next to her again. "Tell me what you're trying to say."

Fiona stared at her for the longest time, finally nodded. "We'll tell you everything. You won't believe us, but we'll tell you." Fiona turned slowly, her eyes meeting Don's. Whatever was communicated between them was done silently. It was Don who spoke next.

"Usually, two times a year—sometimes three—Belden and the hunters bring back young girls or women. They bring them to the caves. Mother Hogan has this ritual that she calls Celebration Week."

"This has been going on for years. Well before our time," Fiona added.

"The girls are offered up as a sacrifice to...well, to whatever lives in the cave," Don said.

"A sacrifice?"

"Mother Hogan makes them drink one of her potions, then Belden takes them past the cavern and into the main tunnel of the cave." Fiona looked down, her eyes nearly closed. "Sometimes there is screaming. It goes on for so long sometimes," she said, her voice nearly a whisper. "They're made to run. For the chase."

"They're killed?" Paige asked quietly.

Fiona looked up. "They're eaten."

Paige's eyebrows shot up. "These potions that Mother Hogan mixes up. What is she? A witch?"

Fiona actually smiled. "Yes. She could be."

Paige and CJ exchanged glances again, but CJ was not ready to reveal their mission. She gave a subtle shake of her head, seeing Paige's answering nod. CJ moved forward, standing in front of Fiona.

"These girls are abducted? What? Random?"

"From what I gather, yes. It's not something that's talked about."

Again, CJ feigned ignorance. "And they're taken into the cave and *eaten* by something?"

Fiona met her eyes. "I know you don't believe us. It's crazy, right?"

"Yeah. Crazy."

"It's also true. Whatever creature lives in the caves controls Mother Hogan."

"We're trying to find a way to stop it," Don said. "We're the only ones who can make it happen. There is no one else. The others, they've been brainwashed for so long, they can't even fathom going against Mother Hogan. Besides, most of them are very old. This is all they know."

"Don and I are among the few who have been to the outside," Fiona said. "We're also the youngest left in the flock. Gretchen is the only other one, but she's a lost cause. She is very loyal to Mother Hogan. Don and I have always been kept separated, never allowed to interact. Because we have been outside. We know of the world. We've been educated."

"If she allowed us to interact," Don said, "we might plot against her. Or just decide to run. Or to tell someone, like we're doing now."

"The rest of them, they all get their direction from Mother Hogan," Fiona said. "All of it. They don't have a single thought that's their own. Everything they do, everything they eat, everything they say, everything they *think* comes from her."

"It's always been that way," Don said. "That's how you're taught. You don't question it. Those who do get culled. Fiona and I have learned to pretend we're as brainwashed as they are. It's the only way to survive. There have been plenty before us who weren't able to. They were culled quickly. And cruelly."

"And that strengthens their fear...and her power," Fiona added.

CJ flicked her eyes at Paige with raised eyebrows. "Culled?"

"Yes," Fiona said. "They're left in the caves. And if it's something really bad," she said, glancing at Don. "Remember Ryan?" Don nodded. Fiona turned to Paige. "Mother Hogan accused Ryan of disobedience, of telling tales to the authorities. We were all made to gather in the chamber. After Mother Hogan listed off his crimes, Belden took him into the cave and tied him up." She closed her eyes, her hand reaching out for Don's. "We were all made to listen to his screams...as he was eaten. You learn quickly after that not to ever question Mother Hogan."

"Holy shit," CJ murmured. "So what is it? What's in the cave?"

"We don't know."

"The screams we hear at night?" Paige asked. "Is that it?"

Fiona nodded. "Yes. That's it. He hunts in the woods here near the school." Fiona looked at Paige directly. "Mother Hogan says we are the guardians of the cave. That's our job. Mother Hogan has powers. They've all had powers."

"They who?" Paige asked.

"Ester's grandmother, her great-grandmother, and those before her. They've all led the flock."

CJ raised an eyebrow. "What kind of powers?"

"She can see things. She knows things. She can move things without touching them."

CJ rubbed her throat, her glance going to Paige. "That day in the café, I felt like someone was choking me. Remember?"

Paige nodded.

"That's one of her favorite tricks," Fiona said.

"And is she, you know, all there?" Paige asked, tapping her head.

"Mother Hogan? No. She's quite mad. She's also very, very smart. That's why we need to get Don out of here. Because she'll *know*." She glanced at Don. "We've had no part in any of this, other than we live here," she said. "Don is the only one who can function outside of Hoganville. The rest, they can't. So you get him out and call the authorities."

"And what about you?" Paige asked.

Fiona shook her head. "What's growing inside of me is not something that can be explained. My fate is sealed."

"You think whatever lives in the caves is..." she said, glancing at her swollen belly.

Fiona nodded.

Paige turned to CJ. "We need to tell them," she whispered.

Paige obviously trusted Fiona and believed what she was saying. The disappearances, yes. But the tale that some creature lived in the caves and ate people? That the creature impregnated Fiona? Well, sure, they'd heard the screams in the woods. And she'd seen *something* that night of the thunderstorm. But did she really believe their wild story? She met Paige's steady gaze, seeing that, yes, Paige did believe their story.

"Okay," she said, relenting. "Tell them."

"Tell us what?" Fiona asked.

Paige glanced between Fiona and Don, finally settling on Fiona. She spread her hands out, motioning to CJ. "We...we *are* the authorities."

Fiona frowned. "What are you talking about?"

Paige squatted down beside her. "Sweetie, we're FBI. I'm not a teacher. We were sent here because of the disappearances."

"You're...you're FBI?"

"Yes."

The anger shown on Fiona's face immediately. She brushed Paige's hand away, clasping her own together tightly.

"So all this time, you've just been playing with me? Pretending to be my friend? Trying to get me to trust you? Your name is probably not even Paige, is it?"

CJ could tell Paige was fighting with herself to maintain a professional persona, but Fiona's words cut deep. Paige lost the fight as she took her hand again.

"My name is Paige. And I haven't been pretending. You are my friend. Sweetie, I'm sorry I couldn't tell you."

"But we've been under investigation?" Fiona tried to stand, but Paige eased her back down.

"And you already know about the girls?" Don asked.

"We don't know any details," Paige said. "One of the girls was a senator's daughter. Her disappearance is what started it all."

CJ hesitated with how much to share with them. Paige obviously trusted Fiona and felt she was telling the truth. CJ, however, had no reason to trust either of them. They could just be blowing smoke up their asses, sent here at the instruction of Ester Hogan. She felt all three of them looking at her and her glance slid to Paige. Paige seemed to understand her hesitation.

"There's no evidence linking Hoganville to anything," Paige continued. "We were sent here to observe, really."

"So you and CJ aren't...well, you've been pretending," Fiona said. "You had me fooled. I guess you had all the teachers fooled."

"I'm sorry," Paige said again. "We needed to fit in. That was the best way."

"It's okay. I understand. You've—" Fiona's words were cut off as she doubled over in pain, her hand pressing hard against her side.

Both Paige and Don tried to comfort her as sweat broke out on her face. CJ stood by helplessly, not knowing what to do.

"We need to get you to a hospital," Paige said. Paige looked at CJ. "Let's just forget all this right now and get her out of here."

CJ shook her head. "We can't."

"We can."

Fiona grasped Paige's arm. "No. I can't go."

"You can. We can get you help."

"No!" Fiona shook Paige's hand away impatiently. "No, I can't. It's too late for that. What's done is done." She took deep breaths, steadying herself. "I'm sorry, Paige. But this is important. This is the only chance. It's got to end here. Now."

"You're in no condition to do anything," Paige said.

"All I have to do is get to the chamber. Mother Hogan will come."

"But—"

"I won't be harmed," Fiona insisted, pointing at her stomach. "Not as long as I carry this."

CJ could tell Paige was still wavering. She gently moved her aside, squatting down next to Fiona. She glanced at Don, seeing fear in his eyes. If all they'd said was true, then he would surely be killed—or *culled*—if he went back. She realized how much faith both he and Fiona were putting in them.

"Tell us what you want us to do," she said to Fiona. "We can call Houston. We can get backup, but it'll take several hours."

"We don't have several hours. You have to get Mother Hogan. She controls everything. But you must be wary of Belden. He will kill you quickly, without thought."

"We can't just go in there and arrest her," CJ said. "We don't have a warrant, for one thing."

Fiona's face turned red as she shook her head. "Not arrest. She'll know you're coming. You must kill her."

"We can't just kill her," Paige said.

Fiona stared at her. "She will give you no choice. You must be ready. This will be the only chance. Once I go there tonight, I won't return. She won't let me leave again. This is how it has to be." She looked at Don. "We need to draw them a map of the tunnels."

"They can get in through my house," Don said.

Fiona shook her head. "No. Once Belden knows you're gone, they would expect that. It must be somewhere else."

CJ glanced at Paige with raised eyebrows. "What tunnels?"

"There are tunnels that link most of the houses to the caves. The café, the grocery store too."

"That's why it seems everyone just disappears," Paige said. "Why the place appears deserted."

"Yes. At certain times she orders us to remain below ground."

CJ looked questioningly at Paige. They needed to call Howley and let him know what was going on. They also needed to talk to Avery. They needed some backup. Could they trust the local sheriff's department? Hell, were they really going in without a warrant? Howley would have both their asses. No, they couldn't involve another agency. No one would believe this crazy story anyway.

"Look, all of this is fascinating, really," CJ said, "but we can't just barge in there—me and Paige—and expect to take them out." She ran her hands through her hair several times.

"Hell, we don't even know what we're going against. Some *thing* lives in the caves? What the hell?"

Fiona squeezed her eyes shut, taking quick breaths again. CJ looked to Paige for help, but Paige was kneeling in front of Fiona, concern overriding her good sense. CJ knew what was coming before Paige even spoke the words.

"You need a hospital. Now. I can't let you go back there."

"That is not an option," Fiona said. "I'll be fine."

"You're not fine. You're—"

"Paige," CJ said. "Let it be."

Paige stood quickly. "I won't let it be. Look at her," she said, pointing.

"Stop it," Fiona said. "Stop it right now. We don't have time for this. My hour approaches. After that, I'll be of no use to anyone."

"She's right," Don said. "It's now or never."

Paige shook her head. "Fiona, I'm afraid for you. If you go back—"

"I know what I'm doing. I know what has to be done. I know my fate. Now are you going to help us or not?"

All eyes turned to Paige. She slowly took in a deep breath, her eyes closed as she let it out. "Jesus," she murmured. She glanced at CJ. "What do you want to do?"

It was CJ's turn to take a deep breath, trying to rein in her thoughts. "We need to let Howley know what's going on. Then we need to alert Avery. Have him—"

"Director Avery?"

"I'm sorry, sweetie," Paige said. "He's FBI too."

"Wow. I had no idea." She leaned back against the sofa, her huge belly protruding badly. "Be careful of Richard, the guard. He is a spy for Belden," she said.

"Yes. We figured as much. He's the one who allowed you and Gretchen to leave the compound at will, despite the gate being locked," CJ said.

"And you know all that too," Fiona said quietly, her eyes slightly accusing.

"I'm sorry."

But Fiona shook her head, dismissing the apology. "Don, let's draw a map of the tunnels. Then you'll need to show them the trail through the woods."

"The trail? At night? Will they be safe?"

"What trail?" CJ and Paige both asked in unison.

CHAPTER FORTY-THREE

The knock on the door was louder, quicker than normal. Ester turned away from the window, knowing Belden was coming with news. Something wasn't right. She could feel it.

"Is there a problem?" she asked as he entered.

"Don is missing," he said.

"Missing?"

"He's not at his home. No one has seen him since this morning."

Ester felt a tightness in her chest. She turned away from him, not wanting him to sense any weakness in her. She parted the blinds; the hot afternoon was giving way to the evening hours. She knew something was amiss. She'd felt it all day. All week really. She just couldn't put her finger on it.

"Fiona should be here by now. But she's not, is she?"

"No, Mother. Not yet."

She saw her plans unraveling and knew she had to do something. She had been wrong to allow Fiona to leave. It was getting too close. But the fear of those from the school nosing around had been too much. Maybe she was letting fear get in the way now too. Maybe Fiona was ill. Maybe Don went to assist her.

No. They would do no such thing without her approval. Her direction. They would not make those decisions without consulting her. They would not disobey. They all knew the consequences of those who disobeyed.

"Don is at the school," she said with certain clarity. She closed her eyes, trying to find him, to *see* him. She saw Fiona instead, in her car. Alone. Her face was wet. Was she crying? She shook her head. No. In pain, perhaps. It was time. But not crying. The flock did not cry. They knew of no such emotion.

"Is he with Fiona?"

"Fiona will be here shortly. She is on her way. Alone." Ester turned from the window, her eyes clear now. "Don has no business at the school. Fiona has not been well. I fear he has taken his role of *doctor* to the extreme. He must be dealt with. You know what to do."

"Yes, Mother."

***

"Meet me at the guard station," Avery said impatiently. He did not like what was going down, but CJ and Paige had given him little option. Howley had not been happy but he too was left with little choice. Fiona was already on her way back to Hoganville. Don Hogan was hiding at the agent's house. Howley had conceded to the plan, however half-baked it sounded. Even by air, they were at least two hours away.

"I'm about to sit down to dinner. Can this wait?"

"I assure you, Chief Aims, this cannot wait. I'm already on my way."

"What is this about?"

"I'll explain when we get there." He disconnected before the chief could ask further questions. Yes, he concurred that Richard Barr was involved. However, just the fact that he allowed Fiona and Gretchen—and sometimes Belden—to come and go at will hardly implicated him in the disappearances. Not to mention the quickly explained torture the girls were put through in the so-called cave. Whether CJ and Paige actually believed such a tale or not, he wasn't certain. They were, however, on their way to Hoganville using a crudely drawn map. As darkness was approaching, he had to admit that he would never attempt such a trek through the woods on foot. Not at night. He and Howley had both advised them to wait until backup arrived, but they feared for Fiona's life.

The guard booth was well-lit and Avery parked next to Richard's car. As he got out, he touched his weapon for reassurance. Not that he expected Richard to protest or make a run for it, nonetheless he felt a comfort from its mere presence. He wouldn't pretend that he was comfortable with what he was doing. He'd never been a field agent, having been content with pushing papers and doing research. But he knew how to handle a weapon. Well, at least at the shooting range, he did. In fact, he was an excellent marksman. He took encouragement from that fact as he opened the door to the guard station.

"Director Avery. What brings you about?"

"Good evening, Richard," he said. "I have some things to discuss with you. Chief Aims should be on his way."

"Is there something wrong?"

There was nothing more Richard Barr needed to know, other than the findings in the gate logs. He decided to use his visit as a disciplinary call.

"There is something wrong, yes. We've done an audit of the gate logs. It seems you have allowed the gate to be opened at odd hours of the night, all without my knowledge. And certainly, going back, it would seem without my predecessor's knowledge as well."

He expected a denial at the very least. Richard simply stared at him, saying nothing. Headlights down the road signaled Chief Aims's approach. Avery moved to the door, motioning him inside.

"Chief Aims, thank you for coming so quickly."

"What's this about, Avery?"

Avery pulled out his credentials, showing them to Aims. "I'm with the FBI," he said. "We did an analysis of the gate logs. It seems—"

"FBI?" Chief Aims laughed. "You're kidding me, right?"

Avery put his credentials away. "No. Mr. Barr has allowed the gate to open after hours. Several times. In fact—"

"Why does the FBI care about that?"

"It's an ongoing investigation. Right now, I simply need you to detain Mr. Barr and make sure he does not contact anyone in Hoganville. We have agents on site."

Chief Aims looked at Richard, grinning. "Did you hear that, Richard? I'm supposed to detain you. Because there are agents here."

Richard laughed. "Yeah. Are you going to cuff me?"

Avery's eyes widened as Aims pulled his service revolver from his hip, causally pointing it at him instead of Richard.

"Well, we're going to cuff somebody, now aren't we? Shall I assume the two new ones, Johnston and Riley, are your agents?" He shook his head. "I knew something wasn't right with her. She was no prison guard. She had no discipline whatsoever."

Richard stood from behind the desk, coming forward. Avery panicked, knowing he was out of his league. This wasn't how it was supposed to go down. He fumbled with his suit jacket, trying to find his weapon, only to have Richard grab his arms roughly and pull them behind him. Aims tossed cuffs his way.

"What are you doing? You can't do this. I said, I'm FBI. You must—"

"Shut up, Avery," Chief Aims said. "I don't care who you are." Aims glanced at Richard. "We need to contact Belden. Let him know he's got two agents roaming around."

"You must not. Chief Aims, this is highly—"

"I said to shut up."

Avery's mouth closed as he felt the cold metal of Aims's pistol resting against his forehead.

CHAPTER FORTY-FOUR

CJ tightened the strap on her thigh holster, glancing at Paige one more time.

"We shouldn't be doing this, you know that, right?"

"Yes, I know."

"It's not too late. We can still wait for backup," she suggested, even though she recognized the determined look on Paige's face.

Paige shook her head immediately. "It is too late. Fiona doesn't have the time for us to wait for backup."

CJ paused behind a tree, the shadows thick now as full darkness was upon them. She didn't know whether to be thankful for the full moon or not. There was enough light that they should be able to navigate most of the trail without flashlights.

There was also enough light that their movements could be followed, if someone—or something—should be watching.

"I can't believe we're out here on this trail," she whispered. "At night."

"You and me both, tiger."

"Howley is not happy with us, you know," CJ said.

"I trust Fiona," Paige said. "Not sure I believe everything they said, but still, this is ground zero as far as the disappearances go."

"And that's the only reason we're going forward with this."

"Do you think the little bit Don told Howley on the phone is enough for a warrant?"

CJ nodded. "I think so. Howley will get something. Why else were we assigned out here in the first place if they weren't willing to act on it? He'll throw around *domestic terrorists*, if nothing else."

"But we did promise him we wouldn't shoot anybody, remember. I don't want to be on every news channel as the one who started a standoff."

"I won't shoot anyone as long as they don't shoot first." CJ was about to continue down the trail when Paige stopped her.

"Fiona...do you think she'll be okay?"

CJ didn't know what answer Paige was expecting. Hell, they'd both seen her. She looked like she was in so much pain, like she was literally about to explode. Was she in labor? Was she about to give birth? And on top of that—what was she about to give birth *to*? But Paige knew all of that as well. She was just looking for some reassurance. CJ wasn't sure she could give it.

"I wish I could promise you that she'll be fine," she said. "She knows that whatever is going to happen to her, with her pregnancy, is going to happen tonight. I'm not certain if she expects us to protect her from Ester Hogan...or from whatever it is that lives in the caves."

Paige stared at her for a long moment, finally nodding. "Okay. Let's go."

The deeper they got into the forest, the heavier the shadows. It was a hot and humid night, the air still and quiet. She felt Paige close behind her and she welcomed her presence. She could feel the woods coming alive—night creatures awakening after their daylight slumber. She was a city girl, sure, but that only meant her imagination was in overdrive. Harmless night creatures like raccoons and opossums rapidly grew fangs and claws as they stalked the forest floor. She stopped suddenly, turning to Paige.

"Raccoons...they don't attack, right?"

Paige nearly laughed. "Sweetheart, I think raccoons will be the least of our worries. But no, I don't believe they attack."

CJ smiled too. "I know I'm being silly. But it's creepy as hell out here."

Paige nodded. "Do you think we should use the flashlight? If we get off of the trail, we're screwed."

"Minimal use," she said. "We're sitting ducks."

As much as she didn't want to use the lights, she had to agree. They'd get lost in an instant. She paused, listening, hearing nothing to indicate they were being followed. Or watched. So she turned on her flashlight, shining it quickly along the ground, seeing that they were indeed still on the trail. It was a trail that appeared to be very well used. She couldn't imagine that people from Hoganville used it, though. What reason would they have to sneak onto the school grounds? Most likely, it had become a game trail, used by deer. And whatever else inhabited these woods at night. She shook that thought away as she turned her light off, turning to Paige instead.

"Have I told you how sexy you look all in black?"

"You like my commando outfit, huh?"

"Very macho. Hair in the ponytail thing, through your cap there, looks nice," she said.

Paige tilted her head. "Are you stalling?"

"Hell, yeah," she whispered. "I swear, if anything moves, I'm going to shoot it."

"You want me to take the lead?"

"You? Paige, you have painted toenails. I really think I should be the one in the lead."

Paige smirked. "Okay, tiger. Then lead on. We don't have all night."

CJ forced herself to move. Each step they took seemed exceptionally loud, each twig that broke echoed through the quiet forest. She could hear their breaths, could feel the nervousness that surrounded them. They were FBI agents, for God's sake. But that didn't bring her any comfort. She'd never been in this situation before. She'd faced hardened criminals, she'd stared down the barrel of a gun, she'd chased down drug lords and crime bosses. But this? Slinking through the woods at night? Hoping to find a tunnel entrance at the old stables? Going underground into the caves? Looking for some...some *creature* that lurked in these woods? No.

Paige's hand squeezed painfully around her arm, stopping her.

"Listen."

CJ tilted her head slightly, her eyes darting around the dark forest, looking for movement. She heard leaves rustling behind them. They both turned and she could feel—hear—the blood pounding in her ears. Her hand slid to the weapon she had strapped to her thigh, ready to pull it out.

Paige fumbled with her own light, pointing it in the direction of the noise. CJ held her breath, waiting. The beam of the light flashed through the trees, then down along the ground. Paige was the first to laugh. CJ followed, although hers was still tinged with nervousness.

"Armadillo," Paige murmured. "Sounded like a bear."

"I can't wait to get back to the city." She turned to go, then stopped. "Wait. Shine the light back over there," she said.

Paige did as she was asked, stopping with a gasp. "Jesus. Is that what I think it is?"

CJ turned on her light too, joining Paige's beam. She walked slowly toward it, her flashlight snaking across the ground. The white skull glowed brightly, the eye sockets, dark and hollow, looking right through them. The gaping mouth seemed to be frozen for eternity in a silent, soulless scream. If she had any lingering doubt about Fiona's story, it vanished quickly into the night air.

"Yeah. It's what you think it is."

She squatted down beside it, brushing the leaves away. There were no other bones visible, nothing to indicate a body was buried here. There was only the skull, nestled snuggly against the roots of the large oak. Maybe it had been dragged there by an animal...or something. She stood up, shrugging off the feeling of being watched.

"Come on," she said. She flashed her light along the trail, walking faster.

The woods were alive with sounds now, drowning out their own footsteps. Frogs, crickets and cicadas all singing in deafening harmony. The screech of an owl nearly caused her to stumble, then Paige again stopped her with a tug on her arm.

"Kill the light," Paige whispered urgently.

CJ did, feeling her heart pounding in her chest. She tilted her head, hearing running not far ahead of them. She ducked farther back into the woods, pulling Paige with her. Up ahead, they saw three shadowy figures nearly jogging along the trail. She crept deeper into the forest, hiding them behind a giant oak. Maybe Fiona was right. Maybe Ester Hogan *could* see things. Maybe she knew they were coming. She recognized the hulk of Belden, which was being followed by two other men. One of the men brandished a flashlight. All three wore dark robes.

She quietly unsnapped her holster, hearing Paige do the same. But the men ran past them, back along the trail from where she and Paige had just come, heading toward the school.

"They know," Paige said quietly.

"They know something, yes." She holstered her weapon again, then shoved on. She navigated without the light, continuing on to Hoganville...and the tunnels.

Only fifteen minutes later the dark shapes of the houses came into view. She held the light close against her, pulling out Don's notes.

Circle around to the left. The boarded up stables will be the fifth building.

She snapped the light off, motioning for Paige to follow. There was no trail to lead them now, and she stepped carefully over fallen limbs. No matter how muted she tried to be, she felt as if each stride was resounding. She silently counted the buildings as they passed, then felt Paige again still her movements.

"Jesus. Now what?"

Back along the trail from where they'd come, a lone figure walked, slowly now, no longer jogging. It was Belden. She tried to make herself as small as possible as she froze in place. There were no trees large enough to hide behind, even if she'd chanced movement. He paused, looking down the trail toward Hoganville, then turning and looking back behind him. He appeared to be alone. He couldn't have made it to the school and back. The other two must have gone on to the school without him. If they went to their house, Don would be a sitting duck. But why would Belden come back?

Belden finally moved, jogging now to the nearest house, then around it. Once he hit the shadows, she could no longer see him. She listened, the sound of his footsteps disappearing as well.

She swallowed nervously, just now aware that she'd been holding her breath. She pulled Paige closer, her mouth against her ear.

"We should call Avery. Don may not be safe."

Paige nodded. "Let's get into the stables first."

She waited a few more seconds, making sure Belden was indeed gone. When there was no movement or sound, she pressed on, cringing as a twig snapped in two with her weight. She kept to the shadows, holding a tree limb out of the way for Paige. The stables were as Don had described them. The boards on the back windows were old and worn, easily pulled out. However, with Belden possibly on the lookout for them, she didn't want to take the chance of announcing their presence with creaky boards and nails.

She crouched low, feeling Paige do the same. She hurried now, along the side of the building, pausing every few feet, listening. When she got to the front corner, she leaned against the wall, the shadows hiding them. She chanced a peek around the corner, seeing no movement. She took a deep breath. It was now or never.

She used her shoulder to try to push the door open. It didn't budge. She used more force, feeling it give way, hearing a loud scraping as the door slid open.

"Shhh," Paige hissed.

CJ pulled her inside and closed the door quickly. It was black dark inside, all the windows boarded up. She waited, the sound of their breathing loud to her ears.

She turned the flashlight on, going to the back stalls where Don said the tunnel could be found.

There's hay piled up. Move the top two bales. You'll see the trap door.

"There," she said. It was as he described it. She and Paige each grabbed an end of the bale and rolled it to the floor, doing the same with the next one. There was a door cut into the wall, not much larger than a small window. She pulled the handle, the rusty hinges nearly screaming in protest as it opened. That gave credence to Don's assertion that the stables were never used. She would assume this door hadn't been opened in more than a decade.

A dank, moist smell hit them. She turned away from it, taking a deep breath. At that moment, the very last thing she wanted to do was to crawl into the tunnel.

Paige stepped back. "Let me call Avery first."

"Yeah. Okay."

CJ flashed the light into the tunnel. Spiderwebs decorated the entrance and stairs dropped down into the cold, dark earth.

"I hate spiders," she murmured.

"No answer," Paige said, holding up her phone. "I have a bad feeling."

CJ nodded. "I do too. But we can't worry about Avery right now. Hopefully he and the chief have secured everything."

"It's Don I'm worried about. We promised Fiona."

CJ looked back into the tunnel, suddenly overcome with a near desperate anxiety. Yeah, they'd promised Fiona a lot of things. She thought Howley was going to have a coronary when she'd told him of their plans. He damn near ordered them to stand down. She wasn't sure what she would have done if he had. Paige had her mind made up. Right now, Paige was in protect mode. Neither of them knew what Fiona had planned, but the look in her eyes told CJ that Fiona had no intention of giving birth. CJ had seen that hopeless, desolate look before in her own sister's eyes. Paige, however, made no mention of it. Her focus right now was getting in there and protecting Fiona from whatever horrors Ester Hogan had planned for her.

She turned to Paige then, pulling her quickly into a tight hug.

"What?"

CJ glanced at the tunnel entrance. "I feel like we're going down into hell."

"I know. I would say let's go and get it over with, but we don't really know what we're getting into."

"No. And even with the guys coming in helicopters, it's still at least another hour before we'll get some backup."

Paige took a deep breath. "Then let's do it. I'm ready to get the hell out of here."

CJ leaned forward and kissed her, then pulled her into another hug.

"Listen, in case something happens, I just want you to know that this...well, this isn't some cheap affair. You're not just a notch, as you once said."

Paige stared at her. "Now? You want to talk about this now?"

Embarrassed, CJ looked at the tunnel entrance again to avoid having to look at Paige. "No. Hell, what was I thinking?" *Yeah, what were you thinking?* She took a step forward, knocking the spider webs down with the flashlight, only to have Paige stop her progress with a hand on her arm. She turned back around, eyebrows raised.

"I don't do cheap affairs." Paige tilted her head. "You know that, right?"

In the shadows, CJ met her gaze. She finally nodded, relieved by what she saw there.

"Then let's get this over with, baby."

"And don't call me *baby*," Paige murmured behind her, and CJ recognized the smile in her voice.

CHAPTER FORTY-FIVE

Fiona grabbed her stomach, taking short, quick breaths. She almost wished she'd taken the pain pill Don had offered her, but she knew she must have her wits about her. No doubt Mother Hogan already knew something was wrong. Had Don been missed yet? If so, Fiona would be the one they turned to for answers.

Her mother met her at the door and by the look in her eyes, Fiona knew Mother Hogan had already questioned her.

"You're late."

Fiona tried to keep her voice even. "Had test papers to grade," she said, a lie she'd made up on the drive over.

"Mother Hogan was concerned. She said you were not feeling well."

Fiona swallowed. "How would she know that?"

Her mother nearly gasped. "You question her? Child, she knows all."

And you know so very little, Fiona thought. Even now, her mother had no clue as to what Fiona's fate was. Did she think Fiona would give birth? Did she have any idea of the...the *thing* she carried? Was she not worried? No. All her mother was worried about was displeasing Mother Hogan. Nothing else.

"If she knows all, then I guess she knows I'm going to the chamber. I suppose I'll see her there."

Fiona headed into the kitchen where the door was that would take her down to the tunnels. Her mother stopped her, holding her arm.

"What is wrong with you? You're acting strange."

"Strange?" Fiona pointed to her stomach. "No. *This* is strange. Yet you make no mention of it. Why?"

"It is not for us to question," her mother said simply.

Fiona drew in a sharp breath as a jolt of pain hit her. "No. Good sheep don't question, do they," she murmured. She glanced at the old grandfather clock that ticked the seconds away quietly, as it had been doing her whole life. Her gaze followed the length of the pendulum, seeing the faded, yellow cloth folded neatly at the bottom of the case, knowing nearly every house had the same clock with the same yellow cloth tucked away there. Would Paige be forced to use the trigger phrase? She glanced at her mother, wondering if that would be the best outcome for her. Death? Or most likely being locked in an asylum for her remaining years. It would be so easy to utter the phrase now, to watch her mother go into a trance, watch as she blindly fumbled with the cloth, pulling out the hard capsule that Mother Hogan had stashed in each clock.

Yellow rock in the clock. Tick. Tock. Yellow. Rock.

But in the end, Fiona couldn't say it. Her own fate might be sealed, but she couldn't be the one to send her mother to her death.

"Goodbye, Mother," she said, wincing as she held her side. "I have a date with Mother Hogan."

"She hasn't summoned you."

"No. I'm doing the summoning this time."

Again, her mother gasped. "You talk like that, you'll bring her wrath," she warned.

Fiona found the strength to laugh. "That's the plan. Now, shouldn't you be starting supper?"

Her mother nodded. "Yes. Of course. I'll do that now."

Fiona watched her for a moment, her movements slow and measured, so as not to have a misstep. No one ever wanted a misstep. She sighed, knowing she would never see her mother again. Strangely, that thought did not make her sad.

She turned, opening the door to the tunnels, glancing back once again, but her mother paid her no mind.

***

Ester paced slowly, back and forth, the opened window letting in the warm night air. It was so still, so humid, she felt perspiration dampening her skin. Fiona was back. She knew that. But something wasn't right. She couldn't *see* her, couldn't *feel* her. Not like she should. Maybe this pregnancy was disrupting her energy flow. Or maybe it was something else.

She listened, hearing footsteps on the stairs. She recognized Belden's heavy step, and she waited for him to knock.

"Yes. Enter."

He looked flushed, his skin glistening with sweat. "Mother," he greeted, his voice sounding slightly out of breath.

"Don?" she asked simply.

He shook his head. "But we'll find him. I have other news, I'm afraid."

She frowned, feeling out of sorts. News? What news could he have that she didn't already know? "Go on," she said.

"Director Avery is a phony," he said.

"A phony?"

"He is an FBI agent."

The words were like a blow to her chest, and she reached out, a claw-like grip closing on Belden's arm.

"How do you know this?"

"He tried to have Chief Aims arrest Richard. Something about the gate."

"He must be eliminated," she said quickly. "We can cull him like the others."

Yes, that was what she would do. Cull him. Make him go away. Then things could get back to normal. After all, Fiona was about to give birth. It was time to celebrate. She didn't have time to deal with the FBI.

"There's more," Belden said, his eyes shifting away from hers nervously.

"Tell me."

"The two women who befriended Fiona. They are also with the FBI."

This news did not startle her. She knew they were not who they claimed to be. It was of no consequence. "They will be culled as well. Bring them and Director Avery here. Tonight."

"That is the problem," he said. "I believe they are already here."

CHAPTER FORTY-SIX

Paige hesitated at the top of the stairs, pausing to look back over her shoulder. She didn't know what she expected to find. The door was closed and the windows were boarded up. Still, she felt like something was watching her, and she nearly shivered with it.

"Come on," CJ said urgently from down below.

Taking a deep breath, Paige took the next step down, pulling the trap door closed behind her. Even though she'd seen CJ breaking up the spiderwebs, she imagined hundreds of spiders lying in wait, ready to jump on her as she crept past.

She took CJ's offered hand, her feet finally hitting the dank earth. She held tight to CJ for a long moment, her eyes adjusting to the semi darkness.

"According to the map," CJ said, holding it under her light, "we should be safe using the flashlights until about here."

Paige followed the progress of CJ's finger, seeing an L-shaped turn that would take them to the chamber. She tried to remember Don's words about the maze of tunnels, but it was all a blur now. She just knew they needed to hurry. It seemed liked hours since they'd parted with Fiona.

"Let's go," she said. "I'm right behind you."

"Oh, sure. Now she wants me in the lead," CJ murmured.

Paige smiled, thankful for CJ's attempt to lighten the mood. She kept her own light zipped in her thigh pocket, instead following close behind CJ as they slowly crept deeper into the earth. The tunnel was small, with barely enough room for them to stand upright. The tunnel had been reinforced with boards, but the quick glimpse she had been able to take suggested they were old and rotting. She had seen horrors before in her job, but nothing could compare to what she was feeling right now. Her fear was genuine, but it wasn't something she could put her finger on. Was it just that they were going into the bowels of the earth, on guard against some creature that might or might not live there? Or was it the unknown powers that Ester Hogan might or might not possess? Was it Belden who was most likely on the hunt for them? Or was it fear for Fiona's fate? Could they save her? All those questions vied for center stage in her mind, pushing down the physical fear she had, the fear of being in the damp, dark tunnel they were attempting to traverse, the fear that it might cave in on them.

They came to a junction, and CJ stopped, pulling out the map again. Paige peered over her shoulder, trying to make sense of the drawings.

"I think we're here," CJ whispered.

"You think?"

"No. I'm pretty sure."

"Give me that," Paige said, taking the map from CJ. It was loosely drawn and obviously not to scale, but she assumed Don would only include the tunnel they needed to take. She turned a circle, trying to get her bearings, but in the dark tunnel she had no idea which direction to go. She silently handed the map back to CJ.

"I don't have a clue."

"See? That's why I'm in the lead."

"Then lead on, tiger. I'm starting to get claustrophobic."

"Yeah. Could they have made this just a little bigger?" CJ murmured as she continued on.

When they came to the sharp L-shaped turn, both stopped quickly and CJ turned off her flashlight. The darkness was cut by a faint light up ahead. Paige blinked several times, adjusting to the muted light. CJ tugged at her arm, motioning for her to follow. Their steps were slower now, careful, and Paige could hear the blood pounding in her ears. She took short, even breaths, trying to quell her nervousness.

As they neared the corner, CJ pressed tight along the wall, moving silently to peek around the edge.

"It looks like an old-fashioned torch," she whispered. "I don't see anyone. The tunnel continues."

Paige nodded, moving forward too. The tunnel appeared to be bigger now, and there was another, smaller tunnel that joined the one they'd come to. The torch was as CJ described, something you might see in an old movie. She wondered what they used for fuel. And on the heels of that thought, she wondered if they were in danger of carbon monoxide poisoning. She smiled at her thoughts, knowing that was the least of their worries right now.

"I'm starting to think this was a terrible idea," CJ said as she walked on.

"I know. But it wasn't like we had a lot of options."

CJ took out the map again, holding it up to the torch. Don had drawn in the other tunnel, so they knew they were on the right course. Only a few more turns and it would open up into what Fiona and Don had called the chamber. The actual cave was beyond that.

"Come on."

Paige nodded, following close behind CJ. Paige wondered why this part of the tunnel was lit by torches. Perhaps it was a main corridor. That thought made her glance over her shoulder, making sure they were still alone. While she didn't see anyone, she certainly felt eyes on her.

"I feel like we're being watched," she whispered, giving voice to her thoughts.

"It's probably just the spiders," CJ murmured with a quiet laugh.

The only sound thereafter was the muffled steps they took. Paige stayed close behind CJ, knowing that the next turn would take them into the open. CJ stopped, motioning Paige against the wall. She listened, hearing voices in the distance.

"Fiona?"

CJ nodded. "And Belden."

"At least we know where he is."

***

"You should not be down here," Belden said.

Fiona's breath was coming in quick, short gasps, the pain nearly unbearable now. Her face was drenched in perspiration, and she wiped a drop of sweat from the corner of her eye.

"Get her," Fiona said again. "I want to see her."

"Mother Hogan left instructions for you to wait. You should not be in the chamber without her."

Fiona shuffled closer to the altar, leaning on the edge to help support herself. She felt a wet stickiness between her legs and knew it was blood. She didn't have much time.

She turned to Belden, hoping to use his fear of Mother Hogan against him. She pointed to her belly.

"I'm about to give birth. If something happens, you'll be to blame. Do you want that?" She took a deep, excruciating breath. "You know what she'll do to you, right?"

Belden hesitated, then his eyes widened as she let out a sharp groan, the pain nearly bringing her to her knees.

"You stay here. I'll get her."

He hurried off, disappearing down the tunnel that would take him to Mother Hogan's estate. She gripped the altar, pulling herself along its length. She closed her eyes tightly, waiting for the pain to subside. When it ebbed somewhat, she stood up straighter, glancing across to the back of the chamber. The dark entrance to the main tunnel stood like a gaping mouth. Beyond it, smaller tunnels converged. Were Paige and CJ close? Had they managed their trip through the woods? Did they find the stables? Was Don's map sufficient for them to find their way? If so, she hoped they were close. She was bleeding, and she felt her strength quickly leaving her. If they wanted to take Mother Hogan at her weakest, it was now. Once it was over with, she feared they would be no match for Mother Hogan's anger.

Each step she took was agonizing, severe shooting pain hitting her core. She glanced down and even in the darkness, she could see the blood staining her Friday work slacks all the way down to her ankles. She felt a great sorrow hit her then and she nearly sobbed with it. So much time wasted. Gone forever. The little normalcy in her life took place at the school, Monday through Friday. She hadn't realized how much she treasured it. If she'd only had the strength all those years ago, she could have maybe lived an ordinary life. She and Don could have run away together. But no. Mother Hogan must have anticipated that. She had to have known that once they'd been outside they would know things. Things the others did not. They were kept separated until the very end. She closed her eyes for a second, then shook her thoughts away. There was no need to bemoan it all now. Her fate was sealed. Her only hope was that it would all end soon. Very soon.

She mustered what strength she had left, holding tight to the altar for support. She felt blindly along the cold stone facing, seeking the crevice where Mother Hogan kept her knife. Her fingers brushed the leather sheath, and she closed her hand around it, pulling it out of its hiding place. She leaned heavily against the altar, her elbows on the edge, keeping her upright.

She took quick, short breaths, feeling her eyelids getting heavy. Amazingly, she felt no more pain. Just a cold numbness that was permeating up her legs. She could feel a slow drip, and she wondered how much blood she'd lost. Her slacks felt soaked. She knew she was cramping, she could feel her insides contracting but she felt no pain.

"Fiona, child, what are you doing?"

Fiona turned her head slowly, seeing Mother Hogan coming toward her, Belden right on her heels. She slid the knife out of its sheath, holding it out so they could see it. As expected, Mother Hogan stopped up short, her eyes widening in disbelief.

"Your...your *baby* is coming," Fiona said, her voice sounding odd to her own ears. She looked away from Mother Hogan's intense gaze, trying to close her mind. She felt a nearly physical tug on the knife, but she held on tightly. Mother Hogan would not win. Oh, where were Paige and CJ? Surely they were close. She couldn't do this on her own, she knew.

"Put the knife down," Mother Hogan said, her voice nearly booming in the chamber.

Fiona shook her head, her grip steady around the smooth handle of the knife. "You have no power over me," she said, surprising herself by her valor. "I am no longer one of your little sheep."

"You do not speak to me that way, child. You must not disobey."

Fiona felt a tear trickle down her cheek and felt her resolve slipping. She feared she wouldn't be strong enough to go through with it. She clenched her teeth, warding off the sudden panic that was gripping her. Her anxiety ebbed as she felt another contraction.

"Look at me," she gasped. "Look at what you've done to me. And for what?"

"It is not for you to question."

Fiona felt the knife loosening in her hand, and she turned her focus to that, willing her fingers to hold tight to the blade. *Mother Hogan has no power over me*, she reminded herself.

"No," she said weakly. "No one ever questions you, do they? Until now."

CHAPTER FORTY-SEVEN

Paige tugged on her arm and CJ turned around, eyebrows raised.

"Do we have a plan?"

"No." She shrugged. "That's pretty much how this whole assignment has been, right?"

"Let's just try not to shoot anyone," Paige said.

"I'm more concerned with Belden. He could snap us in half with his bare hands."

"Right. He could. So you lead, tiger."

CJ silently unsnapped the holster on her thigh, hearing Paige do the same. She crouched low, moving quickly along the wall to the last corner, trying to stay in the shadows. Taking a deep breath, she moved into the large room—the chamber. There was enough light from the torches for her to make out the altar against the far wall. There was Fiona, leaning weakly against it. Ester Hogan—dressed in a dark robe—was facing her. Belden appeared to be flanking to her right. CJ motioned for Paige to go opposite her, toward Ester. CJ hugged the wall to the left, intending to intercept Belden.

It was then she saw the knife, the blade shining brightly as Fiona waved it at Ester.

"Put it down," Ester instructed Fiona in a firm voice. "I command you."

"Get away from me. You don't command me anymore."

CJ glanced at Paige, whose eyes were riveted on Fiona. Now would have been a good time to have a plan.

"Put the knife down, Fiona. *Now*."

CJ didn't think Fiona would try to take down Ester Hogan on her own, but she watched her intently, waiting for some sign to move. Did Fiona know they were there? Could she see them?

"It's too late. I won't be your pawn."

It happened so fast—the knife flashing in the torchlight. Her heart lurched in disbelief as Fiona plunged the blade into her own belly, a terrible mewing sound leaving her lips as she pulled the knife out, only to plunge it in again.

"No!" Paige yelled, running forward. "Fiona...*no!*"

Ester Hogan whipped her head around, her eyes nearly bulging out of her skull. She pointed at them, shrieking loudly.

"*Outsiders! Outsiders! Outsiders! Outsiders! Outsiders!*"

"Oh, fuck."

Before she could take another step, Belden was upon her, one large hand wrapped around her throat choking her as he lifted her off the ground, pressing her back firmly against the wall. She kicked at him, trying desperately to draw breath. She couldn't see Paige, didn't know what was happening. All she heard was Ester Hogan's screeching voice. She brought a knee up, catching Belden under the chin. His grip loosened enough for her to draw in a deep breath. She blinked her eyes, trying to remember the phrase Fiona taught her.

Yellow sock? Yellow rock? Yellow clock? What the hell was it? Yellow fucking...what?

She kicked at him again, catching him in his groin. His hands fell away from her as he doubled over in pain.

***

Paige ran blindly to Fiona, pushing Ester Hogan out of the way with a fierce blow. Fiona lay motionless on the cold ground, blood gushing from her wounds. She blinked slowly, her eyes finding Paige.

"Oh, God, Fiona."

"Don't look at her," Fiona whispered. "Close yourself to her power."

"Don't move. I'll—"

But her words were cut off as she was flung against the far wall. She hit it solidly, the impact nearly knocking the breath from her. She shook her head, finding Ester Hogan's gaze locked on her. Ester had never laid a hand on her, yet she'd been picked up like a ragdoll. She pulled her eyes away from the stare, then dropped to her knees as she felt a vise-like grip around her throat. She stared in utter disbelief. Ester Hogan was at least twenty feet away from her, yet she felt her cold, bony fingers around her neck.

Paige's vision swam as her breath was cut off. She felt along her thigh, finding her weapon still secured in its holster.

***

"Yellow sock," CJ said as she danced around Belden's furious attempt to capture her. "Yellow clock." She ignored a blow to her shoulder, a grin on her face. "Yellow *rock*," she said. *Yeah, that's it.* "Yellow rock in the sock."

Belden stopped, his head tilted, as if searching his memory for some long forgotten riddle. But he shook it off, one long arm grabbing her again and slamming her against the wall.

"Goddamn," she hissed as she felt her ribcage nearly shatter. "Clock. Not sock," she murmured. She met his eyes, seeing a man totally devoid of emotion looking back at her. His hand tightened dangerously around her neck. "Yellow rock in the clock," she choked out, her voice raspy from his grip. Amazingly, Belden's eyes seemed to roll back in his head. "Yeah, that's it. Yellow rock in the clock," she said again. "Tick tock."

"Yellow rock."

"Yeah. Say it with me," she said as his grip loosened. "Yellow rock in the clock. Tick tock. Yellow rock."

"Yellow rock in the clock."

She rubbed her throat when he released her, his eyes glazed over. "Yellow rock."

"In the clock. Tick tock. Yellow rock."

He turned abruptly, his feet moving in a measured cadence, marching back into the mouth of the dark tunnel and disappearing, his mumbled voice chanting the phrase over and over.

She jumped at the sound, then dropped to her knees as a single gunshot echoed over and over again in the closed chamber. She whipped her head around, finding Paige bent over, gasping for breath. Ester Hogan lay motionless on the ground.

CHAPTER FORTY-EIGHT

Paige knelt beside Fiona. Her eyes were closed, but her mouth was open, drawing in shallow breaths. She glanced at CJ, who was standing over the lifeless body of Mother Hogan.

"I thought we weren't supposed to shoot anybody."

"I had no choice."

She touched Fiona's face, seeing her eyelids flutter. She didn't know what to do. The knife was still inside her, buried up to its handle.

"Oh, Fiona. Why?"

"The only way," she whispered.

Paige took her hand, squeezing tightly. "You hang in there. We'll get you to a hospital."

"No. Too late."

"Not too late."

"Paige...thank you, my friend. You were the best thing to ever happen to me."

"No. You stay with me," Paige said instantly, cutting her off. "We'll get you out of here. You and Don both."

"That was always my dream," Fiona said, her voice weak. "To escape." Paige felt Fiona's fingers tighten around her own. "Don't run from CJ," she whispered. "Trust her. The awful things her father did to her...it makes her wary of others. But she wants to love you. Let her."

Paige stared at her in disbelief. "How did you know about her father?"

Fiona's grip loosened and fell away, but her eyes held tight to Paige's. Paige watched as Fiona's hand found the knife, then, in one last gesture, jerked the knife out. Blood gushed, but Fiona never made a sound. She simply lay still, her hand—and the knife—falling futilely to the ground.

Paige stared at her, seeing Fiona's last breath leave her, seeing the life fade from her eyes. Just like that. Gone. By her own hands.

"Paige?"

She felt CJ's touch on her shoulder, and she turned toward it, letting CJ pull her up. She clung to her, burying her face in her shoulder. She felt her heart breaking, yet no tears would come. The scene was surreal. Fiona lying in a pool of her own blood, by her own making. Ester Hogan lying not twenty feet away, a bullet to her heart ending her life without ceremony. Surreal.

"Belden?"

"I did the yellow sock thing. He went into a trance, just like they said he would."

Paige frowned. "Yellow *sock*?"

"Sock, rock, clock. Whatever." CJ held her at arm's length. "Are you okay?" She turned her to the torch, inspecting her neck. "You're bruised."

Paige touched her tender neck. "She never laid a hand on me. I was flung against the wall. And she was choking me. But she never touched me."

"I guess Fiona was right about her powers."

Paige glanced back down at Fiona, slowly shaking her head.

"Why? Why did she do that? We could have helped her."

"Could we?" CJ shrugged. "Maybe. But it could have all just been too much for her. Even if she survived giving birth, then what? She becomes a sideshow in a circus?"

"I don't know. But this just seems—"

Her words were cut off by a hideous roar from back in the cave. She and CJ locked gazes, both of their eyes widening.

"Oh fuck," CJ murmured, pulling Paige with her. "We need to get out of here. *Now!*"

The roar was followed by a high-pitched scream, similar to the ones they'd heard at night. When he was hunting. She ran after CJ, both ducking into the first tunnel they came to. They stopped up short, hiding in the dark shadows. She clutched CJ's arms, peeking around her, her view of the chamber slightly obstructed. She saw his silhouette first, the light from the torch surely distorting his shape. But no. The creature stood on its hind legs, easily ten feet tall.

"Dear God, what *is* it?" she whispered as she shrank back against the wall.

"Hell if I know."

His head was scaly and lizard-like, and he swung his gaze around the chamber, landing first on Ester Hogan, then on Fiona. He let out an awful roar, a pitiful sound full of distress and—dare she say—pain and mourning. Her hand dug into CJ's arm as the creature bent down and scooped Fiona up, her arms swinging lifelessly at her sides. Paige wanted to turn away from the sight but didn't. With another tormented wail, he shuffled off, back into the cave, taking Fiona—and his baby—with him.

"I can't believe I just saw that," CJ said quietly.

"What should we do?"

"We sure as hell aren't going after it."

"But—"

"No way." CJ fumbled for her flashlight, going deeper into the tunnel. "Come on."

"Do we know where we are?"

"Look at this," CJ said, shining the light along the walls.

Whereas the other tunnel they'd come through was haphazardly constructed, this tunnel was reinforced with shiny, varnished wood. Carved into the wood were strange symbols, none of which she'd ever seen before.

"Where do you think this leads?" Paige asked.

"I'm going to guess to Ester's house."

Paige followed, glancing behind them to make sure they weren't being followed. She wondered how they were going to explain everything that had happened. No one was going to believe them. Like CJ, she couldn't quite fathom what she had seen either.

They stopped at the bottom of a short staircase. These stairs too were much nicer than the ones in the stables. Handrails on both sides and again varnished wood. The steps creaked under their weight as they climbed to the top. CJ turned the doorknob slowly. It was unlocked.

Paige took her flashlight out too. The room appeared to have once been a den or living room, although it was sparsely furnished. CJ flashed her light around the room, landing on an open door. Paige followed her, standing in the doorway as CJ went inside. It was an old study. Even in the limited light Paige could see how worn the furniture was. She moved her flashlight to the window, the drapes so faded she couldn't make out their original color. The window was open, letting in what little breeze there was. It was only then that Paige realized how hot and stuffy it was. She wiped at the perspiration on her brow.

"Try the light," CJ said, motioning to the switch on the wall. Paige did, but the room remained dark. "Off the grid," CJ murmured.

"Maybe she only runs a generator when she needs it."

"Probably."

CJ's light moved across the room, landing on a door in the back corner. She opened it, revealing another flight of stairs. This one going up, not down. CJ looked back at her with raised eyebrows. Paige nodded.

It was a narrow staircase and they walked up single file. She wondered if this was a shortcut to Ester's bedroom. CJ opened the door cautiously, pausing to listen but all remained quiet. The door opened into a hallway and the staircase appeared to only be a shorter route to the second floor. There were four doors, two on each side, but it was the fifth door against the opposite end that appeared unusual. The door trim was at least a foot wide, carved with the same symbols that they'd seen in the tunnel.

"Let's check these rooms first," CJ said.

The first was completely empty, including the absence of drapes. A huge spiderweb crossed the window, evidence of the room's non use. CJ went to the next one and Paige crossed the hallway, opening a door on that side. She was expecting another empty room and nearly gasped at what she saw when her flashlight scanned inside. It was a child's room, the furniture small and nondescript. On the bed lay the skeletal remains of a young child, dressed only in a white shirt and shorts.

"CJ," she said. "In here."

CJ peered over her shoulder, then gently moved her aside as she went into the room. Paige hesitated, flashing her light back into the hallway. She couldn't shake the feeling that they weren't alone.

"I would guess maybe six or eight years old," CJ said.

"You think it was Ester's child?"

"I don't know. I can't imagine her as a mother. Can you?"

Paige tilted her head, hearing a welcome sound in the distance. Helicopters. "Listen," she said.

CJ looked up, smiling. "Backup. About damn time."

"Let's check the other rooms," Paige said. "I'm ready to get the hell out of here."

The other two rooms in the hallway were both empty, like the first. There was no sign of Ester's bedroom, leading them to think the decorated door at the end of the hall was hers. Paige stood back, nodding as CJ turned the knob. The door swung open and a rank smell hit them immediately. They both went inside, their lights casting shadows in the room. It was large, much larger than a bedroom. Lined up in a neat row, eight evenly spaced beds dominated the room.

"Jesus," CJ murmured as she walked deeper into the room.

Paige shone her light on each bed, hardly believing what she saw. All eight beds appeared to be hand-carved. The woodworking was exquisite. However, only one bed was empty.

"What the hell is this?"

CJ went to the end, her light shining on the names carved into each bed. "Estaline, Naomi, Opal, Velma, Eustice, Estelle, Rosaline...and Ester."

"Fiona said that things here had always been this way," Paige said. "Do you think these are the reigning Hogans?"

"And when they die, they bring them here? God, can you imagine living in this house with these...these women up here?"

"They're dressed in some sort of ceremonial gowns," Paige noted as her gaze traveled across each skeleton. "If I didn't know better, it looks almost like a wedding gown."

CJ looked up to the ceiling; the helicopters seemed to be right upon them now. "Okay, let's get the hell out of here."

"Where do you think Ester's bedroom is?"

"I imagine downstairs somewhere. Come on." Just then CJ's phone rang, Ice's familiar tone sounding in the quiet room. "Hey, baldy. About time."

***

"Where the hell are you?" Ice asked.

CJ followed Paige back down the stairs. "We're in Ester Hogan's house. The two-story one."

"Yeah. I see it. It's goddamn dark out here," he said.

"They're off the grid, remember? How many agents?"

"Six of us. Howley included."

"Okay. There are about forty residents, we think. Ester Hogan has been eliminated. She's got a bodyguard. Huge guy. Belden. Be careful of him. The rest I don't believe will pose a problem."

"We're checking the houses now."

"We'll be out in a second," she said, disconnecting. She stopped Paige before they went out into the study again. "Hey."

Paige turned around, looking at her questioningly. She seemed to understand CJ's hesitation and killed her light. They embraced tightly, and CJ closed her eyes, feeling her insecurities surfacing again. They'd weathered the tunnel, Belden, Ester

Hogan and even the creature that lived in the cave. But now they had to face Ice, Billy and Howley. They'd changed. They'd both changed. Ice and Billy would notice immediately.

"We can do this," Paige said. "We've played this game a long time."

"They're going to know."

"They may *think* they know. But they won't really know." Paige cupped her face tenderly, her thumb caressing her chin. "We have a lot to talk about, CJ, but now is not the time."

CJ nodded. *God, she's going to break my heart*, she thought. But she smiled good-naturedly. "Okay. Let's get out of here."

Through the study and out into the main room, they found the front door. The hinges protested as it was opened and she assumed Ester rarely—if ever—used the door. One thing she found odd was that nothing was locked. You'd think that as much as they liked to keep themselves isolated, they'd have everything locked up tight.

The air outside was only slightly cooler than inside the stagnant house, but only slightly. She took her cap off, running her hands through her damp hair before putting it back on again.

"Lights over there," Paige said, pointing to the house next door. They were intercepted by Howley before they could get inside.

"What the fuck happened here?" he demanded.

CJ stared at him. "Yeah, we're okay. A little beaten and bruised, but okay," she said sarcastically. "Thanks for asking."

He ignored her, turning to Paige instead. "They're dead."

"They who?"

"Whoever the hell lives here. Dead. I specifically said—"

"Not to shoot anyone," CJ finished. "Ester Hogan was a casualty. It couldn't be avoided. The others, I don't know what you're talking about."

"We haven't encountered anyone other than Ester and Belden," Paige said.

"Who is Belden?"

"He's like her bodyguard," CJ said.

"Two more bodies in this house," Ice yelled.

"Jesus. It's Jim Jones all over again," Howley muttered as he headed in Ice's direction.

CJ and Paige followed. It was an older man and woman, both slumped against the wall. CJ stared at the yellow cloth held tightly in the man's hand. She turned a circle, her light scanning the room, landing on an old grandfather clock, the pendulum stopped.

"Holy shit," she whispered.

"What is it?"

"The clock." She turned to Howley. "Show me another house."

The one next door was the same. Two men. One on the floor, the other slumped on the sofa. Again, a grandfather clock, this one still ticking the time away. CJ turned to Paige.

"The phrase Fiona told us to use. The one that sent Belden into a trance. *Yellow rock in the clock.*"

"It was a suicide trigger," Paige said. "But Belden was the only one who heard it."

"He was saying it over and over again as he left. That must have been part of it. To alert the others. They passed it on."

"Okay, what the hell are you talking about?" Ice asked.

"It was this phrase—"

"Oh my God, CJ. We forgot about Don," Paige said. "And Avery."

"Yeah, where is Avery?" Howley asked. "I can't reach him."

"Us either. He and Chief Aims were going to detain Richard Barr, the guard identified from the gate logs," she said. "We left him at the school. Don was left at our place."

"We've got to go," Paige said, tugging on CJ's arm.

"We don't have a car. And I'm not going back through the woods."

"We'll take Fiona's car," Paige said, looking around. "That is, if we can find it."

Howley held his hands up. "You two, hang on. I need to know what the hell's going on here."

"There are tunnels under the houses that lead to an underground chamber," CJ said.

"A cave," Paige added. "That's where we've been. That's where you'll find Ester Hogan's body. I shot her."

"Unless he came back and took her," CJ said quietly.

"Oh. Yeah. That's a possibility."

"He who?" Howley asked.

Paige and CJ looked at each other. "You want to take this one?" Paige asked.

"Not right now, no. We need to get to the school." She turned to Howley. "With your permission, of course. We need to find Avery and Don."

"I knew not to let you go in by yourselves," he said. "I knew something like this would happen." He let out a frustrated breath. "Okay. Take Ice and Billy. And don't do anything stupid."

CJ paused. "Speaking of that...don't go into the tunnels. It's a maze. And whatever you do, *don't* go into the cave."

CHAPTER FORTY-NINE

The guard shack was lit up but unoccupied. Avery's car was still parked on the side next to Richard's.

"They must be in the chief's car," CJ said as she drove slowly past.

"I got a bad feeling," Paige said. She glanced in the backseat where Ice and Billy sat quietly. "How was the flight?"

"Fast," Billy said.

"So what is it you're not telling Howley?" Ice asked.

She glanced at CJ, then back to Ice. "Something lives in the cave. We've heard it at night a few times. A primal scream. I can't really describe it. We saw it tonight."

Billy leaned closer. "What is it?"

"We don't know," CJ said. "Some...creature."

"You making this shit up?" Ice asked.

Paige grinned. "I wish. So, you miss us?"

"Yeah, we missed you. You miss us?"

"Of course. This one," she said, pointing at CJ, "is no picnic to live with."

"Like you are," CJ chimed in. "You wouldn't believe all the rules she has," she said, looking in the rearview mirror at Ice. "But she's a pretty good cook."

Paige looked at her affectionately, then caught herself, rolling her eyes dramatically for effect. "Then why did you constantly complain about my cooking?"

"Because you're trying to turn me into a vegetarian."

"You?" Ice laughed. "She eats steak twice a week," he said.

Paige glanced back at Ice. "She's into soy now."

"Soy my ass," CJ mumbled. "Where to? Avery's place or ours?"

"Ours. If they were looking for Don, that's the logical place."

"Who is *they*?" Billy asked.

"We have to assume Chief Aims and Richard."

"Don't forget the two robes we saw in the woods with Belden," Paige reminded her.

"That's right. So possibly four men," CJ said.

"What two robes?" Ice asked.

"Two men in black robes," CJ explained. "We saw them on the trail heading to the school. Spooky stuff."

"What were you doing in the woods?" Billy asked.

"Trying to get to the tunnels," Paige said. "It's too much to explain now." She turned to CJ. "I think you should kill the lights. We probably need to approach on foot."

"Yeah. I agree."

CJ pulled the car to the side of the road and stopped. Paige turned in her seat, addressing the guys. "The houses are fairly close together, but staggered. We're the first house on the road. Fiona was across from us."

"What happened to her?"

"She...she died."

"She killed herself," CJ said. "She set Ester Hogan up for us."

"It's a long story," Paige added as she opened her door.

"Yeah. And when we get back to Houston, I'm thinking beers at the bar while you tell us this long story," Ice said as he too got out.

They walked single file on the side of the road. The moon was still high, giving them enough light to see by. Paige let the guys go in front of her as she brought up the rear. She nearly jumped out of her skin when she heard a twig break in the woods not far from them. She jerked her head around, scanning through the trees and seeing nothing.

"What is it?" Billy asked.

"I thought I heard something," she whispered.

CJ stopped and looked back at her. "Okay?"

Paige nodded, although she kept a wary eye on the woods. CJ led them around the back of their little house, past the bedroom window. She ducked below the glass, the others doing the same. It appeared dark and empty. They'd left Don inside with instructions to wait for them.

CJ held up her hand, motioning for them to stop. She turned the knob on the kitchen door, finding it locked. She looked over at Paige with raised eyebrows. No, Paige hadn't locked it. Like the others, they'd gotten in the habit of not locking their doors.

"I don't suppose we have a key," CJ whispered.

"Why don't you have a key to your own house?" Billy asked.

"We don't lock the doors," CJ said as she moved to the kitchen window, cupping her face next to the glass and peering inside. She took her flashlight, shining it through the window. "Shit. Kick the door in," she said quickly.

With one blow of Ice's foot, the flimsy lock gave way. She and CJ went in first, their lights landing on the prone figure lying on the floor.

"Oh God," she murmured.

CJ turned him over. It wasn't Don. It was Avery. His hands were cuffed behind his back. A single bullet to his forehead had blown off the back of his head.

"Jesus," Billy whispered. "Who is it?"

"Avery."

"They've got Don," CJ said. "Apparently both Chief Aims and Richard were loyal to Belden."

"But why?" Paige asked. "What was in it for them? I can't see money exchanging hands."

"Maybe fear," CJ said.

"Or threats," Paige added.

"Okay, I don't know what you guys are talking about, but what's the plan? We need to call Howley. We have an agent down," Ice reminded them.

"Chief Aims is armed. Richard was a guard, he wasn't issued a weapon. The two guys from Hoganville, the two in the robes, we need to assume they are involved as well," CJ said.

"What's with the robes anyway?" Billy asked.

"Remember the story you found about the sheep guy? The men were in robes."

"So are they a cult or what?"

Paige and CJ exchanged glances. "I think if you're going by the mass suicide we just witnessed—Jim Jones style—then yes. But I don't think that was the original intention," she said.

"We'll probably never know for sure." CJ walked to the front door, about to turn the light on when she stopped. "A lot of blood. He was shot here."

"Yeah. So?"

"So Suzette and Becca would have heard the shot," Paige said, completing CJ's thought.

"Call Howley. Let him know what's going on," CJ said to Ice.

"Yeah. It would help if *I* knew what was going on though."

"We're just going to check next door," Paige said. She looked at Billy. "Stay here."

She and CJ went back out through the kitchen door. There were no lights on next door but the next house—where Val and Ella lived—was lit up.

"I don't suppose we care about our cover being blown," CJ said. "Seeing as how we're dressed and all."

"You think the thigh holsters might give us away?" Paige asked with a smile.

They stopped at the back of their house, peeking in through the windows. There was no movement or sound.

"Kinda early to be in bed," CJ said. "You think?"

"I don't know their habits, but yes, I think so. Besides, surely everyone here at the school heard the helicopters land. You'd think they'd be out looking to see what's going on."

"I agree. Let's check next door. Maybe Suzette and Becca went there if they heard a gunshot."

"Do you think maybe Chief Aims and Richard just left the compound?"

"You mean after they killed Avery, they spooked?"

Paige shrugged. "Maybe. But would they have taken Don?"

CJ shook her head. "Regardless, I don't think this is going to end well."

"It already hasn't. Fiona is dead," she reminded her.

"Yeah. I'm sorry. I know you haven't—"

"What? Processed it all? You're right. I haven't." Paige took her cap off and shook out her hair. "This assignment has sucked, hasn't it?"

"Well, it hasn't *all* been bad," CJ said. "Come on."

They kept to the edge of the woods, hidden in the shadows. The blinds were down on all the windows. A peculiarity, to be sure. She and CJ had rarely closed their blinds, taking a cue from their neighbors. To find Valerie and Ella's house shuttered was a surprise.

CJ pulled her deeper into the woods. "Call Billy. Tell him and Ice to get over here. I'm going around to the kitchen. See if I can hear anything. Or maybe see inside."

Paige nodded as she pulled out her phone.

***

CJ moved closer, glad the moon had finally sunk lower in the sky. The pines were blocking out some of its light, making the shadows longer and easier for her to hide in. She listened, hearing a male voice. It sounded like Aims, but she couldn't be certain. She crept closer, her movements slow and measured, her eyes locked on the kitchen window. The mini blinds were pulled down past the windowsill, but she could see along the edges.

She hugged the outside wall now, holding her face against the window.

Son of a bitch.

She could see Suzette and Becca sitting on the floor against the wall. Both of their hands were tied, their eyes wide with fright. There was a body lying on the floor, but she couldn't identify it.

"Belden should be back by now."

"Shut up," Aims said.

"You heard the helicopters, man. We need to get out of here."

"And go where? Run into the woods like those other two idiots? No thank you. We stay here. We have hostages. It's our best bet."

"Yeah, well not if you keep killing them."

CJ turned away from the window, retracing her steps into the woods. Ice and Billy were there, standing beside Paige.

"Two men inside. Chief Aims and Richard Barr. It's a hostage situation. There appears to be at least one casualty."

"Who?" Paige asked.

"I couldn't tell," she said. "Suzette and Becca were accounted for. Their hands were tied. They were on the floor."

"Don?"

"No sign of him."

"What about the two others? The robes?" Ice asked.

"From what I heard, they went back to Hoganville." She looked at Paige. "Through the woods."

"Okay. What's the plan?"

"We haven't had a plan yet. Why start now?"

"Howley said to wait," Ice said.

"Wait on what? Is he going to call in a SWAT team? Or get some fancy hostage negotiator to fly out here? We're in the middle of goddamn nowhere," she reminded them.

"What do you want to do?" Paige asked.

"There are just the two. We can assume they're both armed now. Aims is in charge. Richard wants to leave. Aims is the one throwing the hostage word around. There are four of us. Highly trained," she said with a grin. "Surely we can take them."

"At what risk to the hostages?" Billy asked.

"One of us needs to get inside," Paige said. "Pretend we don't know they're there. Go on the pretense of looking for Suzette and Becca."

"We have to assume that Aims knows about us," CJ said. "Besides, you're not exactly dressed like a teacher right now."

"No, I like the idea," Ice said. "It beats yours."

"You don't even know mine," she said.

"That's because you don't have one."

CJ looked at Paige. "How will it help us if you're inside?"

"Let's use it as a distraction," she said. "I'll go in the front door. They'll want to grab me, frisk me. Ice just kicked our own back door in so we know how well the locks work. You come in through the kitchen."

CJ shook her head. "It's risky. They'll be confused. They'll start shooting."

"Well, like you said, it's only two of them."

CHAPTER FIFTY

Paige reached down where her thigh holster had been, missing the security of it. They'd debated on whether she should leave it on or not. In the end, they decided it was one less gun for Aims to get his hands on. She took a deep breath, then knocked several times in quick succession.

"Val? Ella? Are you there?" she asked loudly. "Suzette and Becca aren't at home." She knocked again before the door was flung open.

Chief Aims looked back at her, his weapon pointed at her face. She hoped she appeared sufficiently surprised.

"Chief Aims? What are you doing?"

"Get inside," he said, slamming the door behind her. "Where's your partner?"

"She's next door. Avery's been shot," she said, glancing around, seeing the frightened eyes of Suzette and Becca. Valerie was in the corner, sobbing quietly. Ella was lying on the floor, blood pooling around her.

"I know who you are. Shut up," he said, pushing her forcibly into the room.

Richard grabbed her, holding her tightly. She bit her lip, wanting nothing more than to disable him with a kick to the groin and a sharp blow to his neck. Instead, she played the game, waiting for the back door to be kicked in.

"Frisk her."

"My pleasure," Richard said.

She stood still as Richard's hands roamed her body, under her breasts and between her legs. She locked gazes with Suzette, seeing confusion in her eyes.

"She's unarmed."

"On the floor with the others," he said, motioning with his gun.

"What are you doing?" she asked.

"What do you think? Now shut up."

"Where's Don?" she asked.

Aims laughed. "The doc? Oh hell, they took him back. Mother Hogan doesn't take kindly to disobedience."

"No? Well, Ester Hogan is dead," she said, seeing the surprise in his eyes.

"Dead? You don't know what you're talking about."

"I shot her. Belden's dead too. They're all dead. Mass suicide."

"I said to shut up," he yelled.

"It's true. You're all alone."

Finally, the kitchen door burst open with a loud crash. A quick, fierce leg whip knocked Richard off his feet. She rolled to the side as gunfire sounded. Chief Aims dropped like a rock to the floor. Just like that, it was over. Richard lay flat, hands locked behind his head, mumbling incoherently as Billy roughly cuffed him.

CJ knelt down beside Ella, checking for a pulse. She shook her head at Paige's silent question.

Paige went to Suzette and Becca, fumbling with the ropes. "Are you okay?"

"Who are you?" Suzette asked.

"FBI," she said, averting her eyes. Now was not the time for questions. "Val? Are you okay?"

Valerie shook her head, lifting her gaze to look at Ella, then dropping her head again, fresh sobs coming.

"What happened?" CJ asked.

"We heard a gunshot," Becca said as she rubbed her wrists. "Coming from your place. Suzette ran over, found Chief Aims standing over Director Avery. They took us over here." She looked at Ella, tears running down her face. "He just shot her. No reason. He just shot her." She turned her tears to Paige. "What's going on?"

"This was an FBI investigation. Avery was an agent too."

"Investigation of what?"

"Hoganville."

"But why?"

"We can't go into details," CJ said. "There's going to be a lot of agents around. There's a lot to tie up. Can you take Val back to your place?"

"Is it safe?" Suzette asked.

"Yes. It's safe now."

"Wait," Paige said. "The other two men...in robes. Where did they go?"

"They took the guy who was at your place. They just left."

"Was he okay?"

"No. He was...he was crying. He was begging them to let him go. Who were they? They were all creepy like in those robes."

"Yeah. They were from Hoganville," Paige said.

Becca picked Valerie up, holding her as they walked out of the house. Suzette turned, glancing back at her.

"Fiona? Is she okay?"

Paige shook her head. "No. No, she's gone."

***

"Here. You talk to him," Ice said, handing the phone to CJ. "He's chewed my ass enough."

CJ rubbed her eyes. "God, this has been a long day." She took the phone, holding it to her ear with a heavy sigh. "Howley?"

"Since when do you no longer have to follow orders?"

"I made a decision in the field. I thought we could still do that," she said.

"Do you know how many goddamn bodies we have over here?"

"Yeah, well, we have three over here. And one missing. There's a trail between here and Hoganville. That's where they took Don. If they made it that far, then they're in the tunnels."

"We haven't found any tunnels. We're still searching house-to-house," he said.

"Who have you called in?"

"Locals. The teams from Dallas and Baton Rouge are on the way too. And I've got three forensic teams coming. After all that, it's just a matter of time before we have hordes of media."

"Yeah, well, that's why you get paid the big bucks." She glanced at Paige across the room. "We're taking the trail through the woods. See if we can find Don. It's a quick, thirty-minute hike." She disconnected before he could say more, tossing the phone back to Ice. "Which of you two girlie boys want to go with us?"

***

"Will you kill your goddamn light, Ice?" CJ whispered.

"Hell, it's spooky out here. You can't see shit."

Paige admitted it was quite a bit darker than when they'd make this trip hours earlier. But having seen all they had this night, it didn't seem quite as spooky to her.

"You do understand we don't want to call attention to ourselves," she said quietly. "And it's not the men we're worried about."

"Yeah, it's the big monster in the woods," he said with a laugh. "You guys really believe that?"

The words had barely left his mouth when a tremendous roar sounded, followed by the primal scream they were used to. She and CJ both looked around them, searching for movement. Ice froze in place.

"What...the fuck...was *that*?"

"Yeah, just that big monster in the woods, baldy. No big deal."

"I'm serious," he said.

"So am I," CJ said. "Come on."

"Are you out of your mind?"

Again, the scream sounded, nearly shaking the trees around them. He was hunting. Had he made a kill? It was then they heard another scream, this one quieter. This one human. She and CJ took off running along the trail, hearing Ice follow close behind.

They came upon the body so quickly, CJ literally stumbled across it, landing in a heap beneath a tree. The robe had been stripped off, his stomach and torso ripped open. CJ jumped to her feet, moving them all off of the trail.

"He's not here. This is too close," she said.

"What are you talking about?" Ice asked.

"The scream we just heard," Paige explained. "This wasn't it."

Ice flashed his light along the body, his breath hissing out at the sight of the man's guts spilled on the ground.

"What the hell did this?"

"I told you," CJ said, "The big monster. And he's pissed."

"I can't believe this," Paige said. "We promised Fiona. We promised Don. For what? We haven't protected either of them."

"We've done the best we can," CJ said. "We couldn't have known about Aims. We couldn't have known these two robes would have come looking for him."

"So, we're going back, right?" Ice said, looking over his shoulder. "I vote we go back."

"Not back," CJ said. "Not until we find Don."

CJ headed down the trail and Paige took Ice's arm, squeezing it tightly. "I'm scared too," she whispered. "But turn your light off."

"What kind of shit did you two get mixed up in?"

"It's just a big blur right about now," she said.

They hadn't walked five minutes before another scream was heard, this one solely human. It was cut off with finality, followed by a loud, piercing scream that echoed through the forest.

"We're close," CJ whispered.

"We're getting close to Hoganville too," Paige said.

"This is some crazy shit," Ice murmured.

Paige grasped CJ's arm as the ground literally shook beneath them, the sound of running and tree limbs snapping all around them.

CJ pulled them off the trail, taking shelter on a slope amongst the roots of a giant tree. The woods seemed alive with sounds, night animals scurrying about while those slumbering were crudely awakened, birds taking flight into the dark skies.

"Oh my God," Ice whispered. "Look at that," he said, pointing to the base of the tree.

Neither CJ nor Paige was surprised. Paige suspected this trail was littered with human skulls. She held her breath; the running was closer now. She made out a shape along the trail, coming toward them.

CJ jumped out from behind the tree, grabbing him. He tried to scream, but she covered his mouth tightly.

"It's us," CJ said.

Don's eyes widened, then relaxed in relief. He fell against her, then went to Paige. She held him tightly, bringing him closer to the tree.

"Are you okay?"

"It's coming. It's chasing me," he gasped. "We need to get out of here."

"I second that," Ice said.

"We can't outrun him," CJ said. "We've got to hide. Everyone, stay still."

The sound of running and limbs breaking peaked, and Paige felt herself shiver with fear. Then the sound faded, going past them.

"Where to?" Paige asked.

"How far are we from the stables?"

Don shook his head. "Ten minutes. But he's too close. I don't think we'd make it."

"Well, we won't make it back to the school," CJ said. "No lights. We go slow." She looked at Ice. "Hell, we have guns. Surely we can take him, right?"

"Who are you?" Don asked, looking at Ice.

"He's with us," Paige said.

"The helicopters?"

"Yes."

"Fiona?"

Paige squeezed his hand and shook her head. "I'm sorry. She didn't make it."

"So she went through with it then? She found the knife?"

"You knew?"

"Yes. She wasn't going to survive giving birth. You must have known that."

"Can we talk about this later?" CJ asked. "Let's go."

Paige again took the rear. She wasn't afraid any longer. Safety in numbers, perhaps, but she didn't fear being snatched up from behind. That, of course, didn't prevent her from constantly glancing over her shoulder. The moon was no longer a factor, having sunk well below the tree line. That fact also led her to wonder if they were even still on the trail.

Don stopped suddenly, his head tilted. "He's close," he whispered.

CJ stopped and turned around slowly. "What should we do?"

"Don't move."

Paige reached out, grasping Don's hand. He squeezed hers tightly, his eyes scanning the forest. She did the same. She could literally hear each breath they each took, could feel the nervousness among them. Through the trees she saw him, running on all fours. She tightened her grip on Don's hand, her eyes following his progress. He stopped suddenly, standing up on his hind legs, his head lifting up, as if sniffing the air. She hardly dared to take a breath, so afraid he'd hear.

They all appeared to be of the same mind, each standing as statues, barely breathing. Her eyes found CJ's, holding them as her heart pounded nervously in her chest. The creature moved again, passing by them, dodging trees as he again ran through the forest. Don was the first to break the silence.

"We should run now," he said, his voice still quiet. "He'll be back."

"Let's go."

CJ again took the lead, using her flashlight to find the trail. They ran fast, jumping over limbs, their feet pounding the ground, not bothering to remain quiet. Paige stumbled, only to have Don grab her and pull her upright.

"Go ahead of me," he said, pushing her.

She ran, following Ice, then nearly stumbled again as the loud, thundering roar sounded behind them.

"Run!" Don shouted, pushing her. "*Run!*"

They were close enough to see the houses of Hoganville, yet they were so far away. She ran blindly, following Ice and CJ, hoping Don was behind her. She could hear the creature gaining ground, could feel the vibrations as they ran. She expected at any moment to feel him grab her from behind.

"This way," CJ shouted, ducking off the trail and heading to the stables.

Another angry roar sounded behind them, and Paige imagined she could feel his breath on her neck. She ran faster, nearly pushing Ice along, thankful to see the dark silhouette of the stables below them. CJ dropped down, stumbling on the hill, nearly rolling the last few feet. Ice grabbed her and picked her up in one motion. Paige turned behind her, seeing Don running with eyes wide with fright. Behind him, she glimpsed the creature, running again on all fours, trying to catch them. Paige turned, grasping Don's hand.

"Over here," CJ yelled, rounding the corner of the stables.

The door opened easily and they all fell inside. But he was behind them, a giant claw-like hand reaching inside. Ice and CJ pushed the door shut, trapping the claw against the side.

"To the tunnels," CJ yelled. "*Now!*"

Paige and Don ran to the back wall, pulling open the trap door. Paige turned, seeing the door being forced open, Ice and CJ unable to hold it.

"Come on. Let's go," she yelled.

She nearly pushed Don down the stairs, waiting as Ice and CJ let the door go, running frantically to her. She jumped blindly down the rickety steps, out of the way as CJ and Ice followed. A maddening scream was heard behind them and the door to the tunnel was ripped from its hinges and tossed aside with ease.

They stumbled in the dark down the tunnel until they realized they weren't being followed. Paige pulled out her flashlight. CJ and Ice did the same.

"He can't fit," CJ said. "The tunnel is too small."

Ice let out a nervous laugh. "Okay. What the *fuck* was that?"

Paige sunk down against the wall, letting out a relieved breath. She felt Don do the same beside her.

"He only has one entry into the cave," Don said quietly. "At least, that's what we think. No one knows where it is though."

Paige felt CJ sit down beside her and she leaned against her, relaxing, not caring that Ice was watching.

"This has been the longest damn day of my life."

"Mine too, tiger."

"Okay, not trying to interrupt anything, but shouldn't we be getting the hell out of here?" Ice asked. "I'm not crazy about small spaces."

CJ stood, holding out a hand to Paige. She took it, letting herself be pulled to her feet. She reached out to Don, returning the favor.

"That was close," he said.

"No shit," CJ murmured.

She retraced the route they'd taken earlier that evening, and soon they found themselves back in the chamber. The torches were still lit and burning brightly. Paige's gaze went to the altar, seeing the blood where Fiona had perished. She looked beyond, expecting to see Ester Hogan's body.

"CJ," she said. "Ester is gone."

They all walked over to the blood stained ground where she had been. There were no tracks. It was as if she had just disappeared.

"Are you sure she was dead?" Don asked. "I mean—"

"Yes," CJ said. "We're sure."

"Fiona?" he asked quietly.

Paige flashed her light back to the altar. "There. She died there."

"He took her back into the cave with him," CJ said.

"Okay, you guys are freaking me out," Ice said.

"Sorry," Paige said. "But we saw him."

"Maybe he came and got Ester too," CJ suggested with a shrug.

"I don't think so," Don said. "Fiona was his bride. She carried his child. Mother Hogan did his bidding, that's all. Mother Hogan was just one of many."

"Look, can we get out of here?" Ice asked. "I'd like to be above ground if we're going to be discussing missing bodies."

"I've never seen you so nervous, baldy," CJ said. "Now do you believe me when I said this assignment sucked?"

"Yeah. I believe you. Now get me the hell out of here. I can face bank robbers, terrorists, murders. You name it. But not this spooky shit."

Don motioned to their left. "The main tunnel will take us—"

"Let's use Ester's tunnel," CJ said, interrupting Don. "It's much nicer."

They again retraced their steps from earlier, going through the tunnel and up the stairs to Ester's house. They were surprised to find Howley and two other agents inside.

"What the hell? I thought you were at the school. You're lucky we didn't shoot you," he said.

"You specifically told us not to shoot anyone," CJ reminded him.

"How did you get here? I told Ice to have you stay put."

"They didn't listen. We came through the woods and then some tunnel," Ice said. "And I don't ever want to do it again."

"Out in the woods? Then you must have heard that sound," he said. "It was like an elephant's roar or something and then this hideous scream."

"Yes, that's a good way to describe it," Paige said.

"What was it?"

"A monster," Ice said simply.

CJ shook her head. "It's some creature that lives in the caves."

"Yeah, like I said. A monster," Ice said again.

"What's with you, Ice? You don't normally spook this easily," Howley said with a laugh. "Probably a mountain lion or something."

"Or something," CJ murmured.

"Well, this is the last house for us to search," Howley explained. "We have forty-four bodies. This is going to be a public relations nightmare." He flashed his light to Don, causing Don to shield his eyes. "Who are you?"

"This is Don," Paige said.

"Oh. You found the doctor. So everyone is accounted for now?"

CJ and Paige glanced at each other, then to Don.

"Well, the two men from here, the ones who took Don, they're not exactly accounted for," she said.

"Meaning?"

"Their bodies are in the woods. Somewhere," CJ said. "Unless he's eaten them."

"Eaten them? Who?"

"More like *what*," Ice said.

"And Fiona's body is gone. He took her back into the cave," CJ said.

"And now Ester's body is missing," Paige said. "I think that's everyone." She looked at Don. "Right?"

"Have you found her son? He lived here with her."

"She had a son?"

"Yes. She kept him here. He was mildly retarded, from what everyone said. He didn't speak. Didn't communicate. He never came out. No one ever saw him." He paused. "Antel was his father."

"Jesus. Antel was Ester's brother," Paige said. "And Fiona's father."

"Yes, well, Mother Hogan was a little crazy herself," he said with a smile. Then he gave a short laugh. "And it feels good to say that and not worry about being culled for disobedience."

"Wait. We found remains of a young child upstairs. In a bed. Could that have been her son?" CJ asked.

"He was born before I was," Don said. "But like I said, no one ever saw him, so yes, she could have killed him as well. No one would have known."

Howley looked at them with a blank expression. "I don't know what the hell you all are talking about. Someone want to explain? Now."

"You know when we started this," CJ said. "You said Ester Hogan was the matriarch, right?"

"Yes."

"So there were others before her. And when they died, they placed them in a bed. In a room. Upstairs."

"You found the burial room?" Don asked quietly.

"So you're telling me there are...remains upstairs?" Howley asked. "This house isn't secure yet?"

"Seven in the one room. Then the child in another."

"Seven?"

"*Skeletal* remains," CJ clarified. "Opal, Velma."

"Estaline and...Estelle?" Paige said.

"Yeah. And Naomi and Eustice," CJ said. "And Rosaline. Seven."

"Eight beds, though. There was a bed for Ester," Paige added.

"Rosaline was Ester's mother," Don stated. "I was a child when she died." He glanced at them, their flashlights all crisscrossing in the room, little flecks of dust floating around them. "The burial room is...sacred. Well, at least it was to Mother Hogan. No one is allowed up there. As far as I know, Belden is the only other one who has been inside. Not even Devin."

"Who's Devin?"

"He's the woodcarver."

"He made the beds?"

Don nodded. "From what I've learned, they all died at a fairly young age. Ester was, by far, the oldest. Of course, her mother was poisoned, so that obviously shortened her life."

"Poisoned?"

"By Ester, no doubt," Paige said.

"Wait a minute," Howley said. "Are you sure the remains are from Hogan women? We're still looking for bodies of the missing girls. That's the point of this, if you'll recall." He turned to Don with raised eyebrows.

"The ones who Belden brought back here," he shook his head. "They were offered as a sacrifice," he said. "In the cave."

"In the cave," Howley repeated. "Where Ice's *monster* lives."

"Yes. They are taken into the cave. Made to run. So he can chase them."

"And?"

"And then he kills them." He looked at Paige. "And then he eats them."

Howley glanced between her and CJ. "What kind of crap is he feeding you?"

"I don't understand," Don said quietly. "What do you mean?"

"He's telling the truth," Paige said. "We've seen him. We've been in the chamber. We've seen the entrance to the cave. We've seen him."

"Me too," Ice said. "He chased us. It's like...man, I can't even describe it. A monster."

"We've come across two skulls out in the woods," CJ added. "I wouldn't be surprised to find more. There's a trail that links back to the school grounds. That's the route we took. I would assume he travels along the same path."

Howley stared at all of them as if they'd grown two heads each. "Okay. We're obviously going to need a thorough briefing. Let's secure this house. Get bodies accounted for, then let the forensics teams in. They should be here soon. We called in the locals too." He rubbed his hair in frustration. "Like I said, public relations nightmare. I just hope we find a trace of young Trumbley. The senator won't let it rest until we do."

"I pity the poor souls who have to go into the cave looking for bodies," CJ murmured.

"Me too," Ice added.

"May I ask a question?" Don asked.

"What is it?"

"You said there were forty-four bodies. What happened?"

"I did the *yellow rock* thing with Belden," CJ said. "You could have warned us it was a suicide trigger phrase."

"We weren't actually sure it would work. Like we told you, Fiona and I were able to block it out. It's hard to believe they're all gone."

"Did you have...family?" Paige asked gently.

He shook his head. "No. My mother's been gone a number of years. And like most, my father was just someone my mother coupled with. He wasn't a part of my life."

"Coupled?" Ice asked.

"Had sex, baldy."

"Come on. Let's get on with it," Howley said.

"Okay, we took the stairs up through the study," CJ said. "It's a narrow passageway. Not quite a secret staircase. I mean, there's a door. But it's narrow. Not meant for frequent travel."

"Let's take the main stairs," Howley said. "Make sure you didn't miss anything."

"We never found her bedroom," Paige said. "It must be down here."

Howley pointed to two of the agents. "You two, check all the rooms down here. Closets too."

Ice cleared his throat. "Is it just me or is anyone else freaking out?"

Paige smiled and rubbed his arm affectionately. "We've just had more time to adjust to it all," she said.

"Maybe if we had some lights, you know. I mean, how do people *live* like this?"

"Actually, most of the houses have solar power or generators," Don said. "Mother Hogan preferred to live in the old way. She used lanterns and candles."

"No offense, man."

"It's okay. Like I said, she was a little crazy."

CJ laughed out loud at that statement. "A *little*?"

"Come on, people," Howley said. "Can we get this over with?"

CJ glanced back over her shoulder. "Paige? You want to take the lead. Show them the rooms."

"No, tiger. You're doing a great job."

With all of their flashlights, it was almost bright on the stairs. But the dust-covered steps led her to believe that Ester used the staircase in her study to travel to the second floor. Of course, since her bedroom was not up there, she may not have had cause to go up very often. Unless she went to...visit, she thought.

"Here," CJ said at the landing, pointing to the burial room. "That's where they all are." She shifted her light down the hallway, walking that way. "And in here," she said, opening the door, "is the child we found."

"May I?" Don asked.

CJ stepped aside, letting him enter.

"Don't touch anything," Howley warned. "Ice, check the other room."

"Oh, man," he mumbled.

Don walked near the bed, bending over to inspect the skeleton as they held their light on it. "It doesn't appear distressed," he said. "Of course, I'm not a real doctor. You probably already know that. But I'd guess he wasn't older than six." He turned around, his gaze going over the room. "It's obviously a child's room. Her son was the only child to live here. It must be him."

"Hey guys," Ice called. "I thought you said there were only seven bodies."

They all hurried from the room, she and CJ stopped up short as they stared at Ester Hogan, dressed in a white gown. She was laid out neatly on the bed that was made for her. The only evidence of her trauma was the light red discoloration staining the gown on her chest.

"What the *hell*?"

Paige shook her head. "She was in the chamber." She turned to Don. "Who could have done this?"

"Belden is the only one who knows. No one else has been in here."

"Belden? The bodybuilder?" Howley shook his head. "No. We found his body."

"Besides, he was the first one—the only one—I told the phrase to," CJ said. "He left the chamber, repeating the stupid little verse over and over again."

"Yes. That's part of it," Don said. "To alert the rest of the flock."

"So who the hell brought her up here?" CJ asked.

No one had an answer. Suddenly Paige felt Don grasp her hand and squeeze tightly.

"I feel her watching me," he whispered. "I feel *someone* watching." He looked around the room, their multitude of flashlights casting odd shadows across the floor and beds. "Doesn't anyone else feel it?"

"Okay," Ice said, slowly backing up to the door. "I've officially reached my limit. There are seven skeletons in those beds over there. And now this? A dead woman, dressed for a wedding? And nobody knows how she got here?" He pointed his light at Don. "And now he's feeling somebody watching us." He turned to Howley. "We don't need to be up here at night. This is some spooky shit."

"It's like when we went to the grocery store that first day," Paige told CJ. "We didn't see a soul, yet we felt eyes on us."

"Avery said the same thing."

"Okay, we're just speculating now," Howley said. "But yeah, I'm a little freaked out too. Let's close this up. We'll let the forensics team in. We probably don't need to be up here anyway."

"Good call," Ice said. "I'll meet you guys at the bottom."

They turned to follow, but Howley stopped them.

"Oh, and Don? We're going to need you to come with us to Houston," he said. "Your debriefing will take several days. If not weeks."

"I understand."

Paige touched his shoulder. "We'll be there with you."

"Thank you. It'll be a little bit out of my comfort zone, to say the least."

CJ laughed. "Yeah. Kinda like this whole thing was for us."

Before closing the door, Paige took one last look inside. She let out a loud gasp. Ester Hogan's eyes were open.

"What is it?"

"Look," she said, holding her light on Ester's face, her dull, lifeless eyes staring at nothing.

"They were closed earlier," CJ whispered.

"I know."

"What are you guys doing?" Howley asked as he waited at the top of the stairs.

"Nothing," they said in unison.

CHAPTER FIFTY-ONE

Ice leaned back in his chair, rolling tiny pieces of paper between his fingers into balls, then tossing them for strikes into the trash can. CJ was tapping away on her keyboard, a smile on her face. Paige was twirling a pen between her fingers, her gaze alternating between her monitor and CJ. Ice flicked his eyes to Billy, who sat watching them both.

"So, CJ, you're in a good mood this morning. Smiling and everything," he said.

She glanced up. "I'm always in a good mood. Besides, when we turn in these reports, we get three days off." She held up three fingers. "Three. While you guys get to stay here and sort through all the mess."

"So that's all it is? I thought maybe you'd gotten laid or something."

"Don't smell tequila on her, and she's wearing clean clothes," Billy said. "No bar last night."

"Like I have to go to the bar to get laid," she said.

Paige looked over at her. "So you *did* get laid?"

Ice was shocked to see a blush cross CJ's face, but she shook it off. "You know, I'm very charming," she said.

"Really?"

"Yeah. And persuasive too."

"Is that so?"

"Absolutely. That's why I can get laid and I don't have to go to the bar."

Paige leaned closer. "So you got laid then?"

Ice couldn't take his eyes off of them. Sure, they were doing their normal thing with the flirting. But something was different. It was their eyes. Their words were teasing, but the look they exchanged was not. He felt the temperature in the room rise, and he shifted uncomfortably in his chair.

"Is that your assumption? That I had sex?"

"Well, since you're so charming and all." Paige finally leaned back. "I never knew that about you. You know, charming and persuasive."

CJ laughed. "See? You learn something new every day."

The door opened to Howley's office, and he and Don came out. Don looked like he'd been beaten.

"Somebody take him to lunch," Howley said. "He needs a break."

"How'd it go?" Paige asked when Howley walked away.

"I don't think he believes me," Don said.

"If we hadn't spent nearly two months there, I wouldn't believe you either," CJ said. "But don't worry. We've got it all in our reports. Including everything that Fiona told us."

"How's the hotel?" Paige asked.

He grinned. "Nice. I can't seem to get away from the television. There are so many things to watch."

"So what are you going to do?" CJ asked. "You know, when this is over with."

He shrugged. "I guess I'll have to get a job. Although, I'm not sure who would hire me. I have no skills. And if a background check was done?" His eyes widened playfully. "Yikes."

They all laughed, including Don.

"You have a medical background. You could always go back to college," Paige suggested. "I might know of a scholarship fund."

CJ arched an eyebrow. "Oh?"

"Well, by all accounts," Ice said, "you're the sole remaining Hogan heir. You have some property you could always sell."

Don laughed at this. "Yes, I could open it up as an amusement park."

"Seriously, what are you going to do with it?" Billy asked. "I mean, it was pretty and all. If you can get past the thing in the woods."

"Mr. Howley said they were considering closing the school," Don said. "Is that true?"

"Two teachers died—Fiona and Ella," CJ said. "He said four others resigned. I'm sure there will be more."

"Well, as long as they think that...that *thing* lives out there, I'm sure they'll all resign," Ice said. "I know I would."

"They've found no trace of it," Billy added. "Are you *sure* you saw something?"

"It's there," CJ said.

"They're going into the cave tomorrow," Ice said. "I'm sure glad I'm not on that team."

"You and me both, baldy."

Paige pushed away from her desk and neatly rolled her chair against it. "I'm taking off," she said. "I've submitted my report."

"I've got a little bit more yet," CJ said.

Paige handed Don her business card. "If you need anything in the next few days, don't hesitate to call me. I'm going to take advantage of Howley's offer of three days off, but I'll be around."

"Thank you. I'll try to stay out of trouble."

"We'll take care of him," Billy said.

Ice watched as Paige glanced once more at CJ, who was pretending to ignore her.

"Okay then. I guess I'll see you guys later."

"Yeah. Later," CJ said, never taking her eyes from her computer monitor.

Billy shot him a look, but Ice only shrugged. A mere two minutes later, CJ got up, a smile still stuck on her face.

"I'm out, girls," she said with a wink. "Don't call me. I won't answer my phone."

She was actually whistling as she walked away.

"What the hell is wrong with them?" Billy murmured.

"What do you mean?" Don asked.

Ice pulled out his visitor's chair with his foot and shoved it toward Don. "Sit down. Gonna be a few minutes before we can split for lunch."

"Thank you," he said. "I really like them. They're nice. Paige more so than CJ, but still."

"Yeah. Paige is a sweetheart," Billy said. "CJ grows on you."

"They play this game with us, see," Ice explained. "They pretend to flirt and tease with each other, but I'm not sure they even like each other."

Don frowned. "What are you talking about? They're together, aren't they?"

"Together?"

"You know...a couple."

"Oh, that. Well, this assignment, yeah. They were posing as a couple, sure. But neither of them wanted to do it," he said.

"That's odd. Fiona said they were...*lovers*," he said in a whisper.

Ice and Billy looked at each other, eyebrows raised. Then Ice shook his head. "No. No way."

"But they've been acting strange," Billy said.

"No. They're just messing with us."

Don looked at them thoughtfully but said nothing. A few minutes later, just as Ice was about to submit his report, the elevator opened and an attractive woman with a younger man in tow got off.

Ice frowned, wondering who'd given them the okay to come up. "Can I help you?"

"Yes, please. I'm looking for Paige Riley," she said.

He shook his head. "You just missed her."

"I was told she was back. Do you know where she is?"

"Excuse me, but who are you?"

The woman held out a nicely manicured hand to him. "Elana Riley. I'm her mother."

"Oh, well, pleased to meet you," he said as he shook her hand. He glanced at the man beside her, waiting for him to speak.

"This is Seth Buchanan, Paige's fiancé," she said. "Do you know where we can find her?"

"Fiancé?"

"Yes. I'm sure she's told you about him."

Billy walked over, sizing him up. "Don't think she's mentioned you," he said. "But I think she went home. She's got time off the next few days."

Ice glared at him as the woman nodded curtly and spun on her heels. Seth gave a slight nod, then followed. As soon as the elevator door closed, Ice punched him in the arm.

"What's wrong with you, man?"

"What do you mean?" Billy said as he rubbed his arm.

"Fiancé? Come on."

***

"I love your place," CJ said as she grabbed Paige, pulling her closer. "Really. But now I want to see your bedroom."

Paige laughed. "How long did you wait before you left?"

"A couple of minutes."

"I'm surprised you made it that long," she murmured as she closed the distance between them, kissing her hard. "Bedroom."

"Absolutely."

She kicked the bedroom door closed behind them, then reached for CJ's shirt, pulling it over her head in one motion. "God, when did you lose your bra?" she asked as she cupped her bare breasts.

"In the car," CJ said, her own hands busy with Paige's blouse.

Pants followed and Paige moved to the bed, pulling CJ down with her. She moaned with pleasure as CJ settled between her legs. "I missed this last night."

"You and me both, baby," CJ said as her mouth closed over one aching nipple.

Paige held her closer, her fingers threading through her hair, her hips beginning a slow roll. The sound of the doorbell made her groan in frustration.

"No, no, no," CJ said as she left her breast. "Don't answer it."

"It's probably my neighbor. She was keeping my mail for me."

"She'll come back."

The doorbell sound again. "She knows I'm here."

CJ rolled off her, her eyes dark with desire. "You have one minute."

Paige smiled. "Thirty seconds. You don't move."

"I'm not going anywhere."

Paige grabbed her robe and slipped it on, then tried to smooth her hair as she walked barefoot through the house. She opened the door without thinking, expecting her neighbor. Her mouth dropped open instead.

"Hello, darling."

"Mother? What are you doing here?" She turned slowly, eyeing the handsome man by her side. "And with Seth, no less."

"What are you doing in a robe?" her mother asked as she pushed inside. "It's the middle of the day."

"Oh, God," Paige whispered. "*Seriously?*" She glanced down the hallway, toward her bedroom...and to where a very naked woman waited for her.

"You looked flushed, my love," Seth said quietly. "Are we interrupting?"

She let out a short laugh. "Oh, you have no idea."

She closed the front door, silently watching as her mother headed into the kitchen and Seth made himself comfortable on her sofa. Paige stood rooted to the spot, her robe covering her nakedness. *Could it get any worse?*

She turned as she heard shuffling down the hallway. CJ came sauntering in, a sheet wrapped adorably around her body, her hair still disheveled from Paige's fingers.

"Paige? Everything okay?"

Paige covered her mouth to hide her smile, then laughed outright. "Okay?" She bit her lip. "Yes, everything is...perfect." She held her hand out. "Come meet my mother. And Seth."

CJ's eyes widened as her gaze slid past Paige and landed on a very amused looking man lounging on her sofa. "Oh...*fuck*," CJ whispered.

Seth stood and came closer, a grin on his face. "Yes, I suppose that *is* what we interrupted." He leaned toward Paige. "She's hot."

"You knew?"

"Of course. Only a lesbian could resist this," he said, motioning at himself in his usual arrogant manner.

Her mother returned holding three glasses of wine. "You knew what, darling?" Her glance moved from Paige to Seth, finally landing on CJ. She looked her up and down, from her bare feet sticking out below the sheet to her tousled hair. "Who in the world...are *you*?"

Oh, this isn't going to end well.